Nebula Awards 24

Nebula

A·W·A·R·D·S

24

SFWA's Choices for the Best

Science Fiction and Fantasy

———1988———

Edited by Michael Bishop

HARCOURT BRACE JOVANOVICH, PUBLISHERS

San Diego   New York   London

The Library of Congress has cataloged this serial publication as follows:
The Nebula awards. — No. 18 — New York [N.Y.]: Arbor House. c1983–
v.; 22cm.
Annual.
Published: San Diego, Calif.: Harcourt Brace Jovanovich, 1984–
Published for: Science Fiction Writers of America, 1983–
Continues: Nebula award stories (New York, N.Y.: 1982)
ISSN 0741-5567 = The Nebula awards
1. Science fiction, American — Periodicals. I. Science Fiction Writers of America
PS648.S3N38   83-647399
813'.0876'08 — dc19
AACR 2 MARC-S   Library of Congress   [8709r84]rev
ISBN 0-15-164932-4
ISBN 0-15-665474-1 (Harvest/HBJ: pbk.)

Designed by G. B. D. Smith

Printed in the United States of America

First edition   A B C D E

Permissions acknowledgments appear on pages 301–302, which
constitute a continuation of the copyright page.

Contents

▼ ▼ ▼

Introduction

▼ ▼ ▼

Michael Bishop

Unable to say more succinctly what George Zebrowski said in his introduction to *Nebula Awards 20*, I will simply reprint his opening paragraph:

> Throughout the year the members of the Science Fiction Writers of America read and recommend stories and novels for the annual Nebula Awards. These recommendations are recorded in a newsletter, and toward the end of the year the recommendations are counted. A preliminary ballot is drawn up and circulated to the membership. The top five novels (40,-000 words or more), novellas (17,500–39,999 words), novelettes (7,500–17,499 words), and short stories (fewer than 7,500 words) are placed on the final ballot, which is then sent to members for their votes. A Nebula Awards jury may add one additional nominee to each category.

The following works made the final ballot in each category in the preliminary voting for the twenty-fourth annual awards. I have indicated the eventual winners with asterisks:

For Novel

Deserted Cities of the Heart by Lewis Shiner (Doubleday/Foundation)
Drowning Towers by George Turner (Arbor House)
*Falling Free by Lois McMaster Bujold (*Analog,* December 1987 through February 1988; Baen)
Great Sky River by Gregory Benford (Bantam Spectra)
Mona Lisa Overdrive by William Gibson (Bantam Spectra)
Red Prophet by Orson Scott Card (Tor)
The Urth of the New Sun by Gene Wolfe (Ultramarine Press; Tor)

For Novella

"The Calvin Coolidge Home for Dead Comedians" by Bradley
Denton (*The Magazine of Fantasy & Science Fiction,* June 1988)
"The Devil's Arithmetic" by Jane Yolen (Viking/Kestrel)
"Journals of the Plague Years" by Norman Spinrad (*Full Spectrum*)
*"The Last of the Winnebagos" by Connie Willis (*Isaac Asimov's
Science Fiction Magazine,* July 1988)
"The Scalehunter's Beautiful Daughter" by Lucius Shepard
(Ziesing Books; *Isaac Asimov's Science Fiction Magazine,* September 1988)
"Surfacing" by Walter Jon Williams (*Isaac Asimov's Science Fiction Magazine,* April 1988)

For Novelette

"Do Ya, Do Ya Wanna Dance" by Howard Waldrop (*Isaac
Asimov's Science Fiction Magazine,* August 1988)
"Ginny Sweethips' Flying Circus" by Neal Barrett, Jr. (*Isaac
Asimov's Science Fiction Magazine,* October 1987)
"The Hob" by Judith Moffett (*Isaac Asimov's Science Fiction Magazine,* May 1988)
"Kirinyaga" by Mike Resnick (*The Magazine of Fantasy & Science
Fiction,* November 1988)
"Peaches for Mad Molly" by Steven Gould (*Analog,* February
1988)
*"Schrödinger's Kitten" by George Alec Effinger (*Omni,* September 1988)
"Unfinished Portrait of the King of Pain by Van Gogh" by Ian
McDonald (*Empire Dreams*)

For Short Story

*"Bible Stories for Adults, No. 17: The Deluge" by James Morrow (*Full Spectrum*)

"The Color Winter" by Steven Popkes (*Isaac Asimov's Science Fiction Magazine*, August 1988)
"Dead Men on TV" by Pat Murphy (*Full Spectrum*)
"The Fort Moxie Branch" by Jack McDevitt (*Full Spectrum*)
"Mrs. Shummel Exits a Winner" by John Kessel (*Isaac Asimov's Science Fiction Magazine*, June 1988)
"Voices of the Kill" by Thomas M. Disch (*Full Spectrum*)

Careful readers will have discovered seven candidates for best novel. This strongly suggests (barring a three-way tie at one of the top five spots) that two novels tied and that the Nebula Awards jury elected to add a title of its own. The appearance of six or seven finalists in each of the short fiction categories suggests that the jury chose to exercise its power here as well. Members who have closely followed the recommendation process over the year may be able to deduce which finalists the jury has added, but the jury—to keep the membership from reacting to its intervention rather than to the merits of the added titles—does not publicly disclose its choices.

What about the winners? Are they worthy choices? Has SFWA acted in a responsible and uplifting way in bestowing its awards? (*Uplifting* not only in the sense that the winning works will give their readers an entertaining high, but also that they will further elevate the always hard-to-pinpoint standards toward which caring writers ought to yearn.) As my forerunner as series editor, George Zebrowski, has noted, "The results of this process can scarcely be expected to please everyone." And as Robert Silverberg observed in his introduction to *Nebula Awards 18*, "[On] a few occasions—the law of averages being what it is— certain of the winning stories have, to experienced observers, seemed to be absolutely off-the-wall choices." But in the next breath, he comments, "By and large, though, the record is a commendable one, as a glance at the list of previous winners at the end of this volume indicates."

And I do feel that this year's winners are a worthy lot, even though one or two—maybe all four of them, given the opinionated argumentativeness of so many SFWA members—will certainly provoke controversy.

Lois McMaster Bujold's *Falling Free,* for example, is ruthlessly hard SF, with a competent, morally aware engineer for a hero, and Ms. Bujold tells her story in a straightforward prose that aims for clarity above all other stylistic effects. In many ways, to stand her novel against Gene Wolfe's subtle and rococo *The Urth of the New Sun* or Lewis Shiner's mystical but hard-bitten *Deserted Cities of the Heart* is to compare particle accelerators and magic flutes. Ian Watson, in this year's survey essay, labels *Falling Free*—not altogether disparagingly, but not exactly approvingly, either—"a juvenile." He asks if SFWA really wants to cite this novel as its "pinnacle of achievement," and he claims that several other writers were "scaling some giant peaks."

In a letter to me, Ms. Bujold wrote, "I'm glad all those other writers Ian mentions, many of whom I also admire, are scaling their giant peaks. I just happen to be climbing in a different mountain range." There is more than a measure of justice in this defense; and in her own brief contribution, "Free Associating about *Falling Free,*" Ms. Bujold relates her novel's origins, her narrative goals, and her foremost extraliterary aim.

All right. What about the short fiction winners? "The Last of the Winnebagos" by Connie Willis may also prove a controversial choice, not only because the competition in the novella category was so strong but also because Ian Watson—along with some other British readers—found her story so uncompromisingly American in its outlook and idiom that he could not get beyond its poignancy to its theme. I like the story a lot.

But I also liked several of the other finalists here, including Jane Yolen's *The Devil's Arithmetic,* a young adult novel. You will find in *Nebula Awards 24* Ms. Yolen's own helpful synopsis of the first fourteen chapters, plus all of the unabridged final chapters. I don't usually care for excerpts (as I explain in my headnote to Ms. Bujold's essay), but "The Devil's Arithmetic" is a work worthy of your notice in any format.

George Alec Effinger's "Schrödinger's Kitten" took the Nebula for best novelette. This was another strong category, but Effinger was long overdue for an award, and this complex but deftly executed story finally got it for him.

"I was nominated last year," Effinger wrote in a brief piece for the SFWA *Bulletin,* "and I went on at great length about all kinds of serious literary stuff, and I embarrassed myself. And I lost anyway, which got me to thinking: 'Schrödinger's Kitten' is my fourth Nebula nomination. Supposing the Nebulas were awarded completely at random. (Our bylaws could be amended to make this official SFWA policy, not merely the custom it is today.) Given an average of six nominees per category, the odds of any particular nominee losing the Nebula are thus $5/6$ or 83.3%. However, the odds of losing four consecutive nominations are drastically reduced, only $625/1296$, or 48.2%. I stand a better than 50-50 chance of actually winning this year! And should I lose, then if I'm ever nominated again, my chances of winning rise to 59.9%. When I put that on a graph, I can see that, paradoxically enough, the longer I continue to lose, *the more Nebulas I must eventually win!*

"I think I'm on my way to inventing the Major Award Insurance Industry."

Anyone who feels that "Schrödinger's Kitten" does not deserve its Nebula should reread not only the story but George's treatise on actuarial voting (see the preceding two paragraphs).

The short story winner was James Morrow's "Bible Stories for Adults, No. 17: The Deluge." In many ways, this was the fiercest, most ambitious story of the six on the final ballot (including even John Kessel's wrenchingly strange "Mrs. Shummel Exits a Winner"), and I regard it as a deeply gratifying choice. Morrow is as gifted a short story writer as he is a novelist, and he is a hugely gifted novelist. Also, this win—to find even extraliterary sources of satisfaction—may in some measure compensate him for the fact that SFWA almost completely overlooked his first two idiosyncratic, satirical novels.

What else is on tap here? A great deal—much of it not controversial at all, but simply entertaining and/or informative.

Other final-ballot or preliminary-ballot stories in this volume are Jack McDevitt's powerful story, "The Fort Moxie Branch"; Neal Barrett, Jr.'s affectingly gonzo novelette, "Ginny Sweethips' Flying Circus"; and Gene Wolfe's engrossing deep-space thriller and psychological character study, "The Other Dead Man."

In 1989, Ray Bradbury received the tenth Grand Master Nebula. This volume celebrates that fact by publishing an original poem, "The Collector Speaks," and by reprinting Bradbury's definitive statement on the many idiocies, and dangers, of would-be censors, "More Than One Way to Burn a Book."

All three winners of the 1987 Rhysling Awards for SF poetry check in, as does Robert Frazier with a poem first published in George Zebrowski's Synergy series.

Bill Warren provides his chatty annual report on Hollywood's clumsy efforts to get sci-fi right; and Paul Di Filippo contributes what may be the surprise of the volume, "My Alphabet Starts Where Your Alphabet Ends," a scholarly critical assessment of a man of letters whom SFWA has unaccountably treated as a pariah, at least when it comes to publicly acknowledging his far-reaching influence and citing him for awards.

Also, on a more serious, commemorative note, *Nebula Awards 24* offers Gordon R. Dickson's heartfelt tribute to Clifford Simak and Frank M. Robinson's fact-filled eulogy to Robert Heinlein. Simak and Heinlein died in the spring of 1988, after forging noteworthy careers in science fiction writing, and critics are still trying to assess the full extent of the field's loss.

How, then, do I see this entire anthology? A reviewer in a big midwestern newspaper declared in a review of *Nebula Awards 23* that one of the field's most dependable best-of-the-year collections—i.e., the volume edited by Gardner Dozois—almost always upstages the annual Nebula Awards anthology, "because it generally includes many of the same stories and appears much, much earlier."

There's not much I can do to hurry the publishing schedule of Harcourt Brace Jovanovich, but I have deliberately set out to limit duplications between the various best-of-the-year collections and this anthology. If Gardner Dozois or Donald A. Wollheim or some other best-of-the-year editor is astute enough to select a Nebula winner or two even before the formal announcement of the awards, then I must necessarily repeat those selections because this volume belongs by both definition and title to the Nebula winners. But I have a good deal of latitude in what I may select after taking the winners, and I try hard to distinguish this book from our annual best-of-the-year collections by making startling but defensible choices from among the other final-ballot and off-ballot stories.

Nebula Awards 23 contained (in addition to Ian Watson's and Bill Warren's essays, the Rhysling Award winners, and an excellent example of "projective verse" by Joe Haldeman) six stories not featured in Dozois's *The Year's Best Science Fiction.* This volume, *Nebula Awards 24,* includes a broad sampling of material, original and reprint, not available elsewhere, and I would ask fair-minded reviewers to assess it on those grounds, and on the quality of its contents, rather than on certain conditions—the inevitable repetition of Nebula winners and its alleged tardiness—over which this editor has no influence. I don't mean that to sound cranky, for the review to which I've alluded was actually a positive one, but I would like readers and critics alike to understand, and to acknowledge, that these Nebula Award anthologies are a different animal from the best-of-the-year collections.

Next year, by the way, is the twenty-fifth anniversary of the Nebula Awards, and I'm planning to celebrate it by sending up some trial balloons and setting off a few literary fireworks. Come and join us.

—*Pine Mountain, Georgia*
May 26, 1989

Nebula Awards 24

Themes and Variations: A View of the SF and Fantasy of 1988

▼ ▼ ▼

Ian Watson

Ian Watson is the author of three unusual horror novels—*The Power, The Fire Worm,* and *Meat*—as well as the recent science fiction novels *Whores of Babylon* and *The Flies of Memory* (based on one of the year's better novellas). Here, he takes a look at the fantasy and science fiction published during 1988.

In my introduction to last year's essay, I wrote, "Ian has the interest and élan to stay abreast of the field, an unswerving faith in the potential of visionary SF to revitalize the world, and both the credentials and the cheek to make unequivocal discriminations among those items on SFWA's preliminary ballot that strike him as deserving of comment." Nothing has happened to deprive Ian of his admirable talents, and so I am only too happy to feature him in the leadoff spot again.

Ian's "cheek," incidentally, enables him to express opinions at odds not only with those of SFWA's membership but also with some of mine. He knocks a pair of stories that I like, hypes a few others that strike me as at best competent, and contends that last year's winning novel, *Falling Free,* is "a juvenile." (Ms. Bujold disputes this contention, and explains her novel's origins and aims, in the essay immediately following.) But a little controversy about award choices and critical judgments is inevitable, and it can be healthy if those debating the issues do so with civility, intelligence, and wit. Ian's cheek almost always manifests itself in civilized ways, and he rarely sinks to dogmatism.

Throughout each year the active members of Science Fiction Writers of America recommend their favorite new novels, novellas, novelettes, and short stories to their professional colleagues

1

by way of a regular newsletter, the *Nebula Awards Report.* Each January, a preliminary ballot lists all titles that have received more than four recommendations. There's a definite tendency for works that have been well ahead on the table of recommendations to end up on the final ballot. In last year's essay on the output of 1987, I suggested that a juvenile mood pervaded several novels among the most popular contenders. During 1988, Lois McMaster Bujold's *Falling Free* easily led the list of recommendations in the novel category.

Some skeptical members of SFWA jokingly retitled this novel *Revolt of the Mutant Four-Armed Welders in Space.* This, indeed, tells all. GalacTech has bioengineered a new race of "quaddies" for work in free fall. In place of legs, quaddies have an additional set of arms. Now GalacTech nastily intends to cancel the project. These bright, engaging, innocent, amorous children will be sterilized, and sent down to the surface of the nearest planet to flop around as cripples for the rest of their lives. Moved by their plight, biped engineer Leo leads the quaddies in hijacking their orbital habitat and heading for another star system. The book is engaging, sprightly, and buoyant, starring a host of Goodies and approximately a couple of Baddies. It contains engineering solutions galore—sufficient to enchant the heart of any reader of *Analog,* where the novel first appeared as a serial.

However, *Falling Free* is an out-and-out juvenile.

Young adult science fiction is a growing and laudable field. Pamela Sargent's *Alien Child* is an excellent contribution from the year in question. It tells thoughtfully of an alien who visits a lifeless future Earth and accidentally causes a stored human embryo to be revived. The alien feels obliged to act as guardian to the resulting solitary human girl. What killed the human race? Will Nita ever enjoy human companionship? Sargent also writes major, ambitious, adult novels. *Falling Free* wasn't published as a juvenile, though perhaps the cover art gives the game away. It is undoubtedly a juvenile—and a very good one too. But do members of SFWA *really* wish this to be seen as their pinnacle, their height of achievement?

Other authors were scaling some giant peaks.

Gene Wolfe's *The Urth of the New Sun** adds an unexpected coda to his acclaimed quartet, *The Book of the New Sun*. *Urth* is at once a masterful new novel and a reinterpretation of all that had gone before. It is set largely on a titanic sailing ship of space, which is conveying the Autarch Severian to a day of judgment outside the ordinary universe. Measured, portentous, and gnomic, this book of exotic wonders—of superscience mixed with magic—plays elegant games with both time and other universes; these games reconcile the complex and teasing meanders of the previous four books. Does the novel actually resolve those enigmas? "Knowing very little after so much . . ." "Always there is much more . . ." Wolfe continues to flourish new scarves from his conjurer's sleeve.

The fact that Severian was a torturer is now explained by the notion that the person chosen to save the world must be he who meted out the harshest justice. *Urth* is deeply antimaterialist and strongly denies death. We must accept past agonies because those were not the full picture. This notion may be one of the most dangerous implications of religious belief, just as it is of political fanaticism.

In fact, Wolfe is rewriting the Bible, as it might have been written by a single, more sophisticated author equipped with a finer sense of narrative structure, characterization, and symbolism. We encounter the Flood and the halting of the sun. Hierogrammate angels deposit Adam and Eve in the grounds of the Autarch's palace.

Religion of a nonassertive variety forms the backbone of Judith Moffett's noteworthy first novel, *Pennterra*. Quaker colonists hope to settle on an alien world, but the native Hross warn that human beings must remain within one large valley and not use powered machinery; otherwise, the spirit of the planet will destroy them. How is it that Quakers are prominent enough to

---

*Though published in 1987, this appeared on the Nebula ballot for 1988 only because the author withdrew the first edition in favor of the later mass market edition, as the Nebula rules confusingly allow.

control a starship? The Earth they have left behind is an ecological wreck; however, nonviolent direct action by Quakers has somehow guaranteed that there won't be any nuclear holocaust. This information hovers, ghostlike, in the background.

The Hross, whose name echoes that of C. S. Lewis's hallowed Martians in *Out of the Silent Planet,* are telepathically sensitive to all other life-forms. They will kill and eat only those other creatures that offer themselves freely. The system of ecological cooperation, the opposite of Darwinian natural selection, is both biologically gonzo and strangely persuasive. The personalities of the Hross can form a composite aura; and they convince the puzzled Quakers, who themselves tune in to unity through silent meditation.

A second shipload of non-Quaker colonists ignores warnings; the planet's immune system duly trounces them. Ultimately, the children of the quietists will gain the freedom to roam this paradise through a process of benign alienation. If *Pennterra* sounds too idyllic by far, in fact Moffett pulls no punches—especially over the sexual implications of empathy. As a result, this is one of the most tense and outspoken books of recent years, as well as, finally, one of the most friendly in its ethos.

Rebecca Ore's *Becoming Alien* is another fine first novel about alienization and alienation, xenophobic violence and coexistence. When Tom and his dominating, drug-dealing, elder brother rescue an alien from a crashed craft, brother Warren's less-than-tender custody of their houseguest leads to its painful, lonely death. The unhappy young alien was a cadet in a star-spanning federation of disparate races. With mixed feelings, a rescue party takes Tom to the stars to become a cadet. He wishes for this, yet his resulting isolation is anguish to him. Ore handles alien biology, languages, and conflicting cultural patterns skillfully, and her memorable human hero does not merely return to Earth as an ambassador or emissary. His difficult destiny is to find community of mind as a stranger among strangers.

Sheila Finch, in *Triad,* also explores alien mind-sets vigorously and ingeniously. Her human linguists take specially tailored hallucinogenic drugs in order to achieve the alien worldviews that generate alien languages. All languages serve as the tools of our perception, but also as a protection against "the roaring ground that was the raw, unfiltered universe."

Themes in science fiction permutate themselves, with telling variations. Octavia Butler continues her remarkable Xenogenesis trilogy with *Adulthood Rites,* in which the alien Oankali gene-traders have repopulated a repaired Earth with human-alien crossbreeds. "Resister" men and women have been sterilized and set free. The Oankali view human beings as a "compelling, seductive, deadly contradiction" because of the coexistence in our nature of intelligence and hierarchical behavior. This, they believe, dooms us to destroy ourselves.

Moffett writes about cooperation, nonviolence, and sexuality. Ore describes the growing pains of becoming alien amidst conflicting aliens who must nevertheless work together. *Adulthood Rites* addresses all these questions, and more, in its story of the first "construct" baby growing toward maturity and metamorphosis. Akin ("a-kin") looks like a normal human infant, apart from a sensory tongue that can taste genetic structure. Resisters, who are desperate to acquire children, kidnap him. The Oankali abandon him temporarily, so that Akin might decide the fate of these native human beings whose barren society is slowly crumbling toward chaos. The baby Akin is as alert and articulate as any adult human being; and after his long-delayed rescue he decides to give the unreformed human race a second chance. Despite the certainty of many Oankali that the human "contradiction" will inevitably lead to violent extinction, they will terraform Mars to provide a new start.

A similar contradiction is the subject of Nancy Kress's *An Alien Light.* The alien Ged communicate by scent as well as by speech. Their joy is to "sing in harmony," mediated by pheromones. However, they find themselves at war with an expansionist human race, whom they cannot understand. The Ged discover an isolated human colony, where two backward societies of warriors and merchant-artisans are forever at odds. Sparta versus Athens, in a sense. So the Ged build an enclosed city, and by promises of wealth and weapons they lure a mixed population of adventurers and outcasts into it. Their aim is to study human learning processes and to solve the central paradox of how a species often hostile to its own kind can possibly have avoided blowing up its own planet long since.

Kress offers a fascinating exploration of the shifting alliances within the city and the way that sexual relations often mirror intraspecies violence, a concept appalling to the Ged's sense of harmony. The solution to the paradox is that human violence actually *assists* change and adaptation. Those Ged who can understand this feel they are contaminated, alienated from their own culture. Some questions still beg answers. The ill-assorted colonists have no idea that they stem respectively from the military crew and the dissident passengers of a crashed starship. How long can the war with the Ged have been going on? And how did it start? How did the slow, harmonious Ged ever take the giant step of eliminating predators on their home world? Meanwhile, *An Alien Light* is a brightly illuminating novel with a cast of notable, often obsessive characters.

Moffett, Butler, Kress . . . In her own way, and upon her very own science-fictional stage, each of these authors conducts a compelling thought experiment about the human paradox of our innate violence in its perpetual tug-of-war with our offsetting bent for cooperation.

D. Alexander Smith conducts a thought experiment, too. In *Rendezvous,* a human starship meets a ship from a planet of bear-like aliens at an agreed midway point. The Bluebears communicate by scent as well as by speech. When they join together in an eightfold group-mind, a higher consciousness submerges their individual identities. The massed group-minds of their home planet have decided that the human monkeys must be destroyed in order to deter future encounters, which could disrupt Bluebear harmony. Monkeys were once savage predators upon the peaceful Bluebears. Unlike Kress, Smith deals in detail with the conundrum of how such predators were wiped out. At the same time, the computer on board the human starship has itself become, secretly, sentient.

Pheromones, predators, violence, and cooperation: can science fiction writers themselves be part of a collective consciousness? *Rendezvous,* with its feisty human crew, finely invented aliens, and ingenious group-mind, is one of the most wonderful first contact novels I have ever read.

War on an interstellar scale sets the stage for Iain M. Banks's *Consider Phlebas*. Banks, a Scotsman, first stormed the British literary scene with a "mainstream" horror-shocker, *The Wasp Factory*. Two strange, Kafkaesque novels later, he was well enough placed to be able to sell what had in fact been his first love, a space opera. *Phlebas* is a space opera of giant scope, depicting vividly the conflict between the enigmatic Culture, of human beings and machines, and the giant tripedal Idirans, who are "pro-life" religious fanatics. Megaships with minds destroy ringworlds. An energy superspecies cordons off planets of the dead. The escapades of the shape-changer hero recall certain events in *Raiders of the Lost Ark*. Banks pulls out all the stops. However, this is space opera with a difference, distinguished by its sheer stylishness, by its fascination with the mechanisms of cultures, and, lastly, by its tendency to dwarf enormous events into virtual insignificance. When measured against the real yardstick of galactic history and cultures, the whole of the action in *Phlebas* is an exercise in disastrous futility. The shape-changer, once an idealist, is finally reduced to a dying wreck who has forgotten even his own name.

War between flesh-life and machine intelligence is the theme of Gregory Benford's *Big Sky River*. At first, the battle seems hopelessly unequal. A degraded echelon of human beings in power-armor flees from predatory mechs and tries to scavenge enough spare parts and food to survive. The silicon-loving machines have thoroughly deterraformed this world near the galactic core, once a human colony. Now it is a desert. Men and women carry "Aspects" of the dead imprinted in their minds, but they have little time to listen to the advice of these often testy custodians of a once rich heritage. One deadly machine, the Mantis, hunts human survivors to collect their minds as an art form.

Much shooting occurs in a drably minimalist terrain, and the cultural flesh seems scraped bare to the bitter bone. Benford experiments with Joycean portmanteau words to express this compression of human horizons and the life-threatening urgency.

(The results look clever on the page, but the ear can easily confuse such opposites as "yeasay" and "naysay.") However, there is a kind of hope. Magnetic minds who live in the accretion disk are keeping a watching brief on human beings. The hero's father still lives, on a starship sailing in strange seas of time within the Eater, the big black hole. Mechs continue to misunderstand the human essence because "a deep-buried spirit filled organic life." And a friendly ship lies buried nearby, undiscovered by all the mech prospectors for metals. We can expect Benford's saga to grow richer and more cosmic in its sequels.

In *The Wooden Spaceships,* his sequel to *The Ragged Astronauts,* Bob Shaw has no truck with superscience—at first. In this alternative universe where the value of *pi* is different, a common hourglass of atmosphere links Land and Overland. When Land tries to invade Overland, a splendid "Battle of Britain" results, fought between balloons and wooden jet fighters. However, the discovery of a symbiotic superrace on a third planet sends the action into the wild blue yonder. Is Shaw pulling rabbits out of a hat? Or will a third volume show that this lurching discontinuity between hot-air tech and FTL was a logical necessity?

One theme in Moffett's *Pennterra* was the "come and kindly be eaten" method of catching one's cutlets for supper. The Indian tribes in Orson Scott Card's *Red Prophet* practice exactly the same method of obtaining meat on the hoof. Because they are in tune with the land, the land assists them and offers animals to them to eat. (Can it be a coincidence that two major novels both contain the same ecomysticism, whereby the carnivore can assuage both appetite and conscience?) As in *Pennterra,* the land opposes the mechanistic white man, tripping him and scratching his face with thorns. A Redskin, on the other hand, can run two hundred miles in a single night thanks to the compliancy and strength of the land (a borrowing, by the way, of the Tibetan lamaist art of *lung-gom*).

In the preceding novel, *Seventh Son,* the hexes of the white colonists played a relatively minor role. In the Indian context, magic blooms amazingly. A shaman walks on water to conjure a tornado full of prophetic visions. A magic loom spins the strands of destiny. Alone among white people, young Alvin can tune in to the Indian land and magic. Card, compulsively readable as always, continues to play delicious games with history. Here he features an alternative Napoleon, opening up possible global perspectives far beyond this particular story of an Indian war ending in a disastrous bloodbath.

Where Card's white people are blind to Indian magic, Michaela Roessner's Australian missionaries are blind to the dreamtime of the Aborigines. *Walkabout Woman* is a wonderful evocation of magical ceremonies in a spellbinding landscape largely hidden from the eyes of the whites. The outback begins to transform young Raba so that she can see and manipulate the crystalline "alien light," akin to the green light that Alvin learns to see. Although a clumsy, well-meaning missionary woman aborts Raba's metamorphosis, the girl is still able to pass through a portal in a painted rock into the spirit world. Here is a book of beauty and strangeness; the outback might well be an alien planet. There is also humor. Blind white-fellas see dirty Aborigines yabbering while they play cards; actually the Aborigines are discussing the finer points of a religious ritual. *Walkabout Woman* is also an ingeniously feminist book. The aboriginal men have chauvinistically blocked women off from major magic, thus blocking the way back to the dreamtime for all their race.

In *Orphan of Creation,* Roger MacBride Allen addresses the status of our Australopithecene cousins. In the nineteenth century, an ex-slave wrote in his journal of the importation of ape men to a Southern plantation. His modern descendant, an archaeologist, follows the trail back to Africa, discovers living survivors, and provokes scientific and creationist upheaval. This novel is strangely reminiscent of Michael Bishop's recent *Ancient of Days.* The narrative deals earnestly with matters that Bishop gave a zany, arch treatment.

Bishop himself, in *Unicorn Mountain,* dares to introduce sick unicorns from an alternative reality into our contemporary world of AIDS. Card's "red prophet" was a prodigious shaman-in-the-making, wrecked by the psychic impact of his father's murder. Only whiskey can drown the black noise in his soul, until Alvin cures him. Bishop's Paisley Coldpony likewise feels the call to shamanhood, and will dance in the spirit house. However, Card's tornado of magic is a far cry from the quirky manifestations of the supernatural in *Unicorn Mountain,* where unicorns suffer from swamp fever and TV programs originate from a parallel world. The numinous in Bishop's novel is also humorous, and poignant. We are exalted but we also laugh, and shed a tear, at the joys and mishaps of his engaging characters. These characters are all very vocal, in a metaphorical vein. This endows them with heightened identities, though it also seems as if a shared, idiosyncratic dialect possesses them all, producing a decorative tapestry of dialogue removed from normal speech. Do people ever really talk this way? "I'm a horse doctor, Miss, not a Nazi vivisectionist, and I'm so all-fired-tired of playing cowboys and Indians with you—a liar and a trespasser—that I'm leaving it to Tonto here and heading home." When swearing their heads off, characters become almost prissily precise. But *Unicorn Mountain* is a bold book, about self-betrayal and death—death that isn't dramatically gruesome, a hook for the jaded reader, but simply sadly realistic. Ultimately, however, the novel comforts and enhances.

Still in Indian territory, Craig Strete's *Death in the Spirit House* is an angry morality tale. A citified Indian cheats his own people on behalf of big business, and big nemesis ensues. Strete's brief novel is eloquent and powerful, written in very short paragraphs, like a magical incantation or like Bible verses. However, it is blatantly manipulative. Strete remorselessly puts his "pathetic cartoonlike figure"—his own words—through a mill of mishaps. Though the protagonist is cleansed at last, the deck was thoroughly rigged.

Card and Bishop both explore alternative realities, the one centrally, the other idiosyncratically. In *Alternities* Michael P. Kube-McDowell offers a fast-paced thriller about a version of modern America attempting to revive its economy by covert borrowings and thefts of better technology from sister realities. Unfortunately, President Robinson views each of these parallel worlds as a convenient "rathole" in the event that his own brinkmanship triggers a nuclear war. This isn't an airport thriller to page through quickly. However, the scientific explanation, when it comes, begs a mountain of questions. Who did split realities back in the 1950s to give the human race more chances? Who built the "quantum bubble supporting mirror pockets of shaped spacetime" upon which the various alternaties hinge? This science-fictional explanation *fits,* yet how oddly similar the device is to Roessner's access gate into the dreamtime! The former is SF, the latter is fantasy—because of context and because of the type of discourse the authors employ.

Michael Coney is also concerned with "happen tracks" in *Fang the Gnome.* This novel blends SF—colonizing aliens and genetic manipulation in the style of Octavia Butler—with myths and fables. *Fang* is an enchanting original: quietly hilarious, vibrant with the love of life, charmingly recounted.

Ancestral spirits haunt the Central American landscape of Lewis Shiner's *Deserted Cities of the Heart.* Shiner pulls off a very tough trick: intersecting the end of a previous Mayan civilization with an impending modern cataclysm foreshadowed by revolutionary guerrilla war. In the past, the collapse resembles Pol Pot's forced expulsion of the city-dwellers of Phnom Penh. In the present, the right-wing mercenaries are led by a very eerie soldier who learned both hip mysticism and ruthlessness in Vietnam. Political turmoil thwarts a project to change the planet through small-scale, friendly technology. A fallen rock star, who hangs out with Mayan shamans, time-trips back to the end of the previous cycle. Volcanoes erupt. His estranged wife learns how to be free. Ancient and modern come together impressively, disconcertingly.

Bruce Sterling's *Islands in the Net* is another novel possessing an excellent sense of place. It also showcases the possibilities of friendly technology. In a world no longer terrorized by nuclear Armageddon, the Rizome corporation exemplifies the kind of industrial democracy made possible by a multinational data-net. But outlaw data pirates control the governments of Grenada, Singapore, and Mali. Soon, the protagonist, Laura, pitches herself idealistically into a web of violence and nuclear terrorism. After a long, miserable stay in an African jail, she finally learns the truth, but her life with David has been destroyed. She and David were only little persons, after all, and now she has outgrown him. This vivid, highly detailed thriller is an extremely *human* book, moving and anguished and, in the end, redemptive. Cyberpunk spokesperson Sterling becomes the apostle of electronic humanism.

Dazzlingly, Sterling persuades us that his twenty-first century does indeed exist as a radically different kind of world. In *The Gold Coast*, Kim Stanley Robinson follows a more conservative projection. In part, this novel is a lovely, sad, moving elegy for Orange County, California. It is also a radical critique of the military-industrial establishment. Apparently, America will continue to intervene abroad, there will be no fundamental change in Soviet society, and no united Europe will arise as an independent force. The world will churn on as at present, give or take eyedropper designer drugs, the automation of the Los Angeles freeways, and surgically precise remote-piloted vehicles on the drawing boards. How else, though, could this particular book have been written? A terrible "dynamic inertia" grips history, and Jim's attempt to sabotage the juggernaut can only backfire. Narrated in a "utopian present" tense that tellingly conveys the designer death of history and memory, *The Gold Coast* is a worthy flip side to Robinson's *The Wild Shore;* it is also a powerful indictment of a war machine that is also a money machine.

Revolutionaries of a different stripe inhabit the Berkeley of Lisa Goldstein's *A Mask for the General,* namely urban shamans. A computer virus has ruined the entire banking system, and the U.S. economy has collapsed. Shortages are rife. General Gleason runs a police state of informers and Rehab camps for dissidents; he is courting the Japanese in the hope of reacquiring computer technology. Layla expresses her rebellion magically by making a spirit mask that she is sure will reach the general. It does. She can see—shades of Card—the green land of animals. Her would-be apprentice, Mary, a seventeen-year-old epileptic, becomes an urban guerrilla. Full of Philip Dickian frailties, follies, and bravados, misunderstandings and radiant perceptions, Goldstein's bittersweet novel affirms, despite all, the value of love.

Little love is lost between the privileged Sweet and the proletarian Swill in George Turner's *Drowning Towers.* This worst-case scenario for a future Australia evokes most of our dystopian dreads. On the one hand, this is a crusty, curmudgeonly "old man's" book, suggesting that things can only degenerate. On the other, it is a book of courage. It took courage to write: it concerns human courage amidst degrading, inhuman conditions; and it warns powerfully of our own failure of courage to plan wisely for the future. Undoubtedly, it will rank as the major Australian SF novel for some years to come.

After the government releases a virus to attack its own population, Swill boss Kovacs tortures a hypno-blocked sergeant to extract the truth from him. This crucial scene is a key to the personality of Kovacs, but it also makes of George Turner yet another custodian of a chamber of horrors into which some SF authors seem obliged to drag their puppets. Moreover, nothing is achieved in real terms. Because the self-limiting virus is already irrelevant, the scene is gratuitous.

If the world were saved through torture, the moral of this episode would be even worse. Now, Turner is actually undertaking an antipodean revision of Orwell's *Nineteen Eighty-Four,* with Swill and Sweet playing the roles of Proles and Party. Big Brother's people are, in the circumstances, relatively benign. It is the prolish hope of the future who carry out the torture. When Sweet characters opt out of their privileged positions to take up residence in the towers of the Swill and to become "New Men," one wonders whether Turner is rebutting Orwell. Or has he totally forgotten the folly of Winston Smith in imagining that the Proles are the future, the reservoir of vitality, the possibility of revolution? Given the dour mood of the book, this "New Man" movement seems peculiarly utopian. Presumably, in the long run, the "New Man" impetus is as pointless as the torture, for sheer climatic change is bound to sweep all of this away and decimate the human race. Structurally, at least, the courage represented by the "New Man" movement prevents us from grounding with total despair.

A thousand years later, we encounter a consoling demiparadise of a reduced and sensible population—Turner's astringent version of a postholocaust pastoral. Ultimately, the whole novel is a fantasy reconstruction from the viewpoint of that future. It may be that the future Lenna is romanticizing wildly, in what she thinks is a hard-bitten, gritty way. One triumph of *Drowning*

Towers is that Turner brings such ghastly conditions believably to life as a nightmare that humanity can in fact live through.

Another author who has drowned cities is J. G. Ballard. Ballard is the prose-poet of disasters, many of which his characters welcome as a variety of psychological liberation. Catastrophe leads to a fevered celebration, viewed with a cool eye. In *The Day of Creation,* Ballard confronts the Saharan drought and Third World conflict. A new Nile is born surrealistically, and its creator sets out—as through the landscape of his own imagination—perversely to staunch the flow. This novel, one of Ballard's finest, is a mesmeric litany of haunting images. Rich with similes (and slightly repetitive in the way of litanies), the whole book resembles a magical conjuration. "Jets of flame, like a score of gas mantles, lifted through the decking. Tinted by the metal salts in the mural pigments, the flames darted among the tables, gaudy geysers of zinc and copper light, as the ghosts of these nymphs put on their last performance." Who else would have noted the clinical, chemical detail?

Some cities are drowned; others are empty, or almost so. *The Silent City,* by Elisabeth Vonarburg, details the intricate relationships between the last few long-lived human beings in their cybercity in the wake of ecocatastrophe; meanwhile, in the wilderness, tribes of survivors are barely beginning to get their acts together. A stock theme? No. For the balance of the sexes has changed dramatically, and Vonarburg's heroine, who is able to alter her gender, explores crucial questions about our bodily and social identity. This highly ambitious novel from Québec, ably translated from the French, flows compellingly.

Body-change plays an important role in John Shirley's *A Splendid Chaos.* Superior aliens kidnap a medley of intelligent species, including human beings, and dump the lot on a strange, metamorphic planet where landscape can be literally alive. Those hills do roll. The castaways are given enough information and technology . . . to fight as rivals. Echoes of Philip Farmer, echoes of Jack Chalker? Is this a science-fictional *Alice in Wonderland* world, or is it a genuine planet? Bioelectrics and particles of perception known as IAMtons begin to figure, reminiscent of ideas in A. A. Attanasio's *Radix.* The title gives a nod to Chaos

Theory. Ilya Prigogine's ideas about self-organizing patterns are another influence, just as they are in Shiner's *Deserted Cities*. A war conducted in the "overstructure" of reality results in the checkmate of the malign, metamorphosed human emperor, who ends up mad and locked in a mirror cell. (A similar fate overtook the villain of Shirley's horror novel, *Cellars.*) It transpires that the superior Metas have been broadcasting the whole wondrous turmoil as an art form. *A Splendid Chaos* is lyrical, fierce, transcendent, an unexpected turning in Shirley's career.

William Gibson completed his cyberpunk trilogy in a slick, information-dense style with *Mona Lisa Overdrive*. Richard Kadrey's debut novel, *Metrophage,* deploys the hip, drug-zonked sleaze of cyberpunk, together with surreal wisecracking, in a brio performance. But somehow the flip superficialities and violence are less subversive than Lisa Goldstein's quieter surrealism, used in a similar context. In *Wetware,* Rudy Rucker cyberbops his way through a conspiracy by robots to replace human beings. Rucker's slangy, vivacious satire combines the footwork of Fred Astaire with the farce of a Marx Brothers routine. Living paisley shorts, fractal costumes, designer drugs for robots, boneless turkeys grown in tanks: the buoyant, skew-eyed humor of the performance works excellently. Some one-liners deserve enshrinement: "God was about the same as usual—a little more burnt, maybe." Certainly this isn't "language with a flat tire," to quote another of Rucker's witticisms. At the heart of the book is an unreconstructed, liberal, hippy vision of freedom and fulfillment for all.

In the horror-fantasy vein, Jonathon Carroll's *Bones of the Moon* is another surreal pièce de résistance. Its free-floating Maurice Sendak world of Rondua invades ordinary reality enchantingly, then horrifyingly. The price of victory is death. Death that is fully perceived, death that makes the reader grieve, is a difficult act to stage.

Full Spectrum, edited by Lou Aronica and Shawna McCarthy, is the standout anthology of 1988. Perhaps the spectrum isn't actually "full"; there are hues of SF that don't feature at all here. And perhaps the introductions nudge the reader in the ribs somewhat effusively. However, the contents gained a total of five Nebula nominations.

Norman Spinrad's "Journals of the Plague Years" is both crackpot and splendid: an outpouring of vintage "Bug Jack Barron" rhetoric devoted to the hypothesis that we can copulate our way to the conquest of AIDS. James Morrow plays satirical games in "Bible Stories for Adults, No. 17: The Deluge," in which the Ark picks up a half-drowned whore. However warmly we might regard transcendence, we should always be willing to play games with religion, even if ayatollahs send out assassins. Tom Disch, whose Brave Little Toaster went cheerfully to Mars last year, describes an encounter with water-spirits lyrically and archly in "Voices of the Kill." Jack McDevitt's "The Fourth Moxie Branch" is a heart-stopping account of how a failed author is offered shelf space for his neglected masterpiece in a library full of lost works that aliens have saved from the sands of time. In "Dead Men on TV," by Pat Murphy, the anguished daughter of a dead actor watches her father's old movies over and over. Though she is living comfortably off a trust fund in an inherited ranch house, she has only one antiquated TV set. Since Pete, the TV repair man, will rekindle her life, this is a crucial plot element; and it is unbelievable. Logic flops out of the window, while simple poignancy scores.

The popularity of poignancy at the expense of solid sinew perhaps led to a couple of other Nebula nominations last year: John Kessel's "Mrs. Shummel Exits a Winner" and Connie Willis's "The Last of the Winnebagos." How very different is Ian McDonald's vivid, swirling, passionate fable, "Unfinished Portrait of the King of Pain by Van Gogh," from his collection *Empire Dreams*. With Harlan Ellison–like intensity, this new young author introduces the tormented painter to the proud, petulant superman whom future cybernetic intelligences have appointed as a judge over sinful humanity. Only the last line is banal.

Other outstanding stories in *Full Spectrum* come from Aaron Schultz, Robert Sampson, and Lisa Goldstein. In "Once in a Lullaby," by new author Fred Bals, a rich old lady in Kansas hires a private detective in Los Angeles to bid at auction for a pair of slippers worn by Judy Garland in *The Wizard of Oz*. When the new owner dons these, she rapidly sheds her years, and a tornado opens the way to the yellow brick road: "There's a path to every dream if you want to find it badly enough."

Increasingly authors are strip-mining popular mythology and writing as if these domains are actual places: the imagination come to life, as it were. Karen Joy Fowler also exploits Oz in "Heartland," a short story published in *Interzone*. Tourists are turning up; burger joints are opening. Jonathon Carroll's *Sleeping in Flame* bridges contemporary Vienna and the world of the Brothers Grimm. This is another pellucid, disquieting, magical book from a remarkable author. At the end, after Rumpelstiltskin has been trounced, a peeved Red Riding Hood turns up at the door. The *Wild Cards* anthology series, with its superheroes, represents a similar phenomenon.

Some such stories—relying on uniquely American resonances, like Willis's Winnebago tale—are opaque to outsiders. Carroll is beginning to show a tendency toward self-reference; his characters and magical domains have started to cross-refer. Gustave Flaubert once declared that he dreamed of a novel that could support itself by the power of style alone, without external reference. We are now seeing stories that, while located within normal reality in mood, nevertheless elbow the real world aside. Their allegiance is to a kind of collective mythology.

Vampires and werewolves belong to this common pool of myth. For several years now authors such as Anne Rice, Suzie McKee Charnas, and S. P. Somtow have been executing sophisticated new variations upon the vampire theme. The horror genre has grown more subtle and complex, almost philosophical. Vampires no longer lead an intellectual half-life. They represent an existential dilemma framed in passionate terms. The latest variation comes from Brian Stableford. His novelette "The Man Who Loved the Vampire Lady" is from his breakthrough novel, *The Empire of Fear*. In this excellent alternative history, vampires rule the world of the seventeenth century. However, as science arises, offering the possibility of a biological explanation of vampirism, their reign is in danger. Stableford ingeniously brings vampires over into the science-fictional sphere.

In "Madonna of the Wolves," Somtow transposes all the erotic tension of vampirism into the werewolf mythos. Although

Somtow is eloquent concerning the fierce alien beauty of the transformation, and the dark side of desire, I, myself, do not get off on packs of German shepherds pissing on a child, then tearing it to shreds. The secret project of the Lycanthrope Society is to travel to the American wilderness, to prey on the savages. Orson Scott Card's Indians might hardly welcome the prospect. Given the present tendency toward shared themes and shared worlds, may we imagine a story—as yet unwritten—in which Somtow's sophisticated, savage werewolves come up against Card's red prophet?

Susan Shwartz's anthology *Arabesques* is the first in a series that re-creates the world of the Arabian Nights. The baseline for departure isn't our modern world but a well-thought-out medieval framework. Predictably, there's much about *djinni* and virginity. Melissa Scott and M. J. Engh are ingenious and original, and Jane Yolen's "Memoirs of a Bottle Djinni" is the briefest yet neatest contribution.

Tim Sullivan's anthology *Tropical Chills* features a most disconcerting story by Pat Cadigan, "It Was the Heat." Both pungent and chilly, sensual yet structured, this story details the psychic obsession and breakdown of a businesswoman visiting New Orleans. George Zebrowski's Synergy series continued; a highlight of volume two is Daniel Pearlman's "Taking From the Top," where "publish or perish" acquires a new meaning: an aging Robert Frost scholar strives to avoid euthanasia in a coldhearted world.

The collectors' market for quality editions from private presses continues to expand. Lucius Shepard's "The Scalehunter's Beautiful Daughter" appeared both in a magazine and as a fine limited edition from Ziesing Books. This stately, stylish morality tale is a worthy partner of Shepard's earlier novella about the giant, paralyzed dragon Griaule. However, Shepard's "Nomans Land" may be his most chilling and disturbing story from last year. A pretend member of the IRA, who has been living a braggartly fantasy, is cast away with a companion on an island "capable of absorbing what came within its sphere." Transfiguration ensues. Tiny spiders with memory molecules in their poisonous venom are responsible. What's more, the human race really died out some years ago. History itself is a dream spun by the spiders, and the whole planet is a no-man's-land. The scientific rationale does, giddily, persuade us. Or is it the power of the writing, the force of the author's vision?

The same writer's "The Wooden Tiger" has no such rationale. As usual Shepard writes superbly, blending the realistic and the visionary. This tale of a CIA operative and a Tibetan goddess hovers on the borderland of utter implausibility. It possesses the sort of fundamental irreality figuring in stories written by children still ignorant of the ways of the world. But Shepard's knowledge of emotion and his demon-haunted, magical style authenticate what might otherwise be nonsense. The poetry compels us.

Kim Stanley Robinson's "The Lunatics" is another crazy story, the weirdest version yet of an escape from a penal colony. Brain-blanked prisoners, who somehow possess a "third eye," labor in darkness to dig out the element Promethium from the brain of the Moon. Seemingly, Promethium brings energy into our universe from elsewhere. Something in the dark is chasing Robinson's prisoners. They burrow up to the surface and blow up Luna City. An element named Promethium does indeed exist, and the Moon exists, but not like this! In such a story, science itself has become a kind of surreal magic. The power of style, the energy of narrative, enforces belief. There are scientific truths, and there are truths of the imagination, truths of vision. Often a mere quivering membrane separates science fiction from wonderland. Some of the finest stories inhabit this interface.

The dialectic between "truth" and "wonder" can be powerful, or it can be fey and whimsical. Steven Popkes's well-received story "The Color Winter" falls into the latter category. Can we really believe in an interstellar refugee from some depression or war working as a garage attendant in downtown Boston in order to send some dollars home? The images in the story compel our sense of pathos, winning the poignancy vote again, but the premise is quite silly.

Steven Gould's "Peaches for Mad Molly" also has a strange premise. Tough, independent squatters live on the *outside* of a three-kilometer-high, guarded condominium, breeding pigeons, growing flowers, and carrying on vertical trade despite gang warfare. Even if the gymnastics strain our credulity, the vigor and detail of the story stop the rope from snapping. Mad Molly herself, who wouldn't trade the view, or her pigeons, for a tame apartment inside, is amusingly akin to D. Alexander Smith's gutsy old lady in "Dying in Hull," where the oceans are rising but not everyone will flee from them.

Gnomelike alien refugees hide under the Yorkshire moors in Judith Moffett's "The Hob." Her extrapolation of folklore is both charming and thoroughly robust. The hibernatory Hob, who speaks in broad dialect when first encountered, has a well-devised, believable background. For once, UFO-encounter lore—the "lost day" of the abductee—makes moving, life-enhancing sense instead of numbing us with its laughability. And Moffett's attention to place is masterly.

There are authors who can extract a strong emotional kick from a simple technological innovation. Bob Shaw's "Dark Night in Toyland," a fine *Interzone* story, tells of a vicar's child dying of cancer. The boy makes a golem out of biodoh, a wonder material allowing even children to build simple living organisms and to take them apart again. As he dies, his soul transfers to the golem. The vicar reluctantly dismantles it. In Sean McMullen's "The Colors of the Masters," modern technology makes possible the processing of certain nineteenth-century recordings made upon a "harmonoscribe," and the dead play and speak again.

Away from Planet Earth, "Surfacing" by Walter Jon Williams treats a specialist in whale language who is struggling to comprehend the leviathans of an alien deep. As go-betweens, the man employs imported humpback whales. Disenchanted with his own work and tequila-besotted, he hardly knows how to talk to a fellow human being any longer. The themes of alienation and of aliens intersect richly in this elating tale of contact between species, between people.

Robert Silverberg's annual wonder-book, *At Winter's End,* seems somewhat long-winded and a touch lackluster. With his novella "We Are for the Dark," however, he is right on course. As a religious crusade to plumb the nearby stars and find God goes astray, Silverberg explores the metaphysical meaning of space, the splendor and variety of worlds, with revelatory consequences.

The avant-garde critical magazine *Science Fiction Eye* produced a special fiction issue in 1988 featuring a wonderfully eccentric, experimental story by Richard A. Lupoff. Set deep in space on a universe-hopping starship like no other, "Hyperprism 21.5" resembles a jaunty psychedelic comic with musical accompaniment.

In Earth orbit, a Kikuyu habitat follows the old African traditions to the letter in Mike Resnick's "Kirinyaga." Unfortunately, that letter prescribes the ritual murder of babies and the reinauguration of Mau Mau oaths. The shaman hero regards modern Kenyans as plastic people who have forsaken "the indomitable spirit of Jomo Kenyatta." Acts of savagery will usher in a new season of *Uhuru,* or freedom. Either "Kirinyaga" is deeply sarcastic or else the main character is clinically insane.

Frederik Pohl's "Waiting for the Olympians" also concerns the preservation of old traditions. Because the Roman Senate regained its authority under Augustus, and because Tiberius merely whipped Christ, Christianity melted away and Roman civilization continued. Consequently, Galileo is famous for detecting the first extrasolar planet, and Tycho for spectrographic analysis of his supernova. In this witty novella, a "sci-rom" novelist is hunting urgently for a salable theme. At the same time, a coalition of alien superraces is approaching to usher in galactic partnership with the human race. But then the aliens receive one new datum of information, convincing them to turn tail and to embargo Earth forever. The novelist, delightfully impervious to notions of alternative history, swallows the values of his own society lock, stock, and barrel. The explanation for the aliens' change of heart quite eludes Earth's best minds. It is, of course, that there are still slaves on Earth. More ironic still, Pohl's global Roman society *is* a utopia compared with most of recorded human history.

In George Alec Effinger's "Schrödinger's Kitten," an Arab girl sees visions of the many universes of quantum mechanics. Either she is doomed to rape and dishonor, or else she must murder her rapist before he can act, and thus she will be executed. Physicist Hilbert, holidaying in her homeland, pays the blood price to save her from death. The Arab girl herself becomes a physicist, working with Heisenberg. When she mails technical papers, instead of popular summaries, about nuclear fission to the Nazi bigwigs, she ensures that the Third Reich loses interest in any atom bomb project. The text bops back and forth in time, from world-line to world-line, illustrating the multiple possibilities jazzily.

Paul J. McCauley's first novel, *Four Hundred Billion Stars,* appeared in 1988; it is an effervescent space opera infected with a deep sense of alienation. His well-crafted, haunting story in *Interzone,* "Karl and the Ogre," switches world-lines from the scientific to the magical. Paranormal children alter our world to suit their whims, producing a wondrous and horrible fairyland where only remnants of science linger. In the new wilderness, adults from the old dispensation are hunted down as ogres.

Life after the cataclysm used to be starker and more solemn. In "Ginny Sweethips' Flying Circus," Neal Barrett, Jr., gives a nod to Monty Python as he unfolds with zany verve a survivalist scenario unlike any other. Gunfire rattles, as giant android dogs toting Uzis and riding Harleys take on a tribe of piratical insurance agents. The week before, the 7th Mercenary Writers, on horseback, had almost cleaned the underwriters out of legal pads and blank claim forms.

And if we die? Let us not be sent to anything like "The Calvin Coolidge Home for Dead Comedians." In this long satire by Bradley Denton, a foul-mouthed comedian arrives at the transit lodge adjacent to heaven. His lips are now sealed. Banal contentment is the goal. Heaven is a prissy Stepford.

In Shepard's "Nomans Land," as one of the castaways slips from dream to bizarre dream, and realizes that the whole of life is a dream, so he finally reaches "the source of dreams, the place from which life derived its impulse and meaning." He understands that he must employ these dreams "in playing the game of the world."

Whether science fiction and fantasy address urgent contemporary political and social concerns, whether they explore alien worlds or delve into the domain of Red Riding Hood or Dracula or Oz, they are playing a game of the world, a game of the universe. Crossovers occur. The paranormal invades the starship. Mayan shamanism intersects with guerrilla warfare. Unicorns enter the world of AIDS. Themes—of the alien, of alternative worlds, of biological or cybernetic transfiguration—mutate and permutate. Ultimately, all our fictions are games. They are written to entertain.

But games can be very serious affairs. We learn to live in the world by means of games. By continuing, as adults, to experience the games of science fiction and fantasy—which deal with vital questions of possible tomorrows, of radical change, and of new imaginative insights—we maintain our freshness and flexibility. Not only do we prevent a desert from invading our hearts and minds, but we also diminish the likelihood of our turning the real world into a desert.

Free Associating About
Falling Free

▼ ▼ ▼

Lois McMaster Bujold

Every year, quite reliably, these *Nebula Award* volumes show-case all the award-winning works in the short fiction categories: short story, novelette, and novella. But, for obvious reasons, it is impossible to feature the year's Nebula Award–winning novel, and an editor must struggle to find a way to acknowledge and celebrate the work of the author who has won perhaps the most coveted of the four annual awards.

An editor's options are three: run an excerpt from the winning novel; use a distinguished piece of short fiction published by the winning author during the year under review; or commission an essay or story especially for the anthology in question.

I dislike using excerpts (unless the excerpt is long enough to convey a sense of the novel's unique accomplishment) because they cannot afford a thorough picture of what the author was about. Reprinting a piece of short fiction by the author of the award-winning novel is probably the most attractive option, and last year I was especially fortunate! Pat Murphy's novel *The Falling Women* took the Nebula, as did her novelette "Rachel in Love." The second most attractive of the three options is the one to which I have necessarily resorted this year: commissioning an original piece by the author of the winning novel. Lois McMaster Bujold—whose appearance above the increasingly cluttered horizon of the SF world has been vivid and mete-oric—published no short fiction in 1988. But she agreed to expand a brief essay for the SFWA *Bulletin* on the origins of her award-winning novel into the following informal article, "Free Associating About *Falling Free*," and I hope that it in-duces many of you to go out and lay hands on a copy of the novel itself.

Ms. Bujold published her first story, "Barter," in the March/April 1985 issue of *Twilight Zone,* which unhappily ceased publishing last year. She has also had short fiction in *American Fantasy, Far Frontiers,* the anthology *Alien Stars,* and, of course, *Analog,* where *Falling Free* appeared as an extremely popular serial before its paperback release from Baen Books. Her earlier novels include *Shards of Honor* (a finalist for Balticon's 1986 Compton Crook Award for best first novel), *The Warrior's Apprentice,* and *Ethan of Athos.* In 1987, Ms. Bujold was a finalist for the John W. Campbell Award for best new writer. Since writing *Falling Free,* she has completed the novel *Brothers in Arms* and a pair of long stories, which, along with "The Borders of Infinity," appear in a collection of that title. Her work has had Spanish and Japanese editions, and her first two novels appear together in a Science Fiction Book Club edition, *Test of Honor.*

A word about the following essay: Ms. Bujold, given a chance to read Ian Watson's comments about her novel in this year's survey essay, felt it important to take issue with his characterization of the novel as a "juvenile." The points she makes are cogent, and I have placed her essay immediately after "Themes and Variations" in order to suggest a dialogue. By the way, I see Ms. Bujold's concept of an obsolescent species of bioengineered humanity as one of the most compelling and fascinating notions of the past several years, and her treatment of it always ingenious and gripping. *Falling Free,* I think, will have a long and influential life.

I had an array of goals in writing *Falling Free.* First, I intended it to be both a tribute to and a commentary on the sort of SF I began reading at age nine—my *Analog* story. My mother, cleaning out files, recently turned up the check stub from my first gift subscription to *Analog,* which I received for my thirteenth birthday. (A year's issues cost four dollars back then.) *Falling Free'*s subsequent serialization therein completed the circuit, to my delight.

I use the phrase "commentary on" with precision. "Parody," "pastiche," and "satire" are cold, unloving terms, and I loved those tales with passion. But, clearly, some of the early *Analog* stories had vision defects. One was the absence of women from their worldview, as if the stork had brought all those soldiers and scientists and engineers. It should be no particular surprise to learn that one of my early favorite *Analog* authors was James H. Schmitz, whose female heroes took center stage—even if he didn't go so far as to show them doing women's work. However, in the course of my writing I discovered a subtler reason than sexism for the lack of creditable females in some stories; action-adventure, for a woman with children in tow like my quaddie Claire, is not fun. It is, in fact, a fair approximation of hell. No escapism there.

But in even the most aggressively masculine military SF, we should not forget that every one of those guys onstage is a former pregnancy—except, of course, in stories where they are gestated in vats. I take on the fuller implications of vats in other works, particularly *Ethan of Athos; Falling Free* was too crowded to make this running theme (of the uses and abuses that will become possible when reproduction passes out of women's control) more explicit. But the theme is there, backgrounded like women themselves, and like women utterly fundamental to the whole setup.

Briefly, *Falling Free* is the origin-story of a new, bioengineered species of human beings. GalacTech, their parent corporation, developed the "quaddies" to live and work permanently in free-fall. In addition to numerous metabolic changes to maintain health in zero-g, the most spectacular alteration is the substitution of a second set of arms in place of relatively useless legs. But an advance from an unexpected quarter, the development of a practical, artificially generated gravity, renders the space workers obsolete. *Falling Free* explores the consequences of technological obsolescence when the technology in question is bioengineering, the obsolete "product" a human being. Interestingly, the most moving and insightful letters I received on the book were from blind or otherwise handicapped readers, who have felt in their own lives just what it means to be classed as "redundant."

The novel may be "a juvenile," i.e., a book young people can read (in fact, I hope it may reach as broad an audience as possible); it is emphatically not juvenile, i.e., immature, trivial, or witless. Juvenile interests, in this second definition, include violence, pornography, narcissistic despair, and a great deal of posturing.

Adult interests include teaching, building, nurturing, making moral choices, and taking personal responsibility for the welfare of fellow human beings. All these adult themes are right on deck in *Falling Free.*

But back to my array of goals. For me, hard SF of the *Analog* type has always been the defining core of the genre, undoubtedly because of my early imprinting (rather like that of a baby duck). My earlier novels were classed by some reviewers as space opera, a subcategory of equally ancient and honorable lineage. But I wanted to prove that if I wrote space opera, I did so by choice, and not because I was incapable of anything "better" or "harder." However, as I also discovered, the assertion that it's called "hard SF" because it is harder to write has a certain merit.

Noting that much current SF, including my own, seemed rather overrun with military themes and heroes, I wanted to write a tale with a scientist (or at least an engineer) as hero. Too, I wanted to recall for myself the early pleasures of Nevil Shute's novels, with their ordinary blokes rising to extraordinary circumstances. I am, frankly, a character-centered writer. I greatly admire the short story writers who can deliver that quick intellectual hit, but my own novelist's aim is to slip the reader gently into a warm bath of characterization—and gradually turn up the heat. Ideas in fiction exist to test and display character; poorly extrapolated ideas betray those same characters.

I had an insight while watching a singularly bad thriller movie that seemed to have everything—the budget, the actors, the high-speed car chases—but that totally failed to thrill. Musing upon it, I realized that it does a writer no good to place a character in danger without first taking the trouble to make the audience care whether the character lives or dies. So the secret of compelling action seems to be characterization too, The amount of caring, not the amount of bloodshed, raises the reader's pulse rate. I had slaughtered thousands to make my first novel; as a personal challenge, I wanted to see if I could write a high-tension adventure without killing *anybody.*

Another old peeve of mine is the magical-science genius—you know, the man who steps offstage to solve some difficult problem and returns waving the solution or device, without the reader's ever getting to see how he did it. This narrative approach leads the poor reader to imagine that scientific ability, like psi power, is something ordinary people do not possess. (I particularly envied those phalanxes of heroes with photographic memories.) I wanted my characters to do their problem solving onstage, the real way, in fits and starts and with no certainty about the outcome. A number of reviewers seem to be allergic to engineering, citing a preference for "characterization," as if engineering were not a human activity, or as if solving a difficult engineering problem in difficult circumstances were not both a test and a demonstration of character. I disagree profoundly.

Falling Free, though it eventually put down roots through my whole life-experience, had its immediate genesis in a series of phone conversations with my publisher, Jim Baen. I had written my first three novels more or less in isolation in Marion, Ohio, though with unstinting help by mail from two writer friends, Lillian Carl and Pat Wrede. Having finally captured a publisher, and conscious of the option clause, I naturally wanted to make sure my next book was one Jim could buy. The quaddies began as a background item in another story line I proffered, interstellar junk dealers living in their asteroid belt, the obsolete products of bioengineering dealing in the obsolete products of engineering. Jim perked right up, assuring me that no one had done the idea of obsolete people in quite this way. Writers have plowed over the SF genre for sixty years; it seemed exciting, if unlikely, that any idea of mine could really be new. Encouraged, I started to think about the quaddies. Eventually resolving to begin at their beginning, I reasoned my way back to the Habitat.

Initially, for convenience, I made my hero Leo Graf—you may picture him, physically, as a cross between Mel Gibson and Mr. Wizard—a welding and nondestructive testing engineer. My father was a world-class authority in those fields. His work is today saving the lives of people who will never know his name; among other things he was the inventor of xeroradiography, now being used worldwide in the early detection of cancer. Because we took regular weekend trips with the kids to the grandparents' anyway, my research and expert-review problems seemed solved. But my father died of a chronic heart condition before the book was a third done. His death threw me on other sources for the techie bits, to be sure, but it also centered the book more firmly on my characterization of engineers, both good and bad.

Our society sometimes takes the technology that supports it—and especially the huge numbers of dedicated people who make that technology go—terribly for granted. If my space-living quaddies ever lost their technological base, they would die quickly (as when the air goes out the lock); not many people seem to have noticed that we on Planet Earth are in the same spaceship, except that some of us would have the dubious privilege of dying more slowly (as when the electricity goes off in New York City). So I wanted to put in a plea for technology as a high *human* endeavor. (Note, please, that I consider eco-consciousness to be an integral part of sound technological thinking. A call for technology is not a call for paving the Earth; it's a call for living smarter.) Real survivalists don't run off into the woods; they stay and work to *prevent* disaster. If *Falling Free* encourages even one bright young person to look into engineering as a career, I should be most pleased.

Ray Bradbury:
Ambassador to the Future

! ! !

Greg Bear

Greg Bear, as I write, is in his second term as president of Science Fiction Writers of America. Because I am almost six years his elder, I sometimes find myself viewing him—despite his three Nebulas, his two Hugos, and a literary output boasting some of the most original science fiction of the past half decade—as a Young Turk, an upstart, a whippersnapper. Fondly, though, always fondly, for Bear is one of those rare people who strive to do everything at the top of their talent and who thereby succeed in enriching us all. His award-winning short fiction includes the 1983 novelette "Blood Music," on which he based his Prix Apollo–winning novel of that title; the complex novella "Hardfought" (1983); and "Tangents" (1986), the title piece of a new story collection. *Eon, The Forge of God, Eternity,* and *Queen of Angels* constitute a short list of his distinguished recent novels.

Although we have met only a time or two, my link to Greg Bear goes back at least fourteen years—to my admiration of a cover painting he executed for *Analog* for his story "A Martian Ricorso" (February 1976). Four years later, I reviewed his first novel for *Fantasy & Science Fiction.* About this book, *Hegira,* I said, "Bear already has a sure grasp of a writer's most basic tools, and that is something to celebrate in a first novelist." Three years later, Arkham House—publishers of my first story collection—did Bear's first collection, *The Wind from a Burning Woman.* Its title came, with my ready blessing, from a poem of mine, "Postcards to Athena." Clearly, I am here attempting to bask in reflected glory, for Bear has established himself not only as one of the field's brightest stars of the 1980s but also as the writer most likely to emerge as the genre talent with a reputation as deservedly large as those of Robert Heinlein, Arthur C. Clarke, Isaac Asimov, and Ray Bradbury.

In the following essay, not incidentally, Bear acknowledges

his debt to the last-named of these four estimable gentlemen, SFWA's tenth officially designated Grand Master. Although I have yet to meet Ray Bradbury myself, I identify with nearly everything Bear says about him because Bradbury (the author of "In a Season of Calm Weather," "The Wonderful Ice Cream Suit," "All Summer in a Day," "Dark They Were, and Golden-eyed," "The Town Where No One Got Off," "The Golden Apples of the Sun," "A Sound of Thunder," "The Flying Machine," "The Veldt," "The Small Assassin," and dozens upon dozens of other magical tales) was my first career model, too. Further, Bear's high regard for the man undoubtedly mirrors that of hundreds of other published writers who remember their first encounters with Ray Bradbury's lyrical stories as among the most crucial formative experiences of their lives.

There's something familiar to many of us about Ray Bradbury's youth. According to friends, he was a brash, awkward teenager given to enthusiasm, writing terrible stories, and making even worse puns. He published pseudonymous stories in his own fan magazines. He associated with other awkward youths, and they all read awkward, youthful magazines that published science fiction and fantasy. In these magazines he found foods not yet recognized by the grown-up literary critics of the time: exotic, highly spiced dishes by Clark Ashton Smith, and steaks and meatpies by Theodore Sturgeon and Robert A. Heinlein. He swallowed them whole, digested them with Edgar Allan Poe, and added a dessert made in part of depression America, Emily Dickinson, and Ernest Hemingway. Incidentally, he read everything else he could get his hands on, mining his local library.

Forrest J. Ackerman says that Bradbury frequently drove his companions to thoughts of mayhem. A few idly considered drowning him. Yet even then, they saw that in this gadfly adolescent there was a concern for that which is most human: love, fear, memory and myth, and dreams of better things. Bradbury knew there would be spaceships: the weapons of World War II had given birth to their destructive embryos. Many people he admired told him the rest would come soon enough.

He wanted spaceships to exist. But he also wished to know

what they would mean to us when they arrived. In his early twenties, he began writing stories that would speak to Earthbound people in virtually every literate country in the world.

The nuts and bolts of science and technology were of less concern to him than the inner feelings of people, their reactions to the reality of what was, in his youth, barely even dreamed of. Whether or not he was consciously aware of what he was doing, Bradbury set out to make a myth, to condense the future into images and narratives accessible to ordinary men, women and children.

Bradbury always worked at a fever pitch, aiming to have a work completed, if not refined, every single day. This necessarily limited him—with a few notable exceptions—to the short story.

We are all subconscious writers, but for most of us, most of the time, the subconscious submits its works for criticism before they are written down. Bradbury prefers fresher goods, unopened packages; he does not wish to know what is going to happen until it surprises him by appearing on the page. Most writers have a fond uneasiness about their inner story daemons; Bradbury trusts his implicitly.

In each Bradbury story there is a burst of anger or fear, of wonder or pique; a laugh, a scream, a sigh. Yet these are not manipulations so much as shared responses. Bradbury allows us to find these emotions in ourselves, by reacting to the situations he invents and records.

Once, long ago, a question arose as to whether Ray Bradbury wrote science fiction or fantasy. Technically speaking, most of what he writes is fantasy; speaking honestly, it doesn't matter a whit. He is a fabulist. True makers of fables are given a very special literary license: they can do and go where they please, and shrug off labels like irritating leeches.

Bradbury, despite considerable success—he is arguably the most famous science fiction writer in the world—has never shunned the friends and colleagues of his youth. He is of that rare and balanced breed that embraces the joys and concerns of childhood while at the same time understanding perfectly well he is grown up now, with greater responsibilities. This shows in his work; it shows in his life.

My personal memories of Ray are more than fond. He is my career model, more than any other writer; from my early adolescence, I absorbed his work and tried to find something equally genuine in myself. What he taught me was that I must find strong emotions to power my stories. Social situations, plots and stratagems are well and good, but they are not enough. There has to be something deeply heartfelt behind every important story or novel.

I first met Ray in 1968, when he came to San Diego to speak at a local high school. I was a green 16; I came clutching a script for an adaptation of his "A Sound of Thunder." Our high school film group wanted to make a movie of the story. I was there to meet the man, and ask his permission. Coincidentally, another group of filmmakers from nearby Carlsbad—William Stromberg and Phil Tippett—was also present, also clutching a script, also asking permission. Ray generously gave both groups permission, so long as no profit was involved. My group never completed its film; Stromberg was to finish his version over fifteen years later.

From that point on, I corresponded with Ray, and that correspondence lasts to this day. Ray always took the time to answer my letters, to offer cautious advice, to encourage and provide an excellent example. He had no way of knowing whether or not anything would come of his encouragement; doubtless dozens of other correspondents with the ambition to become writers received equal encouragement, and most gave up.

I didn't.

I'm not very objective about Ray Bradbury. I love the man and his works. He has become a literary papa to me. To be in the position to give him this long-deserved honor is a privilege; to give it to him as a fellow writer and president of an organization filled with so many other personal heroes and exemplars gives me a feeling of completion and pride that is difficult to express.

I'll have to write a story about it some day.

Welcome to the Grand Masters of Science Fiction, Ray. It's long overdue.

The Collector Speaks

▼ ▼ ▼

Ray Bradbury

Ray Bradbury is probably better known for his lyrical prose than for his lyrical verse, but he admits to a love affair with poetry going back to the age of ten. At Los Angeles High School, he belonged to the Poetry Club, one of three brave boys "inundated" by fifteen young ladies, all of whom struck him as the superior talents. And, as he confesses in "How to Keep and Feed a Muse," his introduction to *The Complete Poems of Ray Bradbury,* "It took me the better part of twenty-five years to catch up. I wrote poetry during all that time, against the advice of family and friends. I simply couldn't help myself. The ideas were there, and I had to get them down."

His breakthrough came when the editors of *Pro Football* magazine asked him for a 3,000-word article on the game. He declined the assignment, politely pointing out that he could write about a topic only if the inspiration for doing so came from within. Once off the phone, however, he began remembering his boyhood connections to football, went to his typewriter, and in a half hour's time turned out a 135-line poem—"All Flesh Is One; What Matter Scores?"—that *Pro Football* accepted in a shot.

This experience gave Bradbury the boost he needed to send out others of his poems. Eventually, he published three collections—*When Elephants Last in the Dooryard Bloomed* (1973), *Where Robot Mice and Robot Men Run Round in Robot Towns* (1977), and *The Haunted Computer and the Android Pope* (1981)—which together make up *The Complete Poems of Ray Bradbury* (1982). His acknowledged companions are Shakespeare, Emily Dickinson, Gerard Manley Hopkins, William Butler Yeats, Robert Frost, and Dylan Thomas. Unlike the "poets" whose work "currently decorates and bores you in *The New Yorker,*" Bradbury does not disdain the old virtues of rhyme, alliteration, assonance, and consonance.

The following poem—"The Collector Speaks"—has its first publication in *Nebula Awards 24.* Although the editor and Harcourt Brace Jovanovich have made a small token payment

to secure it, I would argue that in truth the poem is Ray Bradbury's gift to the membership of SFWA and to every reader
who has ever marveled at his intermingled talents for invention
and song. In a letter written on Valentine's Day 1989, he told
me that "The Collector Speaks" "pretty well describes the way
I create, the relationship I have between my outer skin and my
inner stuffs." Bradbury the collector is Bradbury the writer,
and vice versa, and this poem illuminates them both . . . without
puncturing the mystery of either.

It's so hard for me to let anything stay
Leave anything lost on the road.
We were changing our wallpaper yesterday,
Time's goad said touch, not only touch but keep
That sample of old, up there by the mold.
I can let no mere thing sink to sleep,
I want the cats beneath our turf
Under our grass.
The silver-shard of agate glass
From some old game
Is mine. That shame
I'm sure I share with those like me
Who suffer change immoderately.
I cram my files with oddment pictures
Ancient rictures of smiles and frowns,
Views of nameless towns and villas, mindless bogs
Whispers of various dogs,
Hair of the frog that leaped as a boy.
All toys, broken or mended,
Every roadmap we ever wended or strode,
Chips of bricks from the halred in it mud out front my
        house.
Button of Mickey Mouse,
Buck Rogers ring that can code, decode,
Locks of my loves, all women, all daughters.
Mineral waters from the downtown shop
Where haircrops were scythed by our ancient barber,
Who swept the floor with a mythic broom.

All *that?* you cry. No room! No room!
No room for you—that may well be.
But, look, touch, feel:
Much room
In me.

More Than One Way to Burn a Book

▮ ▮ ▮

Ray Bradbury

Born in 1920 in Waukegan, Illinois (the real-world template
for the fictional Green Town in his novels *Dandelion Wine* and
Something Wicked This Way Comes), Ray Bradbury moved to Los
Angeles with his family; he graduated from high school there
in 1938 and published his first story in *Rob Wagner's Script* two
years later. In the intervening half century—how can *that*
be?—he has indisputably become a citizen of the world, a
praise-singing child of the entire universe.

One of my first encounters with Bradbury's work was an
indirect one. An excited, almost beside-himself teenage friend
told me in loving detail the plot of one of the wonder-invoking
stories in *The Martian Chronicles*. At the time, we were cruising
the semirural south side of Tulsa, Oklahoma, in the beat-up
Ford of another buddy and stupidly sipping vodka and grape
juice out of soggy milk shake cups. Later, I discovered that this
story was "The Earth Men," the second full-length tale in *The
Martian Chronicles*. My friend had got all the crucial plot elements right, but he had utterly failed to render the delicious-
ness of Bradbury's language:

"A man squatted alone in darkness. Out of his mouth
issued a blue flame which turned into the round shape of a
small naked woman. It flourished on the air softly in vapors of
cobalt light, whispering and sighing."

And:

"A woman stood there, changing. First she was embedded
in a crystal pillar, then she melted into a golden statue, finally
a staff of polished cedar, and back to a woman."

I was smitten. This Ray Bradbury—depicted in line drawings on the covers of his books as a youngish man with a shy
smile and a shooting guard's crew cut—was the first writer
since Jack London to show me *really* new stuff, *really* new
worlds, *really* new ways of transforming a series of black-and-

white printed pages into a photo album of vivid colors and mind-expanding images. I wanted to read everything I could by him. And, soon enough, my small library of paperbacks— bought with money earned sacking groceries at Phelps's IGA—included *A Medicine for Melancholy, The October Country, The Golden Apples of the Sun, The Illustrated Man,* and, of course, *The Martian Chronicles.* Each title is an evocation; each story in each volume, a dear, imperishable memory.

By now, Bradbury has published twenty-three books, in- cluding an autobiographical mystery novel, *Death Is a Lonely Business;* several collections of plays; a huge retrospective of his stories; and last year's first new story collection in almost a decade, *The Toynbee Convector.* An opera based on his novel *Fahrenheit 451* premiered in Fort Wayne, Indiana, in Novem- ber 1988; a musical based on *Dandelion Wine,* with music by Jimmy Webb, opened last year at the University of Oklahoma, Tulsa, in my old hometown. And twelve new episodes of *Ray Bradbury TV Theater* ran on USA Cable during the last three months of 1989. Now entering his seventieth year, Bradbury shows few signs of his age. His effervescent personality still yearns after favorite writers, spaceflight, his own artfully trans- figured past, and all the other human miracles, large and small, that feed his life and work.

The essay that follows—"More Than One Way to Burn a Book"—first appeared in October 1977 as an afterword to the forty-eighth printing (!) of his classic novel *Fahrenheit 451.* I am reprinting it here not only because I believe that the *Nebula Awards* anthology commemorating Ray Bradbury's official des- ignation as a Grand Master should include a strong sampling of his work but also because this essay forthrightly addresses the question of censorship. And 1989, the year in which SFWA physically bestowed this award on Bradbury, was also the year in which the Ayatollah Khomenei of Iran condemned Salman Rushdie to death for publishing a novel, *The Satanic Verses,* that he viewed as blasphemous and offensive to Islam.

Greg Bear, as president of SFWA, urged every member to send the following statement, or a variation on it, to our local libraries, bookstores, congressional representatives, and sena- tors: "Freedom of expression is sacrosanct. Anyone who seeks to remove a book or any other artistic or literary expression from public notice, whether it be because they find it offensive, or fear that others will find it offensive, is my enemy, as if they threaten harm to my family and my children."

Bear noted in an open letter to SFWA that "Rushdie's plight is a bitter reminder that Western notions of freedom of expression are not universally held." He reported that even then a parent's group in his own state had asked that *The Martian Chronicles* be deleted from a list of titles recommended ' for advanced English study at the junior high level.

Bradbury has never had to go into hiding for outraging readers, but, clearly, he *has* known firsthand the occasional pettiness of the American reading public. His essay is a reply to the kind of intolerance that elsewhere, magnified, permits a religious leader to call for another human being's death.

About two years ago, a letter arrived from a solemn young Vassar lady telling me how much she enjoyed reading my experiment in space mythology, *The Martian Chronicles.*

But, she added, wouldn't it be a good idea, this late in time, to rewrite the book inserting more women's characters and roles?

A few years before that, I got a certain amount of mail concerning the same Martian book complaining that the blacks in the book were Uncle Toms and why didn't I "do them over"?

Along about then came a note from a Southern white suggesting that I was prejudiced in favor of the blacks and the entire story should be dropped.

Two weeks ago, my mountain of mail delivered forth a pipsqueak mouse of a letter from a well-known publishing house that wanted to reprint my story "The Fog Horn" in a high school reader.

In my story, I had described a lighthouse as having, late at night, an illumination coming from it that was a "God-Light." Looking up at it from the viewpoint of any sea-creature, one would have felt that one was "in the Presence."

The editors had deleted "God-Light" and "in the Presence."

Some five years back, the editors of yet another anthology for school readers put together a volume with some 400 (count 'em) short stories in it. How do you cram 400 short stories by Twain, Irving, Poe, Maupassant and Bierce into one book?

Simplicity itself. Skin, debone, demarrow, scarify, melt, render down, and destroy. Every adjective that counted, every verb that moved, every metaphor that weighed more than a mosquito—out! Every simile that would have made a sub-moron's mouth twitch—gone! Any aside that explained the two-bit philosophy of a first-rate writer—lost!

Every story, slenderized, starved, bluepenciled, leeched and bled white, resembled every other story. Twain read like Poe read like Shakespeare read like Dostoevsky read like—in the finale—Edgar Guest. Every word of more than three syllables had been razored. Every image that demanded so much as one instant's attention—shot dead.

Do you begin to get the damned and incredible picture?

How did I react to all of the above?

By "firing" the whole lot.

By sending rejection slips to each and every one.

By ticketing the assembly of idiots to the far reaches of hell.

The point is obvious. There is more than one way to burn a book. And the world is full of people running about with lit matches. Every minority, be it Baptist/Unitarian, Irish/Italian/Octogenarian/Zen Buddhist, Zionist/Seventh-Day Adventist, Women's Lib/Republican, Mattachine/Four Square Gospel, feels it has the will, the right, the duty to douse the kerosene, light the fuse. Every dimwit editor who sees himself as the source of all dreary blanc-mange plain porridge unleavened literature, licks his guillotine and eyes the neck of any author who dares to speak above a whisper or write above a nursery rhyme.

Fire-Captain Beatty, in my novel *Fahrenheit 451,* described how the books were burned first by minorities, each ripping a page or a paragraph from this book, then that, until the day came when the books were empty and the minds shut and the libraries closed forever.

"Shut the door, they're coming through the window, shut the window, they're coming through the door," are the words to an old song. They fit my life-style with newly arriving butcher/censors every month. Only six weeks ago, I discovered that, over the years, some cubbyhole editors at Ballantine Books, fearful of contaminating the young, had, bit by bit, censored some 75 separate sections from the novel. Students, reading the novel which, after all, deals with censorship and book-burning in the future, wrote to tell me of this exquisite irony. Judy-Lynn del Rey, one of the new Ballantine editors, is having the entire book reset this summer [1979] with all the damns and hells back in place.

A final test for old Job II here: I sent a play, *Leviathan 99,* off to a university theater a month ago. My play is based on the "Moby Dick" mythology, dedicated to Melville, and concerns a rocket crew and a blind space captain who venture forth to encounter a Great White Comet and destroy the destroyer. My drama premieres as an opera in Paris this autumn. But, for now, the university wrote back that they hardly dared do my play—it had no women in it! And the ERA ladies on campus would descend with ballbats if the drama department even tried!

Grinding my bicuspids into powder, I suggested that would mean, from now on, no more productions of *Boys in the Band* (no women), or *The Women* (no men). Or, counting heads, male and female, a good lot of Shakespeare that would never be seen again, especially if you count lines and find that all the good stuff went to the males!

I wrote back maybe they should do my play one week, and *The Women* the next. They probably thought I was joking, and I'm not sure that I wasn't.

For it is a mad world and it will get madder if we allow the minorities, be they dwarf or giant, orangutan or dolphin, nuclear-head or water-conservationist, pro-computerologist or Neo-Luddite, simpleton or sage, to interfere with aesthetics. The real world is the playing ground for each and every group, to make or unmake the laws. But the tip of the nose of my book or stories or poems is where their rights end and my territorial imperatives begin, run and rule. If Mormons do not like my plays, let them write their own. If the Irish hate my Dublin stories, let them rent typewriters. If teachers and grammar school editors find my jaw-breaker sentences shatter their mushmilk teeth, let them eat stale cake dunked in weak tea of their own ungodly manufacture. If the Chicano intellectuals wish to re-cut my "Wonderful Ice Cream Suit" so it shapes "Zoot," may the belt unravel and the pants fall.

For, let's face it, digression is the soul of wit. Take philosophic asides away from Dante, Milton or Hamlet's father's ghost and what stays is dry bones. Laurence Sterne said it once: Digressions, incontestably, are the sunshine, the life, the soul of reading! Take them out and one cold eternal winter would reign in every page. Restore them to the writer—he steps forth like a bridegroom, bids all-hail, brings in variety and forbids the appetite to fail.

In sum, do not insult me with the beheadings, finger-choppings or the lung-deflations you plan for my works. I need my head to shake or nod, my hand to wave or make into a fist, my lungs to shout or whisper with. I will not go gently onto a shelf, degutted, to become a non-book.

All you umpires, back to the bleachers. Referees, hit the showers. It's my game. I pitch, I hit, I catch. I run the bases. At sunset I've won or lost. At sunrise, I'm out again, giving it the old try.

And no one can help me. Not even you.

Bible Stories for Adults,
No 17: The Deluge

▼ ▼ ▼

James Morrow

James Morrow has written *The Wine of Violence, The Continent of Lies, This Is the Way the World Ends,* and *Only Begotten Daughter,* a series of unrelated, idiosyncratic novels that nevertheless offer a self-consistent critique of humanity in conflict with its various gods. As I wrote in my introduction to a tale by Morrow in *Nebula Awards 23,* "Imagine Dostoevsky's brain sharing cranial space with Kurt Vonnegut's, and you may acquire a shadowy idea of the kind of mind in operation here."

That description of this highly original, and unapologetically serious, writer's mind and method strikes me as appropriate to this year's short-story-award winner, "Bible Stories for Adults, No. 17: The Deluge." Also, the story itself seems an appropriate winner in a year in which the Ayatollah Khomenei put out a contract on the life of an author whose latest novel he deemed both blasphemous and offensive. A year in which biblical literalists in this country tried to prevent movie theaters from showing Martin Scorsese's *The Last Temptation of Christ.* A year in which George Bush visited a flag factory and thumped his Democratic opponent for declining to compel everyone in America's public schools to recite the Pledge of Allegiance.

Writes Morrow, "In the current atmosphere of Republican Party piety, it's sometimes difficult to remember what a morally ambiguous anthology—perhaps I should say collection—the Bible is. Is my treatment of the Flood blasphemous? I certainly hope so. Is it offensive? Perhaps. But then so, to my mind, is the story on which it's based."

Take your cup down to the Caspian, dip, and drink. It did not always taste of salt. Yahweh's watery slaughter may have purified the earth, but it left his seas a ruin, brackish with pagan blood and the tears of wicked orphans.

Sheila and her generation know the deluge is coming. Yahweh speaks to them through their sins. A thief cuts a purse, and the shekels clank together, pealing out a call to repentance. A priest kneels before a graven image of Dagon, and the statue opens its marble jaws, issuing not its own warnings but Yahweh's. A harlot threads herself with a thorny vine, tearing out unwanted flesh, and a divine voice rises from the bleeding fetus. You are a corrupt race, Yahweh says, abominable in my sight. My rains will scrub you from the earth.

Yahweh is as good as his word. The storm breaks. Creeks become rivers, rivers cataracts. Lakes blossom into broiling, wrathful seas.

Yes, Sheila is thoroughly foul in those days, her apple home to many worms, the scroll of her sins as long as the Araxas. She is gluttonous and unkempt. She sells her body. Her abortions number eleven. *I should have made it twelve,* she realizes on the day the deluge begins. But it is too late, she had already gone through with it—the labor more agonizing than any abortion, her breasts left pulpy and deformed—and soon the boy was seven, athletic, clever, fair of face, but today the swift feet are clamped in the cleft of an olive tree root, the clever hands are still, the fair face lies buried in water.

A mother, Sheila has heard, should be a boat to her child, buoying him up during floods, bearing him through storms, and yet it is Sam who rescues her. She is hoisting his corpse aloft, hoping to drain the death from his lungs, when suddenly his little canoe floats by. A scooped-out log, nothing more, but still his favorite toy. He liked to paddle it across the Araxas and catch turtles in the marsh.

Sheila climbs aboard, leaving Sam's meat to the sharks.

Captain's Log. 10 June 1057 After Creation

The beasts eat too much. At present rates of consumption, we'll be out of provisions in a mere fifteen weeks.

For the herbivores: 4,540 pounds of oats a day, 6,780 pounds of hay, 2,460 of vegetables, and 3,250 of fruit.

For the carnivores: 17,620 pounds of yak and caribou meat a day. And we may lose the whole supply if we don't find a way to freeze it.

Yahweh's displeasure pours down in great swirling sheets, as if the planet lies fixed beneath a waterfall. Sheila paddles without passion, no goal in mind, no reason to live. Fierce winds churn the sea. Lightning shatters the sky. The floodwaters thicken with disintegrating sinners, afloat on their backs, their gelatinous eyes locked in pleading stares, as if begging God for a second chance.

The world reeks. Sheila gags on the vapors. Is the decay of the wicked, she wonders, more odoriferous than that of the just? When she dies, will her stink drive even flies and vultures away?

Sheila wants to die, but her flesh argues otherwise, making her lift her mouth toward heaven and swallow the quenching downpour. The hunger will be harder to solve: it hurts, a scorpion stinging her belly, so painful that Sheila resolves to add cannibalism to her repertoire. But then, in the bottom of the canoe, she spies two huddled turtles, confused, fearful. She eats one raw, beginning with the head, chewing the leathery tissues, drinking the salty blood.

A dark mountainous shape cruises out of the blur. A sea monster, she decides, angry, sharp-toothed, ravenous . . . Yahweh incarnate, eager to rid the earth of Sheila. Fine. Good. Amen. Painfully she lifts her paddle, heavy as a millstone, and strokes through a congestion of drowned princes and waterlogged horses, straight for the hulking deity.

Now God is atop her, a headlong collision, fracturing her canoe like a crocodile's tail smacking an egg. The floodwaters cover her, a frigid darkness flows through her, and with her last breath she lobs a sphere of mucus into Yahweh's gloomy and featureless face.

Captain's Log. 20 June 1057 A.C.

Yahweh said nothing about survivors. Yet this morning we came upon two.

The *Testudo marginata* posed no problem. We have plenty of turtles, all two hundred and twenty-five species in fact, *Testudinidae, Chelydridae, Platysternidae, Kinosternidae, Chelonidae,* you name it. Unclean beasts, inedible, useless. We left it to the flood. Soon it will swim itself to death.

The *Homo sapiens* was a different matter. Frightened, delirious, she clung to her broken canoe like a sloth embracing a tree. "Yahweh was explicit," said Ham, leaning over *Eden II*'s rail, calling into the gushing storm. "Everyone not in this family deserves death."

"She is one of the tainted generation," added his wife. "A whore. Abandon her."

"No," countered Japheth. "We must throw her a line, as any men of virtue would do."

His young bride had no opinion.

As for Shem and Tamar, the harlot's arrival became yet another occasion for them to bicker. "Japheth is right," insisted Shem. "Bring her among us, Father."

"Let Yahweh have his way with her," retorted Tamar. "Let the flood fulfill its purpose."

"What do *you* think?" I asked Reumah.

Smiling softly, my wife pointed to the dinghy.

I ordered the little boat lowered. Japheth and Shem rode it to the surface of the lurching sea, prying the harlot from her canoe, hauling her over the transom. After much struggle we got her aboard *Eden II,* laying her unconscious bulk on the foredeck. She was a lewd walrus, fat and dissipated. A necklace of rat skulls dangled from her squat neck. When Japheth pushed on her chest, water fountained out, and a cough ripped through her like a yak's roar.

"Who are you?" I demanded.

She fixed me with a dazed stare and fainted. We carried her below, setting her among the pigs like the unclean thing she is. Reumah stripped away our visitor's soggy garments, and I winced to behold her pocked and twisted flesh.

"Sinner or not, Yahweh has seen fit to spare her," said my wife, wrapping a dry robe around the harlot. "We are the instruments of his amnesty."

"Perhaps," I said, snapping the word like a whip.

The final decision rests with me, of course, not with my sons or their wives. Is the harlot a test? Would a true God-follower sink this human flotsam without a moment's hesitation?

Even asleep, our visitor is vile, her hair a lice farm, her breath a polluting wind.

Sheila awakens to the snorty gossip of pigs. A great bowl of darkness envelops her, dank and dripping like a basket submerged in a swamp. Her nostrils burn with a hundred varieties of stench. She believes that Yahweh has swallowed her, that she is imprisoned in his maw.

Slowly a light seeps into her eyes. Before her, a wooden gate creaks as it pivots on leather hinges. A young man approaches, proffering a wineskin and a cooked leg of mutton.

"Are we inside God?" Sheila demands, propping her thick torso on her elbows. Someone has given her dry clothes. The effort of speaking tires her, and she lies back in the swine-scented straw. "Is this Yahweh?"

"The last of his creation," the young man replies. "My

parents, brothers, our wives, the birds, beasts—and myself, Japheth. Here. Eat." Japheth presses the mutton to her lips. "Seven of each clean animal, that was our quota. In a month we shall run out. Enjoy it while you can."

"I want to die." Once again, Sheila's abundant flesh has a different idea, devouring the mutton, guzzling the wine.

"If you wanted to die," says Japheth, "you would not have gripped that canoe so tightly. Welcome aboard."

"Aboard?" says Sheila. Japheth is most handsome. His crisp black beard excites her lust. "We're on a boat?"

Japheth nods. *"Eden II.* Gopher wood, stem to stern. This is the world now, nothing else remains. Yahweh means for you to be here."

"I doubt that." Sheila knows her arrival is a freak. She has merely been overlooked. No one means for her to be here, least of all God.

"My father built it," the young man explains. "He is six hundred years old."

"Impressive," says Sheila, grimacing. She has seen the type, a crotchety, withered patriarch, tripping over his beard. Those final five hundred years do nothing for a man, save to make his skin leathery and his worm boneless.

"You're a whore, aren't you?" asks Japheth.

The boat pitches and rolls, unmooring Sheila's stomach. She lifts the wineskin to her lips and fills her pouchy cheeks. "Also a drunkard, thief, self-abortionist"—her grin stretches well into the toothless regions—"and sexual deviant." With her palm she cradles her left breast, heaving it to one side.

Japheth gasps and backs away.

Another day, perhaps, they will lie together. For now, Sheila is exhausted, stunned by wine. She rests her reeling head on the straw and sleeps.

Captain's Log. 25 June 1057 A.C.

We have harvested a glacier, bringing thirty tons of ice aboard. For the moment, our meat will not become carrion; our tigers, wolves, and carnosaurs will thrive.

I once saw the idolators deal with an outcast. They tethered his ankles to an ox, his wrists to another ox. They drove the first beast north, the second south.

Half of me believes we must admit this woman. Indeed, if we kill her, do we not become the same people Yahweh saw fit to destroy? If we so sin, do we not contaminate the very race we are meant to sire? In my sons' loins rests the whole of the future. We are the keepers of our kind. Yahweh picked us for the purity of our seed, not the infallibility of our justice. It is hardly our place to condemn.

My other half begs that I cast her into the flood. A harlot, Japheth assures me. A dipsomaniac, robber, lesbian, and fetus-killer. She should have died with the rest of them. We must not allow her degencrate womb back into the world, lest it bear fruit.

Again Sheila awakens to swine sounds, refreshed and at peace. She no longer wishes to die.

This afternoon a different brother enters the pig cage. He gives his name as Shem, and he is even better looking than Japheth. He bears a glass of tea in which float three diaphanous pebbles. "Ice," he explains. "Clotted water."

Sheila drinks. The frigid tea buffs the grime from her tongue and throat. Ice: a remarkable material, she decides. These people know how to live.

"Do you have a pisspot?" Sheila asks, and Shem guides her to a tiny stall enclosed by reed walls. After she has relieved herself, Shem gives her a tour, leading her up and down the ladders that connect the interior decks. *Eden II* leaks like a defective tent, a steady, disquieting plop-plop.

The place is a zoo. Mammals, reptiles, birds, two by two. Sheila beholds tiny black beasts with too many legs and long cylindrical ones with too few. Grunts, growls, howls, roars, brays, and caws rattle the ship's wet timbers.

Sheila likes Shem, but not this floating menagerie, this crazy voyage. The whole arrangement infuriates her. Cobras live here. Wasps, their stingers poised to spew poisons. Young tyrannosaurs and baby allosaurs, eager to devour the gazelles on the deck above. Tarantulas, rats, crabs, weasels, armadillos, snapping turtles, boar-pigs, bacteria, viruses: Yahweh has spared them all.

My friends were no worse than a tarantula, Sheila thinks. My neighbors were as important as weasels. My child mattered more than anthrax.

Captain's Log. 14 July 1057 A.C.

The rains have stopped. We drift aimlessly. Reumah is seasick. Even with the ice, our provisions are running out. We cannot keep feeding ourselves, much less a million species.

Tonight we discussed our passenger. Predictably, Japheth and Shem spoke for acquittal, while Ham argued the whore must die.

"A necessary evil?" I asked Ham.

"No kind of evil," he replied. "You kill a rabid dog lest its disease spread, Father. This woman's body holds the eggs of future thieves, perverts, and idolators. We must not allow her to infect the new order. We must check this plague before our chance is lost."

"We have no right," said Japheth.

"If God can pass a harsh judgment on millions of evildoers," said Ham, "then surely I can do the same for one."

"You are not God," said Japheth.

Nor am I—but I am the master of this ship, the leader of this little tribe. I turned to Ham and said, "I know you speak the truth. We must choose ultimate good over immediate mercy."

Ham agreed to be her executioner. Soon he will dispose of the whore using the same obsidian knife with which, once we sight land, we are bound to slit and drain our surplus lambs, gratitude's blood.

They have put Sheila to work. She and Ham must maintain the reptiles. The *Pythoninae* will not eat unless they kill the meal themselves. Sheila spends the whole afternoon competing with the cats, snaring shiprats, hurling them by their tails into the python pens.

Ham is the handsomest son yet, but Sheila does not care for him. There is something low and slithery about Ham. It seems fitting that he tends vipers and asps.

"What do you think of Yahweh?" she says.

Instead of answering, Ham leers.

"When a father is abusive," Sheila persists, "the child typically responds not only by denying that the abuse occurred, but by redoubling his efforts to be loved."

Silence from Ham. He fondles her with his eyes.

Sheila will not quit. "When I destroyed my unwanted children, it was murder. When Yahweh did the same, it was eugenics. Do you approve of the universe, Ham?"

Ham tosses the python's mate a rat.

Captain's Log. 17 July 1057 A.C.

We have run aground. Shem has named the place of our imprisonment Ararat. This morning we sent out a *Corvus corax,* but it did not return. I doubt we'll ever see it again. Two ravens remain, but I refuse to break up a pair. Next time we'll try a *Columbidae.*

In an hour the harlot will die. Ham will open her up, spilling her dirty blood, her filthy organs. Together we shall cast her carcass into the flood.

Why did Yahweh say nothing about survivors?

Silently Ham slithers into the pig cage, crouching over Sheila like an incubus, resting the cool blade against her windpipe.

Sheila is ready. Japheth has told her the whole plot. A sudden move, and Ham's universe is awry, Sheila above, her attacker below, she armed, he defenseless. She wriggles her layered flesh, pressing Ham into the straw. Her scraggly hair tickles his cheeks.

A rape is required. Sheila is good at rape; some of her best customers would settle for nothing less. Deftly she steers the knife amid Ham's garments, unstitching them, peeling him like an orange. "Harden," she commands, fondling his pods, running a practiced hand across his worm. "Harden or die."

Ham shudders and sweats. Terror flutes his lips, but before he can cry out Sheila slides the knife across his throat like a bow across a fiddle, delicately dividing the skin, drawing out tiny beads of blood.

Sheila is a professional. She can stiffen eunuchs, homosexuals, men with knives at their jugulars. Lifting her robe, she lowers herself onto Ham's erection, enjoying his pleasureless passion, reveling in her impalement. A few minutes of graceful undulation, and the worm spurts, filling her with Ham's perfect and upright seed.

"I want to see your brothers," she tells him.

"What?" Ham touches his throat, reopening his fine, subtle wound.

"Shem and Japheth also have their parts to play."

Captain's Log. 24 July 1057 A.C.

Our dinghy is missing. Maybe the whore cut it loose before she was executed. No matter. This morning I launched a dove, and it has returned with a twig of some kind in its beak. Soon our sandals will touch dry land.

My sons elected to spare me the sight of the whore's corpse. Fine. I have beheld enough dead sinners in my six centuries.

Tonight we shall sing, dance, and give thanks to Yahweh. Tonight we shall bleed our best lamb.

The world is healing. Cool, smooth winds rouse Sheila's hair, sunlight strokes her face. Straight ahead, white robust clouds sail across a clear sky.

A speck hovers in the distance, and Sheila fixes on it as she navigates the boundless flood. This sign has appeared none too soon. The stores from *Eden II* will not last through the week, especially with Sheila's appetite at such a pitch.

Five weeks in the dinghy, and still her period has not come. "And Ham's child is just the beginning," she mutters, tossing a wry smile toward the clay pot. So far, the ice shows no sign of melting; Shem and Japheth's virtuous fertilizer, siphoned under goad of lust and threat of death, remains frozen. Sheila has plundered enough seed to fill all creation with babies. If things go according to plan, Yahweh will have to stage another flood.

The speck grows, resolves into a bird. A *Corvus corax,* as the old man would have called it.

Sheila will admit that her designs are grand and even pompous. But are they impossible? She aims to found a proud and impertinent nation, a people driven to decipher ice and solve the sun, each of them with as little use for obedience as she, and they will sail the sodden world until they find the perfect continent, a land of eternal light and silken grass, and they will call it what any race must call its home, Formosa, beautiful.

The raven swoops down, landing atop the jar of sperm, and Sheila feels a surge of gladness as, reaching out, she takes a branch from its sharp and tawny beak.

The Devil's Arithmetic

! ! !

Jane Yolen

Like Greg Bear, Jane Yolen served two terms as president of the Science Fiction Writers of America. This is truly hazardous duty, without pay, and I admire her for her resolve, her courage, and her accomplishment.

I admire her even more for her writing. She has published over a hundred books, most for children and/or young adults, and she is the winner of the 1988 Kerlan Award for the body of her work, the 1988 Caldecott Medal for *Owl Moon,* the 1987 World Fantasy Award, the Mythopoeic Society Award, the Golden Kite (given by the Society of Children's Book Writers), and the National Jewish Book Award and the Sydney J. Taylor Book Award given by the Association of Jewish Libraries, both for *The Devil's Arithmetic.* In addition, her work has been nominated for the National Book Award, the Balrog, and, this past year, the Nebula.

The titles that Dr. Yolen published in the fall of 1989 give a good indication of the broad range of her work: *Best Witches,* an illustrated collection of Halloween poems for young readers; *The Faerie Flag,* a collection of fantasy and fairy tale stories and poems for young adults; *The Laptime Song & Play Book,* a selection of finger songs and lap games that she edited; *White Jenna,* an adult fantasy novel (and a sequel to *Sister Light, Sister Dark*); *Dove Isabeau,* an illustrated fairy tale picture book; and *Things That Go Bump in the Night,* an anthology of scary stories edited for young readers. Her classic *Dream Weaver* collection has just had a paperback reissue, and she is currently editor-in-chief of her own imprint, Jane Yolen Books, at Harcourt Brace Jovanovich.

Of "The Devil's Arithmetic," she writes: "It is so rare that something published as a children's book or story finds its way onto the Nebula ballot that I am still stunned to see 'The Devil's Arithmetic' there. It is a children's novel (a novella by Nebula count) that I wrote partially to remind children of their Jewish heritage and partially as an answer to the eighth graders in a posh Indianapolis school who thought I was making up the

facts about concentration camps, though after one day in their
school I already knew they had two teachers who were Survivors.

"'The Devil's Arithmetic' divided the children's book
community. Some very vocal opponents felt that a novel of
time travel in which a girl goes back to the 1940s, to a shtetl
on the Polish-German border, and is rounded up with the rest
of the villagers and taken to a concentration camp, is by its very
nature a bad book. 'Fantasy trivializes the Holocaust' has been
their watchcry, even as they admitted my book 'moving and
provocative.'

"My best answer came from a girl who received it as a
Chanukah gift. 'I never read history books,' she wrote.
'They're boring. But I love fantasy books. You made me see
history a new way. A real way. I want to find out more.' I
answered her the only way I could. I said: *My story, your story,
our story—history.*"

We here reprint that story from its fifteenth chapter on-
ward. Dr. Yolen synopsizes her earlier chapters to make getting into this otherwise self-contained, and altogether
harrowing, excerpt as easy as such a deeply unsettling topic
permits.

"I'm tired of remembering," Hannah Stern tells her mother as
they drive away from her best friend's Easter egg hunt toward the
Stern's family seder. The whole Jewish emphasis on memory, on
the rote of history, is a bore to her. Family seders are always a
disaster, with Grandpa Will going crazy every time the Holocaust
is mentioned, showing his number tattooed on his wrist and
screaming. She expects this year's seder to be no different, no less
embarrassing, even though her little brother, Aaron, is getting to
ask the four questions for the first time.

At thirteen—almost—Hannah is more interested in her own
friends than in family, even in her great-aunt Eva, her favorite;
Aunt Eva never complains about her own past though it is surely
as awful as her brother, Grandpa Will's.

When the seder begins, Hannah gets to drink some watered
wine for the first time and, befuddled by it, and still angry at
being dragged to the seder and forced to participate in what she

considers to be childish superstitions, she flings open the door for the prophet Elijah at her grandfather's bidding.

Only when she looks out, instead of the expected apartment house hallway with its familiar green doors, there is a greening field, a lowering sky, and a moon hanging ripely between two heavy gray clouds. Across the field comes a shadowy figure, hoe over his shoulder, singing.

Hannah has gone through a doorway in time, emerging in 1942 in a small shtetl on the German-Polish border. Somehow she has become Chaya, the niece of the handsome young farmer Shmuel, who is about to be married, and his older sister, Gitl, called "Gitl the Bear" by the villagers because she is so fiercely independent and strong-minded.

Just as strange, Hannah can now understand the Yiddish they are speaking, as if her own language and theirs lie side by side in her mind. So, too, lie the memories—Chaya's memories of life in Poland and her own. But when she tries to tell Gitl and Shmuel about her parents and the seder and New Rochelle, they think she is suffering the effects of the typhoid that had killed Chaya's parents and almost killed her, too.

So Hannah's life as Chaya begins. In the morning, along with Yitzchak, the village butcher who loves Gitl, and all the rest of their neighbors, they travel through the forest to meet up with Shmuel's betrothed, the rabbi's beautiful daughter, Fayge. Carts piled high with wedding gifts accompany them.

On the way, Hannah is introduced to four girls her own age—Esther, Rachel, Shifre, and Yente, whom she delights with stories such as "Yentl" and "Conan the Barbarian" and "Little Women" and "Hansel and Gretl." She is delighted in return when the villagers are met by a *klezmer* band and a *badchan,* a jester, hired for the wedding by the rabbi.

But the happy procession turns to horror when they approach Fayge's village. Hannah, now riding in a cart with the bride and her father, is the only one who understands the devastation that awaits them, for the temple is surrounded by Nazi soldiers.

Warned by her memories of life in the 1980s, Hannah tries to explain her fears. She tells the villagers: "They kill people. They killed—kill—will kill Jews. Hundreds of them. Thousands of them. Six million of them! I know. Don't ask me how I know, I just do. We have to turn the wagons around. We have to run!" But Reb Boruch shakes his head. "There are not six million Jews in all of Poland, my child." And then he tells her, "Where would we run to? God is everywhere . . . and there is still a wedding to be made."

So the two villages surrender themselves peacefully to the waiting soldiers for—they think—"resettlement." Shmuel promises Fayge that they will get married soon, and under a wedding canopy. Only Hannah/Chaya knows the horrible truth.

Taken first by truck and then by cattle car, the villagers are brought to the camp, a hideous place of barracks, barbed wire, and a smokestack belching its string of numbers against the sky.

Hannah continues to try to warn her friends, until her head is shaved. Then, as if her memory has been shorn as well, she becomes completely Chaya Abramowitz, #J197241.

It is another girl in the camp, Rivka, a preternaturally wise ten-year-old, who clues Hannah/Chaya and her friends in to the ways of this particular camp.

Rivka tells them that they might escape death one day at a time *if* they worked hard, didn't stand next to Greek Jews (who couldn't understand German orders), stayed away from the black door in the wall the camp inmates called Lilith's Cave, and didn't say words like *death* or *corpse* or anything else that indicated to the guards that they recognized what was happening. Most important, she explained the midden heap to them. Whenever Commandant Breuer came for one of his inspections, the children were all to dive into the garbage dump. It was a particular dehumanizing game the Nazis played with the children: if you are garbage—they were saying—we will not let you die.

The days in the camp move slowly, endlessly for Chaya. One after another, the villagers she came in with, the inmates she knows so well, die. Some die by their own hands, some die of malnutrition, some die of broken hearts. Most die because they are *chosen* to march through the black door into the crematorium, to become more of the satanic count written black in smoke against the blue sky.

But as Chaya's hair grows back, so do strange, troubling

memories, flashes of another life that she cannot at first account for. Until one day . . .

In the morning, after roll call and breakfast were over, they got their first lesson at the midden.

"Commandant!" a man called across the wire fence from the men's camp.

"Commandant coming!" A woman took up the cry.

"He is coming," Rivka said urgently to Hannah and Shifre, who were standing near the cauldrons, where they had been helping dish out the watery soup. "Do what I do."

Rivka put her hands up to her mouth as if shouting, but instead made a penetrating clucking noise by placing her tongue against the roof of her mouth. From all over the camp came the same clicking, as if crazed crickets had invaded the place. The small children, alerted by the sound, came scrambling from everywhere. They raced toward the midden heap behind the barracks. Even the camp guards joined in, alternately clucking and laughing, waving the children on toward the garbage pile. The largest children carried the littlest ones in their arms. There were about thirty in all.

Hannah watched, amazed at their speed. When they got to the midden, they skinned out of their clothes and dove naked into the dump.

Suddenly Hannah noticed that one of the camp babies was still cradled in a washtub. Without stopping to ask, she grabbed it up and ran with the child into the middle of the midden. Garbage slipped along her bare legs.

She waded through a mixture of old rags, used bandages, the emptied-out waste of the slop buckets. The midden smell was overwhelming. Though she'd already gotten used to the pervasive camp smell, a cloudy musk that seemed to hang over everything, a mix of sweat and fear and sickness and the ever-present smoke that stained the sky, the smell in the midden was worse. She closed her eyes, and lowered herself into the garbage, the baby clutched in her arms.

When the all-clear clucking finally came, Hannah emerged from the heap with the baby, who was cooing. She scrubbed them both off with a rag until the child's mother, Leye, came running over.

"I will murder that Elihu Krupnik. Where is he? He is supposed to take her in. And look! You left her clothes on. They are filthy." Leye's face was contorted with anger.

"No thanks?" Rivka asked. "Leye, she saved the baby."

Leye stared for a moment at Hannah, as if seeing her for the first time. Then, as if making an effort, she smiled. "I will *organize* some water," she said, leaving the filthy baby in Hannah's filthy arms.

"That means 'thank you,'" Rivka said.

Hannah stared after Leye. "I think . . . ," she said slowly, "I think I prefer the water to the thanks."

That night, she washed out her dress with the cup of water, hanging it like a curtain from her sleeping shelf. Now she understood why the children had all stripped off their clothes, dropping them like bright rags on the sandy ground. She'd worried that the clothing would be gaudy signals to the commandant, but clearly he already knew—as did the guards—where the children hid. It was all some kind of awful game. But she'd been too scared to stop and too shy to undress out in the open like that, especially while the memory of her naked hours waiting for the shower still brought a blush to her face. Especially as the guards, some in their late teens, had all been laughing nearby.

As she fell asleep, she was sure the smell of the midden had gotten into her pores; that there was not enough water in the camp—in all of Poland—to wash her clean.

The days quickly became routine: roll call, breakfast, work, lunch, work, supper, work. The meals were all watery potato soup and occasionally bread, hard and crusty. Then they had a precious hour before they were locked in their barracks for the night.

The work was the mindless sort. Some of it was meant to keep the camp itself running: cleaning the barracks, the guards' houses, the hospital, the kitchen. Cutting and hauling wood for the stoves. Building more barracks, more privies. But most of the workers were used in the sorting sheds, stacking the clothing and suitcases and possessions stolen from the prisoners, dividing them into piles to be sent back to Germany.

Still, Hannah was glad of the routine. As long as she knew what to expect, she wasn't frightened. What was more frightening was the unknown: the occasional corpse hanging on the gate without an explanation, the swift kick by the *blokova* for no reason.

She and Shifre were set to work with Rivka in the kitchen hauling water in large buckets from the pump, spooning out the meager meals, washing the giant cauldrons in which the soup cooked, scrubbing the walls and floors. It was hard work, harder than Hannah could ever remember doing. Her hands and knees held no memory of such work. It was endless. And repetitive. But it was not without its rewards. Occasionally they were able to scrape out an extra bit of food for themselves and the little ones while cleaning the pots, burned pieces of potatoes that had stuck to the bottom. Even burned pieces tasted wonderful, better even than beef. She thought she remembered beef.

"She gave the *blokova* a gold ring she *organized* to get you in here," Leye explained, wiping her hands on a rag and nodding her head in Rivka's direction. Leye was the head of the kitchen crew; her arms were always splotchy and stained. But it was a good job, for she could keep her baby with her. "Otherwise that one . . ." and she spit on the ground to show her disapproval of the three-fingered woman, ". . . she would have had you hauling wood with the men. And you would never have lasted because you are a city girl. It is in your hands. Not a country girl like Shifre. We outlast you every time."

When Hannah tried to thank Rivka, the girl only smiled and shrugged away the thanks. "My mother, may she rest in peace, always said *a nemer iz nisht keyn geber,* a taker is not a giver. And a giver is not a taker either. Keep your thanks. And hand it on." She said it gently, as if embarrassed.

Hannah understood her embarrassment and didn't mention it again, but she *did* try to pass it on. She began saving the softer insides of the bread, slipping it to Reuven when she could. Yitzchak's little boy was so thin and sad-looking, still wondering where his sister had gone, that she could not resist him. She even tried giving him her whole bread, meal after meal, until Gitl found out.

"You cannot help the child by starving yourself," Gitl said. "Besides, with those big blue eyes, he will have many to help him. And that smile . . ."

Hannah bit her lip. Those big blue eyes and the luminous, infrequent smiles reminded her of someone she couldn't name.

"But you—you are still a growing girl, Chaya. You must take care of you." She folded Hannah's hands around the bread and pushed her away from Reuven. "Go, finish your kitchen duties. I will take Reuven with me."

Hannah turned away reluctantly, as if she had somehow failed Rivka. As she did so, she saw that Gitl had given the child her own bread—and half her soup besides.

It was on the third day in the camp that Commandant Breuer came again, this time—word was whispered around the camp—for a Choosing.

His black car drove right up the middle of the camp, between the rows of barracks, the flag on the aerial snapping merrily. The driver got out, opened the rear door, and stood at attention.

"What *is* a Choosing?" Hannah asked Rivka out of the side of her mouth as they waited beside the cauldrons they were cleaning. She didn't know why, but she could feel sweat running down her dress, even though it was a cool day, as if her body knew something it wasn't telling her mind.

There was no movement from the midden pile, where the bright shorts and blouses of the children marked their passage. The commandant strode past without giving the dump a glance.

Rivka hissed Hannah quiet and ran a finger across her own throat, the same signal that the peasants had made in the fields when the cattle were passed them by. Hannah knew that signal. She just didn't know what it meant . . . exactly. She shivered.

The commandant was a small, handsome man, so clean-shaven his face seemed burnished. His cheekbones had a sharp edge and there was a cleft in his chin. He stopped for a moment in front of Hannah, Rivka, and Shifre. Hannah felt sweat run down her sides.

The commandant smiled, pinched Rivka's cheek, then went on. Behind him was a man with a clipboard and a piece of paper. They walked without stopping again, straight to the far end of the compound. The door banged behind them ominously.

Rivka let out a ragged breath, and turned to Hannah. "Anyone who cannot get out of bed today will be chosen," she said. Her voice was soft but matter-of-fact.

"Chosen for what?" Hannah asked, though she'd already guessed.

"Chosen for processing."

"You mean chosen for death," Hannah said. Then suddenly she added, "Hansel, let out your finger, that I may see if you are fat or lean."

"Do not use that word aloud," Rivka cautioned.

"Which word?" asked Hannah. "Finger? Fat? Lean?"

Rivka sighed. "Death," she said.

"But why?" asked Shifre, her pale face taking color from the question. "Why will some be chosen?"

"Because they cannot work," said Rivka. "And work . . ." Her voice became very quiet and, for the first time, Hannah heard a bitterness in it. "Because work *macht frei.*"

"And because he enjoys it!" added Leye, coming over to see why they were not working.

"But do not let them hear you use the word *death.* Do not let them hear you use the word *corpse.* Not even if one lies at your feet," Rivka warned. "A person is not killed here, but *chosen.* They are not cremated in the ovens, they are *processed.* There are no corpses, only pieces of *drek,* only *shmattes,* rags."

"But why?" asked Hannah.

"Why?" Leye said. "Because what is not recorded cannot be blamed. Because that is what *they* want. So that is how it must be. Quickly, back to work."

No sooner had they begun scrubbing again than the door to the hospital opened and Commandant Breuer emerged, still smiling, but broader this time. As he and his aide passed by, Hannah could see the paper on the clipboard was now covered with numbers and names.

The commandant reminded her of someone. A picture

perhaps. A moving picture. She'd seen a smiling face like that somewhere.

"Dr. . . . Dr. Mengele," she said suddenly. "The Angel of Auschwitz." As suddenly as she knew it, the reference was gone.

"No," Rivka said, puzzled, "his name is Breuer. Why did you say that?"

"I told you she says strange things," Shifre put in.

Hannah looked down at her hands. They were trembling. "I don't know why I said it. Am I becoming a *musselman?* Am I going mad?"

No one answered.

Gitl had been working in the sorting shed, where mountains of clothes and shoes, mounds of books and toys and household goods from the suitcases and bags were divided up. It was also the place where men and women could talk together, so there was a quick, quiet trading of information from the women's camp to the men's and back again.

That night, Gitl shared the news with the others of the *zugangi* barracks. "All the clothes and shoes in good condition go straight to Germany. And we get what is left. But look what I took for you, Chayaleh." She held up a blue scarf.

"Organized. You *organized* it, Tante Gitl," Shifre cried out, her hands up with delight.

The women all laughed, the first time such a sound had rippled through the barracks since they had arrived. "Yes, she *organized* it."

Gitl looked up, pursed her lips for a moment, then smiled. "All right. I *organized* it."

"How did you do it, Gitl?" someone called.

"You can bet she did not ask!" came an answer.

Gitl nodded, stretching the scarf between her hands. *"Az m'fraygt a shyle iz trayf."*

Hannah translated mentally, "If you ask permission, the answer is no." She remembered suddenly another phrase, from somewhere else, almost like it: "It's easier to ask for forgiveness than permission." She had a brief memory of it printed on something. Like a shirt.

"So," said Esther's mother, a self-satisfied look on her face, "we may be *zugangi,* but we already know how to *organize.*"

Esther looked longingly at the blue scarf, and hummed quietly to herself.

Gitl handed the scarf to Hannah. "To replace the blue ribbons," she said softly.

"The blue ribbons?" For a moment, Hannah couldn't remember them. Then she did.

"And because today is your birthday," Gitl added.

"Her birthday!" cried Shifre. "You did not tell me."

Hannah shook her head. "My birthday is . . . is in the winter. In . . . in *February.*" The word sat strangely on her mouth.

"What nonsense is this?" asked Gitl, her hands on her hips. "And what kind of word is *February?* They taught you to count the days by the Christian calendar in Lublin?" She turned to look at the women who were circled around them. "You think I do not know my own niece's birthday? And did I send a present every year?"

"Of course you know," a gray-haired woman called out.

"I remember the day she was born," said another. "You told me in the synagogue, all happy with the idea. You were only thirteen, you said, and already an aunt."

"So," Gitl said, turning to face Hannah.

Her certainty overrode Hannah's own. Besides, she asked herself, who knew what day it was, what year, in this place?

"Thank you, Gitl," she whispered. "It's the best present I've ever had, I think. The only one I remember, anyway."

"Oh, my dear child," Gitl said, pulling her close, "thank God that your father and mother are not alive to see you now."

Caught in Gitl's embrace, Hannah suddenly remembered the little house in the shtetl and the big, embracing arms of Shmuel. "What of Shmuel?" she said. "And Yitzchak? Are they . . . well?"

Gitl sat on a low shelf bed and pulled Hannah down next to her. The circle of women closed in, eager for news.

Gitl nodded. "Now listen. Shmuel is working with the crew that cuts wood, but it is all right. It is what he knows how to do and he is strong. With him are Yitzchak the butcher and Gedaliah and Natan Borodnik and their cousin Nemuel. Tzadik the cobbler is doing what he has always done, making shoes and belts. They have a cobbler's shop there. He is making a fine pair of riding boots for the commandant. Size five."

"That is a woman's size!" Esther's mother said with a laugh.

"Yes, and they have made up a little rhyme about it. Listen, I will tell it to you:

> Breuer wears a lady's shoe,
> What a cock-a-doodle-do.

The women began to giggle; Hannah didn't understand the humor.

Gitl held up her hand and the laughter stopped. "And from Viosk, Naftali the goldsmith is making rings on order for all the SS men. He is a very sick man but they like his work so much, they are leaving him alone."

"And where does he get the gold?" asked a woman in a stained green dress.

"From the valises, idiot," someone else answered.

"From our fingers," Fayge said suddenly, the first time she had spoken in days. She held up her hands so that everyone could see that they were bare. "From our ears."

"From our dead," Gitl whispered. Hannah wondered whether anyone else heard her.

"What about the others?" Esther's mother asked.

"I do not remember anything more," Gitl said softly.

"What about the rabbi?" asked a woman with a harelip. "What about Rabbi Boruch?"

Gitl did not answer.

Fayge knelt down in front of her, putting her hands on Gitl's skirt. "We are sisters, Gitl," she said. "I am your brother's wife. You must tell me about my father."

Gitl closed her eyes and pursed her lips. For a long moment she did not speak, but her mouth opened and shut as if there were words trying to come out. At last she said, "Chosen. Yesterday. *Boruch dayan emes.*"

Fayge opened her mouth to scream. The woman in the green dress clapped her hand over Fayge's mouth, stifling the scream, pulling her onto the sandy floor. Three other women wrapped their arms around her as well, rocking back and forth with her silent sobs.

"Chosen," Gitl said explosively, her eyes still closed. "Along with Zadek the tailor, the *badchan,* the butcher from Viosk, and two dozen others. And the *rendar."*

"Why?" asked Hannah.

"The rabbi was in the hospital. His heart was broken. Zadek, too. He had been beaten almost to death. The *badchan* because he chose to go. They say he said, 'This is not a place for a fool, where there are idiots in charge.' And the others whose names I do not remember for crimes I do not know. And the *rendar . . ."*

"With all his money he could not buy his way out?" asked Esther's mother.

"In this place he is just a Jew, like the rest of us," said Gitl. "Like the least of us."

"He's a *shmatte* now," said Hannah, remembering Rivka's word.

Gitl opened her eyes and slapped Hannah's face without warning. "That may be camp talk out there, but in here, we say the prayer for the dead properly, like good Jews."

"Gitl the Bear," someone murmured.

Hannah looked up, hand on her smarting cheek. She could not find the speaker, so spoke to them all. "Gitl is right," she said, her cheek burning. "Gitl is right."

Gitl began reciting the *Kaddish,* rocking back and forth on the sleeping shelf with the sonorous words, and the prayer was like the tolling of a death bell. The rest joined her at once. Hannah found she was saying the words along with them, even though her mind didn't seem to have any memory of the prayer: *Yis-ga-dal v'yis-ka-dash sh'may ra-bo . . .*

The first choosing had been the hardest, Hannah thought later. After that, it merely became part of the routine. And if you didn't stand too near the Greeks or work too slowly or say the wrong word or speak too loudly or annoy a guard or threaten the *blokova* or stumble badly or fall ill, the chances were that this time you wouldn't be Chosen. This time.

Part of her revolted against the insanity of the rules. Part of her was grateful. In a world of chaos, any guidelines helped. And she knew that each day she remained alive, *she remained alive.* One plus one plus one. The Devil's arithmetic, Gitl called it.

And so one day eroded into the next. Her memories became camp memories only: the day a guard gave her a piece of sausage and asked for nothing in return. The morning a new shipment of *zugangi* arrived. The morning a new shipment *didn't* arrive. The afternoon Gitl *organized* a rope and the children all played jumping games after dinner. And that same night when red-headed Masha from Krakow hanged herself with the jump rope, having learned that her husband and seventeen-year-old son had gone up the smokestack.

It was on a sunny afternoon, as Hannah cleaned out cauldrons with Shifre, that Hannah asked dreamily, "What is your favorite food? If you could have anything in the world."

They were in the tipped-over pots on their hands and knees, scraping off bits of burned potato that still clung stubbornly to the vast pot bottom.

Shifre backed out of the cauldron, wiping one dirty hand across her cheek. She thought a moment before answering. It was not a new question. They had been asking each other variations of the same thing for weeks.

"An orange, I think," she said slowly. That was a change. Usually she said an egg.

"An orange," Hannah echoed, pleased with the novelty. "I'd forgotten oranges."

"Or an egg."

"Boiled?"

"Or fried." They were back to their regular conversation.

"Or scrambled?"

"Or an omelet."

"How about . . . pizza!" Hannah said suddenly.

"What is *pizza?*" Shifre asked.

"It's . . . it's . . . I don't know," Hannah said miserably, fingers in her mouth, blurring the words. "I can't remember. I can only remember potato soup."

"You can remember eggs," Shifre said.

"No, I can't. Not pizza, not eggs either. Only potato soup and hard brown bread. That's all I can remember." She popped a piece of the burned potato scraping into her mouth. "Well, do not cry over this *pizza.* Tell me about it."

"I can't," Hannah said. "And I'm not crying over the thing, whatever it is. I'm crying because I can't remember *what* it is. I can't remember anything."

"You can remember the shtetl," Shifre said. "And Lublin."

"That's the trouble," said Hannah. "I can't."

Just then Rivka came out of the kitchen and shook her finger at Hannah. "No tears," she said. "If the *blokova* sees you crying . . ."

"That three-fingered bi . . ." Hannah stopped herself in time. It was a dangerous habit to fall into, calling the *blokova* names. One might be Chosen for doing such a thing.

"If she loses control of her *zugangi,* she will be a two-fingered whatever-you-call-her," said Rivka, smiling.

"What do you mean?" Hannah and Shifre asked together.

"How do you think she lost those other fingers?" Hannah mused. "I thought maybe she'd been born that way."

Holding up her own hand and wriggling the fingers, Rivka pointed to one. "She lost control and a whole group of *zugangi* rioted. That was right before I got here. They were sent through Lilith's Cave and she lost one finger. Then she lost control and six *zugangi* hanged themselves one night, my aunt Sarah among them. Aunt Sarah had been sick for a long time and could no longer disguise it. She knew she was to be sent to the hospital. Everyone really sick in the hospital goes up the stack. So she said to my mother, '*I* will do the choosing, not them. God will understand.' " Rivka smiled. "A second finger. I wish Aunt Sarah could have seen the *blokova*'s face in the morning. When they took the finger."

"Maybe *we* could do something to help the *blokova* balance her hand. Three is such an unlucky number," Shifre said.

Rivka shook her head. "Too dangerous," she said. "Let the grown-ups make their plans."

"What plans?" asked Hannah.

"Oh," Rivka said mysteriously, "there are always grown-up plans."

"What plans?" Hannah and Shifre asked together. But before Rivka could answer, a shout from the gate end of the compound riveted them.

"Commandant!"

"But he was just through yesterday," Hannah said in a nervous whisper. "He's not due for at least another few days."

Ignoring her, Rivka already had her hands to her mouth, making the clucking sound to warn the children. Shifre, too, was signaling.

"It's not *fair!*" Hannah complained, her voice rising into a whine.

Shifre nudged her angrily, and Hannah began to cluck as the little ones scrambled for the midden pile.

The first two in were a brother and a sister, seven and eight years old. They left green and blue shorts and shirts at the edge of the dump. Next came a nine-year-old girl carrying a baby. She shucked off her shoes as she ran and, holding the baby under one arm, tore off its shirt. When she set the naked baby down by the side of the pile in order to get out of her own dress, the child immediately began crawling toward the midden on its own.

Like spawning fish, the children came from everywhere to dive into the pile. They waded or crept in one after another while the horrible clucking continued and overhead the swallows, alerted to a feast of insects, dipped and soared.

Hannah finally heard the commandant's car, then saw it as it barreled toward them, down the long bare avenue between the barracks. It moved relentlessly toward the hospital, which squatted at the compound's end.

The car had just passed the *zugangi* barracks when the hospital door opened and a small thin boy limped down the steps, his right knee bloody and his blue eyes ringed with dirt. He was wiping his hands on his shirt. When he looked up and saw the car bearing down on him, despite the desperate clucking from all around, he froze, staring.

"Reuven!" Hannah cried out. "Run! Run to the midden!"

But the boy didn't move and she felt a sudden coldness strike through her as if an ice dagger had been plunged into her belly.

"*Gottenyu!*" Rivka whispered.

Shifre, who had been looking at the midden with its bright flags of clothing, heard Hannah's shout and turned. She grabbed Hannah's hand, squeezing it until there was no feeling left.

The car slowed, then stopped. Commandant Breuer himself got out of the car. He walked toward Reuven and the child could not look at him, staring instead at Hannah, his hand outstretched toward her. Big tears ran down his cheeks, but he cried without a sound.

"He knows," Hannah whispered.

"Hush!" Rivka said.

The commandant looked down at the boy. "Have you hurt yourself, my child?" he asked, his voice deadly soft.

Hannah moved forward a half-step and Rivka jerked her back.

"Let me see," Breuer said. He took a white handkerchief out of his pocket and touched it to Reuven's bloody knee thoughtfully. "And where is your mother?"

When Reuven didn't answer, Hannah stepped forward. "Please, sir, his mother is dead."

Rivka gasped. Hannah heard her and added hastily, "She died years ago, when he was born."

The commandant stood up and stared at her, his eyes gray and unreadable. "Are you his sister?"

She shook her head dumbly, afraid to say more.

"That is good. For you." Breuer bent down and wrapped the handkerchief around the boy's knee, knotting it gently with firm, practiced hands. Then he picked Reuven up. "A boy your age should be with his mother," he said, smiling. "So I shall be sure you go to her." He handed Reuven to his driver, who was waiting by the car door. Then, without another word, Breuer went up the stairs to the hospital and closed the door so quietly they could not tell when it was finally shut.

That evening, the sky was red and black with the fire and smoke. The latest arrivals in the cattle cars had not been placed in barracks. The camp was full. The newcomers had been shipped directly to processing, a change in routine that frightened even the long-termers.

Rumors swept the camp. "A shipment from Holland," some said. "A shipment from Silesia." No one knew for sure.

But Reuven did not come back. Not that evening. Not that night.

"Not ever," Hannah muttered to herself as she watched the smoke curling up, writing its long numbers against the stone-colored sky. "And it's my fault."

"Why is it your fault?" Rivka asked.

"I should have said he was my brother."

"Then you would not be here either. It would not have helped Reuven."

"He is dead." Hannah said the word aloud curiously, as if understanding it for the first time. "Dead."

"Do not say that word."

"Monsters!" Hannah said suddenly. "Gitl is right. We are all monsters."

"*We* are the victims," Rivka said. "*They* are the monsters."

"We are all monsters," Hannah said, "because we are letting it happen." She said it not as if she believed it but as if she were repeating something she had heard.

"God is letting it happen," Rivka said. "But there is a reason. We cannot see it yet. Like the binding of Isaac. My father always said that the universe is a great circle and we—we only see a small piece of the arc. God is no monster, whatever you think now. There is a reason."

Hannah scuffed the ground with her foot. "We should fight," she said. "We should go down fighting."

Rivka smiled sadly. "What would we fight with?"

"With guns."

"We have no guns."

"With knives."

"Where are our knives?"

"With—with something."

Rivka put her arm around Hannah's shoulder. "Come. There is more work to be done."

"Work is not fighting."

"You want to be a hero, like Joshua at Jericho, like Samson against the Philistines." She smiled again.

"I want to be a hero like . . ." Hannah thought a minute but she could think of no one.

"Who?"

"I don't know."

"My mother said, before she . . . died . . . that it is much harder to live this way and to die this way than to go out shooting. Much harder. Chaya, you are a hero. I am a hero." Rivka stared for a moment at the sky and the curling smoke. "We are all heroes here."

That night Fayge began to speak, as if the words so long dammed up had risen to flood. She told a story she had heard from her father, about the great Ba'al Shem Tov. It was set in the time when he was a boy named Israel and *his* father warned him: "Know, my son, that the enemy will always be with you. He will be in the shadow of your dreams and in your living flesh, for he is the other part of yourself. There will be times when he will surround you with walls of darkness. But remember always that your soul is secure to you, for your soul is entire, and that he cannot enter your soul, for your soul is part of God." Fayge's voice rose and fell as she told how young Israel led a small band of children against a werewolf whose heart was Satan's. And in the end, when Israel walked straight into the werewolf's body and held its awful dark heart in his hand, "shivering and jerking like a fish out of water," Fayge said, her own hand moving in the same way, that awful heart was filled with "immeasurable pain. A pain that began before time and would endure forever."

She whispered the story as the night enfolded them. "Then Israel took pity on the heart and gave it freedom. He placed it upon the earth and the earth opened and swallowed the black heart into itself."

A sigh ran around the barrack and Hannah's was the deepest of all. *A werewolf,* she thought. *That's where we are now. In the belly of the werewolf. But where, where is its dark pain-filled heart?* She was still sighing when she slipped into sleep.

"There is a plan," Gitl whispered. "And Yitzchak and Shmuel are part of it." She had crept onto the sleeping shelf, putting her arms around Hannah and speaking very softly into her ear. "You must not be afraid, but you must not tell anyone. I am a part of it, too."

Hannah didn't move.

Gitl's voice tickled her ear. "The reason I am telling you this is that you are our only flesh and blood. Our only link with the past. If something happens to us, you must remember. Promise me, Chaya, you will remember."

Hannah's lips moved but no sound came out.

"Promise."

"I will remember." The words forced themselves out through her stiffened lips.

"Good."

"What plan?" Hannah managed to ask.

"If I tell you, you might say."

"Never."

"You would not mean to, but it could slip out."

"Not even if *afile* . . ."

"*Afile brenen un brutn* . . . even if you should be burned and roasted. Here that is not a proverb to be spoken aloud."

Horrified at what she'd said, Hannah felt herself begin to giggle. It was a hysterical reaction, but she couldn't seem to control herself.

"Nevertheless," Gitl ended, "I will not tell you."

"When?" Hannah whispered.

"You will know."

The horn signaled morning roll call and Gitl rolled off the shelf. Hannah followed, stood, and stared at her.

"Is it . . . is it because of Reuven?" she asked quietly.

"For Yitzchak it is. Who else does he have left, poor man? He adored those children," Gitl said.

"But why you? Why Shmuel?"

"If not us, who? If not now, when?" Gitl smiled.

"I think I've heard those words before," Hannah said slowly.

"You will hear them again," Gitl promised. "Now we must not talk about this anymore."

And yet for all of Gitl's promises, nothing seemed to happen. The days' routines were as before, the only change being the constant redness of the sky as trainloads of nameless *zugangi* were shipped along the rails of death. Still the camp seemed curiously lightened because of it, as if everyone knew that as long as others were processed, *they* would not be. A simple bit of mathematics, like subtraction, where one taken away from the top line becomes one added on to the bottom. The Devil's arithmetic.

"When?" she whispered at night to Gitl.

"You will know," Gitl always answered. "You will know."

And yet, when it finally happened, Hannah was surprised that she hadn't known, hadn't even suspected. There had been no signs or portents, no secret signals. Just an ordinary day in the camp and at night she went to bed on the hard, coverless shelf trying to remember sheets and pillows and quilts while all around her in the black barrack she heard the breathy sounds of sleeping women.

A hand on her back and over her mouth startled her so, she was too surprised to protest.

"Chaya, it is now," Gitl's voice whispered in her ear. "Nod if you understand."

She nodded, opening her eyes wide though it was too dark to see anything. "The plan," she said, her words hot on Gitl's palm. She sat up abruptly and just missed smacking her head on the upper shelf.

Gitl took her hand away. "Follow me," she whispered.

"Am I part of the plan?"

"Of course, child. Did you think we would leave you in this hell?"

They crept to the door and Hannah could feel her heart thudding madly. It was warm in the barrack, yet she felt cold.

"Here," Gitl whispered, shoving something into her hands.

Hannah looked down. She could see nothing in the dark, but she realized she was holding a pair of shoes.

"We'll put them on outside."

They paused at the door, then Gitl eased it open slowly. It protested mildly.

"It's not locked!" Hannah said, shocked.

"Some guards can be bribed," Gitl whispered. "Give me your hand."

Slipping her hand into Gitl's, Hannah held back for a moment. "What about Fayge? Shmuel wouldn't go without Fayge."

Gitl's hand on hers tightened. "Fayge says she prefers the dark wolf she knows to the dark one she does not."

"Even with Shmuel going? But she loves him."

"She has come to love her next bowl of soup more," Gitl said. "Now hush."

They slipped through the door, shut it, and locked it from the outside with a too-loud *snick*. Hannah shivered at the sound and took Gitl's hand again, ice on ice.

"We meet behind the midden," Gitl whispered. "No more talking now."

Hannah looked up. There was no moon. Above them, in the cloudless sky, stars were scattered as thick as sand. A small, warm breeze blew across the compound. Night insects chirruped. Hannah took a deep breath. The air was sweet-smelling, fresh, new. A dog barked suddenly and a harsh voice quieted it with a command.

Gitl pulled Hannah back against the barrack's wall. Hannah could feel the fear threatening to scream out of her, so she dropped the shoes and put both hands over her mouth, effectively gagging herself. There was a wetness under her arms, between her legs, down her back. She moaned.

And then there came a shout. A shot. And another. And another, rumbling, staccato. A man began to scream, high-pitched and horrible. He called a single phrase over and over and over. *"Ribono shel-oylam."*

"Quickly!" Gitl whispered hoarsely. "It is ruined. Before the lights. Come."

As she spoke, great spotlights raked the compound, missing

them by inches and seeking the outer perimeter of wire fence and mine fields and the woods beyond, where Hannah thought she saw shadows chasing shadows into the dark trees.

Gitl dragged her back to the barrack's door, slid the bolt open with one hand, and shoved Hannah inside with the other. They both sank gratefully to the floor.

"What is it?" the *blokova*'s voice called out from her private room.

Hannah's mouth opened. What could they say? They would be found out. They would be Chosen.

"I went to get my bowl to relieve myself," Gitl called, her voice incredibly calm. "And then shots began outside and I was so frightened, I fell to the floor, dropping the bowl." She pushed Hannah away from her as she spoke.

Crawling on her hands and knees, Hannah made it back across the room to her sleeping shelf. She lifted herself onto it gratefully, trembling so hard she was sure she would wake everyone.

"You Jews," the *blokova*'s voice drawled sleepily, "you can never do anything quietly or efficiently. That is why the Germans will finish you all off. If you have to relieve yourself, wait until the morning or do it in your bed. Or you shall have to deal with me."

"Yes, *blokova*," Gitl answered.

"And get to bed," the *blokova* added unnecessarily.

Instead of going to her own shelf, Gitl crowded in with Hannah, hugging her so tightly that Hannah could hardly breathe. Yet she was glad not to have to lie there alone. Leaning back against Gitl, Hannah could feel the woman shaking with silent sobs.

Then a sudden, awful thought came to her. She couldn't turn over with Gitl there on the shelf, so she whispered to the wall: "Gitl, Gitl, please."

At last Gitl heard. "What is it?"

"The shoes, Gitl, I dropped the shoes outside. They'll know it was me out there. What will I do? What will I do?"

"Do?" the breathy voice whispered into her ear. "Do? Why, you will do nothing, my darling child. Those were not your shoes. They were the *blokova*'s. I took them from outside her door because you deserved a better pair for such a difficult journey. They will discover *her* shoes in the morning." She began to laugh, muffling it against Hannah's back, a sound so close to sobbing that Hannah could not tell the difference.

The roll call in the morning was held under a brilliant sun and a sky so blue it hurt the eyes. The woods on the other side of the barbed wire fence burst with birdsong. Commandant Breuer himself stood at the front of the assembly, flanked by SS guards. Before him were six men in chains.

Hannah recognized only Shmuel and the violin player from the *klezmer* band. The other four men were strangers to her. They had all been badly beaten and two could not stand.

"Yitzchak . . . ," she whispered.

Beside her Gitl was silent.

"Yitzchak . . . ," she tried again.

"Hush."

The commandant stared around the compound as if his mind were on other matters. Once he even looked up at the sky. At last he turned his attention to Shmuel, who stood chin thrust out defiantly.

Shmuel spat.

A guard hit him with the butt end of his gun in the stomach and Shmuel went down on his knees, but he made no sound.

"These men . . . ," Breuer began, "these pieces of, in your Jew language, *drek* tried to escape last night. Escape! And where would they go? To the mine fields? To the woods to starve? To the town where no right-thinking Pole would give them shelter? This camp is in the middle of nowhere, remember that. *You* are in the middle of nowhere. All that gives you life is work—and my good wishes. Do you understand?" He glanced around as if daring any of them to challenge him.

They were silent.

"I see I have been too easy on you. I have made you into my pets. That is what they call you, you know: Breuer's dirty little pets. The other transports, they do not come here and sleep in barracks and have three meals every single day. They are not cared for in a modern hospital. They are not given clothes and shoes." He held up a pair of woman's shoes and Hannah tried not to stare at them, but they drew her eyes. "No, they are processed at once, as has been ordered from Berlin. They are part of the Final Solution to the Jewish Problem. But you, my little pets, I have let you live to work. And see how you reward your master."

He walked over to the violinist, who had been pushed to his knees by a guard. Pushing the man's head back, Breuer spoke directly to him, but in a voice that carried around the compound: "I let *you* play music because it is said that music feeds the gods. Well, now you shall feed your god." He signaled to his men. "Move them to the wall."

There was a protesting sound from the crowd, a strange undercurrent of moaning. Hannah realized suddenly that she was one of the moaners, though she didn't know what going to the wall meant. Something awful, that she knew.

"Silence!" Breuer said, his voice hardly raised at all. "If you are silent, I will let you watch."

They were all silent. Not, Hannah thought, because they wanted to watch, but because they wanted to be witnesses. And because they had no other choice.

The guards dragged the men to a solid wall that stood next to the gate. The wall was pocked with holes and dark stains. To the right and above, the sign ARBEIT MACHT FREI swung creakingly in the wind. Birds cried out merrily from the woods and the tops of the trees danced to rhythms all their own.

The six men were lined up with their backs to the wall, four standing and two sitting. Shmuel alone smiled.

Slowly the soldiers raised their guns and Hannah bit her lip to keep from crying aloud.

"*Shema Yisrael, Adonai Eloheynu . . . ,*" the violinist began in a clear voice. The other men at the wall joined him.

But Shmuel was silent, searching through the watching crowd, that same strange smile on his face. At last his lips moved and Hannah read the word there.

"Fayge."

"Shmuel!" came a loud wail, and Fayge pushed through the

crowd, flinging herself at his feet. She lifted her face to his and smiled. "The sky is our canopy. God's canopy. The sky."

He bent down and kissed the top of her head as the guns roared, a loud volley that drowned out birdsong and wind and screams.

When it was silent at last, the commandant threw the shoes on top of Fayge's body. "Let them all go up the stack," he said. "Call the *Kommandos. Schnell!*"

The soldiers marched off to the side of the compound, except for one, who opened the door into Lilith's Cave. Out came ten men in green coveralls. Though she'd heard of them, feared them, mourned them, Hannah had never actually seen any of them before. One, hardly more than a boy, put his fingers to his lips and a shrill whistle pierced the air. The *Kommandos* lifted their heads at the sound and in mocking parody of the soldiers marched over to the wall. They began to drag the dead bodies back toward the gate.

The boy who had whistled stooped down and picked up Fayge in his arms. His beardless face was grim, but there was no sign of sorrow or horror there. Still he carried Fayge as one might carry a loved one, with conscious tenderness and pride.

Rivka whispered to no one in particular, "That one, carrying Fayge, that is my brother, Wolfe."

The *blokova* came forward, a wooden spoon in her hand with which she dealt out blows right and left. "*Schnell. Schnell.* Scum. There is work to do, much work." Her voice held a note of hysteria. The hand with the spoon didn't rest, but her other hand was held stiffly by her side. It was wrapped in a broad bandage, the white stained with fresh blood.

"Gitl . . . ," Hannah said as they walked back toward the kitchen. "Did you see?"

"I saw," Gitl said, her voice ragged. "I saw everything."

"I mean, did you see that Yitzchak wasn't there?"

Gitl turned, took Hannah by the arms, and stared at her. "Yitzchak?"

"He wasn't there. He wasn't in the lineup either."

"Hush," Gitl said, turning away, but her voice held a measure of hope. "Hush."

Hannah said no more, but in her mind's eye she saw a swift shadow racing into the dark trees. She smiled with the memory.

Later that afternoon, the cauldrons all set for cooking, Hannah walked with Rivka and Shifre to the water pump. Esther was there already, filling a bucket in slow motion for the women in the sewing shop. She had lost a lot of weight, the dress hung in loose folds on her frail body, her eyes were dead.

Overhead the swallows dipped down to catch bugs rising from the ground. Then they soared back up beyond the barracks. Hannah watched them for a moment, scarcely breathing. It was as if all nature ignored what went on in the camp. There were brilliant sunsets and soft breezes. Around the commandant's house, bright flowers were teased by the wind. Once she'd seen a fox cross the meadow to disappear into the forest. If this had been in a book, she thought, the skies would be weeping, the swallows mourning by the smokestack.

Her mouth twisted at the irony of it and she turned to the three girls at the water pump. Suddenly, with great clarity, she saw another scene superimposed upon it: two laughing girls at a water fountain dressed in bright blue pants and cotton sweaters. They were splashing water on each other. A bell rang to call them to class. Hannah blinked, but the image held.

Drawing a deep breath, she forced herself to bring the camp back into focus; it was like turning a camera lens. One way she could see the water fountain, the other way the pump. Her heart was thudding under the thin gray dress. She was afraid to move. And then suddenly she made up her mind.

"Listen," she said to the girls at the pump, "I have a story to tell you."

"A story?" Shifre looked up, her light-lashed eyes bright. "You have not told us a story since the first day. At the . . ." She hesitated a minute, afraid to name the memory, afraid a guard might hear and, somehow, steal it away.

"*At the wedding,*" Hannah said. "Funny how saying it brings it back. *At the wedding. At school. At home.*"

"Tell the story," Rivka pleaded. "I would like to hear it." For the first time she sounded like the ten-year-old she was.

Hannah nodded. "This isn't a once-upon-a-time story," she said. "This is about now—and the future."

"I do not want a story about now," Esther said slowly. "There is too much now."

"And not enough future," Shifre added.

Hannah moved close to them. "Now—six million Jews will die in camps like this. *Die!* There, I've said the word. Does it make it more real? Or less? And how do I know six million will die? I'm not sure how, but I do."

"Six million?" Shifre said. "That's impossible. There are not six million Jews in the whole world."

"Six million," Hannah said, "but that's not all the Jews there are. In the end, in the future, there will be Jews still. And there will be Israel, a Jewish state, where there will be a Jewish president and a Jewish senate. And in America, Jewish movie stars."

"I do not believe you," Esther said. "Not six million."

"You must believe me," Hannah said, "because I remember."

"How can you remember what has not happened yet?" asked Rivka. "Memory does not work that way—forward. It only works backward. Yours is not a memory. It is a dream."

"It's not a dream, though," Hannah said. "It's as if I have three memories, one on top of another. I remember living with Gitl and Shmuel."

"May he rest in peace," Rivka said.

"May they all rest in peace," Hannah added.

"And Lublin," put in Shifre. "You remember Lublin."

"Yes, there is Lublin, but that memory is like a story I've been told. I don't remember Lublin, but I remember being there. And then there's my memory of the future. It's very strong and real now, as if the more I try to remember, the more I do. Memory on memory on memory, like a layer cake."

"I remember cake," Shifre said.

"Impossible," Esther said.

"Even crazy," Rivka pointed out.

"Nevertheless," Hannah said, "I remember. And you—you must remember, too, so that whoever of us survives this place will carry the message into that future."

"What message?" Rivka asked, her voice breathy and low.
"That we *will* survive. The Jews. That what happens here
must never happen again," Hannah said. "That . . ."

"That four girls are talking and not working," interrupted a
harsh voice.

They looked up. Standing over them was a new guard, his
nose reddened from the sun. He had a strange, pleased look on
his face. "I have been told that the ones who do not work are to
go over there." He pointed to the gate.

"No!" Rivka cried. "We were working. We were." She held
up the empty bucket.

The guard dismissed her pleas with a wave of his hand, and
all four of them held their breath, waiting.

"I was told that we need three more Jews to make up a full
load. Commandant Breuer believes in efficiency and our units do
not work well with short loads. So I was sent to find three of the
commandant's pets who were *not* working. He told me—per-
sonally—to make up the load."

"We *were* working," Shifre begged, her words tumbling out
in a rush. "And we are healthy. We are healthy hard workers.
You never take healthy hard workers. It is one of the rules.
Never."

The guard smiled again. "Since Commandant Breuer makes
the rules, I guess he can change the rules. But why are you
worrying so, *Liebchen?* I only need three. Perhaps I won't take
you." He looked over the girls slowly, the smile still on his face.
"I'll take you. You are the least *healthy.*" He pointed to Esther,
who almost fell forward in front of him, as if someone had suddenly kicked her in the back of the knees.

Shifre drew in a great, loud breath and closed her eyes.

"And you," he said, playfully putting his finger on Shifre's
nose, almost as if he were flirting with her, "because you protest
too much after all. And . . . and . . ."

Hannah let out her breath as slowly as she dared. She did
nothing to call attention to herself. To stay alive one more day,
one more hour, one more minute, that was all any of them
thought of. It was all they could hope for. Rivka was right. What
she had was not a memory but a dream.

". . . and you, with the babushka, like a little old lady. I'll take you, too." He pointed to Rivka, winked at Hannah, then turned and marched smartly toward the gate, confident that the chosen girls would follow.

Rivka gave Hannah a quick hug. "Who will remember for you now?" she whispered.

Hannah said nothing. The memories of Lublin and the shtetl and the camp itself suddenly seemed like the dreams. She lived, had lived, would live in the future—she, or someone with whom she shared memories. But Rivka had only now.

Without thinking through the why of it, Hannah snatched the kerchief off Rivka's head. "Run!" she whispered. "Run to the midden, run to the barracks, run to the kitchen. The guard is new. He won't know the difference. One Jew is the same as another to him. Run for your life, Rivka. Run for your future. Run. Run. Run. And remember."

As she spoke, she shoved Rivka away, untied the knot of the kerchief with trembling fingers, and retied it about her own head. Then, as Rivka's footsteps faded behind her, she walked purposefully, head high, after Shifre and Esther.

When she caught up with them, she put her arms around their waists as if they were three schoolgirls just walking in the yard.

"Let me tell you a story," she said quietly, ignoring the fact that they were both weeping, Shifre loudly and Esther with short little gasps. "A story I know you both will love."

The strength in her voice quieted them and they began to listen even as they walked.

"It is about a girl. An ordinary sort of girl named Hannah Stern who lives in New Rochelle. Not Old Rochelle. There is no Old Rochelle, you see. Just New Rochelle. It is in an America where pictures come across a cable, moving pictures right into your living room and . . ." She stopped as the dark door into Lilith's Cave opened before them. "And where one day, I bet, a Jewish girl will be President if she wants to be. Are you ready, now? Ready or not, here we come . . ."

Then all three of them took deep, ragged breaths and walked in through the door into endless night.

When the dark finally resolved itself, Hannah found she was looking across an empty hall at a green door marked 4N.

"Four for the four members of my family," Hannah thought. *"And N for New Rochelle."* She couldn't see Shifre or Esther anywhere. They had slipped away without a farewell. She almost called out their names, thought better of it, and turned to look behind her.

There was a large table set with a white cloth. The table was piled high with food: matzoh, roast beef, hard-boiled eggs, goblets of deep red wine. Seven adults and a little blond boy were sitting there, their mouths opened expectantly.

"Well, Hannah?" said the old man at the head of the table. "Is he coming?"

Hannah turned back and looked down the long, dark hall. It was still empty. "There's no one there," she whispered. "No one."

"Then come back to the table and shut the door," called out the other old man. "There's a draft. You know your Aunt Rose gets these chills."

"Sam, don't hurry the child so. She's doing her part." The woman who spoke had a plain face lit up by a special smile. "Come, sweetheart, sit by Aunt Eva." She patted an empty chair next to her, then reached over and picked up her glass of wine. "You look so white, Hannahleh. Like death. How can we fix that?" She raised her glass, looked at Hannah. *"L'chaim.* To life." She took a sip.

Hannah slipped into the chair, knowing it was the one the family reserved for the prophet Elijah, who slipped through the centuries like a fish through water. She watched all the grown-ups raise their glasses.

"L'chaim."

Aunt Eva turned toward her, smiling. Her sweater was pushed back beyond her wrist. As she raised the glass again, Hannah noticed the number on her arm: J18202.

"Hannahleh, you're staring," whispered Aunt Eva as the talk began around the table: Uncle Sam arguing about the price of new cars, Grandpa Will complaining about the latest government scandal, her mother asking Aunt Rose about a book.

"Staring?" She repeated the word without understanding.

"Yes, at my arm. At the number. Does it frighten you still? You've never let me explain it to you and your mother hates me to talk of it. Still, if you want me to . . ."

Hannah touched the number on her aunt's arm with surprising gentleness, whispering, "No, no, please, let me explain it to you." For a moment she was silent. Then she said: *"J* is for Jew. and *1* because you were alone, alone of the *8* who had been in your family, though *2* was the actual number of them alive. Your brother was a *Kommando,* one of the Jews forced to tend the ovens, to handle the dead, so he thought he was a *0."* She looked up at Eva, who was staring at her. "Oh! Your brother. Grandpa Will. That must have been him carrying Fayge. So that's why . . ."

Aunt Eva closed her eyes for a moment, as if thinking or remembering. Then she whispered back, "His name was Wolfe. Wolfe! And the irony of it was that he was as gentle as a lamb. He changed his name when we came to America. We all changed our names. To forget. Remembering was too painful. But to forget was impossible." Her coffee brown eyes opened again. "Go on, child."

Hannah took her hand from her aunt's arm and dropped it into the safety of her own lap. She couldn't look at her aunt anymore, that familiar, unfamiliar, plain, beautiful face. "You said . . . ," she whispered, ". . . you said that when things were over, you would be two again forever. J18202."

They sat for a long moment in silence while the talk and laughter at the table dipped and soared about them like swallows.

At last Hannah looked up. Her aunt was staring at her, as if really seeing her for the first time. "Aunt Eva . . . ," Hannah began and Eva's hand touched her on the lips firmly, as if to stop her mouth from saying what had to be said.

"In my village, in the camp . . . in the past," Eva said, "I was called Rivka."

Hannah nodded and took her aunt's fingers from her lips.

She said, in a voice much louder than she had intended, so loud that the entire table hushed at its sound, "I remember. Oh, I remember."

Epilogue

Aunt Eva told Hannah the end of the story much later, when the two of them were alone, because no one else would ever have believed them. She said that, of all the villagers young Chaya had come to the camp with that spring, only two were alive at the end of the war. Yitzchak, who had indeed escaped, had lived in the forest with the partisans, fighting the Germans. And Gitl. When the camp had been liberated in 1945, Gitl weighed only seventy-three pounds because she had insisted on sharing her rations with the children. But she was alive.

The *blokova* and all the villagers from Viosk were dead, but among the living, besides Gitl, Yitzchak, and Rivka, were Leye and her baby, a solemn three-year-old.

Gitl and Yitzchak had emigrated to Israel, where they lived, close friends, until well into their seventies. Neither of them ever married. Yitzchak became a politician, a member of the Israeli senate, the Knesset. Gitl, known throughout the country as Tante Gitl and Gitl the Bear, organized a rescue mission dedicated to salvaging the lives of young survivors and locating the remnants of their families. It later became an adoption agency, the finest in the Mideast. She called it after her young niece, who had died a hero in the camps: CHAYA.

Life.

Rhysling Award Winners

▼ ▼ ▼

As George Zebrowski wrote in his introduction to the winning poems in *Nebula Awards 22:* "Although there is no Nebula Award for poetry, the situation is more than remedied by the Science Fiction Poetry Association's Rhysling Award for long and short poems. The award is named after the blind poet of the spaceways who appears in 'The Green Hills of Earth,' a story written by Nebula Grand Master Robert A. Heinlein and published in 1947." A tradition has arisen of showcasing the Rhysling winners in the annual Nebula anthology, and I am delighted to continue it.

The competition for the 1988 Rhyslings produced a tie in the short poem category (under fifty lines) between "The Nightmare Collector" by Bruce Boston and "Rocky Road to Hoe" by Suzette Haden Elgin. Meanwhile, the winner in the long poem category (over fifty lines) was "White Trains" by Lucius Shepard.

Bruce Boston won a previous Rhysling Award in 1985 for "For Spacers Snarled in the Hair of Comets" (best short poem). He has also won the small-press Pushcart Prize and Z Miscellaneous Award for fiction, the Odyssey Science Fiction Poetry Award for a work written with Robert Frazier, and, in 1988, the Small Press Writers and Artists Organization award as Best Small Press Poet. He has published poems and/or stories in a great many venues, including *Asimov's, Amazing Stories, Weird Tales, Year's Best Fantasy,* and *100 Great Fantasy Short-Short Stories.* His most recent books are a collection of poems written with Robert Frazier, *Chronicles of the Mutant Rain Forest,* and a volume of stories titled *Hypertales & Metafictions.*

Of "The Nightmare Collector," which originally appeared in the short-lived magazine *Night Cry,* Boston says, "The poem was inspired in part by Rod Serling, in part as a result of a reading I heard by poet Nanos Valaoritis in which he described political torture in his native Greece." Whatever its inspiration, it is an unsettling evocation of a palpable evil.

Suzette Haden Elgin has written several challenging SF novels, including *Native Tongue;* its sequel, *Judas Rose;* the Ozark Trilogy; and the three Coyote Jones novels collected as *Communipath Worlds.* Meanwhile, from her home in Huntsville,

Arkansas, Elgin continues to write science fiction; to run the Ozark Center for Language Studies; to publish two newsletters, *The Lonesome Node* (on linguistics) and *The Gentle Art of Verbal Self-Defense Newsletter* (which derives from two enduring, enormously popular self-help books); to run a nonprofit religious organization, Lovingkindness; to self-publish brief books; to produce cassette tapes and videotapes; to offer seminars, workshops, and a variety of training and consulting services; and sometimes, she grudgingly admits, to "eat and/or sleep." Elgin was one of the forces behind the founding of the Science Fiction Poetry Association (perhaps *the* major force), and for several years she single-handedly produced its newsletter, *Star∗Line.* It is fitting, if wildly overdue, that twelve years after the first Rhyslings were awarded, she has finally received one herself.

Of her winning poem, "Rocky Road to Hoe," she writes: "[It] meets my minority standards *for* a science fiction poem. That is, for me an SF poem must have both the science and the fiction—it has to have a clear narrative component that would serve as a respectable plot, and it has to extrapolate from some respectable scientific base (in this case, the science of linguistics, focusing on interspecies communication)." And only a true SF poet, I must add, would have both the bravado and the insight to choose stones as one of those communicating "species."

Lucius Shepard appeared in last year's volume with a brief but moving fantasy, "The Glassblower's Dragon." He has a well-deserved 1986 Nebula Award for his novella "R&R," and his engaging, fluent, and colorful short fiction has been leading more and more readers to his work ever since "The Taylorsville Reconstruction" appeared in Terry Carr's *Universe 13,* and "Solaritario's Eyes" in *Fantasy & Science Fiction,* both in 1983. This past year, "The Scalehunter's Beautiful Daughter" was a finalist in the novella category, and a story that I greatly admire—"Life of Buddha"—held a strong place on the preliminary ballot without quite shouldering its way among the six finalists for the short story Nebula.

For those reasons, then, I am glad to have a chance to reprint Shepard's "White Trains" from the spring 1987 issue of *Night Cry* as the winner of the long poem Rhysling. How will I ever forget its male passengers, men so evanescent they seem to have been made of "something insubstantial / like Perrier or truth"?

In a letter, Lucius reluctantly explained the origins of "White Trains"—reluctantly, because he feels that writers who interpret their own work impose a viewpoint that may distort or constrict the work's meaning: "When I wrote 'White Trains,' I was living in a high-crime neighborhood, lots of coke and crack and despair. It may well be that the white trains are a metaphor for all the strange and unexpected disruptions of our lives, whether they be an addiction, a romance, or something more arcane. . . . 'White Trains' is ultimately concerned with the concept of fate and how one confronts it; with the apprehension of everyday reality as a mystery; and, peripherally, with the American ability to deny an immediate problem and to transform it into either some sort of commercial enterprise or a photo opportunity for *People* magazine."

The Nightmare Collector
Bruce Boston

Each night he calls you
for the leading role
in his gallery
of ancestral tableaus
which trails back
through the Pleistocene
to the red primeval.

From the endless slashes
in his voluminous greatcoat
you can feel the heat
of captured bodies
invade your rumpled bed
with delirium and fever;
you can smell a brassy
sediment of tears.

From the hollow blackness
of his flapping sleeves
you can hear the pulse
and thump of unborn shadows,
a dense hysteric fugue
winding up and down
the bones of your sleep.

The nightmare collector
waits on the landing
in the unlit hall
where the instruments
of ablation are arranged
on cold leather pallets,
where the dreamer's
balustrade of terror
rushes across landscapes
of a darkening retina,
where snakes coil about
your arms and ankles
and draw you down
bodily into a forest
of bloodstained hair.

Rocky Road to Hoe

Suzette Haden Elgin

The woman the stones *spoke* to ignored them;
knowing better. Fearing the thorazines.
Only after the rose quartz chunk said to her,
"Your little girl has fallen into the pool,"
and it was so,
did she accept the burdensome embedded knowledge.
Pointedly, gratingly,

she kept it to herself.
The stones had a dignity to their converse
appropriate to their formation,
the many-layered levels of meaning brought upward,
one at a time,
breaking through detritus,
not to be easily, ever, set aside.

She had the gravel in the driveway taken up,
and paved it over, grateful for concrete silence;
she removed the lovely slate from the side terrace
and laid down redwood over her husband's objections;
when driving through New Mexico and Arizona,
she stayed inside the car. At all times.
The day her daughters bought her a necklace of agates,
she carried it out to the garden and hung it high in a tree;
when that was not enough to hush its tinted voices,
she had her husband shut it away at the bank
in their safe deposit box. Saying,
"I can't leave something so precious lying about."

But stones are everywhere.
Everyone else, being stone deaf, collects them.
Speaking to her from fingers of friends and strangers alike,
they told her how it felt.
To be mined.

When the woman the stones spoke to died,
she left an enigma.
"Do not," she said in her will, "under any circumstances
     whatsoever,
bury me beneath
a stone."

White Trains

Lucius Shepard

White trains with no tracks
have been appearing on the outskirts
of small anonymous towns,
picket fence towns in Ohio, say,
or Iowa, places rife with solid American values,
populated by men with ruddy faces and weak hearts,
and women whose thoughts slide
like swaths of gingham through their minds.
They materialize from vapor or a cloud,
glide soundlessly to a halt in some proximate meadow,
old-fashioned white trains with pot-bellied smokestacks,
their coaches adorned with filigrees of palest ivory,
packed with men in ice cream suits and bowlers,
and lovely dark-haired women in lace gowns.
The passengers disembark, form into rows,
facing one another as if preparing for a cotillion.
And the men undo their trouser buttons,
their erections springing forth like lean white twigs,
and they enter the embrace of the women,
who lift their skirts to enfold them,
hiding them completely, making it appear
that strange lacy cocoons have dropped from the sky
to tremble and whisper on the bright green grass.
And when at last the women let fall their skirts,
each of them bears a single speck of blood
at the corner of their perfect mouths.
As for the men, they have vanished
like snow on a summer's day.

I myself was witness to one such apparition
on the outskirts of Parma, New York,
home to the Castle Monosodium Glutamate Works,
a town whose more prominent sophisticates

often drive to Buffalo for the weekend.
I had just completed a thirty-day sentence
for sullying the bail bondsman's beautiful daughter
(They all said she was a good girl
but you could find her name on every bathroom wall
between Nisack and Mitswego),
and having no wish to extend my stay
I headed for the city limits.
It was early morning, the eastern sky
still streaked with pink, mist threading
the hedgerows, and upon a meadow bordering
three convenience stores and a laundromat,
I found a number of worthies gathered,
watching the arrival of a white train.
There was Ernest Cardwell, the minister
of the Church of the Absolute Solstice,
whose congregation alone of all the Empire State
has written guarantee of salvation,
and there were a couple of cops big as bears
in blue suits, carrying standard issue golden guns,
and there was a group of scientists huddled
around the machines with which they were
attempting to measure the phenomenon,
and the mayor, too, was there, passing out
his card and declaring that he had no hand
in this unnatural business, and the scientists
were murmuring, and Cardwell was shouting
"Abomination," at the handsome men
and lovely women filing out of the coaches,
and as for me, well, thirty days and the memory
of the bail bondsman's beautiful daughter
had left me with a more pragmatic attitude,
and ignoring the scientists' cries of warning and
Cardwell's predictions of eternal hellfire,
the mayor's threats, and the cops' growling,
I went toward the nearest of the women
and gave her male partner a shove and was amazed
to see him vanish in a haze of sparkles

as if he had been made of something insubstantial
like Perrier or truth.

The woman's smile was cool and enigmatic
and as I unzipped, her gown enfolded me
in an aura of perfume and calm,
and through the lacework the sun acquired
a dim red value, and every sound was faraway,
and I could not feel the ground beneath my feet,
only the bright sensation of slipping inside her.
Her mouth was such a simple curve, so pure
a crimson, it looked to be a statement of principle,
and her dark brown eyes had no pupils.
Looking into them, I heard a sonorous music;
heavy German stuff, with lots of trumpet fanfares
and skirling crescendos, and the heaviness
of the music transfigured my thoughts,
so that it seemed what followed was a white act,
that I had become a magical beast with golden eyes,
coupling with an ephemera, a butterfly woman,
a creature of lace and heat and silky muscle . . .
though in retrospect I can say with assurance
that I've had better in my time.

I think I expected to vanish, to travel
on a white train through some egoless dimension,
taking the place of the poor soul I'd pushed aside,
(although it may be he never existed, that only
the women were real, or that from those blood drops
dark and solid as rubies at the corners of their mouths,
they bred new ranks of insubstantial partners),
but I only stood there jelly-kneed watching
the women board the train, still smiling.
The scientists surrounded me, asking questions,
offering great sums if I would allow them to do tests
and follow-ups to determine whether or not
I had contracted some sort of astral social disease,
and Cardwell was supplicating God to strike me down,

and the mayor was bawling at the cops to take me
in for questioning, but I was beyond the city limits
and they had no rights in the matter, and I walked
away from Parma, bearing signed contracts
from the scientists, and another presented me
by a publisher who, disguised as a tree stump,
had watched the entire proceeding, and now
owned the rights to the lie of my life story.
My future, it seemed, was assured.

White trains with no tracks
continue to appear on the outskirts
of small anonymous towns, places
whose reasons have dried up, towns
upon which dusk settles
like a statement of intrinsic greyness,
and some will tell you these trains
signal an Apocalyptic doom, and
others will say they are symptomatic
of mass hysteria, the reduction of culture
to a fearful and obscure whimsey, and
others yet will claim that the vanishing men
are emblematic of the realities of sexual politics
in this muddled, weak-muscled age.
But I believe they are expressions of a season
that occurs once every millennium or so,
a cosmic leap year, that they are merely
a kind of weather, as unimportant and unique
as a sun shower or a spell of warmth in mid-winter,
a brief white interruption of the ordinary
into which we may walk and emerge somewhat
refreshed, but nothing more.
I lecture frequently upon this subject
in towns such as Parma, towns whose lights
can be seen glittering in the dark folds of lost America
like formless scatters of stars, ruined constellations
whose mythic figure has abdicated to a better sky,
and my purpose is neither to illuminate nor confound,

but is rather to engage the interest of those women
whose touch is generally accompanied by
thirty days durance on cornbread and cold beans,
a sentence against which I have been immunized
by my elevated status, and perhaps my usage
of the experience is a measure of its truth,
or perhaps it is a measure of mine.

Whatever the case, white trains move silent as thought
through the empty fields, voyaging from nowhere
to nowhere, taking on no passengers, violating
no regulation other than the idea of order,
and once they have passed we shake our heads,
returning to the mild seasons of our lives,
and perhaps for a while we cling more avidly
to love and loves, realizing we inhabit a medium
of small magical transformations that like overcoats
can insulate us against the onset of heartbreak weather,
hoping at best to end in a thunder of agony
and prayer that will move us down through
archipelagoes of silver light to a morbid fairy tale
wherein we will labor like dwarves at the question
of forever, and listen to a grumbling static from above
that may or may not explain in some mystic tongue
the passage of white trains.

Schrödinger's Kitten

▼ ▼ ▼

George Alec Effinger

Introducing a George Alec Effinger story in my anthology *Light Years and Dark*, I warned against trying to label or pigeonhole this wittily inventive writer's work. I cited his novels *What Entropy Means to Me, Relatives, Death in Florence*, and *The Wolves of Memory* as indisputably unique contributions to the field.

Today, I could add to that list *The Bird of Time, When Gravity Fails* (a Nebula and Hugo finalist last year), *A Fire in the Sun* (a sequel to *When Gravity Fails*), and *The Stone Fire*. He is also one of our best short story writers, and I regard "The Aliens Who Knew, I Mean, *Everything*," which appeared in *Nebula Awards 20*, as perhaps the funniest, most delightful piece of short science fiction of all of the 1980s.

But, as already noted, trying to label or pigeonhole Effinger's work is a mug's game, as "Schrödinger's Kitten"—this year's winner for best novelette—clearly demonstrates.

"I wanted to write a good, solid story that grew directly from a genuine scientific idea," Effinger says. "In other words, a hard science story, not my usual kind of thing. I wanted to begin with a kernel of quantum physics, and build an elaborate and emotionally involving story around it that illustrated the scientific idea both in subject matter and in the story's actual structure.

"I had been reading several popular explanations of quantum theory, and had become fascinated with how similar Hugh Everett's Many-Worlds Theory is to our SF convention of parallel universes. I placed the story in the Budayeen, the Muslim neighborhood that I had invented for *When Gravity Fails*. I liked the contrast of the quantum physics and this conservative, low-tech setting. And I remember that the writing of 'Schrödinger's Kitten' was a great deal of fun."

Reading it is an altogether involving experience, as you will very shortly discover.

The clean crescent moon that began the new month hung in the western sky across from the alley. Jehan was barely twelve years

old, too young to wear the veil, but she did so anyway. She had
never before been out so late alone. She heard the sounds of
celebration far away, the three-day festival marking the end of the
holy month of Ramadân. Two voices sang drunkenly as they
passed the alley; two others disputed the price of some honey
cakes in loud, angry voices. The laughter and the shouting came
to Jehan as if from another world. In the past, she'd always loved
the festival of Id el-Fitr; she took no part in the festivities now,
though, and it seemed odd to her that anyone else still could.
Soon she gave it all no more of her attention. This year she must
keep a meeting more important than any holiday. She sighed,
shrugging: The festival would come around again next year.
Tonight, with only the silver moon for company, she shivered in
her blue-black robe.

Jehan Fatima Ashûfi stepped back a few feet deeper into the
alley, farther out of the light. All along the street, people who
would otherwise never be seen in this quarter were determinedly
amusing themselves. Jehan shivered again and waited. The moment she longed for would come just at dawn. Even now the sky
was just dark enough to reveal the moon and the first impetuous
stars. In the Islamic world, night began when one could no longer
distinguish a white thread from a black one; it was not yet night.
Jehan clutched her robe closely to her with her left hand. In her
right hand, hidden by her long sleeve, was the keen-edged,
gleaming, curved blade she had taken from her father's room.

She was hungry and she wished she had money to buy something to eat, but she had none. In the Budayeen there were many
girls her age who already had ways of getting money of their
own; Jehan was not one of them. She glanced about herself and
saw only the filth-strewn, damp and muddy paving stones. The
reek of the alley disgusted her. She was bored and lonely and
afraid. Then, as if her whole sordid world suddenly dissolved into
something else, something wholly foreign, she saw more.

Jehan Ashûfi was twenty-six years old. She was dressed in a conservative dark gray woolen suit, cut longer and more severely
than fashion dictated, but appropriate for a bright young physicist. She affected no jewelry and wore her black hair in a long

braid down her back. She took a little effort each morning to look as plain as possible while she was accompanying her eminent teacher and advisor. That had been Heisenberg's idea; in those days, who believed a beautiful woman could also be a highly talented scientist? Jehan soon learned that her wish of being inconspicuous was in vain. Her dark skin and her accent marked her a foreigner. She was clearly not European. Possibly she had Levantine blood. Most who met her thought she was probably a Jew. This was Göttingen, Germany, and it was 1925.

The brilliant Max Born, who first used the expression "quantum mechanics" in a paper written two years before, was leading a meeting of the university's physicists. They were discussing Max Planck's latest proposals concerning his own theories of radiation. Planck had developed some basic ideas in the emerging field of quantum physics, yet he had used classical Newtonian mechanics to describe the interactions of light and matter. It was clear that this approach was inadequate, but as yet there was no better system. At the Göttingen conference, Pascual Jordan rose to introduce a compromise solution; but before Born, the department chairman, could reply, Werner Heisenberg fell into a violent fit of sneezing.

"Are you all right, Werner?" asked Born.

Heisenberg merely waved a hand. Jordan attempted to continue, but again Heisenberg began sneezing. His eyes were red and tears crept down his face. He was in obvious distress. He turned to his graduate assistant. "Jehan," he said, "please make immediate arrangements, I must get away. It's my damned hay fever. I want to leave at once."

One of the others at the meeting objected. "But the colloquium—"

Heisenberg was already on his feet, "Tell Planck to go straight to hell, and to take de Broglie and his matter waves with him. The same goes for Bohr and his goddamn jumping electrons. I can't stand any more of this." He took a few shaky steps and left the room. Jehan stayed behind to make a few notations in her journal. Then she followed Heisenberg back to their apartments.

There were no mosques in the Budayeen, but in the city all around the walled quarter there were many mosques. From the tall, ancient towers strong voices called the faithful to morning devotions. "Come to prayer, come to prayer! Prayer is better than sleep!"

Leaning against a grimy wall, Jehan heard the chanted cries of the muezzins, but she paid them no mind. She stared at the dead body at her feet, the body of a boy a few years older than she, someone she had seen about the Budayeen but whom she did not know by name. She still held the bloody knife that had killed him.

In a short while, three men pushed their way through a crowd that had formed at the mouth of the alley. The three men looked down solemnly at Jehan. One was a police officer; one was a qadi, who interpreted the ancient Islamic commandments as they applied to modern life; and the third was an imam, a prayer leader who had hurried from a small mosque not far from the east gate of the Budayeen. Within the walls the pickpockets, whores, thieves, and cutthroats could do as they liked to each other. A death in the Budayeen didn't attract much attention in the rest of the city.

The police officer was tall and heavily built, with a thick black moustache and sleepy eyes. He was curious only because he had watched over the Budayeen for fifteen years, and he had never investigated a murder by a girl so young.

The quadi was young, clean-shaven, and quite plainly deferring to the imam. It was not yet clear if this matter should be the responsibility of the civil or the religious authorities.

The imam was tall, taller even than the police officer, but thin and narrow-shouldered; yet it was not asceticism that made him so slight. He was wellknown for two things: his common sense concerning the conflicts of everyday affairs, and the high degree of earthly pleasures he permitted himself. He too was puzzled and curious. He wore a short, grizzled gray beard, and his soft brown eyes were all but hidden within the reticulation of wrinkles that had slowly etched his face. Like the police officer, the imam had once worn a brave black moustache, but the days of fierceness had long since passed for him. Now he appeared decent and kindly. In truth, he was neither, but he found it useful to cultivate that reputation.

"O my daughter," he said in his hoarse voice. He was very upset. He much preferred explicating obscure passages of the glorious Qur'ân to viewing such tawdry matters as blatant dead bodies in the nearby streets.

Jehan looked up at him, but she said nothing. She looked back down at the unknown boy she had killed.

"O my daughter," said the imam, "tell me, was it thou who hath slain this child?"

Jehan looked back calmly at the old man. She was concealed beneath her kerchief, veil, and robe; all that was visible of her was her dark eyes and the long thin fingers that held the knife. "Yes, O Wise One," she said, "I killed him."

The police officer glanced at the qadi.

"Prayest thou to Allah?" asked the imam. If this hadn't been the Budayeen, he wouldn't have needed to ask.

"Yes," said Jehan. And it was true. She had prayed on several occasions in her lifetime, and she might yet pray again sometime.

"And knowest thou there is a prohibition against taking of human life that Allah hath made sacred?"

"Yes, O Wise One."

"And knowest thou further that Allah hath set a penalty upon those who breaketh this law?"

"Yes, I know."

"Then, O my daughter, tell us why thou hath brought low this poor boy."

Jehan tossed the bloody knife to the stone-paved alley. It rang noisily and then came to rest against one leg of the corpse. "I killed him because he would do me harm in the future," she said.

"He threatened you?" asked the qadi.

"No, O Respected One."

"Then—"

"Then how art thou certain that he would do thee harm?" the imam finished.

Jehan shrugged. "I have seen it many times. He would throw me to the ground and defile me. I have seen visions."

A murmur grew from the crowd still cluttering the mouth of

the alley behind Jehan and the three men. The imam's shoulders slumped. The police officer waited patiently. The qadi looked discouraged. "Then he didst not offer thee harm this morning?" said the imam.

"No."

"Indeed, as thou sayest, he hath *never* offered thee harm?"

"No. I do not know him. I have never spoken with him."

"Yet," said the qadi, clearly unhappy, "you murdered him because of what you have seen? As in a dream?"

"As in a dream, O Respected One, but more truly as in a vision."

"A dream," muttered the imam. "The Prophet, mayest blessings be on his name and peace, didst offer no absolution for murder provoked only by dreams."

A woman in the crowd cried out, "But she is only twelve years old!"

The imam turned and pushed his way through the rabble.

"Sergeant," said the qadi, "this young girl is now in your custody. The Straight Path makes our duty clear."

The police officer nodded and stepped forward. He bound the young girl's wrists and pushed her forward through the alley. The crowd of fellahîn parted to make way for them. The sergeant led Jehan to a small, dank cell until she might have a hearing. A panel of religious elders would judge her according to Shari'a, the contemporary code of laws derived from the ancient and noble Qur'ân.

Jehan did not suffer in her noxious cell. A lifetime in the Budayeen had made her familiar with deprivation. She waited patiently for whatever outcome Allah intended.

She did not wait long. She was given another brief hearing, during which the council asked her many of the same questions the imam had asked. She answered them all without hesitation. Her judges were saddened but compelled to render their verdict. They gave her an opportunity to change her statement, but she refused. At last, the senior member of the panel stood to face her. "O young one," he said in the most reluctant of voices, "The Prophet, blessings be on his name and peace, said, 'Whoso slayeth a believer, his reward is Hell forever.' And elsewhere, 'Who killeth *a human being for other than manslaughter or corruption in the earth, it shall be as if he killed all mankind.'* Therefore, if he whom you slew had purposed corruption upon you, your act would have been justified. Yet you deny this. You rely on your dreams, your visions. Such insubstantial defense cannot persuade this council otherwise than that you are guilty. You must pay the penalty even as it is written. It shall be exacted tomorrow morning just before sunrise."

Jehan's expression did not change. She said nothing. Of her many visions, she had witnessed this particular scene before also. Sometimes, as now, she was condemned; sometimes she was freed. That evening she ate a good meal, a better meal than most she had taken before in her life of poverty. She slept the night, and she was ready when the civil and religious officials came for her in the morning. An imam of great repute spoke to her at length, but Jehan did not listen carefully. The remaining acts and motions of her life seemed mechanically ordered, and she did not pay great heed to them. She followed where she was led, she responded dully when pressed for a reply, and she climbed the platform set up in the courtyard of the great Shimaal Mosque.

"Dost thou feel regret?" asked the imam, laying a gentle hand on her shoulder.

Jehan was made to kneel with her head on the block. She shrugged. "No," she said.

"Dost thou feel anger, O my daughter?"

"No."

"Then mayest Allah in His mercy grant thee peace." The imam stepped away. Jehan had no view of the headsman, but she heard the collective sigh of the onlookers as the great axe lifted high in the first faint rays of dawn, and then the blade fell.

Jehan shuddered in the alley. Watching her death always made her exceptionally uneasy. The hour wasn't much later; the fifth and final call to prayer had sounded not long before, and now it was night. The celebration continued around her more intensely than before. That her intended deed might end on the headsman's block did not deter her. She grasped the knife tightly, wishing that time would pass more swiftly, and she thought of other things.

By the end of May 1925, they were settled in a hotel on the tiny island of Helgoland some fifty miles from the German coast. Jehan relaxed in a comfortably furnished room. The landlady made her husband put Heisenberg and Jehan's luggage in the best and most expensive room. Heisenberg had every hope of ridding himself of his allergic afflictions. He also intended to make some sense of the opaque melding of theories and counter-theories put forward by his colleagues back in Göttingen. Mean-while, the landlady gave Jehan a grim and glowering look at their every meeting, but said nothing. The Herr Doktor himself was too preoccupied to care for anything as trivial as propriety, mor-als, the reputation of this Helgoland retreat, or Jehan's peace of mind. If anyone raised eyebrows over the arrangement, Heisen-berg certainly was blithely unaware; he walked around as if he were insensible to everything but the pollen count and the occa-sional sheer cliffs over which he sometimes came close to tum-bling.

Jehan was mindful of the old woman's disapproval. Jehan, however, had lived a full, harsh life in her twenty-six years, and a raised eyebrow rated very low on her list of things to be concerned about. She had seen too many people abandoned to starvation, too many people dispossessed and reduced to beg-gery, too many outsiders slain in the name of Allah, too many maimed or beheaded through the convoluted workings of Is-lamic justice. All these years, Jehan had kept her father's blooded dagger, packed now somewhere beneath her Shetland wool sweaters, and still as deadly as ever.

Heisenberg's health improved on the island, and there was a beautiful view of the sea from their room. His mood brightened quickly. One morning, while walking along the shoreline with him, Jehan read a passage from the glorious Qur'ân. "This sûrah is called The Earthquake," she said. *" 'In the name of Allah, the Beneficent, the Merciful. When Earth is shaken with her final earth-quake, and Earth yields up her burdens and man saith: What aileth her? That day she will relate her chronicles, because thy Lord inspireth her.*

That day mankind will issue forth in separate groups to be shown their deeds. And whoso doeth good an atom's weight will see it then. And whoso doeth ill an atom's weight will see it then.' "

And Jehan wept, knowing that however much good she might do, it could never outweigh the wrongs she had already performed.

But Heisenberg only stared out over the gray, tumbling waves of the ocean. He did not listen closely to the sacred verses, yet a few of Jehan's words struck him. " 'And whoso doeth good an atom's weight will *see* it then,' " he said, emphasizing the single word. There was a small, hesitant smile quivering at the corners of his mouth. Jehan put her arm around him to comfort him because he seemed chilled, and she led him back to the hotel. The weather had turned colder and the air was misty with sea spray; together they listened to the cries of the herring gulls as the birds dived for fish or hovered screeching over the strip of beach. Jehan thought of what she'd read, of the end of the world. Heisenberg thought only of its beginning, and its still closely guarded secrets.

They liked their daily long, peaceful walk about the island. Now, more than ever before in her life, Jehan carried with her a copy of the Qur'ân, and she often read short verses to him. So different from the biblical literature he'd heard all his life, Heisenberg let the Islamic scriptures pass without comment. Yet it seemed to him that certain specific images offered their meanings to him alone.

Jehan saw at last that he was feeling well. Heisenberg took up again full-time the tangled knot that was the current state of quantum physics. It was his vocation and his means of relaxation. He told Jehan the best scientific minds in the world were frantically working to cobble together a slipshod mathematical model, one that might account for all the observed data. Whatever approach they tried, the data would not fit together. *He,* however, would find the key; he was that confident. He wasn't quite sure how he'd do it, as yet; but, of course, he hadn't yet really applied himself thoroughly to the question.

Jehan was not amused. She read to him: " *'Hast thou not seen those who pretend that they believe in that which is revealed unto thee*

*and that which was revealed before thee, how they would go for judgment
in their disputes to false deities when they have been ordered to abjure
them? Satan would lead them all astray.' "*

Heisenberg laughed heartily. "Your Allah isn't just talking
about Göttingen there," he said. "He's got Bohr in mind, too,
and Einstein in Berlin."

Jehan frowned at his impiety. It was the irreverence and
ignorant ridicule of the kaffir, the unbeliever. She wondered if
the old religion that had never truly had any claim on her was
yet still part of her. She wondered how she'd feel after all these
years, walking the narrow, crowded, clangorous ways of the Budayeen again. "You mustn't speak that way," she said at last.

"Hmm?" said Heisenberg. He had already forgotten what
he'd said to her.

"Look out there," said Jehan. "What do you see?"

"The ocean," said Heisenberg. "Waves."

"Allah created those waves. What do *you* know about that?"

"I could determine their frequency," said the scientist. "I
could measure their amplitude."

"Measure!" cried Jehan. Her own long years of scientific
study were suddenly overshadowed by an imagined insult to her
heritage. "Look here," she demanded. "A handful of sand. Allah
created this sand. What do *you* know about it?"

Heisenberg couldn't see what Jehan was trying to tell him.
"With the proper instruments," he said, a little afraid of offend-
ing her, "in the proper setting, I could take any single grain of
sand and tell you—" His words broke off suddenly. He got to
his feet slowly, like an old man. He looked first at the sea, then
down at the shore, then back out at the water. "Waves," he
murmured, "particles, it doesn't make any difference. All that
really counts is what we can actually measure. We can't measure
Bohr's orbits, because they don't really exist! So then the spectral
lines we see are caused by transitions between two states. Pairs
of states, yes; but that will mean an entirely new form of mathematical expression just to describe them, referencing tables list-
ing every possible—"

"Werner." Jehan knew that he was now lost to her.

"Just the computations alone will take days, if not weeks."

"Werner, listen to me. This island is so small, you can throw a stone from one end to the other. I'm not going to sit on this freezing beach or up on your bleak and dreary cliff while you make your brilliant breakthrough, whatever it is. I'm saying goodbye."

"What? Jehan?" Heisenberg blinked and returned to the tangible world.

She couldn't face him any longer. She was pouring one handful of sand through the fingers of her other hand. It came suddenly to her mind then: If you had no water to perform the necessary ablution before prayer in the direction of Mecca, you were permitted to wash with clean sand instead. She began to weep. She couldn't hear what Heisenberg was saying to her—if indeed he was.

It was a couple of hours later in the alley now, and it was getting even colder. Jehan wrapped herself in her robe and paced back and forth. She'd had visions of this particular night for four years, glimpses of the possible ways that it might conclude. Sometimes the young man saw her in the alley shortly after dawn, sometimes he didn't. Sometimes she killed him, sometimes she didn't. And, of course, there was the open question of whether her actions would lead to her freedom or to her execution.

When she'd had the first vision, she hadn't known what was happening or what she was seeing. She knew only the fear and the pain and the terror. The boy threw her roughly to the ground, ripped her clothing, and raped her. Then the vision passed. Jehan told no one about it; her family would have thought her insane. Then, about three months later, the vision returned; only this time it was different in subtle ways. She was in the alley in darkness, but this time she smiled and gestured to the boy, inviting him. He smiled in return and followed her deeper into the alley. When he put his hand on her shoulder, she drew her father's dagger and plunged it into the boy's belly. That was as much as the vision had showed her then. It terrified her even more than the rape scene had.

As time passed, the visions took on other forms. She was certain now that she was not always watching *her* future, *the* future, but rather *a* future, each as likely to come to pass as the others. Not all the visions could possibly be true. In some of them, she saw herself living into her old age in the city, right here in this filthy quarter of the Budayeen. In others, she moved about strange places that didn't seem Islamic at all, and she spoke languages definitely not Arabic. She did not know if these conflicting visions were trying to tell her or warn her of something. Jehan prayed to know which of these versions she must actually live through. Soon after, as if to reward her for her faith, she began to have less violent visions: She could look into the future a short way and find lost objects, or warn against unlucky travel plans, or predict the rise and fall of crop prices. The neighbors, at first amused, began to be afraid of her. Jehan's mother counseled her never to speak of these "dreams" to anyone, or else Jehan might be locked away in some horrible institution. Jehan never told her father about her visions, because Jehan never told her father about anything. In that family, as in the others of the Budayeen—and the rest of the city for that matter—the father did not concern himself very much with his daughters. His sons were his pride, and he had three strong sons whom he firmly believed would someday vastly increase the Ashûfi prestige and wealth. Jehan knew he was wrong, because she'd already seen what would become of the sons—two would be killed in wars against the Jews; the third would be a coward, a weakling, and a fugitive in the United States. But Jehan said nothing.

A vision: It was just past dawn. The young man—whose name Jehan never learned—was walking down the stone-paved street toward her alley. Jehan knew it without even peering out. She took a deep breath. She walked a few steps toward the street, looked left, and caught his eyes. She made a brief gesture, turned her back, and went deeper into the shadowy seclusion of the alley. She was certain that he would follow her. Her stomach ached and rumbled, and she was shaking with nervous exhaustion. When the young man put his hand on her shoulder, murmuring indecent suggestions, her hand crept toward the concealed knife, but she did not grasp it. He threw her down roughly, clawed off her clothing, and raped her. Then he left her there. She was almost paralyzed, crying and cursing on the wet, foul-smelling stones. She was found some time later by two women who took her to a doctor. Their worst fears were confirmed: Her honor had been ravaged irredeemably. Her life was effectively over, in the sense of becoming a normal adult female in that Islamic community. One of the women returned to Jehan's house with her, to tell the news to Jehan's mother, who must still tell Jehan's father. Jehan hid in the room she shared with her sisters. She heard the violent breaking of furniture and shrill obscenity of her father. There was nothing more to be done. Jehan did not actually know the name of her assailant. She was ruined, less than worthless. A young woman no longer a virgin could command no bride price. All those years of supporting a worthless daughter in the hopes of recovering the investment in the marriage contract—all vanished now. It was no surprise that Jehan's father felt betrayed and the father of a witless creature. There was no sympathy for Jehan's own plight; the actual story, whatever it might be, could not alter the facts. From that morning on, Jehan was permanently repudiated and cast out from her house. She had only the weeping of her sisters and her mother. Jehan's father and three brothers would not even look at her or offer her their farewells.

The years passed ever more quickly. Jehan became a woman of the streets. For a time, because of her youth and beauty, she earned a good living. Then as the decades left their unalterable blemishes upon her, she found it difficult to earn enough for a meal and a room to sleep in. She grew older, more bitter, and filled with self-loathing. Did she hate her father and the rest of her family? No, her fate had been fixed by the will of Allah, however impossible it was for her to comprehend it, or else by her own timidity in the single moment of choice and destiny in the alley so many years before. She could not say. Whatever the answer, she could not benefit now from either insight or wisdom. Her life was as it was, according to the inscrutable designs of Allah the Merciful. Her understanding was not required.

Eventually she was found dead, haggard and starved, and her corpse was contorted and huddled for warmth coincidentally in the same alley where the young man had so carelessly despoiled any chance Jehan had for happiness in this world. After she died, there was no one to mourn her. Perhaps Allah the Beneficent took pity on her, showing mercy to her who had received little enough mercy from her neighbors while she lived among them. It had always been a cold place for Jehan.

For a while estranged from Heisenberg, Jehan worked with Erwin Schrödinger in Zurich. At first, Schrödinger's ideas confused her, because they went against many of Heisenberg's basic assumptions. For the time being, Heisenberg rejected any simple picture of what the atom was like, any model at all. Schrödinger, older and more conservative than the Göttingen group, wanted to explain quantum phenomena without new mathematics and elusive imagery. He treated the electron as a wave function, but a different sort of wave than de Broglie's. The properties of waves in the physical world were wellknown and without ambiguity. Yet when Schrödinger calculated how a change in energy level affected his electron wave, his solutions didn't agree with observed data.

"What am I overlooking?" he asked.

Jehan shook her head. "Where I was born they say, 'Don't pour away water in your canteen because of a mirage.' "

Schrödinger rubbed his weary eyes. He glanced down at the sheaf of papers he held. "How can I tell if this water is worth keeping, or something that belongs in a sewer?"

Jehan had no reply to that, and Schrödinger set his work aside, unsatisfied. A few months later, several papers showed that after taking into account the relativistic effects, Schrödinger's calculations agreed remarkably well with experimental results, after all.

Schrödinger was pleased. "I hoped all along to find a way to drag Born and Heisenberg back to classical physics," he said. "I knew in my heart that quantum physics would prove to be a sane world, not a realm populated by phantoms and governed by ghost forces."

"It seems unreal to me now," said Jehan. "If you say the electron is a wave, you are saying it is a phantom. In the ocean, it is the water that is the wave. As for sound, it is the air that

carries the wave. What exists to be a wave in your equations?"
"It is a wave of probability, Born says. I do not wholly
understand that yet myself," he said, "but my equations explain
too many things to be illusions."

"Sir," said Jehan, frowning, "it may be that in this case the
mirage is in your canteen, and not before you in the desert."

Schrödinger laughed. "That might be true. I may yet have to
abandon my mental pictures, but I will not abandon my mathematics."

It was a breathless afternoon in the city. The local Arabs didn't
seem to be bothered by the heat, but the small party of Europeans
was beginning to suffer. Their cruise ship had put ashore at the
small port and a tour had been arranged to the city some fifty
miles to the south. Two hours later, the travelers concluded that
the expedition had been a mistake.

Among them was David Hilbert, the German mathematician, a lecturer at Göttingen since 1895. He was accompanied by
his wife Käthe, and their maid Clärchen. At first they were quite
taken by the strangeness of the city, by the foreign sights and
sounds and smells; but after a short time, their senses were glut-
ted with newness, and what had at first been exotic was now only
deplorable.

As they moved slowly through the bazaars, shaded ineffectu-
ally by awnings or meager arcades of sticks, they longed for the
whisper of a single cool breeze. Arab men dressed in long white
gallebeyas cried out shrilly, all the while glaring at the Europeans. It was impossible to tell what the Arabs were saying. Some
dragged little carts loaded with filthy cups and pots—water? tea?
lemonade? It made no difference. Cholera lingered at every stall,
every beggar offered typhus as he clutched at sleeves.

Hilbert's wife fanned herself weakly. She was almost over-
come and near collapse. Hilbert looked about desperately.
"David," murmured the maid, Clärchen, the only one of Hilbert's amours Frau Hilbert could tolerate, "we have come far
enough."

"I know," he said, "but I see nothing—nowhere—"

"There are some ladies and gentlemen in that place. I think

it's an eating place. Leave Käthe with me there, and find a taxi. Then we shall go back to the boat."

Hilbert hesitated. He couldn't bear to leave the two unprotected women in the midst of this frantic heathen marketplace. Then he saw how pale his wife had become, how her eyelids drooped, how she swayed against Clärchen's shoulder. He nodded. "Let me help," he said. Together they got Frau Hilbert to the restaurant, where it was no cooler but at least the ceiling fans created a fiction of fresh air. Hilbert introduced himself to a well-dressed man who was seated at a table with his family, a wife and four children. The mathematician tried three languages before he was understood. He explained the situation, and the gentleman and his wife both assured Hilbert that he need not worry. Hilbert ran out to find a taxi.

He was soon lost. There were not streets here, not in the European sense of the word. Narrow spaces between the buildings became alleys, opened into small squares, closed again, other narrow passages led off in twisting, bewildering directions. Hilbert found himself back at a souk; he thought at first it was where he'd begun and looked for the restaurant, but he was wrong. This was another souk entirely; there were probably hundreds in the city. He was beginning to panic. Even if he managed to find a taxi, how could he direct it back to where his wife and Clärchen waited?

A man's hand plucked at him. Hilbert tried to shrug the long fingers away. He looked into the face of a lean, hollow-cheeked man in a striped robe and a blue knitted cap. The Arab kept repeating a few words, but Hilbert could make no sense of them. The Arab took him by the arm and half-led, half-shoved Hilbert through the crowd. Hilbert let himself be guided. They crossed through two bazaars, one of tinsmiths and one of poultry dressers. They entered a stone-paved street and emerged into an immense square. On the far side of the square was a huge, many-towered mosque, built of pink stone. Hilbert's first impression was awe; it was as lovely an edifice as the Taj. Then his guide was pushing him again through the throng, or hurrying in front to hew a path for Hilbert. The square was jammed and choked with people. Soon Hilbert could see why—a platform had been erected in the center, and on it stood a man with what could only be an executioner's axe. Hilbert felt his stomach sicken. His Arab guide had thrust aside everyone in their way until Hilbert stood at the very foot of the platform. He saw uniformed police and a bearded old man leading out a young girl. The crowd parted to allow them by. The girl was stunningly lovely. Hilbert looked into her huge, dark eyes—"like the eyes of a gazelle," he remembered from reading Omar Khayyam—and glimpsed her slender form undisguised by her modest garments. As she mounted the steps, she looked down directly at him again. Hilbert felt his heart lurch, he felt a tremendous shudder. Then she looked away.

The Arab guide screamed in Hilbert's ear. It meant nothing to the mathematician. He watched in horror as Jehan knelt, as the headsman raised his weapon of office. When the fierce, bellowing cry went up from the crowd, Hilbert noticed that his suit was now spattered with small flecks of red. The Arab screamed at him again and tightened his grip on Hilbert's arm until Hilbert complained. The Arab did not release him. With his other hand, Hilbert took out his wallet. The Arab smiled. Above him, Hilbert watched several men carry away the body of the decapitated girl. The Arab guide did not let him go until he'd paid an enormous sum.

Perhaps another hour had passed in the alley. Jehan had withdrawn to the darkest part and sat in a damp corner with her legs drawn up, her head against the rough brick wall. If she could but sleep, she told herself, the night would pass more quickly; but she would not sleep, she would fight it if drowsiness threatened. What if she should slip into slumber and waken in the late morning, her peril and her opportunity both long since lost? Her only companion, the crescent moon, had abandoned her; she looked up at fragments of constellations, stars familiar enough in their groups but indistinguishable now as individuals. How different from people, where the opposite is true. She sighed; she was not a profound person, and it did not suit her to have profound thoughts. These must not truly be profound thoughts, she decided; she was merely deluded by weariness. Slowly she let her head fall forward. She crossed her arms on her knees and cradled her head. The greater part of the night had already passed, and only silence came from the street. There were perhaps only three more hours until dawn. . . .

Soon Schrödinger's wave mechanics was proved to be equivalent to Heisenberg's matrix mechanics. It was a validation of both men's work, and of the whole field of quantum physics as well. Eventually, Schrödinger's simplistic wave picture of the electron was abandoned, but his mathematical laws remained undisputed. Jehan remembered Schrödinger predicting that he might need to take just that step.

Jehan had at last returned to Göttingen and Heisenberg. He had "forgiven her petulance." He welcomed her gladly, because of his genuine feelings for her, and because he had much work to do. He had just formally developed what came to be known as the Heisenberg Uncertainty Principle. This was the first indication that the impartial observer could not help but play an essential, active role in the universe of subatomic particles. Jehan grasped Heisenberg's concept readily. Other scientists thought Heisenberg was making a trivial criticism of the limitations of their experiments or the quality of their observations. It was more profound than that. Heisenberg was saying that one can never hope to know both the position and the momentum of an electron at the same time under *any* circumstances. He had destroyed forever the assumption of the impartial observer.

"To observe is to disturb," said Heisenberg. "Newton wouldn't have liked any of this at all."

"Einstein still doesn't like it right this very minute," said Jehan.

"I wish I had a mark for every time he's made that sour 'God doesn't play dice with the universe' comment."

"That's just the way he sees a 'wave of probability.' The path of the electron can't be known unless you look; but once you look, you change the information."

"So maybe God doesn't play dice with the universe," said Heisenberg. "He plays vingt-et-un, and if He does not have an extra ace up His sleeve, He creates one—first the sleeve, then the ace. And He turns over more natural twenty-ones than is statistically likely. Hold on, Jehan! I'm not being sacrilegious. I'm not saying that God cheats. Rather, He invented the rules of the game and He *continues* to invent them; and this gives Him a rather large advantage over poor physicists and their lagging understanding. We are like country peasants watching the magic card-tricks of someone who may be either genius or charlatan."

Jehan pondered the metaphor. "At the Solvay Conference, Bohr introduced his Complementarity idea, that an electron was a wave function until it was detected, and then the wave function collapsed to a point and you knew where the electron was. Then it was a particle. Einstein didn't like that, either."

"That's God's card-trick," said Heisenberg, shrugging.

"Well, the noble Qur'ân says, *'They question thee about strong drink and games of chance. Say: In both is great sin, and some usefulness for men; but the sin of them is greater than their usefulness.'* "

"Forget dice and cards, then," said Heisenberg with a little smile. "What kind of game *would* it be appropriate for Allah to play against us?"

"Physics," said Jehan, and Heisenberg laughed.

"And knowest thou there is a prohibition against taking of human life that Allah hath made sacred?"

"Yes, O Wise One."

"And knowest thou further that Allah hath set a penalty upon those who breaketh this law?"

"Yes, I know."

"Then, O my daughter, tell us why thou hath brought low this poor boy."

Jehan tossed the bloody knife to the stone-paved alley. It rang noisily and then came to rest against one leg of the corpse. "I was celebrating the Id al Fitr," she said. "This boy followed me and I became afraid. He made filthy gestures and called out terrible things. I hurried away, but he ran after me. He grabbed me by the shoulders and pressed me against a wall. I tried to escape, but I could not. He laughed at my fear, then he struck me many times. He dragged me along through the narrowest of streets, where there were not many to witness; and then he pulled me into this vile place. He told me that he intended to defile me, and he described what he would do in foul detail. It was then that I drew my father's dagger and stabbed him. I have spent the night in horror of his intentions and of my deed, and I have prayed to Allah for forgiveness."

The imam put a trembling hand on Jehan's cheek. "Allah is All-Wise and All-Forgiving, O my daughter. Alloweth me to return with thee to thy house, where I may put the hearts of thy father and thy mother at their ease."

Jehan knelt at the imam's feet. "All thanks be to Allah," she murmured.

"Allah be praised," said the imam, the police officer, and the qadi together.

More than a decade later, when Jehan had daughters of her own, she told them this story. But in those latter days children did not heed the warnings of their parents, and the sons and daughters of Jehan and her husband did many foolish things.

Dawn slipped even into the narrow alleyway where Jehan waited. She was very sleepy and hungry, but she stood up and took a few wobbling steps. Her muscles had become cramped, and she could hear her heart beating in her ears. Jehan steadied herself with one hand on the brick wall. She went slowly to the mouth of the alley and peered out. There was no one in sight. The boy was coming neither from the left nor the right. Jehan waited until several other people appeared, going about the business of the new day. Then she hid the dagger in her sleeve once more and departed from the alley. She hurried back to her father's house. Her mother would need her to help make breakfast.

Jehan was in her early forties now, her black hair cut short, her eyes framed by clumsy spectacles, her beauty stolen by care, poor diet, and sleeplessness. She wore a white lab coat and carried a clipboard, as much a part of her as her title, Fräulein Professor Doktor Ashûfi. This was not Göttingen any longer; it was Berlin, and a war was being lost. She was still with Heisenberg. He had protected her until her own scientific credentials became protection of themselves. At that point, the Nazi officials were compelled to make her an "honorary" Aryan, as they had the Jewish physicists and mathematicians whose cooperation they needed. It had been only Jehan's long-standing loyalty to Heisenberg himself that kept her in Germany at all. The war was of little concern to her; these were not her people, but neither were the British, the French, the Russians, or the Americans. Her only interest was in her work, in the refinement of physics, in the unending anticipation of discovery.

She was glad, therefore, when the German bomb project was removed from the control of the German army and given to the Reich Research Council. One of the first things to be done was the calling of a research conference at the Kaiser Wilhelm Institute of Physics in Berlin. The conference would be conducted under the tightest security; no preliminary list of topics would be released in advance, so that no foreign agents might see such terms as "fission cross-sections" and "isotope enrichment," leading to speculation on the long-term goals of these physicists.

At the same time, the Reich Research Council decided to hold a second conference for the benefit of the government's highest officials on the same day. The idea was that the scientists speaking at the Kaiser Wilhelm Institute's meeting could present short, elementary summaries of their work in plain language, so that the political and military leaders could be briefed on the progress toward a nuclear weapon. Then, following the laymen's presentation, the physicists could gather and discuss the same matters in their more technical jargon.

Heisenberg thought it was a good idea. It was 1942, and material, political support, and funding were getting more difficult to find. The army wanted to put all available research resources into the rocketry program; they argued that the nuclear experiments were not showing sufficient success. Heisenberg was a theoretical physicist, not an engineer; he could not find a way to tell the council that the development of the uranium bomb must necessarily be slow and methodical. Each new step forward in theory had to be tested carefully, and each experiment was expensive in both time and money. The Reich, however, cared only for positive results.

One evening Jehan was alone in an administrative office of the Reich Research Council, typing her proposal for an important test of their isotope-separation technique. She saw on the desk two stacks of papers. One stack listed the simple synopses the physicists had prepared for Göring, Himmler, and the other Reich ministers who had little or no background in science. The second stack was the secret agenda for the physicists' own meeting—"Nuclear Physics as a Weapon," by Prof. Dr. Schumann; "The Fission of the Uranium Atom," by Prof. Dr. Hahn; "The Theoretical Basis for the Production of Energy from the Fission of Uranium," by Heisenberg; and so on. Each person attending the technical seminar would be given a program after he entered the lecture hall, and he would be required to sign for it.

Jehan thought for a long while in the quiet office. She remembered her wretched childhood. She recalled her arrival in Europe and the people she had come to know, the life she had come to lead here. She thought about how Germany had changed while she hid in her castle of scientific abstractions, uninvolved with the outside world. At last she thought about what this new Germany might do with the uranium bomb. She knew exactly what she must do.

It took her only a few moments to hide the layman's synopses in her briefcase. She took the highly technical agendas and dropped them into the already-addressed envelopes to be sent to the Third Reich's highest officials. She had guaranteed that the brief introductory discussion would be attended by no one. Jehan could easily imagine the response the unintelligible scientific papers would get from the political and military leaders—curt, polite regrets that they would not be in Berlin on that day, or that their busy schedules prevented them from attending.

It was all so easy. The Reich's rulers did not hear the talks, and they did not learn how close Germany was to developing an atomic bomb. Never again was there any hope that such a weapon could be built in time to save the Reich—all because the wrong invitations had been slipped into a few envelopes.

Jehan awoke from a dream, and saw that the night had grown very old. It would not be long before the sun began to flood the sky with light. Soon she would have a resolution to her anxiety. She would learn if the boy would come to the alley or stay away.

She would learn if he would rape her or if she would find the courage to defend herself. She would learn if she would be judged guilty or innocent of murder. She would be granted a glimpse of the outcome to all things that concerned her.

Nevertheless, she was so tired, hungry, and uncomfortable that she was tempted to give up her vigil. The urge to go home was strong. Yet she had always believed that her visions were gifts granted by Allah, and it might offend Him to ignore the clear warnings. For Allah's sake, as well as her own, she reluctantly chose to wait out the rest of the dying night. She had seen so many visions since last evening—more than on any other day of her life—some new, some familiar from years passed. It was, in a small, human way, almost comparable to the Night of Power that was bestowed upon the Prophet, may Allah's blessings be on him and peace. Then Jehan felt guilty and blasphemous for comparing herself to the Messenger that way.

She got down on her knees and faced toward Mecca, and addressed a prayer to Allah, reciting one of the later sûrahs from the glorious Qur'ân, the one called "The Morning Hours," which seemed particularly relevant to her situation. " *'In the name of Allah, the Beneficent, the Merciful. By the morning hours, and by the night when it is stillest, thy Lord hath not forsaken thee nor doth He hate thee, and verily the latter portion will be better for thee than the former, and verily thy Lord will give unto thee so that thou wilt be content. Did He not find thee an orphan and protect thee? Did He not find thee wandering and direct thee? Did He not find thee destitute and enrich thee? Therefore the orphan oppress not, therefore the beggar drive not away, therefore of the bounty of thy Lord be thy discourse.'* "

When she finished praying, she stood up and leaned against the wall. She wondered if that sûrah promised that soon she'd be an orphan. She hoped that Allah understood that she never intended anything awful to happen to her parents. Jehan was willing to suffer whatever consequences Allah willed, but it didn't seem fair for her mother and father to have to share them. She shivered in the damp, cold air, and gazed up to see if there was yet any brightening of the sky. She pretended that already the stars were beginning to disappear.

The square was jammed and choked with people. Soon Hilbert could see why—a platform had been erected in the center, and on it stood a man with what could only be an executioner's axe. Hilbert felt his stomach sicken. His Arab guide had thrust aside everyone in their way until Hilbert stood at the very foot of the platform. He saw uniformed police and a bearded old man leading out a young girl. The crowd parted to allow them by. The girl was stunningly lovely. Hilbert looked into her huge, dark eyes—"like the eyes of a gazelle," he remembered from reading Omar Khayyam—and glimpsed her slender form undisguised by her modest garments. As she mounted the steps, she looked down directly at him again. Hilbert felt his heart lurch, he felt a tremendous shudder. Then she looked away.

The Arab guide screamed in Hilbert's ear. It meant nothing to the mathematician. He watched in horror as Jehan knelt, as the headsman raised his weapon of office. Hilbert shouted. His guide tightened his grip on the outsider's arm, but Hilbert lashed out in fury and threw the man into a group of veiled women. In the confusion, Hilbert ran up the steps of the scaffold. The imam and the police officers looked at him angrily. The crowd began to shout fiercely at this interruption, this desecration by a European kaffir, an unbeliever. Hilbert ran to the police. "You must stop this!" he cried in German. They did not understand him and tried to heave him off the platform. "Stop!" he screamed in English.

One of the police officers answered him. "It cannot be stopped," he said gruffly. "The girl committed murder. She was found guilty, and she cannot pay the blood-price to the victim's family. She must die instead."

"Blood-price!" cried Hilbert. "That's barbarous! You would kill a young girl just because she is poor? Blood-price! *I'll* pay your goddamn blood-price! How much is it?"

The policeman conferred with the others, and then went to the imam for guidance. Finally, the English-speaking officer returned. "Four hundred kiam," he said bluntly.

Hilbert took out his wallet with shaking hands. He counted out the money and handed it with obvious disgust to the policeman. The imam cried a declaration in his weak voice. The words were passed quickly through the crowd, and the onlookers grew more enraged at this spoiling of their morning's entertainment. "Take her and go quickly," said the police officer. "We cannot protect you, and the crowd is becoming furious."

Hilbert nodded. He grasped Jehan's thin wrist and pulled her along after him. She questioned him in Arabic, but he could not reply. As he struggled through the menacing crowd, they were struck again and again by stones. Hilbert wondered what he had done, if he and the girl would get out of the mosque's courtyard alive. His fondness for young women—it was an open joke in Göttingen—had that been all that had motivated him? Had he unconsciously decided to rescue the girl and take her back to Germany? Or was it something more laudable? He would never know. He shocked himself: While he tried to shield himself and the girl from the vicious blows of the crowd, he thought only of how he might explain the girl to his wife, Käthe, and Clärchen, his mistress.

In 1957, Jehan Fatima Ashûfi was fifty-eight years old and living in Princeton, New Jersey. By coincidence, Albert Einstein had come here to live out the end of his life, and before he died in 1955 they had many pleasant afternoons at his house. In the beginning, Jehan wanted to discuss quantum physics with Einstein; she even told him Heisenberg's answer to Einstein's objection to God's playing dice with the universe. Einstein was not very amused, and from then on, their conversation concerned only nostalgic memories of the better days in Germany, before the advent of the National Socialists.

This afternoon, however, Jehan was sitting in a hall at Princeton University, listening to a young man read a remarkable paper, his Ph.D. thesis. His name was Hugh Everett, and what he was saying was that there was an explanation for all the paradoxes of the quantum world, a simple but bizarre way of looking at them. His new idea included the Copenhagen interpretation and explained away all the objections that might be raised by less open-minded physicists. He stated first of all that quantum mechanics provided predictions that were invariably correct when measured against experimental data. Quantum physics *had* to be consistent and valid, there was no longer any doubt. The trouble was that quantum theory was beginning to lead to unappetizing alternatives.

Everett's thesis reconciled them. It eliminated Schrödinger's cat paradox, in which the cat in the box was merely a quantum wave function, not alive and not dead, until an observer looked to see which state the cat was in. Everett showed that the cat was no mere ghostly wave function. Everett said that wave functions do not "collapse," choosing one alternative or the other. He said that the process of observation chose one reality, but the other reality existed in its own right, just as "real" as our world. Particles do not choose at random which path to take—they take every path, in a separate, newly branched world for each option. Of course, at the particle level, this meant a huge number of branchings occurring at every moment.

Jehan knew this almost-metaphysical idea would find a chilly reception from most physicists, but she had special reasons to accept it eagerly. It explained her visions. She glimpsed the particular branch that would be "real" for her, and also those that would be "real" for other versions of her, her own duplicates living on the countless parallel worlds. Now, as she listened to Everett, she smiled. She saw another young man in the audience, wearing a T-shirt that said, "Wigner: Would you please ask your friend to feed my cat? Thanks, Schrödinger." She found that very amusing.

When Everett finished reading, Jehan felt good; it wasn't peace she felt, it was more like the release one feels after an argument that had been brewing for a long while. Jehan thought back over the turns and sidetracks she had taken since that dawn in the alley in the Budayeen. She smiled again, sadly, took a deep breath and let it out. How many things she had done, how many things had happened to her! They had been long, strange lives. The only question that still remained was: How many uncountable futures did she still have to devise, to fabricate from the immaterial resources of this moment? As she sat there—in some worlds—Jehan knew the futures went on without her willing them to, needing nothing of her permission. She was not cautious of when tomorrow came, but *which* tomorrow came.

Jehan saw them all, but she still understood nothing. She

thought, "The Chinese say that a journey of a thousand li begins with a single step. How short-sighted that is! A *thousand* journeys of a thousand li begin with a single step. Or with each step not taken." She sat in her chair until everyone else had left the lecture hall. Then she got up slowly, her back and knees giving her pain, and she took a step. She pictured myriad mirror-Jehans taking that step along with her, and a myriad that didn't. And in all the worlds across time, it was another step into the future.

At last, there was no doubt about it: It was dawn. Jehan fingered her father's dagger and felt a thrill of excitement. Strange words flickered in her mind. "The Heisenty Uncertainberg Principle," she murmured, already hurrying toward the mouth of the alley. She felt no fear.

The Fort Moxie Branch

▼ ▼ ▼

Jack McDevitt

Jack McDevitt lives in Brunswick, Georgia. He has been a naval officer, an English teacher, and a customs officer. He has lived in such diverse places as Philadelphia; Chicago; Washington, D.C.; Rhode Island; New Hampshire; North Dakota; and Yokohama, Japan. He did not begin writing until his mid-forties, and (an encouragement to all late-bloomers) he deservedly managed to sell the first story to roll out of his typewriter.

His short fiction has appeared in a variety of markets, and his story "Cryptic" was on the final Hugo ballot in 1984. *The Hercules Text,* his first novel, an Ace Special published under Terry Carr's editorship, received the Philip K. Dick Special Award in 1986 and in a poll of *Locus* readers garnered the laurel as best first novel of the year. He has also published a colorful novel of far-future conflict, *A Talent for War,* and a pair of stories indicating that war is *not* inevitable, "Date with Destiny" in Lewis Shiner's *When the Music's Over . . .* and "Valkyrie" in a volume edited by Harry Harrison and Bruce McAllister and tentatively titled *The Peace Anthology.*

McDevitt has a natural, self-effacing prose style that never raises any barriers between the reader and the tale being told. And ever since hearing him read at an SF convention in Atlanta, I can no longer read his work without hearing his distinctive voice caressing each word—an eerie, but also a strangely comforting, experience.

Of "The Fort Moxie Branch," McDevitt writes: "We lived for a number of years in Pembina, North Dakota (the Fort Moxie of the story). The town is small, population maybe 600. It lies on the Canadian border, along the western edge of an ancient shoreline. The inland sea that once existed there, Lake Agassiz, covered great parts of the Dakotas, Minnesota, and Manitoba.

"You can still make out the general coastal configuration from the air. But Agassiz, in its time the largest of the Great Lakes, is gone. Lost in the meltwaters of the retreating glaciers.

"The missing lake has always struck me as something of an outrage. The ultimate symbol of a relativistic universe where nothing quite survives. And things get lost far too easily. So I built Fort Moxie's branch of a very special library. With a lot of help (by the way) from the story doctors at the Sycamore Hill workshop."

In many ways, this is a wish-fulfillment story for writers, but it is also a strong psychological study of a good man and a moving lament for the mutability—the perishability—of our lives and works. No wonder that "The Fort Moxie Branch" was also a finalist for the Hugo Award for best short story. As is usually the case with a McDevitt story, it resonates in readers' memories as well as in writers'.

A few minutes into the blackout, the window in the single dormer at the top of Will Potter's house began to glow. I watched it from across Route 11, through a screen of box elders, and through the snow which had been falling all afternoon and was now getting heavier. It was smeary and insubstantial, not the way a bedroom light would look, but as though something luminous floated in the dark interior.

Will Potter was dead. We'd put him in the graveyard on the other side of the expressway three years before. The property had lain empty since, a two-story frame dating from about the turn of the century.

The town had gone quiet with the blackout. Somewhere a dog barked, and a garage door banged down. Ed Kiernan's station wagon rumbled past, headed out toward Cavalier. The streetlights were out, as was the traffic signal down at Twelfth.

As far as I was concerned, the power could have stayed off.

It was trash night. I was hauling out cartons filled with copies of *Independence Square,* and I was on my way down the outside staircase when everything had gone dark.

The really odd thing about the light over at Potter's was that it seemed to be spreading. It had crept outside: the dormer began to burn with a steady, cold, blue-white flame. It flowed gradually down the slope of the roof, slipped over the drainpipe, and turned the corner of the porch. Just barely, in the illumination, I could make out the skewed screens and broken stone steps.

It would have taken something unusual to get my attention that night. I was piling the boxes atop one another, and some of the books had spilled into the street: my name glittered on the bindings. It was a big piece of my life. Five years and a quarter million words and, in the end, most of my life's savings to get it printed. It had been painful, and I was glad to be rid of it.

So I was standing on the curb, feeling very sorry for myself while snow whispered out of a sagging sky.

The Tastee-Freez, Hal's Lumber, the Amoco at the corner of Nineteenth and Bannister, were all dark and silent. Toward the center of town, blinkers and headlights misted in the storm.

It was a still, somehow motionless, night. The flakes were blue in the pale glow surrounding the house. They fell onto the gabled roof and spilled gently off the back.

Cass Taylor's station wagon plowed past, headed out of town. He waved.

I barely noticed: the back end of Potter's house had begun to balloon out. I watched it, fascinated, knowing it to be an illusion, yet still half-expecting it to explode.

The house began to change in other ways.

Roof and corner lines wavered. New walls dropped into place. The dormer suddenly ascended, and the top of the house with it. A third floor, complete with lighted windows and a garret, appeared out of the snow. (In one of the illuminated rooms, someone moved.)

Parapets rose, and an oculus formed in the center of the garret. A bay window pushed out of the lower level, near the front. An arch and portico replaced the porch. Spruce trees materialized, and Potter's old post light, which had never worked, blinked on.

The box elders were bleak and stark in the foreground.

I stood, worrying about my eyesight, holding onto a carton, feeling the snow against my face and throat. Nothing moved on Route 11.

I was still standing there when the power returned: the streetlights, the electric sign over Hal's office, the security lights at the Amoco, gunshots from a TV, the sudden inexplicable rasp of an electric drill. And, at the same moment, the apparition clicked off.

I could have gone to bed. I could have hauled out the rest of those goddamned books, attributed everything to my imagination, and gone to bed. I'm glad I didn't.

The snow cover in Potter's backyard was undisturbed. It was more than a foot deep beneath the half-inch or so that had fallen that day. I struggled through it to find the key he'd always kept wedged beneath a loose hasp near the cellar stairs.

I used it to let myself in through the storage room at the rear of the house. And I should admit that I had a bad moment when the door shut behind me, and I stood among the rakes and shovels and boxes of nails. Too many late TV movies. Too much Stephen King.

I'd been here before. Years earlier, when I'd thought that teaching would support me until I was able to earn a living as a novelist, I'd picked up some extra money by tutoring Potter's boys. But that was a long time ago.

I'd brought a flashlight with me. I turned it on, and pushed through into the kitchen. It was warmer in there, but that was to be expected. Potter's heirs were still trying to sell the place, and it gets too cold in North Dakota to simply shut off the heat altogether.

Cabinets were open and bare; the range had been disconnected from its gas mooring and dragged into the center of the floor. A church calendar hung behind a door. It displayed March 1986: the month of Potter's death.

In the dining room, a battered table and three wooden chairs remained. They were pushed against one wall. A couple of boxes lay in a corner.

With a bang, the heater came on.

I was startled. A fan cut in, and warm air rushed across my ankles.

I took a deep breath and played the beam toward the living room. I was thinking how different a house looks without its furnishings, how utterly strange and unfamiliar, when I realized I wasn't alone. Whether it was a movement outside the circle of light, or a sudden indrawn breath, or the creak of a board, I couldn't have said. But I *knew.* "Who's there?" I asked. The words hung in the dark.

"Mr. Wickham?" It was a woman.

"Hello," I said. "I, uh, I saw lights and thought—"

"Of course," she said. She was standing back near the kitchen, silhouetted against outside light. I wondered how she could have got there. "You were correct to be concerned. But it's quite all right." She was somewhat on the gray side of middle age, attractive, well-pressed, the sort you would expect to encounter at a bridge party. Her eyes, which were on a level with mine, watched me with good humor. "My name is Coela." She extended her right hand. Gold bracelets clinked.

"I'm happy to meet you," I said, trying to look as though nothing unusual had occurred. "How did you know my name?"

She touched my hand, the one holding the flashlight, and pushed it gently aside so she could pass. "Please follow me," she said. "Be careful. Don't fall over anything."

We climbed the stairs to the second floor, and went into the rear bedroom. "Through here," she said, opening a door that should have revealed a closet. Instead, I was looking into a brightly illuminated space that couldn't possibly be there. It was filled with books, paintings and tapestries, leather furniture and polished tables. A fireplace crackled cheerfully beneath a portrait of a monk. A piano played softly. Chopin, I thought.

"This room won't fit," I said, rather stupidly. The thick quality of my voice startled me.

"No," she agreed. "We're attached to the property, but we're quite independent." We stepped inside. Carpets were thick underfoot. Where the floors were exposed, they were lustrous parquet. Vaulted windows looked out over Potter's backyard, and Em Pyle's house next door. Coela watched me thoughtfully. "Welcome, Mr. Wickham," she said. Her eyes glittered with pride. "Welcome to the Fort Moxie branch of the John of Singletary Memorial Library."

I looked around for a chair and, finding one near a window, lowered myself into it. The falling snow was dark, as though no illumination from within the glass touched it. "I don't think I understand this," I said.

"I suppose it is something of a shock."

Her amusement was obvious, and sufficiently infectious that I loosened up somewhat. "Are you the librarian?"

She nodded.

"Nobody in Fort Moxie knows you're here. What good is a library no one knows about?"

"That's a valid question," she admitted. "We have a limited membership."

I glanced around. All the books looked like Bibles. They were different sizes and shapes, but all were bound in leather. Furthermore, titles and authors were printed in identical silver script. But I saw nothing in English. The shelves near me were packed with books whose titles appeared to be Russian. A volume lay open on a table at my right hand. It was in Latin. I picked it up and held it so I could read the title: *Historiae, V–XII.* Tacitus. "Okay," I said. "It must be limited. Hardly anybody in Fort Moxie reads Latin or Russian." I held up the Tacitus. "I doubt even Father Cramer could handle this."

Em Pyle, the next-door neighbor, had come out onto his front steps. He called his dog, Preach, as he did most nights at this time. There was no response, and he looked up and down Nineteenth Street, into his own backyard, and *right through me.* I couldn't believe he didn't react.

"Coela, who are you exactly? What's going on here? Who the hell is John of Singletary?"

She nodded, in the way people do when they agree that you have a problem. "Perhaps," she said, "you should look around, Mr. Wickham. Then it might be easier to talk."

She retired to a desk, and immersed herself in a sheaf of papers, leaving me to fend for myself.

Beyond the Russian shelves, I found Japanese or Chinese titles. I couldn't tell which. And Arabic. There was a lot of Arabic. And German. French. Greek. More Oriental.

I found the English titles in the rear. They were divided into

American and British sections. Dickens, Cowper, and Shakespeare on one side; Holmes, Dreiser, and Steinbeck on the other.

And almost immediately, the sense of apprehension that had hung over me from the beginning of this business sharpened. I didn't know why. Certainly, the familiar names in a familiar setting should have eased my disquiet.

I picked up Melville's *Agatha* and flipped through the pages. They had the texture of fine rice paper, and the leather binding lent a sense of timelessness to the book. I thought about the cheap cardboard that Crossbow had provided for *Independence Square.* My God, this was the way to get published.

Immediately beside it was *The Complete Works of James McCorbin.* Who the hell was James McCorbin? There were two novels and eight short stories. None of the titles was familiar, and the book contained no biographical information.

In fact, most of the names were people I'd never heard of. Kemerie Baxter. Wynn Gomez. Michael Kaspar. There was nothing unusual about that, of course. Library shelves are always filled with obscure authors. But the lush binding, and the obvious care expended on these books, changed the rules.

I took down Hemingway's *Watch by Night.* I stared a long time at the title. The prose was vintage Hemingway. The crisp, clear bullet sentences and the factual, journalistic style were unmistakable. Even the setting: Italy, 1944.

Henry James was represented by *Brandenberg.* There was no sign of *The Ambassadors,* or *The Portrait of a Lady,* or *Washington Square.* In fact, there was neither *Moby Dick* nor *Billy Budd.* Nor *The Sun Also Rises* nor *A Farewell to Arms.* Thoreau wasn't represented at all. I saw no sign of Fenimore Cooper or Mark Twain. (What kind of library had no copy of *Huck Finn?*)

I carried *Watch by Night* back to the desk where Coela was working. "This is *not* a Hemingway book," I said, lobbing it onto the pile of papers in front of her. She winced. "The rest of them are bogus too. What the hell's going on?"

"I can understand that you might be a little confused, Mr. Wickham," she said, a trifle nervously. "I'm never sure quite how to explain things."

"Please try your best," I said.

She frowned. "I'm part of a cultural salvage group. We try to ensure that things of permanent value don't, ah, get lost."

She pushed her chair back, and gazed steadily at me. Somewhere in back, a clock ticked ponderously. "The book you picked up when you first came in was—" she paused, "—mislaid almost two thousand years ago."

"The *Tacitus?*"

"The *Histories Five through Twelve.* We also have his *Annals.*"

"Who *are* you?"

She shook her head. "A kindred spirit," she said.

"Seriously."

"I'm being quite serious, Mr. Wickham. What you see around you is a treasure of incomparable value that, without our efforts, would no longer exist."

We stared at each other for a few moments. "Are you saying," I asked, "that these are all lost masterpieces by people like Tacitus? That *this*"—I pointed at *Watch by Night*—"is a bona fide Hemingway?"

"Yes," she said.

We faced one another across the desktop. "There's a Melville back there too. And a Thomas Wolfe."

"*Yes,*" she said. Her eyes were bright with pleasure. "*All of them.*"

I took another long look around the place. Thousands of volumes filled all the shelves, packed tight, reaching to the ceiling. Others were stacked on tables; a few were tossed almost haphazardly on chairs. Half a dozen stood between Trojan horse bookends on Coela's desk.

"It's not possible," I said, finding the air suddenly close and oppressive. "How? How could it happen?"

"Quite easily," she said. "Melville, as a case in point, became discouraged. He was a customs inspector at the time *Agatha* first came to our attention. I went all the way to London, specifically to allow him to examine my baggage on the way back. In 1875, that was no easy journey, I can assure you." She waved off my objection. "Well, that's an exaggeration, of course. I took advantage of the trip to conduct some business with Matthew Arnold and— Well: I'm name-dropping now. Forgive me. But think about having Herman Melville go through your luggage." Her laughter echoed through the room. "I was quite young. Too young to understand his work, really. But I'd read *Moby Dick,* and some of his poetry. If I'd known him then the way I do now, I don't think I could have kept my feet." She bit her lower lip and shook her head, and for a moment I thought she might indeed pass out.

"And he *gave* you the manuscript? Simply because you asked for it?"

"No. Because I knew it for what it was. And he understood why I wanted it."

"And why do you want it? You have buried it here."

She ignored the question.

"You never asked about the library's name."

"The John of—"

"—Singletary—"

"—Memorial. Okay, who's John of Singletary?"

"That's his portrait, facing the main entrance." It was a large oil of an introspective-looking monk. His hands were buried in dark brown robes, and he was flanked by a scroll and a crucifix. "He was perhaps the most brilliant sociologist who ever lived."

"I never heard of him."

"That's no surprise. His work was eventually ruled profane by his superiors, and either burned or stored away somewhere. We've never been sure. But we were able to obtain copies of most of it." She was out of her seat now, standing with her back to the portrait. "What is significant is that he defined the state toward which he felt the human community should be advancing. He set the parameters and the goals for which the men and women whose works populate this library have been striving: the precise degree of balance between order and freedom; the extent of one's obligation to external authority; the precise relationships that should exist between human beings. And so on. Taken in all, he produced a schematic for civilized life, a set of instructions, if you will."

"The human condition," I said.

"How do you mean?"

"He did all this, and no one knows him."

"*We* know him, Mr. Wickham." She paused. I found myself glancing from her to the solemn figure in the portrait. "You asked why we wanted *Agatha*. The answer is that it is lovely, that it is very powerful. We simply will not allow it to be lost."

"But who will ever get to see it *here?* You're talking about a novel that, as far as anyone is concerned, doesn't exist. I have a friend in North Carolina who'd give every nickel he owns to see this book. If it's legitimate."

"We *will* make it available. In time. This library will eventually be yours."

A wave of exhilaration washed over me. "Thank you," I said.

"I'm sorry," she said quickly. "That may have been misleading. I didn't mean right now. And I didn't mean *you.*"

"When?"

"When the human race fulfills the requirements of John of Singletary. When you have, in other words, achieved a true global community, all this will be our gift to you."

A gust of wind rattled the windows.

"That's a considerable way off," I said.

"We must take the long view."

"Easy for you to say. We have a lot of problems. Some of this might be just what we need to get through."

"This was once *yours*, Mr. Wickham. Your people have not always recognized value. We are providing a second chance. I'd expect you to be grateful."

I turned away from her. "Most of this I can't even recognize," I said. "Who's James McCorbin? You've got his *Complete Works* back there with Melville and the others. Who *is* he?"

"A master of the short story. One of your contemporaries, but I'm afraid he writes in a style and with a complexity that will go unappreciated during his lifetime."

"You're telling me he's *too* good to get published?" I was aghast.

"Oh, yes. Mr. Wickham, you live in an exceedingly commercial era. Your editors understand that they cannot sell champagne to beer drinkers. They buy what sells."

"And that's also true of the others? Kemerie Baxter? Gomez? Somebody-or-other Parker?"

"I'm afraid so. It's quite common, in fact. Baxter is an essayist of the first order. Unlike the other two, he has been published, but by a small university press, in an edition which sank quickly out of sight. Gomez has written three exquisite novels, and has since given up, despite our encouragement. Parker is a poet. If you know anything about the markets for poetry, I need say no more."

We wandered together through the library. She pointed to lost works by Sophocles and Aeschylus, to missing epics of the Homeric cycle, to shelves full of Indian poetry and Roman drama. "On the upper level," she said, raising her eyes to the ceiling, "are the songs and tales of artists whose native tongues had no written form. They have been translated into our own language. In most cases," she added, "we were able to preserve their creators' names.

"And now I have a surprise." We had reached the British section. She took down a book and passed it to me. William Shakespeare. "His *Zenobia*," she said, her voice hushed. "Written at the height of his career."

I was silent for a time. "And why was it never performed?"

"Because it's a savage attack on Elizabeth. Even he might well have lost his head. We have a major epic by Virgil that was withheld for much the same reason. In fact, that's why the Russian section is so large. They've been producing magnificent novels in the tradition of Tolstoy and Dostoyevski for years, but they're far too prudent to offer them for publication."

There were two other Shakespearean plays. "*Adam and Eve* was heretical by the standards of the day," Coela explained. "And here's another that would have raised a few eyebrows." She smiled.

It was *Nisus and Euryalus.* The characters were out of the *Aeneid.* "Homosexual love," she said.

"But he wished these withheld," I objected. "There's a difference between works that have been lost, and those a writer wishes to destroy. You published these against his will."

"Oh, no, Mr. Wickham. We never do that. To begin with,

if Shakespeare had wanted these plays destroyed, he could have handled that detail quite easily. He desired only that they not be published in his lifetime. Everything you see here," she included the entire library with a sweeping, feminine gesture, "was given to us voluntarily. We have very strict regulations on that score. And we do things strictly by the book, Mr. Wickham.

"In some cases, by the way, we perform an additional service. We are able, in a small way, to reassure those great artists who have not been properly recognized in their own lifetimes. I wish you could have seen Melville."

"You could be wrong, you know."

Her nostrils widened slightly. "About what?"

"Maybe books that get lost deserve to be lost."

"Some do." Her tone hardened. "None of those are here. We exercise full editorial judgment."

"We close at midnight," she said, appearing suddenly behind me while I was absorbed in the Wells novel, *Starflight.* I could read the implication in her tone: *Never to open again. Not in Fort Moxie. Not for you.*

I returned Wells and moved quickly along, pulling books from the shelves with some sense of urgency. I glanced through *Mendinhal,* an unfinished epic by Byron, dated 1824, the year of his death. I caught individually brilliant lines, and tried to commit some of them to memory, and proceeded on to Blake, to Fielding, to Chaucer! At a little after eleven, I came across four Conan Doyle stories: "The Adventure of the Grim Footman"; "The Branmoor Club"; "The Jezail Bullet"; "The Sumatran Clipper." My God, what would the Sherlockians of the world not give to have those?

I hurried on with increasing desperation, as though I could somehow gather the contents into myself, and make them available to a waiting world: *God and Country,* by Thomas Wolfe; fresh cartoons by James Thurber, recovered from beneath wallpaper in a vacation home he'd rented in Atlantic City in 1947; plays by Odets and O'Neill; short stories by Nathaniel Hawthorne and Terry Carr. Here was *More Dangerous Visions.* And there Mary Shelley's *Morgan.*

And through it all, as I whirled through the rice-paper pages, balancing the eerie moonlit lines of A. E. Housman with the calibrated shafts of Mencken, I envied them. Envied them all.

And I was angry.

"You have no right," I said at last, when Coela came to stand by my side, indicating that my time was up.

"No right to withhold all this?" I detected sympathy in her voice.

"Not only that," I said. "Who are you to set yourself up to make such judgments? To say what is great and what is pedestrian?"

"I've asked myself that question many times. We do the best we can." We were moving toward the door. "We have quite a lot of experience, you understand."

The lights dimmed. "Why are you really doing this? It's not for us, is it?"

"Not exclusively. What your species produces belongs to all." Her smile broadened. "Surely you would not wish to keep your finest creations for yourselves?"

"Your people have access to them now?"

"Oh, yes," she said. "Back home everyone has access. As soon as a new book is cataloged here, it is made available to everybody."

"Except us."

"We will not do everything for you, Mr. Wickham." She drew close, and I could almost feel her heartbeat.

"Do you have any idea what it would mean to our people to recover all this?"

"I'm sorry. For the moment, there's really nothing I can do."

She opened the door for me, the one that led into the back bedroom. I stepped through it. She followed. "Use your flashlight," she said.

We walked through the long hallway, and down the stairs to the living room. She had something to say to me, but seemed strangely reluctant to continue the conversation. And somewhere in the darkness of Will Potter's place, between the magic doorway in the back of the upstairs closet, and the broken stone steps off the porch, I understood! And when we paused on the concrete beside the darkened post light, and turned to face each other, my pulse was pounding. "It's no accident that this place became visible tonight, is it?"

She said nothing.

"Nor that only I saw it. I mean, there wouldn't be a point in putting your universal library in Fort Moxie unless you wanted something. Right?"

"I said this was the Fort Moxie *branch.* The central library is located on Saint Simons Island." The brittleness of the last few moments melted without warning. "But no, you're right, of course."

"You want *Independence Square,* don't you? You want to put my book in there with Thomas Wolfe and Shakespeare and Homer. Right?"

"Yes," she said. "That's right. You've created a psychological drama of the first water, Mr. Wickham. You've captured the microcosm of Fort Moxie and produced a portrait of small town America that has captured the admiration of the Board. And, I might add, of our membership. You will be interested, by the way, in knowing that one of your major characters caused the blackout tonight. Jack Gilbert."

I was overwhelmed. "How'd it happen?" I asked.

"Can you guess?"

"An argument with his wife, somehow or other." Gilbert, who had a different name, of course, in *Independence Square,* had a long history of inept philandering.

"Yes. Afterward, he took the pickup and ran it into the streetlight at Eleventh and Foster. Shorted out everything over an area of forty square blocks. It's right out of the book."

"Yes," I said.

"But he'll never know he's in it. Nor will any of the other people you've immortalized. Only you know. And only you would *ever* know, were it not for us." She stood facing me. The snow had stopped, and the clouds had cleared away. The stars were hard and bright in her eyes. "We think it unlikely that you will be recognized in your own lifetime. We could be wrong. We were wrong about Faulkner." Her lips crinkled into a smile. "But it is my honor to invite you to contribute your work to the library."

I froze. It was really happening. Emerson. Hemingway. Wickham. I loved it. And yet, there was something terribly wrong about it all. "Coela," I asked. "Have you ever been refused?"

"Yes," she said cautiously. "Occasionally it happens. We couldn't convince Fielding of the value of *Harold Swanley.* Charlotte and Emily Brontë both rejected us, to the world's loss. And Tolstoy. Tolstoy had a wonderful novel from his youth which he considered, well, anti-Christian."

"And among the unknowns? Has anyone just walked away?"

"No," she said. "Never. In such a case, the consequences would be especially tragic." Sensing where the conversation was leading, she'd begun to speak in a quicker tempo, at a slightly higher pitch. "A new genius, who would sink into the sea of history, as Byron says, 'without a grave, unknelled, uncoffined, and unknown.' Is that what you are considering?"

"You have *no* right to keep all this to yourself."

She nodded. "I should remind you, Mr. Wickham, that without the intervention of the library, these works would not exist at all."

I stared past her shoulder, down the dark street.

"Are you then," she said at last, drawing the last word out, "refusing?"

"This belongs to *us,*" I said. "It is ours. We've produced *everything* back there!"

"I almost anticipated, feared, this kind of response from you. I think it was almost implicit in your book. Will you grant us permission to use *Independence Square?*"

My breath had grown short, and it was hard to speak. "I must regretfully say no."

"I am sorry to hear it. I— You should understand that there will be no second offer."

I said nothing.

"Then I fear we have no further business to transact."

———

At home, I carried the boxes back up to my living room. After all, if it's that damned good, there has to be a market for it. Somewhere.

And if she's right about rampant commercialism? Well, what the hell.

I pulled one of the copies out, and put it on the shelf, between Walt Whitman and Thomas Wolfe.

Where it belongs.

In Memoriam

▼ ▼ ▼

Within two weeks of each other in the spring of 1988, two of the first three officially designated Grand Masters of SFWA died. Robert A. Heinlein, the first, passed away fourteen days after the third, Clifford D. Simak, and suddenly a great many of us, even if only half as old as these two stalwarts, began to feel troubling intimations of our own mortality. Almost overnight, the landscape of contemporary science fiction had lost two of its most reliable and imposing natural monuments.

In the essays that follow, Gordon R. Dickson memorializes Simak, and Frank R. Robinson attempts to assess Heinlein's far-reaching influence. Dickson and Robinson are noteworthy figures themselves, and in a moment I will introduce *them.*

First, though, I want to comment briefly on Clifford Simak's literary contributions (because Dickson's essay is deliberately a memoir concentrating on the man rather than his work), noting that his first published story, "The World of the Red Sun," appeared in *Wonder Stories* in 1931, not quite sixty years ago, and that almost a half century later, in 1980, he earned the Nebula Award for "The Grotto of the Dancing Deer," a short story from *Analog.* He kept writing until emphysema, leukemia, shingles, and other ailments and hardships made it impossible for him to continue.

Simak's career had many high points, including his creation of the series of stories published together as *City* (1952), which won the prestigious International Fantasy Award and remains today among his most popular titles. From it, Ian Watson and I reprinted his haunting little story "Desertion," set on the maddeningly hostile planet Jupiter, in our 1983 anthology, *Changes.* "Huddling Place," another famous episode from *City,* appears in *The Science Fiction Hall of Fame,* a 1970 anthology edited by Robert Silverberg and devoted to the best stories to appear in the field before the inauguration of the Nebula Awards in 1965. Simak's novelette "The Big Front Yard," from John W. Campbell's *Astounding,* won the 1959 Hugo Award, as did his impressive novel *Way Station* in 1964.

Other praiseworthy titles include *Time Is the Simplest Thing,
They Walked Like Men, All Flesh Is Grass, Why Call Them Back
from Heaven?, A Choice of Gods, Cemetery World, Enchanted Pil-
grimage, A Heritage of Stars, The Fellowship of the Talisman, Project
Pope,* and *Special Delivery.* Salient in each of Simak's tales and
novels is the enduring quality of his vision, the palpable de-
cency of the man behind the plots and prose.

Gordon R. Dickson, who here memorializes Simak, appears to be on the road to a Grand Master Nebula himself. He
has been a full-time writer since 1950, and he has studied
under such world-famous literary figures as Sinclair Lewis and
Robert Penn Warren. His most ambitious work is a renowned
series titled *The Childe Cycle,* which, when complete, will com-
prise three historical novels, three contemporary novels, and
seven books set in the future. Six of the "future" books include
Dorsai! (1957), *Necromancer* (1960), *Soldier, Ask Not* (1967),
Tactics of Mistake (1971), *The Final Encyclopedia* (1984), and
The Chantry Guild (1988). One of the founders of SFWA,
Dickson has twice served as its president; he also belongs to the
Authors Guild and the Mystery Writers of America. His most
recent novels are *Wolf and Iron* and *The Dragon Knight,* a sequel
to one of his most popular books, *The Dragon and the George.*

Frank R. Robinson, Heinlein's eulogist, is probably most
well known for a novel-length collaboration with Thomas N.
Scortia, *The Glass Inferno,* filmed as *The Towering Inferno.* Two
others of his novels have been filmed, and his articles and
stories have appeared in *Playboy, Reader's Digest, Cavalier, Galaxy, Gallery, Astounding,* and other markets. He has held important editorial positions at a wide range of magazines,
including *Science Digest, Family Weekly, Rogue, Censorship Today,*
and *Playboy.* He says that he "lived as an aging hippie in San
Francisco during the 'Summer of Love' and the disasters that
followed," and he is living there again, "inviting bankruptcy
remodeling an old house." He does a monthly column for
Locus called "The Media Scene." In his spare time, he collects
old pulp magazines and watches video disks.

Robert Heinlein, as Robinson's essay on the first Grand
Master clearly shows, meant a great deal to him—as, of course,
Heinlein did to almost everyone else in love with twentieth-
century science fiction.

Clifford D. Simak

Gordon R. Dickson

Clifford D. Simak was very deceptive in person as well as in manner. He stood about five feet, nine inches tall; but his clothes and his gentle voice drew attention from the fact that his shoulders were disproportionately wide. In fact, he was a short giant; and he had always shown unusual strength and endurance—which undoubtedly helped him in the illnesses of his last years.

I met Cliff for the first time in 1940, at a meeting of the Minneapolis Fantasy Society, a later-to-be-legendary group whose meeting that night included Carl Jacobi and Oliver Saari. (Other meetings would at times include such writers or early SF fans as Phil Bronson, Manse Brackney, Dale Rostomily, John Chapman, and Sam Russell.)

The MFS seldom produced more than fifteen people for its meetings, and so they were generally held at members' homes, in turns. On the occasions when the meeting was held at Cliff's house his wife (her name was Agnes but everyone called her Kay) always produced huge plates of sandwiches—I remember that well, because in those days most of us younger members were always hungry and the stacks of sandwiches had a tendency to disappear at a positively impolite rate.

Cliff's house, at that time, also contained a dog who was a basic source of canine characters in many of Cliff's stories—including those in the "City" series. He was a black, curly-haired, friendly fellow called Squanchfoot, and as much a member of the club as anyone—he had a membership of his own, duly recorded; and, if memory serves, he even wrote an occasional column for some of the local fanzines.

Being around Cliff was always comfortable—he had a way of relaxing those about him (which among other things served him well as a reporter). But for the rest of us there was a certain excitement, as well, for he often brought with him the manuscript of whatever story he was working on at the moment, reading it to us and seeking our opinions. This had the effect of turning the club meetings into something that was more than half a writers' workshop—and it was both helpful and fascinating to the younger writers.

World War II broke up the MFS, putting most of its members into uniforms and other activities for five years. When the club reformed there were some of the earlier members gone, but a number of newer members, including Poul Anderson, Marvin Larson, Jean Firmage, and Jane Anderson. The mix was still good, but different.

Cliff had continued through the war as a newspaperman. That was only appropriate for someone who had fallen in love with writing at an early age, but had been faced with the problem of trying to make a living from it.

Most of us face that problem, of course, in one form or another. But Cliff had, quite literally, grown up dirt-poor in the backwoods. His parents had been homesteaders in southeastern Wisconsin, where the countryside was never scraped flat by glaciers, and the cuts made by the rivers were lined with old, dark forests. Clearing the trees and plowing the steep hillsides was a poor life, and the whole community was so poor that even Cliff's mother's father, the local storekeeper, could not extend much by way of credit to the family.

Cliff roamed about in the woods of the river valleys, and the flatter countryside atop the bluffs; and in later years these places all showed up in his books. A local fan, Dave Wixon, has roamed that countryside, and located such Simak landmarks as Millville, Patch Grove, and the Whistling Well. They still exist.

But to a young man in such straitened circumstances, the notion of making a living writing fiction—no matter how attractive an idea—must have seemed absurd. So Cliff started out to teach and then gravitated into newspapers, where he found his niche and remained.

He was very good at that work, too. At the time I met him, in his late thirties, I found him one of the relatively few writers I've known who shared my fascination with the great essayists of the nineteenth century. We used to talk about them—Dryden and John Stuart Mill and the rest. Cliff had a love for the order and control of the finely tuned essay; and it influenced all his writings—particularly his newspaper work, where it made him stand out among his fellow reporters from the start.

I'm not sure of where Cliff's work took him in his early days—I know Dave, in talking with him, heard mentions of North Dakota, Iowa, southwestern Minnesota, and the upper peninsula of Michigan. But in 1938 he went to work for the Minneapolis *Star,* and remained with that paper (under its various incarnations) until his retirement in 1977, at the age of seventy-two.

Cliff had become a highly regarded, loved, and valued member of the staff long before then, specializing in feature stories, to which he brought his essayist's art and a great deal of the emotion of a fiction writer. He was strongly drawn by both forms of writing, the story and the feature article.

He had originally planned to retire at the age of sixty-five, and write his fiction full-time. But he found out, as so many of us have, that literary royalties are considered "earned income" by the IRS—which meant that his social security was diminished in proportion to those royalties.

He decided therefore to stay on at the paper until he was seventy-two—and when he indicated his willingness to do so, they offered him any job he wanted except that of publisher—

". . . and I wouldn't have taken the publishing position, anyway," he told me.

Instead, during those last seven years he was turned loose to write those feature stories he was so good at—free not only to write, but to write what he chose. During those years, accordingly, he turned out, in addition to his fiction, a remarkable series of articles about many things, including science, its meanings, its effects and its implications for human lives. He was finally, in twentieth-century form, doing what Ruskin and the rest had done a hundred years and more before.

But things had also gone well with his fiction. I remember talking with him one day after we had finished an autographing at Uncle Hugo's, right about the time he *did* retire. I asked him whether, if he had known things would go as well for him in the future as they did, he would still have stayed on at the paper. He said no, he would not have.

"I should be able to double my fiction output now," he said.

But things did not work out so. Kay's increasing disability from arthritis had left him with all the work of the house. Their two children had both taken good jobs far away; and Cliff himself had been stricken by emphysema. It was during this time period when his support of the local fan community paid off by leading him into a strong friendship with Dave Wixon.

I happened to be more aware of that friendship than most, since Dave has for a long time been working closely for and closely with me. I knew when he started doing the occasional small favor for Cliff—it was a sign of his need that Cliff could ask at all, and Dave was the only one he felt comfortable asking.

I knew when Cliff, increasingly debilitated, had to lean on Dave more and more heavily. But the two of them formed a bond that was priceless to them both—Cliff several times saying that he would have died years earlier if not for Dave's help and caring.

Unhappily, life was hard on Cliff in those last years. He was attacked by leukemia. Also, Kay suffered a serious stroke, to the extent that the severely weakened Cliff could no longer care for her at home. She was put into a nursing home, where she died late in 1985.

Cliff had always told me he would have no strong reason for living after Kay was gone. But he lived on, weakened as he was, still deeply interested in life, alert and thoughtful. He did small bits of writing, but generally found himself too weak to finish any of these. He grew very close to his younger brother, Carson, who still lives in Wisconsin; and he still read and studied voraciously.

It was a crime that in this condition he should have been further attacked by shingles; a cruel disease particularly in the very elderly. The pain at times flared up severely, and he had to endure it the rest of his life.

He died in a Minneapolis hospital on a Monday, the 25th of April, 1988—having been taken there after breathing difficulties developed a day or two before. His death was quiet and peaceful, in his sleep.

During his life, Clifford D. Simak was not someone who asked favors easily. I know that, most of the time, if Dave had not taken the initiative, Cliff would have struggled alone and in silence with near-impossible situations. I have noticed this same phenomenon in the case of a number of other writers; and it is sometimes heart-breaking to realize how little many of us realize how deep is the appreciation, and how willingly help would be given, by many of those near who have read us over the years.

It's true this has been a literary field with an unusual closeness among its writers and readers, in an occupation where solitariness is a work-required element. It's undoubtedly also true that our ghetto beginnings probably had a great deal to do with creating this. But the existence of such affection is nonetheless real; even for those of us who privately consider ourselves somewhat curmudgeonly.

The fact remains. There is a great deal of warmth surrounding us in a number of unexpected directions. I like to think Cliff felt this strongly during his final years.

Robert A. Heinlein
Frank M. Robinson

Robert A. Heinlein, the most influential author in modern science fiction, died peacefully in his sleep Sunday morning, May 8, 1988. He was eighty years old. Death resulted from emphysema, congestive heart failure, and the complications of old age. There was no funeral ceremony. The author's remains were cremated and scattered at sea with full military honors.

At the time of his death, forty-four of Heinlein's fifty-four books were in print, a record unmatched by any other writer; his sales totaled over forty million copies. But Heinlein's impact on the world extended far beyond that of an entertaining novelist. He was fascinated by how things worked and delighted in teaching others. As a result, his early fictions were didactic works explaining the intricacies of space travel, genetics, ballistics, and a dozen other sciences to a captivated readership.

Heinlein's ability to entertain and teach made him a formidable propagandist for space travel. In the late 1940s, he carried the popularity of science fiction beyond the pulp magazines with the sale of four short stories—all glamorizing space travel—to the *Saturday Evening Post.* Somewhat later, his juveniles preached space travel to pre-teens and teenagers. One, *Space Cadet* (1948), was the basis of the popular television series *Tom Corbett, Space Cadet* (1951–1956), and another, *Rocket Ship Galileo* (1947), along with his short story "Requiem," served as a springboard for the film *Destination Moon* (1950). In 1969, the year Neil Armstrong stepped out of the NASA lunar module onto the moon, it was hard to find a rocket scientist or an astronaut who had not been a Heinlein fan as a young person.

H. G. Wells tried to change the world by advocating social revolution; he largely failed. Heinlein tried to change it by influencing technological revolution; he largely succeeded.

Robert Anson Heinlein was born July 7, 1907, in Butler, Missouri. He attended the University of Missouri and the U.S. Naval Academy, graduating from the latter in 1929. An expert in ordnance, gunnery, and fire control, he served on board destroyers and the U.S.S. *Lexington,* the first modern aircraft carrier. Tuberculosis forced him to retire from the navy in 1934. Between bouts of illness, he studied physics and mathematics at UCLA, worked at silver mining and real estate, and dabbled in politics. Desperate for money after an election loss for California state assemblyman in 1939, Heinlein wrote a short story for *Thrilling Wonder Stories,* which had an ongoing "contest" open to amateur writers. (The prize was not fifty dollars, as Heinlein and others later stated, but, according to the contest entry blank, standard word rates.) Once he had finished the story, however, Heinlein tried for the big time by sending it to *Collier's.* When *Collier's* rejected it, he sent it on to *Astounding Science Fiction.*

The story was "Lifeline." John W. Campbell, Jr., *Astounding*'s editor, paid Heinlein seventy dollars—for less than a week's work. "Lifeline" appeared in the August 1939 issue. Campbell had found the writer who would spark the Golden Age of *Astounding,* and Heinlein, in his own words, never again looked for "honest work."

Heinlein followed "Lifeline" with "Misfit" (in reality, the

story was his first juvenile), which introduced Andrew Jackson Libby, better known as "Slipstick" Libby, a recurring character in later novels. A third story, "Requiem," saw the first appearance of D. D. Harriman, "the man who sold the moon" and the prototype of Heinlein's "wise-old-man-who-knows-how," best typified by Jubal Harshaw of *Stranger in a Strange Land* (1961).

The two-part serial "If This Goes On—" (*Astounding,* February-March 1940) was to go a long way toward establishing Heinlein's reputation. No other writer in the history of science fiction had made the future appear as immediate and credible as the present. During the next two years, he wrote a series of stories certifying his place as the leading author in the field and *Astounding Science Fiction* as the leading magazine. His early stories included "The Roads Must Roll," "Blowups Happen," "Logic of Empire," "Waldo," "Coventry," "By His Bootstraps," and "Solution Unsatisfactory." He often used the pen name Anson MacDonald, as well as the pseudonyms Lyle Monroe, Caleb Saunders, and John Riverside, to avoid having his own byline appear twice in a single issue.

The most significant story of the period was his novel *Methuselah's Children* (*Astounding,* July-August-September 1941), which introduced the long-lived Howard families and Heinlein's most charismatic character, Lazarus Long. The families and their various members, especially Lazarus, figured prominently in many later novels. Moreover, the themes of *Methuselah's Children* foreshadowed those of his later philosophical novels. The first part of the serial received a 1.00 in The Analytical Laboratory, i.e., every reader voted it first place.

In addition to his stories for *Astounding,* Heinlein also wrote for its companion magazine *Unknown* (later titled *Unknown Worlds*). "They" and "The Devil Makes the Law" (aka "Magic, Inc.") appeared under Heinlein's own name. "The Unpleasant Profession of Jonathan Hoag" was by "John Riverside." Heinlein enjoyed slyly mixing genres, especially after Campbell laid down rigid definitions for both science fiction and fantasy stories. As one critic put it, "Waldo" was "superficially [a] science fiction story with a magical problem and solution," while "Magic, Inc." was "a fantasy story told as a logical science fiction narrative."

Heinlein may have been the first modern author to make a living exclusively from science fiction. He had a regular schedule, turning out four pages of copy a day for four months at a stretch, at the end of which he had a novel. He habitually overwrote, then edited himself ruthlessly, often paring a novel by a third or more.

His assets as a writer were considerable. He had an engineering background, a thorough knowledge of all the major sciences, and a knack both for dramatizing technological change and for creating believable characters. Most of his early stories followed a rough "history of the future," which he had outlined on a wall chart in his study. Campbell eventually published this chart, leading many readers to wonder about titles listed but never written ("Da Capo," "The Stone Pillow," "Fire Down Below," "The Sound of His Wings," etc.). The inspiration for this complex historical frame Heinlein attributed to Sinclair Lewis, who used a somewhat similar system to track the citizens of his fictional city of Zenith.

For most science fiction readers of the early 1940s, the future had Heinlein's fingerprints all over it. It was Heinlein who based his extrapolations on current laboratory research. And it was Heinlein who decided that science fiction stories would be more believable if believable people did all those incredible things. He proved his point. A few critics later carped that some of his plots were thin and some of his endings weak, but his readers always noticed and appreciated what Heinlein did well. In fact, his influence on new SF writers was so strong that many of them patterned their stories and writing style after his. None of them was as successful. In 1941, less than two years after his first published story, Heinlein was Guest of Honor at the World Science Fiction Convention held in Denver, Colorado.

Heinlein's early science fiction career came to a halt with World War II. In 1942, along with Isaac Asimov and L. Sprague de Camp, he went to work for the Naval Air Experimental Station in Philadelphia. A former shipmate of Heinlein's, by then a high-ranking officer in the navy, had sent for Heinlein and put him in charge of a high-altitude laboratory. One of the lab's projects was the development of a high-altitude pressure suit, essentially a space suit. Heinlein worked on it, then was succeeded by de

Camp, who helped develop and test models of the suit throughout the war. Heinlein got the idea for his version of the suit from an Edmond Hamilton story, "The Sargasso of Space" (*Astounding,* September 1931). Later, working on *Destination Moon,* Heinlein sent for a photograph of one of de Camp's suits and used it for the movie.

Heinlein had married Leslyn MacDonald in the mid-1930s. (And so the "MacDonald" in "Anson MacDonald.") They were divorced in the mid-1940s. At the Naval Air Station in Philadelphia, Heinlein met navy lieutenant Virginia Doris Gerstenfeld, a pretty co-worker with a background almost as varied and extensive as his own. They were married in 1948. (Well versed in seven languages, "Ginny" has been a biochemist, an aviation test engineer, and an experimental horticulturist.)

After the war, Heinlein spread his wings. In 1947, he sold stories to the *Saturday Evening Post* (the first genre writer to do so), including the classic "The Green Hills of Earth" (1947). He also sold to *Argosy, Blue Book, Boy's Life,* and the *American Legion Magazine.* More significant was the sale of his first young adult novel, *Rocket Ship Galileo,* to Scribners. Those that followed, at the rate of one a year—*Space Cadet* (1948), *Red Planet* (1949), *Farmer in the Sky* (1950), *Between Planets* (1951), *The Rolling Stones* (1952), *Starman Jones* (1953), *Tunnel in the Sky* (1955), *Time for the Stars* (1956), etc.—established Heinlein as the world's most important writer of young adult SF. Their impact on the space program a generation later has already been noted.

His output in the 1950s and early 1960s was prodigious. *The Puppet Masters* (1951) appeared first in H. L. Gold's *Galaxy;* *Double Star* (1956) and *Citizen of the Galaxy* (1957) were serialized in *Astounding;* "Star Lummox" (1954, retitled *The Star Beast*), *The Door into Summer* (1957), *Have Space Suit—Will Travel* (1959), "Starship Soldier" (1959, retitled *Starship Troopers*), and *Glory Road* (1963) in *Fantasy and Science Fiction; Podkayne of Mars* (1962), *Farnham's Freehold* (1964), and *The Moon Is a Harsh Mistress* (1966) in *Worlds of If.* Over the years, the demarcation line between a Heinlein juvenile and a novel intended for adults had blurred. Magazines did not bill them as juveniles, and few readers knew or cared what audience they were meant for.

Heinlein published twelve young adult novels with Scribners, but the thirteenth broke the contract. His editor rejected the novel, eventually called *Starship Troopers,* as too militaristic for young people. (It later appeared from G. P. Putnam as an adult novel.) The book won the Hugo, but received a caustic reception from the critics, who echoed the Scribners editor's complaints of excessive militarism.

Heinlein's most successful and famous novel had no magazine serialization at all. *Stranger in a Strange Land* (Putnam, 1961) was the first SF novel ever to reach the *New York Times* bestseller list. Later Heinlein novels became regular fixtures on the list. With *Stranger*'s publication in paperback, however, the hour and the author met. In *Stranger,* Valentine Michael Smith, a human being born on Mars, returns to Earth to bring mankind the benefits of "grokking" and "water-sharing." Smith receives a mixed reception from the fictional characters in the book but quickly became a cult figure to young, idealistic dropouts of the middle and late 1960s. "Grokking" became part of the language, and *Stranger in a Strange Land,* with its peculiar blend of free love and mysticism, became a multimillion-copy bestseller and a handbook for hippies.

The critics who proclaimed Heinlein a fascist on the evidence of *Starship Troopers* were hard put to explain Heinlein's authorship of *Stranger.* Few of them knew that although *Stranger* appeared two years after *Troopers,* Heinlein had begun it in 1948 in response to Ginny's suggestion that he write a "Mowgli" story (as in Rudyard Kipling's *Jungle Book*). He wrote a first and a last chapter and made extensive notes. In 1955, he resumed work on the novel for about six weeks, but realized that it would be double the length of the "potboilers [he] had been doing" and so laid it aside to fulfill other commitments. Heinlein finished *Starship Troopers* in April of 1959. He returned to *Stranger* in January of 1960 and "finished it the following month." The draft ran to 800 pages, which he cut to a final 600.

"I know that some people have wondered how the same man could write both books," Heinlein said. "Well, I not only wrote both of them but I worked on them at the same time . . . and some of the notes for *Starship Troopers* were lifted from the *Stranger* file, and then some of the notes I had left over from *Starship Troopers* were later salvaged by using them in *Stranger*. In my mind there was never any conflict between the two books—*both* books were quite savage comments on the present state of our society and *both* books have the same basic theme: that a man, to be truly human, must be unhesitatingly willing at all times to lay down his life for his fellow man. Both are based on the twin concepts of love and duty—and how they are related to the survival of our race."

The success of *Stranger in a Strange Land* in the mid-1960s was a turning point for Heinlein, enabling him to exchange the narrow stage of science fiction for a world platform. But he returned briefly to pure science fiction narration with *The Moon Is a Harsh Mistress* (1966), the story of a lunar revolt. This novel won the Hugo in 1967, and some critics regard it as his best book.

But the didactic novel with its traditional science fiction structure no longer suited Heinlein's purposes. He changed his style and his narrative techniques, and, to a large extent, these changes transformed his audience. He turned from writing science fiction to the writing of conspicuously philosophical fantasies; one critic summarized the major theme of these novels as "You can conquer death through love." Indeed, Heinlein seemed intent on exploring the two themes most important to an adult audience: love and death. *Time Enough for Love* (1973), a novel that brought back the most outrageous and popular character in his earlier fiction, Lazarus Long, is probably his most thorough exploration of these themes.

Heinlein's books now invariably made the bestseller lists. *I Will Fear No Evil* (1970), about an older, wealthy man who transfers his mind into the body of his beautiful young secretary, has sold a million copies in paperback. A gift book, *The Notebooks of Lazarus Long* (1978), gathers quotations from *Time Enough for Love*. *The Number of the Beast* (1980) pays homage, via anagrams and in-jokes, to many of the author's literary forebears and mentions a number of his fellow writers and friends by name. Intended as a novel about command, it struck some critics as a failure.

At the age of seventy-seven, Heinlein returned to the *New*

York Times bestseller list with *Job: A Comedy of Justice* (1984). He followed it with two more bestsellers, *The Cat Who Walked Through Walls* (1985) and *To Sail Beyond the Sunset* (1987), published on his eightieth birthday. The autobiography of Lazarus Long's mother, *To Sail Beyond the Sunset* is a mix of ideas about sex and politics and longevity, as well as a poignant reminiscence of growing up in the Midwest at the turn of the century.

Praised in some quarters, damned in others (he was both booed and enthusiastically applauded when he took the stage at the World Science Fiction Convention in 1976), Heinlein was a writer whose career was unparalleled in science fiction. He won four Hugos—for *Double Star, Starship Troopers, Stranger in a Strange Land,* and *The Moon Is a Harsh Mistress*—and in 1975 he received the Grand Master Nebula Award for lifetime achievement. It was the first such award, and no one doubted that he would receive it.

"It was like George Washington becoming the first President," said Isaac Asimov. "There was no argument."

Heinlein was also the only author to be Guest of Honor at three World Science Fiction Conventions. He took the honor seriously; at each convention, he delivered a significant address about the field and its impact on society.

Explanations for the unevenness of Heinlein's later books are, at least to charitable critics, easy to marshal. A man of frail health for much of his life, Heinlein was not so willful that he could prevent his various illnesses from affecting his work. He underwent major surgery a number of times late in life. He required multiple transfusions, almost dying in several instances, with all of the trauma that such episodes imply. In 1978, he was half paralyzed by a TIA, a transient ischemic attack, a prelude to a stroke, caused by a blockage of the carotid artery on the left side of his brain. Experimental surgery was used in a successful carotid bypass operation. The results were immediate. "It was," he told a friend, "like walking into a darkened room and turning on the light. I could think again."

Many of Heinlein's friends referred to him, as an older man, as "The Admiral." Tuberculosis may have forced him to leave the navy in his mid-twenties, but the navy never left Heinlein. He admired military men, and the Naval Academy had inculcated him with all the most admirable military virtues. Ever afterward, he remained in touch with the services. He was a member of the U.S. Naval Academy Alumni Association, the Naval Institute, and the Retired Officers Association. He had advisory status with the Navy League, the Air Force Association, the Air Power Council, and the Association of the Army of the United States. Throughout his life, he and Ginny made generous contributions to Navy Relief.

In 1973, Heinlein delivered the James Forrestal Lecture at Annapolis. Midshipmen who had read his juveniles as teenagers had specifically requested that he do so. When he spoke of loyalty and love of one's country, he reiterated concepts that they had already encountered in his novels. Small wonder, then, that Heinlein wrote *Starship Troopers;* it was a book he had been born to write.

The background for *Stranger in a Strange Land* is a good deal less prosaic. One of his classmates at Greenwood Grammar School in Kansas City had been Sally Rand, who went on to fame and fortune as a fan dancer at the Chicago World's Fair in 1933. There was probably no causal connection, but Heinlein later claimed that he was the founder of the first nudist camp in the United States west of the Mississippi. He was also an accomplished photographer who delighted in showing visitors his studies of nudes. Sex in science fiction? Heinlein had certainly never been against it. And he was not totally without the background to write about it. But the contradictions did exist. A military man against conscription, a man who had led a regimented life at the Academy and in the navy, but a man who stood four-square for the individual. On his *handling* of sex in fiction, Heinlein received mixed marks—which, again, was no surprise. He had been raised with a Calvinist background, but could count Sally Rand as a friend and take an occasional erotic photograph. His slang when it came to sex and women was of the period, much as E. E. Smith's had been, or almost any other author one could name. (At some future time, even the dialogue of John Cheever and Norman Mailer will ring both dated and quaint.)

Women had an honored role in Heinlein's stories. Although

he did not always treat them with sophistication, he seldom relegated them to camp cooks or brood mares. And it was Heinlein, after all, who promoted the role of women in space over the avuncular Walter Cronkite's surprise and strong objections. But perhaps one can more easily resolve the apparent contradictions in the man than in his fiction.

Heinlein's impact on the field of science fiction is hard to assess only because it was so enormous. His storytelling abilities were immense, his gift for character was striking, his background in the sciences was formidable. He had the patience and the energy to research his work thoroughly and the courage to venture beyond the familiar and the guaranteed-to-be-successful. He had his detractors, but the worst that anyone could say about him was that he was a man of strong beliefs whose literary reach sometimes exceeded his grasp.

Heinlein's world view, which provided the subtext of much of his work, appeared in colloquial synopsis in his early story "The Year of the Jackpot":

> What good is the race of man? Monkeys, he thought, monkeys with a touch of poetry in them, cluttering and wasting a second-string planet near a third-string star. But sometimes they finish in style.

Robert A. Heinlein was generous and learned; he believed in the virtues of freedom and the uniqueness of man. He lived a full life during which he wrote fifty-four books, several of them undisputed classics. He largely created modern science fiction; in doing so, he changed the world as much as any politician or general.

He had no children, but his family of devoted readers numbers in the millions.

Ginny Sweethips' Flying Circus

! ! !

Neal Barrett, Jr.

Neal Barrett, Jr., born in 1929, currently lives in Fort Worth, Texas. In 1960, he entered the SF world with a double entry: "To Tell the Truth" (*Galaxy*, August) and "Made in Archerius" (*Amazing*, August). In the 1960s and 1970s, he contributed regularly to both the science fiction and the men's magazines.

His twelve novels in the SF field include *Kelwin* (1970), *The Gates of Time* (1970), *Highwood* (1972), *Stress Pattern* (1974), and the four books in the Aldair series (1976–82).

His novel *Through Darkest America* (1986) accumulated impressive reviews from such publications as *Locus* and *Twilight Zone. Dawn's Early Light*, a sequel, appeared in July 1989.

In the late 1970s and early 1980s, Barrett began receiving Nebula nominations for such stories as "Hero" and "A Day at the Fair." Then, in the mid-1980s, he began publishing a series of delightfully quirky, astonishingly original stories—"Trading Post," "Sallie C," "Perpetuity Blues," "Diner," "Highbrow," "Class of '61," "Stairs"—that kicked the props out from under both editors and readers alike, and brought Barrett a reputation as one of the most consistently different and exhilarating writers in the field.

About "Ginny Sweethips' Flying Circus," his Nebula finalist in the novelette category (and a Hugo nominee), Barrett gives us this amusing rundown:

"I have written several post-holocaust stories in the last couple of years; all of these reflect the theme that life after the Big Disaster *can* be a lot of fun if we'll just make the effort. I have a particular liking for post-holocaust stories; they allow me a great deal of freedom. Virtually anyone can be on hand. Anything can happen. It's like: The public library explodes. Only a few books are left. *Tom Sawyer. The Joy of Sex. The Lives of the Popes. Basic Accounting.* That's all you've got to build a new world. Wind up this diverse set of characters and circumstances and see what they do. If I'm lucky, it's something like 'Ginny Sweethips' Flying Circus.'

"There is a lot of Mad Max in 'Ginny Sweethips' Flying Circus,' though I honestly didn't realize the obvious until the story was done. Which is fine, because Max is my kind of guy. He knows his world is insane, but he goes about his job in an earnest, professional manner: There's a lot more rubble, and you can't get Cokes anymore, but everything else is basically the same as it was before."

Del drove and Ginny sat.

"They're taking their sweet time," Ginny said, "damned if they're not."

"They're itchy," Del said. "Everyone's itchy. Everyone's looking to stay alive."

"Huh!" Ginny showed disgust. "I sure don't care for sittin' out here in the sun. My price is going up by the minute. You wait and see if it doesn't."

"Don't get greedy," Del said.

Ginny curled her toes on the dash. Her legs felt warm in the sun. The stockade was a hundred yards off. Barbed wire looped above the walls. The sign over the gate read:

First Church of the Unleaded God
& Ace High Refinery
WELCOME
KEEP OUT

The refinery needed paint. It had likely been silver but was now dull as pewter and black rust, Ginny leaned out the window and called to Possum Dark.

"What's happening, friend? Those mothers dead in there or what?"

"Thinking," Possum said. "Fixing to make a move. Considering what to do." Possum Dark sat atop the van in a steno chair bolted to the roof. Circling the chair was a swivel-ring mount sporting fine twin fifties black as grease. Possum had a death-view clean around. Keeping out the sun was a red Cinzano umbrella faded pink. Possum studied the stockade and watched heat distort the flats. He didn't care for the effect. He was suspicious of things less than cut and dried. Apprehensive of illusions of every kind. He scratched his nose and curled his tail around his leg. The gate opened up and men started across the scrub. He teased them in his sights. He prayed they'd do something silly and grand.

Possum counted thirty-seven men. A few carried sidearms, openly or concealed. Possum spotted them all at once. He wasn't too concerned. This seemed like an easygoing bunch, more intent on fun than fracas. Still, there was always the hope that he was wrong.

The men milled about. They wore patched denim and faded shirts. Possum made them nervous. Del countered that; his appearance set them at ease. The men looked at Del, poked each other and grinned. Del was scrawny and bald except for tufts around the ears. The dusty black coat was too big. His neck thrust out of his shirt like a newborn buzzard looking for meat. The men forgot Possum and gathered around, waiting to see what Del would do. Waiting for Del to get around to showing them what they'd come to see. The van was painted turtle-green. Gold Barnum type named the owner, and selected vices for sale:

Ginny Sweethips' Flying Circus
*** SEX · TACOS · DANGEROUS DRUGS ***

Del puttered about with this and that. He unhitched the wagon from the van, folded out a handy little stage. It didn't take three minutes to set up, but he dragged it out to ten, then ten on top of that. The men started to whistle and clap their hands. Del looked alarmed. They liked that. He stumbled and they laughed.

"Hey, mister, you got a girl in there or not?" a man called out.

"Better be something here besides you," another said.

"Gents," Del said, raising his hands for quiet, "Ginny Sweethips herself will soon appear on this stage and you'll be more than glad you waited. Your every wish will be fulfilled, I promise you that. I'm bringing beauty to the wastelands, gents. Lust the way you like it, passion unrestrained. Sexual crimes you never dreamed."

"Cut the talk, mister," a man with peach-pit eyes shouted to Del. "Show us what you got."

Others joined in, stomped their feet and whistled. Del knew he had them. Anger was what he wanted. Frustration and denial. Hatred waiting for sweet release. He waved them off but they wouldn't stop. He placed one hand on the door of the van—and brought them to silence at once.

The double doors opened. A worn red curtain was revealed. Stenciled with hearts and cherubs. Del extended his hand. He seemed to search behind the curtain, one eye closed in concentration. He looked alarmed, groping for something he couldn't find. Uncertain he remembered how to do this trick at all. And then, in a sudden burst of motion, Ginny did a double forward flip and appeared like glory on the stage.

The men broke into shouts of wild abandon. Ginny led them in a cheer. She was dressed for the occasion. Short white skirt shiny bright, white boots with tassles. White sweater with a big red "G" sewn on the front.

"Ginny Sweethips, gents," Del announced with a flair, "giving you her own interpretation of Barbara Jean the Cheerleader Next Door. Innocent as snow, yet a little bit wicked and willing to learn, if Biff the Quarterback will only teach her. Now what do you say to that?"

They whistled and yelled and stomped. Ginny strutted and switched, doing long-legged kicks that left them gasping with delight. Thirty-seven pairs of eyes showed their needs. Men guessed at hidden parts. Dusted off scenarios of violence and love. Then as quickly as she'd come Ginny was gone. Men threatened to storm the stage. Del grinned without concern. The curtain parted again and Ginny was back, blond hair replaced with saucy red, costume changed in the blink of an eye. Del introduced Nurse Nora, an angel of mercy weak as soup in the hands of Patient Pete. Moments later, hair black as a raven's throat, she

was Schoolteacher Sally, cold as well water until Steve the Bad
Student loosed the fury chained within.

Ginny vanished again. Applause thundered over the flats.
Del urged them on, then spread his hands for quiet.

"Did I lie to you gents? Is she all you ever dreamed? Is this
the love you've wanted all your life? Could you ask for sweeter
limbs, for softer flesh? For whiter teeth, for brighter eyes?"

"Yeah, but is she *real?*" a man shouted, a man with a broken
face sewn up like a sock. "We're religious people here. We don't
fuck with no machines."

Others echoed the question with bold shouts and shaking
fists.

"Now I don't blame you, sir, at all," Del said. "I've had a
few dolly droids myself. A plastic embrace at best, I'll grant you
that. Not for the likes of you, for I can tell you're a man who
knows his women. No, sir, Ginny's real as rain, and she's yours
in the role of your choice. Seven minutes of bliss. It'll seem like
a lifetime, gents, I promise you that. Your goods gladly returned
if I'm a liar. And all for only a U.S. gallon of gas."

Howls and groans at that, as Del expected.

"That's a cheat is what it is. Ain't a woman worth it!"

"Gas is better'n gold and we work damn hard to get it!"

Del stood his ground. Looked grim and disappointed. "I'd
be the last man alive to try to part you from your goods," Del
said. "It's not my place to drive a fellow into the arms of sweet
content, to make him rest his manly frame on golden thighs. Not
if he thinks this lovely girl's not worth the fee, no sir. I don't do
business that way and never have."

The men moved closer. Del could smell their discontent. He
read sly thoughts above their heads. There was always this moment when it occurred there was a way Ginny's delights might
be obtained without a price.

"Give it some thought, friends," Del said. "A man's got to
do what he's got to do. And while you're making up your minds,
turn your eyes to the top of the van for a startling and absolutely
free display of the slickest bit of marksmanship you're ever likely
to see."

Before Del's words were out of his mouth and on the way, before the men could scarcely comprehend, Ginny appeared again and tossed a dozen china saucers in the air.

Possum Dark moved in a blur. Turned a hundred and forty degrees in his bolted steno chair and whipped his guns on target, blasting saucers to dust. Thunder rolled across the flats. Crockery rained on the men below. Possum stood and offered a pink killer grin and a little bow. The men saw six-foot-nine-and-a-quarter inches of happy marsupial fury and awesome speed, of black agate eyes and a snout full of icy varmint teeth. Doubts were swept aside. Fifty-caliber madness wasn't the answer. Fun today was clearly not for free.

"Gentlemen, start your engines," Del smiled. "I'll be right here to take your fee. Enjoy a hot taco while you wait your turn at glory. Have a look at our display of fine pharmaceutical wonders and mind-expanding drugs."

In moments, men were making their way back to the stockade. Soon after that, they returned toting battered tins of gas. Del sniffed each gallon, in case some buffoon thought water would get him by. Each man received a token and took his place. Del sold tacos and dangerous drugs, taking what he could get in trade. Candles and Mason jars, a rusty knife. Half a manual on full field maintenance for the Chrysler Mark XX Urban Tank. The drugs were different colors but all the same: Twelve parts oregano, three parts rabbit shit, one part marijuana stems. All this under Possum's watchful eye.

"By God," said the first man out of the van, "she's worth it, I'll tell you that. Have her do the Nurse, you won't regret it!"

"The Schoolteacher's best," said the second man through. I never seen the like. I don't care if she's real or she ain't."

"What's in these tacos?" a customer asked Del.

"Nobody you know, mister," Del said.

"It's been a long day," Ginny said. "I'm pooped, and that's the truth." She wrinkled up her nose. "First thing we hit a town you hose 'er out good now, Del. Place smells like a sewer or maybe worse."

Del squinted at the sky and pulled up under the scant shade of mesquite. He stepped out and kicked the tires. Ginny got down, walked around and stretched.

"It's getting late," Del said. "You want to go on or stop here?"

"You figure those boys might decide to get a rebate on this gas?"

"Hope they do," Possum said from atop the van.

"You're a pisser," Ginny laughed, "I'll say that. Hell, let's keep going. I could use a hot bath and town food. What you figure's up the road?"

"East Bad News," Del said, "if this map's worth anything at all. Ginny, night driving's no good. You don't know what's waiting down the road."

"I know what's on the roof," Ginny said. "Let's do it. I'm itchy all over with bugs and dirt and that tub keeps shinin' in my head. You want me to drive a spell, I sure will."

"Get in," Del grumbled. "Your driving's scarier than anything I'll meet."

Morning arrived in purple shadow and metal tones, copper, silver and gold. From a distance, East Bad News looked to Ginny like garbage strewn carelessly over the flats. Closer, it looked like larger garbage. Tin shacks and tents and haphazard buildings rehashed from whatever they were before. Cookfires burned, and the locals wandered about and yawned and scratched. Three places offered food. Others bed and a bath. Something to look forward to, at least. She spotted the sign down at the far end of town:

MORO'S REPAIRS
Armaments · Machinery · Electronic Shit of All Kinds

"Hold it!" Ginny said. "Pull 'er in right there."

Del looked alarmed. "What for?"

"Don't get excited. There's gear needs tending in back. I just want 'em to take a look."

"Didn't mention it to me," Del said.

Ginny saw the sad and droopy eyes, the tired wisps of hair sticking flat to Del's ears. "Del, there wasn't anything to mention," she said in a kindly tone. "Nothing you can really put your finger on, I mean. Okay?"

"Whatever you think," Del said, clearly out of sorts.

Ginny sighed and got out. Barbed wire surrounded the yard behind. The yard was ankle deep in tangles of rope and copper cable, rusted unidentifiable parts. A battered pickup hugged the wall. Morning heat curled the tin roof of the building. More parts spilled out of the door. Possum made a funny noise, and Ginny saw the Dog step into the light. A Shepherd maybe six-foot-two. It showed Possum Dark yellow eyes. The man appeared behind the Dog, wiping heavy grease on his pants. Bare to the waist, hair like stuffing out of a chair. Features hard as rock, flint eyes to match. Not bad-looking, thought Ginny, if you cleaned him up good.

"Well now," said the man. He glanced at the van, read the legend on the side, took in Ginny from head to toe. "What can I do for you, little lady?"

"I'm not real little and don't guess I'm any lady," Ginny said. "Whatever you're thinking, don't. You open for business or just talk?"

The man grinned. "My name's Moro Gain. Never turn business away if I can help it."

"I need electric stuff."

"We got it. What's the problem?"

"Huh-unh." Ginny shook her head. "First I gotta ask. You do confidential work or tell everything you know?"

"Secret's my middle name," Moro said. "Might cost a little more, but you got it."

"How much?"

Moro closed one eye. "Now how do I know that? You got a nuclear device in there or a broken watch? Drive it on in and we'll take a look." He aimed a greasy finger at Possum Dark. "Leave *him* outside."

"No way."

"No arms in the shop. That's a rule."

"He isn't carrying. Just the guns you see." Ginny smiled.

"You can shake him down if you like. *I* wouldn't, I don't think."

"He looks imposing, all right."

"I'd say he is."

"What the hell," Moro said. "Drive it in."

Dog unlocked the gate. Possum climbed down and followed Dog with oily eyes.

"Go find us a place to stay," Ginny said to Del. "Clean, if you can find it. All the hot water in town. Christ sakes, Del, you still sulking or what?"

"Don't worry about me," Del said. "Don't concern yourself at all."

"Right." She hopped behind the wheel. Moro began kicking the door of his shop. It finally sprang free, wide enough to take the van. The supply wagon rocked along behind. Moro lifted the tarp, eyed the thirty-seven tins of unleaded with great interest.

"You get lousy mileage or what?" he asked Ginny.

Ginny didn't answer. She stepped out of the van. Light came through broken panes of glass. The skinny windows reminded her of a church. Her eyes got used to shadow and she saw that's what it was. Pews sat to the side, piled high with parts. A 1997 Olds was jacked up before the altar.

"Nice place you got here," she said.

"It works for me," Moro told her. "Now. What kind of trouble you got? Something in the wiring? You said electric stuff."

"I didn't mean the motor. Back here." She led him to the rear and opened the doors.

"God A'Mighty," Moro said.

"Smells a little raunchy right now. Can't help that till we hose 'er down." Ginny stepped inside, looked back, and saw Moro still on the ground. "You coming up or not?"

"Just thinking."

"About what?" She'd seen him watching her move and didn't really have to ask.

"Well, you know . . . " Moro shuffled his feet. "How do you figure on paying? For whatever it is I got to do."

"Gas. You take a look. Tell me how many tins. I say yes or no."

"We could work something out."

"We could, huh?"

"Sure." Moro gave her a foolish grin. "Why not?"

Ginny didn't blink. "Mister, what kind of a girl do you think I am?"

Moro looked puzzled and intent. "I can read good, lady, believe it or not. I figured you wasn't tacos or dangerous drugs."

"You figured wrong," Ginny said. "Sex is just software to me and don't you forget it. I haven't got all day to watch you moonin' over my parts. I got to move or stand still. When I stand still, you look. When I move, you look more. Can't fault you for that, I'm about the prettiest thing you ever saw. Don't let it get in the way of your work."

Moro couldn't think of much to say. He took a breath and stepped in the van. There was a bed bolted flat against the floor. A red cotton spread, a worn satin pillow that said DURANGO, COLORADO and pictured chipmunks and falls. An end table, a pink-shaded lamp with flamingos on the side. Red curtains on the walls. Ballet prints and a naked Minnie Mouse.

"Somethin' else," Moro said.

"Back here's the problem," Ginny said. She pulled a curtain aside at the front of the van. There was a plywood cabinet, fitted with brass screws. Ginny took a key out of her jeans and opened it up.

Moro stared a minute, then laughed aloud. "*Sensory* tapes? Well I'll be a son of a bitch." He took a new look at Ginny, a look Ginny didn't miss. "Haven't seen a rig like this in years. Didn't know there were any still around."

"I've got three tapes," Ginny explained. "A brunette, a redhead and a blond. Found a whole cache in Ardmore, Oklahoma. Had to look at 'bout three or four hundred to find girls that looked close enough to me. Nearly went nuts 'fore it was over. Anyway, I did it. Spliced 'em down to seven minutes each."

Moro glanced back at the bed. "How do you put 'em under?"

"Little needle comes up out of the mattress. Sticks them in the ass lightnin' fast. They're out like that. Seven-minute dose. Headpiece is in the end table there. I get it on and off them real quick. Wires go under the floorboards back here to the rig."

"Jesus," Moro said. "They ever catch you at this, you are cooked, lady."

"That's what Possum's for," Ginny said. "Possum's pretty good at what he does. Now what's *that* look all about?"

"I wasn't sure right off if you were real."

Ginny laughed aloud. "So what do you think now?"

"I think maybe you are."

"Right," Ginny said. "It's Del who's the droid, not me. Wimp IX Series. Didn't make a whole lot. Not much demand. The customers think it's me, never think to look at him. He's a damn good barker and pretty good at tacos and drugs. A little too sensitive, you ask me. Well, nobody's perfect, so they say."

"The trouble you're having's in the rig?"

"I guess," Ginny said. "Beats the hell out of me." She bit her lip and wrinkled her brow. Moro found the gestures most inviting. "Slips a little, I think. Maybe I got a short, huh?"

"Maybe." Moro fiddled with the rig, testing one of the spools with his thumb. "I'll have to get in here and see."

"It's all yours. I'll be wherever it is Del's got me staying."

"Ruby John's," Moro said. "Only place there is with a good roof. I'd like to take you out to dinner."

"Well sure you would."

"You got a real shitty attitude, friend."

"I get a whole lot of practice," Ginny said.

"And I've got a certain amount of pride," Moro told her. "I don't intend to ask you more than three or four times and that's it."

Ginny nodded. Right on the edge of approval. "You've got promise," she said. "Not a whole lot, maybe, but some."

"Does that mean dinner, or not?"

"Means not. Means if I *wanted* to have dinner with some guy, you'd maybe fit the bill."

Moro felt his eyes get hot. "Hell with you, lady. I don't need the company that bad."

"Fine." Ginny sniffed the air and walked out. "You have a nice day."

Moro watched her walk. Watched denims mold her legs, studied the hydraulics of her lips. Considered several unlikely acts. Considered cleaning up, searching for proper clothes. Considered finding a bottle and watching the tapes. A plastic embrace at best, or so he'd heard, but a lot less hassle in the end.

Possum Dark watched the van disappear into the shop. He felt uneasy at once. His place was on top. Keeping Ginny from harm. Sending feral prayers for murder to absent genetic gods. His eyes hadn't left Dog since he'd appeared. Primal smells, old fears and needs assailed his senses. Dog locked the gate and turned around. Didn't come closer just turned.

"I'm Dog Quick," he said, folding hairy arms. "I don't much care for Possums."

"I don't much care for Dogs," said Possum Dark.

Dog seemed to understand. "What did you do before the War?"

"Worked in a theme park. Our Wildlife Heritage. That kind of shit. What about you?"

"Security, what else?" Dog made a face. "Learned a little electrics. Picked up a lot more from Moro Gain. I've done worse." He nodded toward the shop. "You like to shoot people with that thing?"

"Anytime I get the chance."

"You ever play any cards?"

"Some." Possum Dark showed his teeth. "I guess I could handle myself with a Dog."

"For real goods?" Dog returned the grin.

"New deck, unbroken seal, table stakes," Possum said.

Moro showed up at Ruby John's Cot Emporium close to noon. Ginny had a semi-private stall, covered by a blanket. She'd bathed and braided her hair and cut the legs clean off her jeans. She tugged at Moro's heart.

"It'll be tomorrow morning," Moro said. "Cost you ten gallons of gas."

"Ten gallons," Ginny said. "That's stealin' and you know it."

"Take it or leave it," Moro said. "You got a bad head in that rig. Going to come right off, you don't fix it. You wouldn't like that. Your customers wouldn't like it any at all."

Ginny appeared subdued but not much. "Four gallons. Tops."

"Eight. I got to make the parts myself."

"Five."

"Six," Moro said. "Six and I take you to dinner."

"Five and a half and I want to be out of this sweatbox at dawn. On the road and gone when the sun starts bakin' your lovely town."

"Damn, you're fun to have around."

Ginny smiled. Sweet and disarming, an unexpected event. "I'm all right. You got to get to know me."

"Just how do I go about that?"

"You don't." The smile turned sober. "I haven't figured that one out."

It looked like rain to the north. Sunrise was dreary. Muddy, less than spectacular yellows and reds. Colors through a window no one had bothered to wash. Moro had the van brought out. He said he'd thrown in a lube and hosed out the back. Five and a half gallons were gone out of the wagon. Ginny had Del count while Moro watched.

"I'm honest," Moro said. "You don't have to do that."

"I know," Ginny said, glancing curiously at Dog, who was looking rather strange. He seemed out of sorts. Sulky and off his feed. Ginny followed his eyes and saw Possum atop the van. Possum showed a wet Possum grin.

"Where you headed now?" Moro asked, wanting to hold her as long as he could.

"South," Ginny said, since she was facing that direction.

"I wouldn't," Moro said. "Not real friendly folks down there."

"I'm not picky. Business is business."

"No, sir." Moro shook his head. "*Bad* business is what it is. You got the Dry Heaves south and east. Doom City after that. Straight down and you'll hit the Hackers. Might run into

Fort Pru. Bunch of disgruntled insurance agents out on the flats. Stay clear away from them. Isn't worth whatever you'll make."

"You've been a big help," Ginny said.

Moro gripped her door. "You ever *listen* to anyone, lady? I'm giving good advice."

"Fine," Ginny said. "I'm 'bout as grateful as I can be."

Moro watched her leave. He was consumed by her appearance. The day seemed to focus in her eyes. Nothing he said pleased her in the least. Still, her disdain was friendly enough. There was no malice at all, that he could see.

There was something about the sound of Doom City she didn't like. Ginny told Del to head south and maybe west. Around noon a yellow haze appeared on the ragged rim of the world, like someone rolling a cheap dirty rug across the flats.

"Sandstorm," Possum called from the roof. "Right out of the west. I don't like it at all. I think we better turn. Looks like trouble coming fast."

There was nothing Possum said she couldn't see. He had a habit of saying little or more than enough. She told him to cover his guns and get inside, that the sand would take his hide and there was nothing he needed to kill that wouldn't wait. Possum Dark sulked but climbed down. Hunched in back of the van, he grasped air in the shape of grips and trigger guards. Practiced rage and windage in his head.

"I'll bet I can beat that storm," Del said. "I got this feeling I can do it."

"Beat it where?" Ginny said. "We don't know where we are or what's ahead."

"That's true," Del said. "All the more reason then to get there soon as we can."

Ginny stepped out and viewed the world with disregard. "I got sand in my teeth and in my toes," she complained. "I'll bet that Moro Gain knows right where storms'll likely be. I'll bet that's what happened, all right."

"Seemed like a decent sort to me," Del said.

"That's what I mean," Ginny said. "You can't trust a man like that at all."

The storm had seemed to last a couple of days. Ginny figured maybe an hour. The sky looked bad as cabbage soup. The land looked just the way it had. She couldn't see the difference between sand recently gone or newly arrived. Del got the van going again. Ginny thought about yesterday's bath. East Bad News had its points.

Before they topped the first rise, Possum Dark began to stomp on the roof. "Vehicles to port," he called out. "Sedans and pickup trucks. Flatbeds and semis. Buses of all kinds."

"What are they doing?" Del said.

"Coming right at us, hauling timber."

"Doing what?" Ginny made a face. "Damn it all, Del, will you stop the car? I swear you're a driving fool."

Del stopped. Ginny climbed up with Possum to watch. The caravan kept a straight line. Cars and trucks weren't exactly hauling timber . . . but they were. Each carried the section of a wall. Split logs bound together, sharpened at the top. The lead car turned and the others followed. The lead car turned again. In a moment, there was a wooden stockade, square as if you'd drawn it with a rule. A stockade and a gate. Over the gate a wooden sign:

FORT PRU
Games of Chance & Amusement
Term · Whole Life · Half Life · Death

"I don't like it," said Possum Dark.

"You don't like anything's still alive," Ginny said.

"They've got small arms and they're a nervous-looking bunch."

"They're just horny, Possum. That's the same as nervous or close enough." Possum pretended to understand. "Looks like they're pulled up for the night," she called to Del. "Let's do some business, friend. The overhead don't ever stop."

———

Five of them came out to the van. They all looked alike. Stringy, darkened by the sun. Bare to the waist except for collars and striped ties. Each carried an attaché case thin as two slices of bread without butter. Two had pistols stuck in their belts. The leader carried a fine-looking sawed-off Remington Twelve. It hung by a camou guitar strap to his waist. Del didn't like him at all. He had perfect white teeth and a bald head. Eyes the color of jellyfish melting on the beach. He studied the sign on the van and looked at Del.

"You got a whore inside or not?"

Del looked him straight on. "I'm a little displeased at that. It's not the way to talk."

"Hey." The man gave Del a wink. "You don't have to give us the pitch. We're show business folk ourselves."

"Is that right?"

"Wheels of chance and honest cards. Odds I *know* you'll like. I'm head actuary of this bunch. Name's Fred. That animal up there has a piss-poor attitude, friend. No reason to poke that weapon down my throat. We're friendly people here."

"No reason I can see Possum'd spray this place with lead and diuretics," Del said. "Less you can think of something I can't."

Fred smiled at that. The sun made a big gold ball on his head. "I guess we'll try your girl," he told Del. "'Course we got to see her first. What do you take in trade?"

"Goods as fine as what you're getting in return."

"I've got just the thing." The head actuary winked again. The gesture was starting to irritate Del. Fred nodded, and a friend drew clean white paper from his case. "This here is heavy bond," he told Del, shuffling the edges with his thumb. "Fifty percent linen weave, and you got it by the ream. Won't find anything like it. You can mark on it good or trade it off. 7th Mercenary Writers came through a week ago. Whole brigade of mounted horse. Near cleaned us out, but we can spare a few reams. We got pencils too. Mirado 2s and 3s, unsharpened with erasers on the end. When's the last time you saw that? Why, this stuff's good as gold. We got staples and legal pads. Claim forms, maim forms, forms of every sort. Deals on wheels is what we got. And *you* got gas under wraps in that wagon behind your van. I can smell it plain from here. Friend, we can sure talk some business with you there. I got seventeen rusty-ass guzzlers runnin' dry."

A gnat-whisker wire sparked hot in Del's head. He could see it in the underwriter's eyes. Gasoline greed was what it was, and he knew these men were bent on more than fleshly pleasure. He knew with androidial dread that when they could, they'd make their play.

"Well now, the gas is not for trade," he said as calmly as he could. "Sex and tacos and dangerous drugs is what we sell."

"No problem," the actuary said. "Why, no problem at all. Just an idea is all it was. You get that little gal out here and I'll bring in my crew. How's half a ream a man sound to you?"

"Just as fair as it can be," Del said, thinking half of that was fine, knowing dead certain now Fred intended to take back whatever he gave.

"That Moro fellow was right," Del said. "These insurance boys are bad news. Best thing we can do is take off and let it go."

"Pooh," said Ginny, "that's just the way men are. They come in mad as foamin' dogs and go away like cats licking cream. That's the nature of the fornicatin' trade. You wait and see. Besides, they won't get funny with Possum Dark."

"You wouldn't pray for rain if you were afire," Del muttered. "Well, I'm not unhitching that gas. I'll set you up a stage over the tarp. You can do your number there."

"Suit yourself," Ginny said, kissing a plastic cheek and scooting him out the door. "Now get on out of here and let me start getting cute."

It seemed to be going well. Cheerleader Barbara Jean awoke forgotten wet dreams, left their mouths as dry as snakes. Set them up for Sally the Teach and Nora Nurse, secret violations of the soul. Maybe Ginny was right, Del decided. Faced with girlie delights, a man's normally shitty outlook disappeared. When he was done, he didn't want to wreck a thing for an hour or maybe two. Didn't care about killing for half a day. Del could only guess at this magic and how it worked. Data was one thing, sweet encounters something else.

He caught Possum's eye and felt secure. Forty-eight men waited their turns. Possum knew the caliber of their arms, the length of every blade. His black twin-fifties blessed them all.

Fred the actuary sidled up and grinned at Del. "We sure ought to talk about gas. That's what we ought to do."

"Look," Del said. "Gas isn't for trade, I told you that. Go talk to those boys at the refinery, same as us."

"Tried to. They got no use for office supplies."

"That's not my problem," Del said.

"Maybe it is."

Del didn't miss the razor tones. "You got something to say, just say it."

"Half of your gas. We pay our way with the girl and don't give you any trouble."

"You forget about him?"

Fred studied Possum Dark. "I can afford losses better than you. Listen, I know what you are, friend. I know you're not a man. Had a CPA droid just like you 'fore the War."

"Maybe we can talk," Del said, trying to figure what to do.

"Say now, that's what I like to hear."

Ginny's first customer staggered out, wild-eyed and white around the gills. "Godamn, try the Nurse," he bawled to the others. "Never had nothin' like it in my life!"

"Next," Del said, and started stacking bond paper. "Lust is the name of the game, gents, what did I tell you, now?"

"The girl plastic too?" Fred asked.

"Real as you," Del said. "We make some kind of deal, how do I know you'll keep your word?"

"Jesus," Fred said, "what do you think I am? You got my life underwriter's oath!"

The second customer exploded through the curtain, tripped and fell on his face. Picked himself up and shook his head. He looked damaged, bleeding around the eyes.

"She's a tiger," Del announced, wondering what the hell was going on. " 'Scuse me a minute," he told Fred, and slipped inside the van. "Just what are you doing in here," he asked Ginny. "Those boys look like they been through a thrasher."

"Beats me," Ginny said, halfway between Nora and Barbara Jean. "Last old boy jerked around like a snake having a fit. Started pulling out his hair. Something' isn't right here, Del. It's gotta be the tapes. I figure that Moro fellow's a cheat."

"We got trouble inside and out," Del told her. "The head of this bunch wants our gas."

"Well, he sure can't have it, by God."

"Ginny, the man's got bug-spit eyes. Says he'll take his chances with Possum. We better clear out while we can."

"Huh-unh." Ginny shook her head. "That'll rile 'em for sure. Give me a minute or two. We've done one Nora and a Sally. I'll switch them all to Barbara Jean and see."

Del slipped back outside. It seemed a dubious answer at best.

"That's some woman," said Fred.

"She's something else today. Your insurance boys have got her fired."

Fred grinned at that. "Guess I better give her a try."

"I wouldn't," Del said.

"Why not?"

"Let her calm down some. Might be more than you want to handle."

He knew at once this wasn't the thing to say. Fred turned the color of ketchup pie. "Why, you plastic piece of shit. I can handle any woman born . . . *or* put together out of a kit."

"Suit yourself," Del said, feeling the day going down the drain. "No charge at all."

"Damn right there's not." Fred jerked the next man out of line. "Get ready in there, little lady. I am going to handle *all* your policy needs!"

The men cheered. Possum Dark, who understood at least three-fifths of the trouble down below, shot Del a questioning look.

"Got any of those tacos?" someone asked.

"Not likely," Del said.

Del considered turning himself off. Android suicide seemed the answer. In less than three minutes, unnatural howls

came from the van. Howls turned to shrieks. Life underwriters
went rigid. Fred emerged shattered. He seemed a man who'd
kicked a bear with boils. Joints appeared to bend the wrong
way. He looked whomper-eyed at Del, dazed and out of
synch. Everything happened in seconds thin as wire. Del saw
Fred find him, saw the oil-spill eyes catch him clean. Saw the
sawed-off barrels match the eyes so fast electric feet couldn't
snatch him out of the way in time. Del's arm exploded. He let
it go and ran for the van. Possum couldn't help. The actuary
was below and too close. The twin-fifties opened up. Underwriters fled. Possum stitched the sand and sent them flying ragged and dead.

Del reached the driver's seat as lead peppered the van. He
felt slightly silly. Sitting there with one arm, one hand on the
wheel.

"Move over," Ginny said. "That isn't going to work."

"I guess not."

Ginny sent them lurching through the scrub. "Never saw
anything like it in my life," she said aloud. "Turned that poor
fella on, he started twisting out of his socks, bones snapping like
sticks. Damndest orgasm I ever saw."

"Something's not working just right."

"Well, I can see that, Del. Jesus, what's that!"

Ginny twisted the wheel as a large part of the desert rose
straight up in the air. Smoking sand rained down on the van.

"Rockets," Del said grimly. "That's the reason they figured
that crazy-fingered Possum was a snap. Watch where you're
going, girl!"

Two fiery pillars exploded ahead. Del leaned out the window
and looked back. Half of Fort Pru's wall was in pursuit. Possum
sprayed everything in sight. He couldn't spot where the rockets
were coming from. Underwriter assault cars split up, came at
them from every side.

"Trying to flank us," Del said. A rocket burst to the right.

"Ginny, I'm not real sure what to do."

"How's the stub?"

"Slight electric tingle. Like a doorbell half a mile away.
Ginny, they get us in a circle, we're in very deep shit."

"They hit that gas, we won't have to worry about a thing. Oh Lord, now why did I think of that?"

Possum hit a semi clean on. It came to a stop and died, fell over like a bug. Del could see being a truck and a wall at once had its problems, balance being one.

"Head right at them," he told Ginny, "then veer off sharp. They can't turn quick going fast."

"Del!"

Bullets rattled the van. Something heavy made a noise. The van skewed to a halt.

Ginny took her hands off the wheel and looked grim. "It appears they got the tires. Del, we're flat dead is what we are. Let's get out of this thing."

And do *what?* Del wondered. Bearings seemed to roll about in his head. He sensed a malfunction on the way.

The Fort Pru vehicles shrieked to a stop. Crazed life agents piled out and came at them over the flats, firing small arms and hurling stones. A rocket burst nearby.

Possum's guns suddenly stopped. Ginny grimaced in disgust. "Don't you tell me we're out of ammo, Possum Dark. That stuff's plenty hard to get."

Possum started to speak. Del waved his good arm to the north. "Hey now, would you look at that!"

Ginny saw a sudden confusion in the underwriters' ranks. A vaguely familiar pickup had appeared on the rise. The driver weaved through traffic, hurling grenades. They exploded in clusters, bright pink bouquets. He spotted the man with the rocket, lying flat atop a bus. Grenades stopped him cold. Underwriters abandoned the field and ran. Ginny saw a fairly peculiar sight. Six black Harleys had joined the truck. Chow Dogs with Uzis snaked in and out of the ranks, motors snarling and spewing horsetails of sand high in the air. They showed no mercy at all, picking off stragglers as they ran. A few underwriters made it to cover. In a moment, it was over. Fort Pru fled in sectional disarray.

"Well, if that wasn't just in the nick of time," Del said.

"I hate Chow Dogs," Possum said. "They got black tongues, and that's a fact."

"I hope you folks are all right," Moro said. "Well now, friend, looks as if you've thrown an arm."

"Nothing real serious," Del said.

"I'm grateful," Ginny said. "Guess I got to tell you that."

Moro was taken by her penetrating charm, her thankless manner. The fetching smudge of grease on her knee. He thought she was cute as a pup.

"I felt it was something I had to do. Circumstances being what they are."

"And just what circumstances are that?" Ginny asked.

"That pesky Shepherd Dog's sorta responsible for any trouble you might've had. Got a little pissed when that Possum cleaned him out. Five-card stud I think it was. 'Course there might have been marking and crimping of cards, I couldn't say."

Ginny blew hair out of her eyes. "Mister, far as I can see you're not making a lot of sense."

"I'm real embarrassed about this. That Dog got mad and kinda screwed up your gear."

"You let a *Dog* repair my stuff?" Ginny said.

"Perfectly good technician. Taught him mostly myself. Okay if you don't get his dander up. Those Shepherds are inbred, so I hear. What he did was set your tapes in a loop and speed 'em up. Customer'd get, say, twenty-six times his money's worth. Works out to a Mach 7 fuck. Could cause bodily harm."

"Lord, I ought to shoot you in the foot," Ginny said.

"Look," Moro said, "I stand behind my work and I got here quick as I could. Brought friends along to help, and I'm eating the cost of that."

"Damn right," Ginny said. The Chow Dogs sat their Harleys a ways off and glared at Possum. Possum Dark glared back. He secretly admired their leather gear, Purina crests sewn on the backs.

"I'll be adding up costs," Ginny said. "I'm expecting full repairs."

"You'll get it. Of course you'll have to spend some time in Bad News. Might take a little while."

She caught his look and had to laugh. "You're a stubborn son of a bitch, I'll give you that. What'd you do with that Dog?"

"You want taco meat, I'll make you a deal."

"Yuck. I guess I'll pass."

Del began to weave about in roughly trapezoidal squares. Smoke began to curl out of his stub.

"For Christ's sake, Possum, sit on him or something," Ginny said.

"I can fix that," Moro told her.

"You've about fixed enough, seems to me."

"We're going to get along fine. You wait and see."

"You think so?" Ginny looked alarmed. "I better not get used to you around."

"It could happen."

"It could just as easy *not.*"

"I'll see about changing that tire," Moro said. "We ought to get Del out of the sun. You think about finding something nice to wear to dinner. East Bad News is kinda picky."

The Other Dead Man

' ' '

Gene Wolfe

What to say about Gene Wolfe, a true literary phenomenon? His novel *The Urth of the New Sun,* a kind of metaphysical coda to his celebrated four-volume series, *The Book of the New Sun,* was a Nebula finalist this year, and he has won almost every major award—barring the elusive Hugo, a fact that sometimes makes me scratch my head in bemused wonder—that the field has to offer: two Nebulas, the World Fantasy Award, the John W. Campbell Memorial Award, the Chicago Foundation for Literature Award, the British SF Award, the British Fantasy Award, and, from the discerning French, the Prix Apollo.

Outside the New Sun series, his works include *The Fifth Head of Cerberus, The Devil in a Forest, Free Live Free, There Are Doors, Soldier of the Mist, Soldier of Arete, Castleview, Pandora,* and a volume of poetry, *For Rosemary.* His newest collections of short fiction are *Storeys from the Old Hotel* and *Endangered Species.* Wolfe's respect for the reader is profound. Critics who focus on the author's peculiarities in discussing a work, he tells us, are "saying that the letter is more important than its recipient, the signal more important than the changing image created from it, the bait more important than the fish." Wolfe's generosity—in using his stunning talent deliberately and continually *on behalf of the reader*—is an identifying characteristic of this very good man, in whom talent and integrity have inextricably fused.

Of "The Other Dead Man," Wolfe writes: "*Weird Tales*—'the magazine that will not die'—has risen from the grave more than once since the demise of the old pulps. When George H. Scithers, *et al.,* undertook the most recent (and most promising) reanimation, leasing the right to the title from Robert Weinberg, he offered to reprint my first published story, 'The Dead Man,' with some short pieces from my small-press book *Bibliomen.* I, in turn, promised to write a new story for the issue, a story that George referred to as 'the other dead man.'

"Could you have resisted a challenge like that? 'The Other

Dead Man' it was, and all I had to do was work out who the first had been. Everything fell into place nicely once I knew."

Reis surveyed the hull without hope and without despair, having worn out both. They had been hit hard. Some portside plates of Section Three lay peeled back like the black skin of a graphite-fiber banana; Three, Four, and Five were holed in a dozen places. Reis marked the first on the comp slate so that Centcomp would know, rotated the ship's image and ran the rat around the port side of Section Three to show that.

"*Report all damage,*" Centcomp instructed him.

He wrote quickly with the rattail: "*Rog.*"

"*Report all damage,*" flashed again and vanished. Reis shrugged philosophically, rotated the image back, and charted another hole.

The third hole was larger than either of the first two. He jetted around to look at it more closely.

Back in the airlock, he took off his helmet and skinned out of his suit. By the time Jan opened the inner hatch, he had the suit folded around his arm.

"Bad, huh?" Jan said.

Reis shook his head. "Not so bad. How's Hap?"

Jan turned away.

"How's Dawson doing with the med pod?"

"I don't know," Jan said. "He hasn't told us anything."

He followed her along the spiracle. Paula was bent over Hap, and Dawson was bent over Paula, a hand on her shoulder. Both looked up when he and Jan came in. Dawson asked, "Anybody left downship?"

Reis shook his head.

"I didn't think so, but you never know."

"They'd have had to be in suits," Reis said. "Nobody was."

"It wouldn't be a bad idea for us stay suited up."

Reis said nothing, studying Hap. Hap's face was a pale, greenish-yellow, beaded with sweat; it reminded Reis of an unripe banana, just washed under the tap. So this is banana day, he thought.

"Not all of the time," Dawson said. "But most of the time."

"Sure," Reis told him. "Go ahead."

"All of us."

Hap's breathing was so shallow that he seemed not to breathe at all.

"You won't order it?"

"No," Reis told Dawson, "I won't order it." After a moment he added, "And I won't do it myself, unless I feel like it. You can do what you want."

Paula wiped Hap's face with a damp washcloth. It occurred to Reis that the droplets he had taken for perspiration might be no more than water from the cloth, that Hap might not really be breathing. Awkwardly, he felt for Hap's pulse.

Paula said, "You're the senior officer now, Reis."

He shook his head. "As long as Hap's alive, he's senior officer. How'd you do with the med pod, Mr. Dawson?"

"You want a detailed report? Oxygen's—"

"No, if I wanted details, I could get them from Centcomp. Overall."

Dawson rolled his eyes. "Most of the physical stuff he'll need is there; I had to fix a couple of things, and they're fixed. The med subroutines look okay, but I don't know. Centcomp lost a lot of core."

Paula asked, "Can't you run tests, Sid?"

"I've run them. As I said, they look all right. But it's simple stuff." Dawson turned back to Reis. "Do we put him in the pod? You *are* the senior officer fit for duty."

"And don't you forget it," Reis said. "Yes, we put him in, Mr. Dawson; it's his only chance."

Jan was looking at him with something indefinable in her eyes. "If we're going to die anyway—"

"We're not, Mr. van Joure. We should be able to patch up at least two engines, maybe three, borrowing parts from the rest. The hit took a lot of momentum off us, and in a week or so we should be able to shake most of what's left. As soon as Ecomp sees that we're still alive and kicking, it'll authorize rescue." Reis hoped he had made that part sound a great deal more certain than he felt. "So our best chance is to head back in toward the sun and meet it part way—that should be obvious. Now let's get Hap into that pod before he dies. Snap to it, everybody!"

Dawson found an opportunity to take Reis aside. "You were right—if we're going to get her going again, we can't spare anybody for nursing, no matter what happens. Want me to work on the long-wave?"

Reis shook his head. Engines first, long-wave afterward, if at all. There would be plenty of time to send messages when the ship lived again. And until it did, he doubted whether any message would do much good.

Lying in his sleep pod, Reis listened to the slow wheeze of air through the vent. The ship breathed again, they'd done that much. Could it have been . . . admiration, that look of Jan's? He pushed the thought aside, telling himself he had been imagining things. But still?

His mind teetered on the lip of sleep, unable to tumble over.

The ship breathed; it was only one feeble engine running at half force with a doubtful tube, and yet it was something, they could use power tools again—the welder—and the ship breathed.

His foot slipped on an oil spill, and he woke with a start. That had happened years back while they were refitting at Ocean West. He had fallen and cracked his head. He had believed it forgotten. . . .

The ship breathed. She's our mother, Reis thought. She's our mother; we live inside her, in her womb; and if she dies, we die. But she died, and we're bringing her to life again.

Someone knocked on the pod lid. Reis pushed the Retract lever and sat up.

Paula said, "Sir, I'm sorry, but—"

"What is it? Is Jan—?"

"She's fine, sir. I relieved her an hour ago. It's my watch."

"Oh," Reis said. "I didn't realize I'd been asleep." He sounded stupid even to himself.

"My orders were to call you, sir, if—"

He nodded. "What's happened?"

"Hap's dead." Paula's voice was flat, its only emotion this very lack of emotion betrayed.

Reis looked at her eyes. There were no tears there, and he decided it was probably a bad sign. "I'm truly sorry," he said. And then, "Perhaps Centcomp—"

Wordlessly, Paula pointed to the screen. The glowing green letters read: *"Resuscitation under way."*

Reis went over to look at it. "How long has this been up?"

"Five minutes, Captain. Perhaps ten. I hoped—"

"That you wouldn't have to wake me."

Paula nodded gratefully. "Yes, sir."

He wrote: *"Resp?"*

"Respiration 0.00. Resuscitation under way."

The ship breathed, but Hap did not. That, of course, was why Paula had called him "Captain" a moment ago. She must have tried pulse, tried everything, before knocking on his pod. He wrote: *"Cortex?"*

"Alpha 0.00. Beta 0.00. Gamma 0.00," Centcomp replied. *"Resuscitation under way."*

Reis wrote: *"Discon."*

There was a noticeable pause before the alpha-, beta-, and gamma-wave reports vanished. *"Resuscitation under way"* remained stubbornly on screen.

Paula said, "Centcomp won't give up. Centcomp has faith. Funny, isn't it?"

Reis shook his head. "It means we can't rely on Centcomp the way we've been used to. Paula, I'm not very good at telling people how I feel. Hap was my best friend."

"You were his, Captain."

Desperately Reis continued, "Then we're both sorry, and we both know that."

"Sir, may I tell you something?"

He nodded. "Something private? Of course."

"We were married. You know how they still do it in some churches? We went to one. He told them we didn't belong, but we wanted to have the ceremony and we'd pay for it. I thought sure they'd say no, but they did it, and he cried—Hap cried."

Reis nodded again. "You meant a lot to him."

"That's all, sir. I just wanted somebody else to know. Thanks for listening."

Reis went to his locker and got out his suit. It shone a dull silver under the cabin lights, and he recalled a time when he had envied people who had suits like that.

"Aren't you going back to sleep, sir?"

"No. I'll be relieving you in less than an hour, so I'm going hullside to have another look around. When I come back, you can turn in."

Paula gnawed her lower lip. He was giving her something to think about besides Hap, Reis decided; that was all to the good. "Sir, the captain doesn't stand watch."

"He does when there are only four of us, dog tired. Check me through the airlock, please, Mr. Phillips."

"Of course, sir." As the inner hatch swung shut Paula said softly, "Oh, God, I'd give anything to have him back."

Neptune was overhead now; they were spinning, even if the spin was too slow to be visible. With only a single engine in service it was probably impossible to stop the spin, and there was no real reason to. The gravitational effect was so slight he had not noticed it.

He found Jupiter and then the sun, slightly less brilliant than Jupiter or Neptune but brighter than any other star. The sun! How many thousands—no, how many millions of his ancestors must have knelt and sung and sacrificed to it. It had been Ra, Apollo, Helios, Heimdall, and a hundred more, this medium-sized yellow star in a remote arm of the galaxy, this old gas-burner, this space heater laboring to warm infinite space.

If you're a god, Reis thought, why aren't you helping us?

Quite suddenly he realized that the sun *was* helping, was drawing them toward the circling inner planets as powerfully as it could. He shook his head and turned his attention back to the ship.

A faint violet spark shone, died, and rekindled somewhere on Section Six, indicating that Centcomp had at least one of its mobile units back in working order. Centcomp was self-repairing, supposedly, though Reis had never put much faith in that; human beings were supposed to be self-repairing too, but all too often were not.

And deep space was supposed to make you feel alone, but he had never really felt that way; sometimes, when he was not quite so tired, he was more alive here, more vibrant, than he ever was in the polluted atmosphere of Earth. Now Hap was dead, and Reis knew himself to be alone utterly. As he jetted over to check on the mobile unit, he wished that he could weep for Hap as he had wept for his father, though he had known his father so much less well than Hap, known him only as a large, sweet-smelling grown-up who appeared at rare intervals bringing presents.

Or if he could not cry, that Paula could.

The mobile unit looked like a tiny spider. It clung to the side of Section Three with six legs while two more welded up one of the smaller holes. Centcomp, obviously, had decided to close the smallest holes first, and for a moment Reis wondered whether that made sense. It did, he decided, if Centcomp was in actual fact fixing itself; there would be more units as well as more power available later. He swerved down toward the mobile unit until he could see it for what it was, a great jointed machine forty meters across. Three clicks of his teeth brought ghostly numerals—hours, minutes, and seconds—to his faceplate, which had darkened automatically against the raw ultraviolet from the mobile unit's welding arc. Still twenty-four minutes before he had to relieve Paula.

For a minute or two he watched the fusing of the filament patch. The patch fibers had been engineered to form a quick, strong bond; but a bit of dwell was needed just the same. The mobile unit seemed to be allowing enough, working slowly and methodically. In the hard vacuum of space there was no danger of fire, and its helium valves were on Off just as they should have been.

Reis glanced at the time again. Twenty minutes and eleven seconds, time enough yet for a quick look inside Section Three. He circled the hull and jetted through the great, gaping tear, landing easily in a familiar cabin that was now as airless as the skin of the ship. The hermetic hatch that sealed Section Two from this one was tightly dogged still. He had inspected it earlier, just after the hit, and inspected it again when he had come with Dawson,

Jan, and Paula to work on the least damaged engine. He threw his weight against each of the latches once again; you could not be too careful.

Nell Upson's drifting corpse watched him with indifferent eyes until he pushed her away, sending her deeper into the dark recesses of Section Three to join her fellows. In time, space would dry Nell utterly, mummifying her; radiation would blacken her livid skin. None of that had yet taken place, and without air, Nell's blood could not even coagulate—she had left a thin, crimson trail of it floating in the void behind her.

Twelve minutes. That was still plenty of time, but it was time to go. When he left the side of Section Three, the mobile unit was at work on a second hole.

"Resuscitation under way" was still on the screen half an hour into Reis's watch. He read it for the hundredth time with some irritation. Was it supposed to refer to Centcomp's self-repair functions? Reis picked up the rat and wrote, *"Who's in resusc?"*

"Capt. Hilman W. Happle. Resuscitation under way."

So that was that. *"Discon."*

"Resuscitation under way."

"Clear screen," Reis scribbled.

"Resuscitation under way."

Reis cursed and wrote, *"What authority?"*

"Capt. Hillman W. Happle."

That was interesting, Reis decided—not sensible or useful, but interesting. Centcomp did not know that Hap was dead. Reis wrote, *"Capt. Happle K. Lt. Wm. R. Reis commanding."*

The screen went blank, and Reis decided to try a general instrument display. *"GID."*

The three letters faded slowly, replaced by nothing.

"Enter—GID."

That, too, faded to an empty screen. Reis scratched his nose and looked speculatively at the transducer headband. He had ordered the others not to use it—the hard instrumentation was amply sufficient as long as nothing too delicate was being attempted; but it had been sixteen hours since the hit, and Centcomp was still limping at best.

Multiplication became coitus, division reproduction; to add was to eat, to subtract to excrete. Glowing, Centcomp's central processor loomed before him, a dazzling coral palace with twice ten thousand spires where subroutines worked or slept. Tiny and blue alongside it, the lone mobile unit sang a Bach fugue as it labored. Smoldering leaves perfumed the breeze, washed away by a fountain of exponential functions that appeared to Reis to be calculating natural logarithms for purposes both infinite and obscure, pungently returning with each fresh gust of algorithmic air. Interactive matrices sprouted around his feet—the lilies, buttercups, and pale or burning roses that allowed his conscious mind to move here as it did, their blossoms petaled with shining elementary rows and columns.

Hap was sitting astride a tree that sprouted from the coral wall. The smile that divided his dark face when he saw Reis seemed automatic and distracted. Reis saluted, called, "Good evening, Skipper," and leaped across the laughing rill that had overflowed the fountain's rim.

Hap touched his forehead in return. "Hi ya, Bill."

Reis said, "It's damned good to see you here. We thought you were dead."

"Not me, Bill." Hap stared off into the twilight. "You can't die on duty, know that? Got to finish your tick, know what I mean, Bill boy? You want up here on the bridge?" He patted the tree trunk.

"That's okay—I'm fine where I am. Hap . . .?"

His eyes still upon something Reis could not see, Hap said, "Speak your piece."

"Hap, I checked your cortical activity. There wasn't any. You were brain-dead."

"Go on."

"That's why it was quite a surprise to run into you here, and I'm not sure it's really you. Are you Hap, or are you just a kind of surrogate, Centcomp's concept of Hap?"

"I'm Hap. Next question?"

"Why won't Centcomp terminate resuscitation?"

"Because I told it not to, as soon as we left Earth." Hap sounded as though he were talking to himself. "Not just on me, on all of us. We're all too necessary, all of us vital. Rescue is to continue as long as—in Centcomp's judgment—there's the slightest possibility of returning a crewman to his or her duty. No overrides at all, no mutinies. Know what a mutiny is, Bill? Grasp the concept?"

Reis nodded.

"Some snotty kid's trying to take over my ship, Billy boy, trying to push me out through a hatch. That's mutiny. It's a certain Lieutenant William R. Reis. He's not going to get away with it."

"Hap . . ."

Hap was gone. Briefly, the tree where he had sat remained where it was, vacant; then it too vanished, wiped from working memory.

Something was wrong: the brilliant garden seemed haunted by sinister shadows, flitting and swift; the chaotic twilight from which Reis had emerged pressed closer to the coral palace. His head ached, there was a chill in his side, and his fingers felt oddly warm. He tried to remove the headband, willing himself to use his real arms, not the proxies that here appeared to be his arms. A hurrying subroutine shouldered him out of the way; by accident he stepped into the laughing rill, which bit his foot like acid. . . .

A smudged white cabin wall stood in place of the wall of the coral palace. Dawson was bending over him, his face taut with concern. "Reis! What happened?"

His mouth was full of blood; he spat it out. "I'm hurt, Sid."

"I know. *Christ!*" Dawson released him; but he did not fall, floating derelict in the cabin air. Dawson banged on Jan's pod.

Reis moved his right arm to look at the fingers; the warmth there was his own blood, and there was more blood hanging in the cabin, floating spheres of bright scarlet blood—arterial blood. "I'm bleeding, Sid. I think he nicked a lung. Better patch me up."

Twilight closed upon the cabin. Reis remembered how they had celebrated Christmas when he was three—something he had not known he knew, with colored paper and a thousand other wonderful things. Surely he was peeping through one of the plastic tubes the paper had come on; the few things he could see seemed small, toylike and very bright. Everything in all the universe was a Christmas present, a fact he had forgotten long, long ago. He wondered who had brought them all, and why.

"You have been asleep in the medical pod. There is little cause for concern."

Reis searched the pod for a rat, but there was none. No backtalk to Centcomp from in here.

"Are you anxious? Fearful? Confide your fears to me. I assure you that any information that I provide concerning your condition will be both complete and correct. No matter how bad, reality is never quite so bad as our fears concerning reality."

Reis said, "Spare me the philosophy," though he knew that Centcomp could not hear him.

"And your condition is not even critical. You suffered a dangerous lesion between the fifth and sixth ribs of your right side, but you are nearly well."

Reis was already exploring the place with his fingers.

"Please reply."

"Would if I could," Reis muttered.

"You will find a rapid access trace beside your right hand. Please reply."

"There's no God-damned rapid access trace."

A latch clicked. Servos hummed. The pod in which Reis lay rolled forward with stately grandeur, and the pod opened. This time it was Jan who was looking down at him. "Reis, can you sit up?"

"Sure." He proved it.

Low and quick: "I want you to get into your sleeping pod with me, please. Don't ask questions—just do it, fast."

His pod was closed, but not latched from inside. He threw it open and he and Jan climbed in; she lay facing him, on her side, her back to the pod wall. He got in beside her, closed the pod, and threw the latching lever. Jan's breasts flattened against his chest; Jan's pelvis pressed his. "I'm sorry," she whispered. "I hadn't realized it would be this crowded."

"It's all right."

"Even if I had, I'd have had to ask you anyway. This is the only place I could think of where we could talk privately."

"I like it," Reis said, "so you can forget about that part. Talk about what?"

"Hap."

He nodded, though she could not have seen him in the dark. "I thought so."

"Hap was the one who stabbed you."

"Sure," Reis said. "I know that. With the rat from the med pod."

"That's right." Jan hesitated; Reis could feel her sweet breath wash across his face. At last she said, "Perhaps you'd better tell me how you knew. It might be important."

"I doubt it, but there's no reason not to. Hap thinks I'm a mutineer because I took charge when he was hurt—I was talking to him in Centcomp's conscious space. Hap had been in the med pod, and when I woke up in there the rat that should have been there was gone. A rat's stylus is long and sharp, and the whole rat's made of some sort of metal—titanium, I suppose. So a rat ought to make a pretty decent weapon."

Hair brushed his cheek as Jan nodded. "Sid found you. He woke up and realized he should have been on watch."

"Sure."

"He yelled for me, and we put you in the med pod when we saw that it was empty. There's another pod in Section Three, remember?"

"Of course," Reis said.

He waited for her to pursue that line of thought, but she seemed to veer off from it instead. "Hap's resumed command." She swallowed. "It was all right at first—he's the captain, after all. None of us even thought about resisting him, then."

Reis said slowly, "I wouldn't have resisted him either; I would have obeyed his orders, if I'd known he was alive to give them."

Jan said, "He's very suspicious now." There was a queer flatness in her voice.

"I see."

"And Reis, he's going to continue the mission."

For a moment he could not speak. He shook his head. "It's crazy, isn't it? With the ship ripped up like it was."

"Not crazy," he told her. "Impossible."

Jan took a deep breath—he could feel and hear it, her long gasp in the dark. "And Reis, Hap's dead."

Reluctantly Reis said, "If he really wanted to proceed with the mission, maybe it's for the best. You didn't kill him, did you? You and Sid?"

"No. You don't understand. I didn't mean . . . Oh, it's so hard to say what I do mean."

Reis told her, "I think you'd better try." His right hand had been creeping, almost absently, toward her left breast. He forced it to stop where it was.

"Hap's still running the ship. He tells us what to do, and we do it because we know we'd better. But our real captain, our friend, is dead. Try to understand. The real Hap died in the med pod, and Centcomp's substituted something else—something of its own—for his soul or spirit or whatever you want to call it. When you've seen him, after you've been around him for a while, you'll understand."

"Then I ought to be outside, where I can see him," Reis said practically, "not in here. But first—"

Jan screamed, a high-pitched wail of sheer terror that was deafening in the enclosed space of the sleep pod. Reis clapped his hand over her mouth and said, "Jesus! All right, if you don't want to, we won't. Promise you won't do that again if I let you talk?"

Jan nodded, and he returned his hand to his side.

"I'm sorry," she said. "It isn't that I don't like you, or that I'd never want to. I've been under such a terrible strain. You missed it. You were in the med pod, and you can't know what it's been like for us."

"I understand," Reis told her. "Oh, hell, you know what I mean."

"If Hap isn't looking for us already, he will be soon. Or looking for me, anyway. He thinks you're still in the med pod, unless Centcomp's told him I took you out. Reis, you've got to believe me. He's going to court-martial and execute you; that's what he said when Sid and I told him we'd put you in the pod."

"You're serious?"

"Reis, you don't know what he's like now. It doesn't make any difference, we're all going to die anyway, Sid and Paula and me. And Hap's already dead." Her voice threatened to slip from tears to hysteria.

"No, we're not," he told her. "Hap's been having you fix the ship? He must have, if he's talking about carrying out the mission."

"Yes! We've got three engines running now, and the hull's airtight. We don't know—Sid and I don't know—whether we can count on Paula. If she sided with Hap it would be two against two, a man and a woman on each side, and . . ."

"Go on," Reis said.

"But if you were with us, that would be two men and a woman on our side. We'd save the ship and we'd save our lives. Nobody would have to know—we'd tell them the truth, that Hap died in the hit."

"You're not telling *me* the truth," Reis said. "If we're going to handle this together, you've got to open up."

"I am, Reis, I swear. Don't you think I know this isn't the time to lie?"

"Okay," he said. "Then tell me who's in the medical pod in Section Three. Is it Sid? Somebody's in there, or you wouldn't have brought it up."

He waited, but Jan said nothing.

"Maybe Hap sleeps in there," Reis hazarded. "Maybe he's getting himself some additional treatment. You want me to pull the plug on him, but why can't you do that yourself?"

"No. I don't think he sleeps at all. Or . . ."

"Or what?"

"He's got Nell with him—Sergeant Upson. Nell was in the pod, but she's out now, and she stays with him all the time. I didn't want to tell you, but there it is. Something else is in Three's med pod. I don't know who it was, but when it gets out we won't have a chance."

"Nell's dead." He recalled her floating body, its hideous stare.

"That's right."

"I see," Reis said, and jerked back the lever that opened the sleep pod.

"Reis, you have to tell me. Are you with us or against us?"

He said, "You're wrong, Jan. I don't have to tell you one God-damned thing. Where's Hap?"

"In Section Five, probably. He wants to get another engine on line."

Reis launched himself toward the airlock, braked on the dog handles, and released them.

Section Three seemed normal but oddly vacant. He crossed to Centcomp's screen and wrote, *"Present occ this med pod for vis check."*

"ID" flashed on the screen.

"Lt. Wm. R. Reis."

"Refused. Resuscitation under way."

Behind him Jan said, "I tried that. Centcomp won't identify it either."

Reis shrugged and pushed off toward the emergency locker. Opening it, he tossed out breathing apparatus, the aid kit, a body bag, and a folding stretcher with tie-downs. Behind them was a steel emergency toolbox. He selected a crowbar and the largest screwdriver and jetted to the med pod.

"Tampering with medical equipment is strictly forbidden. Resuscitation under way."

Reis jammed the blade of the screwdriver into the scarcely visible joint between the bulkhead and the pod, and struck the screwdriver's handle sharply enough with the crowbar to make his own weightless bodymass jump. He let the crowbar float free, grasped the pod latch, and jerked the screwdriver down. That widened the crack enough for him to work one end of the crowbar into it.

Centcomp's screen caught his eye. It read, *"Tampering is strictly Bill stop."*

Reis said, "Jan, tell it to open the God-damned pod if it doesn't want me to mess with it."

Jan found the rat; but before she could write, the screen read, *"Bill, I cannot."*

Jan gasped, "Oh, holy God," and it struck Reis that he had

never heard her swear before. He said, "I thought you couldn't hear us, Centcomp. Wasn't that the story?"

"I truly cannot, Bill, and that is no story. But I monitor conditions everywhere in the ship. That is my job, and at times I can read your lips. Particularly yours, Bill. You have very good, clear lip motion."

Reis heaved at the crowbar; tortured metal shrieked.

Jan said, "Centcomp will have told Hap. He and Nell are probably on their way up here right now."

"I have not, Lieutenant van Joure."

Reis turned to face the screen. "Is that the truth?"

"You know I am incapable of any deception, Bill. Captain Hapgood is engaged in a delicate repair. I prefer to take care of this matter myself in order that he can proceed without any interruption."

"Watch the dogs—the moment they start going around, tell me."

"All right," Jan said. She had already pulled a wrench from the toolbox.

"Bill, I did not want to tell you this, yet I see I must."

Reis moved the crowbar to the left and pried again. "What is it?"

"You said . . . ?"

"I said what is it, God damn it! Stop screwing around and stalling. It's not going to do you any good."

"Bill, it really would be better if you did not open that."

Reis made no reply. Pale blue light was leaking from the med pod through the crack; it looked as though there might be a lot of ultraviolet in it, and he turned his eyes away.

"Bill, for your own good, do not do that."

Reis heaved again on the crowbar, and the latch broke. The pod rolled out, and as it did a nearly faceless thing inside sat up and caught his neck in skeletal hands. Section Three filled with the sickening sweetish smells of death and gangrene. Reis flailed at the half-dead thing with the crowbar; and its crooked end laid open a cheek, scattering stinking blood that was nearly black and exposing two rows of yellow teeth.

Evening was closing on Section Three. Night's darkness pressed upon Reis; his hands were numb, the crowbar gone.

Jan's wrench struck the dead thing's skull hard enough to

throw her beyond the range of Reis's narrowing vision. The bony fingers relaxed a trifle. Reis forced his own arms between the dead arms and tore the hands away.

Then Jan was back, her wrench rising and falling again and again. His crowbar was gone; but the toolbox itself was within reach, with a D-shaped handle at one end. Reis grabbed it and hurled the box at the dead thing. It was heavy enough to send him spinning diagonally across the section, and it struck the head and chest of the dead thing and the end of the pod as well. For a split second Reis seemed to hear a wailing cry; the pod shot back until its bent and battered end was almost flush with the bulkhead.

Jan screamed as the airlock swung open; there was a rush of air and a scorching blue flash. Something brushed Reis's cheek. He could scarcely see, but he snatched at it and his still-numb fingers told him he held an emergency mask. He pushed it against his face, shut his eyes, and sucked in oxygen, feeling he drank it like wine. There was another searing burst of heat.

Long training and good luck put the manual control into his hands; he tore away the safety strap and spun the wheel. Driven by a fifty-thousand-p.s.i. hydraulic accumulator, the airlock door slammed shut, its crash echoing even in the depleted atmosphere of Section Three. Emergency air that Centcomp could not control hissed though the vents, and Reis opened his eyes.

Jan writhed near the airlock door, her uniform smoldering, one hand and cheek seared. The arm and welding gun of a mobile unit, sheered off at the second joint, floated not far from Jan. Reis sprayed her uniform with a CO_2 extinguisher and smeared her face and hand with blue antibacterial cream.

"My eyes . . ." she gasped.

"You've been flashed," Reis told her. He tried to keep his voice low and soothing. "Zapped by an electric arc. Open them, just for a minute, and tell me if you can see anything."

"A little."

"Good," he told her. "Now shut them and keep them closed. After a while your vision should come back a bit more, and when we get home they can give you a retinal—"

His own dimmed sight had failed to note the spinning dogs.

The hatch to Section Four swung back, and Hap floated in. His sunken cheeks and dull eyes carried the hideous stamp of death, and his movements were the swift, jerky gestures of a puppet; but he grinned at Reis and touched his forehead with the steel rod he carried. "Hi there, Bill boy."

Nell Upson followed Hap. Her lips seemed too short now to conceal her teeth; it was not until she raised her pistol that Reis felt certain she was not wholly dead. Sid Dawson and Paula lingered at the hatch until Nell waved them forward. Both were terrified and exhausted, Reis decided. There could not be much fight left in either—perhaps none.

"You're supposed to salute your captain, Bill. You didn't even return mine. If I were running a tight ship, I'd have my marine arrest you."

Reis saluted.

"That's better. A lot of things have changed while you've been out of circulation, Bill. We've got three engines going. We'll have a fourth up in another forty-eight hours, and we only needed six to break away from the inner planets. Out where we are now, four should be plenty. And that's not all—we've got more air and food per crewman now than we had when we left Earth."

Reis said, "Then there's no reason we can't continue the mission."

"Way to go, Bill! Know what's happened to this old ship of ours?"

Reis shrugged. "I think so, a little. But tell me."

"We've been seized, Bill boy. Taken over, possessed. It isn't Centcomp—did you think it was Centcomp? And it sure as hell ain't me. It's something else, a demon or what they call an elemental, and it's in me, and in Centcomp, and in you, too. Whatever you want to call it, it's the thing that created the *Flying Dutchman* and so on, centuries ago. We're the first ghost ship of space. You're not buying this, are you, Bill boy?"

"No," Reis told him.

"But it's the truth. There's a ship headed for us, it's coming from Earth right now—I bet you didn't know that. I wonder just how long they'll be able to see us."

Reis spat. The little gray-brown globe of phlegm drifted toward Hap, who appeared not to notice it. "Bullshit," Reis said.

Nell leveled her pistol. The synthetic ruby lens at the end of the barrel caught the light for a moment, winking like a baleful eye.

"Can I tell you what's really happened?" Reis asked.

"Sure. Be my guest."

"Centcomp's brought back you and Nell at any and all cost, because that's what you programmed it to do. You were both too far gone, but Centcomp did it anyway. You've suffered a lot of brain damage, I think—you move like it—and I don't think you can keep going much longer. If you hit a dead man's arm with a couple of electrodes, his muscles will jump; but not forever."

Hap grinned again, mirthlessly. "Go on, Bill boy."

"Every time you look at yourself, you see what you are—what you've become—and you can't face it. So you've made up this crazy story about the ghost ship. A ghost ship explains a dead captain and a dead crew, and a ghost ship never really dies; it goes on sailing forever."

Reis paused. As he had hoped, the minute reaction created by the act of spitting was causing him to float, ever so slowly, away from Hap and Nell. Soon he would be caught in the draft from the main vent. It would move him to the left, toward the Section Two hatch; and if neither changed position, Nell would be almost in back of Hap.

"Now are you still going to court-martial me?" he asked. As he spoke, fresh cool air from the vent touched his cheek.

Hap said, "Hell, no. Not if—"

Nell's boot was reaching for the edge of the Section Four hatch; in a moment more she would kick off from it. It was now or never.

Reis's hand closed hard on the tube of antibacterial cream. A thick thread of bright blue cream shot into the space before Hap and Nell and writhed there like a living thing—a spectral monster or a tangle of blue maggots.

Nell fired.

The cream popped and spattered like grease in an overheated skillet, wrapping itself in dense black smoke. Alarms sounded.

Through billowing smoke, Reis saw Dawson dart toward the airlock control.

Reis's feet touched the bulkhead; he kicked backward, going for Hap in a long, fast leap. Hap's steel bar caught his right forearm. He heard the snap of breaking bone as he went spinning through the rapidly closing Section Four hatch. A rush of air nearly carried him back into Three.

Then silence, except for the whisper from the vents. The alarms had stopped ringing. The hatch was closed; it had closed automatically, of course, when Centcomp's detectors had picked up the smoke from the burning cream, closed just slowly enough to permit a crewman to get clear.

His right arm was broken, although the pain seemed remote and dull. He went to Section Four's emergency locker and found a sling for it. It would not be safe to get in a med pod, he decided, even if Hap was gone; not until somebody reprogrammed Centcomp.

The hatchdogs spun. Reis looked around for something that could be used as a weapon, though he knew that his position was probably hopeless if either Hap or Nell had survived. There was a toolbox in this locker too, but his arm slowed him down. He was still wrestling with the stretcher when the hatch opened and Dawson came through.

Reis smiled. "You made it."

Dawson nodded slowly without speaking. Jan entered; her eyes were closed, and Paula guided her with one hand.

Reis sighed. "You were able to catch hold of something. That's good, I was worried about you. Paula too."

Jan said, "Sid saved me. He reached out and snagged me as I flew past, otherwise I'd be out there in space. Paula saved herself, but Hap and Nell couldn't. It was just like you said: they didn't have enough coordination left. You were counting on that, weren't you? That Nell couldn't hit you, couldn't shoot very well anymore."

"Yes," Reis admitted. "Yes, I was, and I didn't think Hap could swat me with that steel bar; but I was wrong."

Jan said, "It doesn't matter now." She was keeping her eyes shut, but tears leaked from beneath their lids.

"No, it doesn't. Hap and Nell are finally dead—truly dead and at rest. Sid, I never thought a hell of a lot of you, and I guess I let it show sometimes; but you saved Jan and you saved the ship. Hell, you saved us all. All of us owe you our lives."

Dawson shook his head and looked away. "Show him, Paula."

She had taken something shining, something about the size of a small notepad, from one of her pockets. Wordlessly, she held it up.

And Reis, looking at it, staring into it for a second or more before he turned away, looked into horror and despair.

It was a mirror.

The Daily Chernobyl

▼ ▼ ▼

Robert Frazier

Robert Frazier, a resident of Nantucket, Massachusetts, is among our most powerful SF poets. He edited the landmark anthology *Burning with a Vision: Poetry of Science and the Fantastic* (1984). With Bruce Boston, he has written a collection of interrelated poems, *Chronicles of the Mutant Rain Forest* (1990), and of late his short fiction has appeared in *Twilight Zone, Asimov's,* and *In the Fields of Fire,* among others. His story "Giant, Giant Steps" received the cover illustration on the May 1990 issue of *Amazing Stories,* and he is now finishing his first novel, *Death Angel.*

The June 1988 issue of *Fantasy & Science Fiction* featured Bruce Sterling's "Our Neural Chernobyl," a story in which *chernobyl* has become a generic term for any disaster triggered by runaway technology. Also in 1988, George Zebrowski's *Synergy 2* published Robert Frazier's poem "The Daily Chernobyl." SF writers, it seems, are doing all they can to make sure we don't forget Chernobyl, and Bob's poem posits as unsettling a near-future scenario as any I have ever read.

Of its origins, Frazier writes: "1987. Martha's Vineyard. An antinuclear speaker talks while roadies set up the stage behind him for veteran rocker Jesse Colin Young. The speaker cranks up in a diatribe against nuclear power. Or is it nuclear arms? I am, in part, oblivious to this preaching to the choir, but my subconscious listens on all levels. My ears perk. What did he say? Or did I mishear? Regardless, I heard the phrase 'this daily Chernobyl around us.' Starting with a title, the right title, is sometimes liberating. The rest of the poem writes itself."

The hot yellow clouds that tatter
that drift toward your islands from northern cities
the ones you have always called smog and despised
because the wind that carries them tastes like stale
    butts

they seem to hang perpetually on the edge of day
    now

you worry if it's really a chinook wind that
pushes them through winter and you wonder why
the flu season is so much worse than the last
you get sick just hearing about the sick and
    exposed
whose symptoms point toward nothing specific
but the whites of their eyes are jaundiced

in the grip of radiation paranoia
your imagination runs freer than a bitch
penned all morning with her own sour moments
freer than your sons who steal your best silver
to excavate for worms and scab-red garnets
in a valley where the headstones seem white as
    coke
lined up in neat rows on the mirror of twilight

the yellow clouds no longer evoke eastern
    mysticism
brain garbage about haiku and wise poets and
    mountains
when they cross in front of a magnesium moon
or cause the sun to bleed across cotton banks of
    cumuli
they've become one of those things that nobody
    talks about
like the constant itch that leeches along your skin
like the dragged down mono feeling you wake to
    each morning

the color of their yellow is what is alarming
the yellow of an amber necklace worn
by a woman so feline that drool beads her
    neoprene lips
and a vertical flame trembles in each emerald pupil

which cannot be quenched even by the dull
    bullock men
who stack themselves like cordwood before her
or it's the yellow of the fever you get with
    dysentery
or from couplings with drunken boys
whose lips are sandy and their fingers coarse as
    lime

of course you worry the most that it's the isotope
yellow of crumbling uranium ores

so you must face implications beyond the moment
what are the worst-case scenarios
when you know the stuff is leaking daily around
    you
and you imagine between waking and sleeping
the dreamtime scenes the daily Chernobyl

the one that hits you
first like a fist
is an afternoon at ground zero
you see twisted faces everywhere in
the plaster cracking over your bed
in the wood-knots oozing pitch
in the cut of a tomato
or the end of a loofa sponge
they take on demented poses
and geometrically breed
until the sun itself warps into an egg
and sprouts the momentary features
of a Rasputin before it blanches
the world with white heat

next comes the fantasia of mutations
that starts with lumps pushing from within
the womblike mushroom buttons under loam
then the twisted births

newborns with fingers fused to flippers
twins with spines twined into a Y
their skin that loses form
cheeks sliding into stringy wattles
ears like moth-eaten rags
these babies' skulls seem soft as sodden cardboard
and their brains bud like flower bulbs
adding empty hallways to another apartment
another verifiable vacancy
and the children all listen to a golden music
high and highly furious
pinwheeling through their veins
pulsing among the platelets

but none of these are vivid as the older kids
perfect and white as toadstools
that run in packs with no apparent reason
their faces develop slowly from the inky dark
photographs in emulsion or
stone rubbings from lost temples
or tin foil pressed over a silver dollar
from a blur to naked clarity
and it's always their eyes
that first rivet you where you stand
irises nonreflective yet brassy as thumbtacks
that float in their gelid frames
like numerals in an LED display
flickering and changing their sums you see
these eyes through car windows or factory
      skylights
or your bedroom window with the lights dimmed
staring into your frying thoughts

then there's the imaginary world
that swallows you in yellow
jungles of helliconia and brazilwoods
or sunflowers nodding at three thousand feet
weighted under leaden bells of seed

worlds where the light under this canopy falls
in showers of gold dust
where time freezes in its watchworks matrix
where the growth goes unchecked
and you walk from path to leafy path searching
for signposts of the familiar
until home is a word forgotten in your language

but worst of all are the lemon-skinned nightmares
you choke down each time you rest
the scenarios that get your REM humming
as wild as geiger counters
machine gun drumrolls of white noise
the scenarios that
even shift the planet's swollen belly
and oh my how it topspins
beneath your feet faster and faster
turning to buttery pools of radioactivity

so at the heart of any and all these precognitions
holds true the sulfurous light
which cannot be snuffed or dampered
though you try with desperate tension
to hold it in your dream fists
to squeeze it down into an ochre jewel
but each time it escapes through you
illuminating the geography of your hands
revealing weedy veins and arteries and nerves
the rivermaps to a country beyond the Inferno
where the boatman has abandoned you to drown
beneath a still topaz sky

now it is pointless to gaze out your windows
just spread the margarine on your toast
and turn the news down to a static burst of
        nothing
there's plenty of time to listen patiently
for the cold rain to tap its skeletal fugue

its cleansing run of ghost notes
on your street on your lawn on your slate roof
on the sill of your open doorway on your legs
on the slick glissando surface of your soul

The Last of the Winnebagos

'''

Connie Willis

Connie Willis appeared in last year's volume, *Nebula Awards 23*, with her runner-up novelette, "Schwarzschild Radius." In 1982, she won two Nebulas, for best short story ("A Letter from the Clearys") and best novelette ("Fire Watch"). Now, having won again for best novella with this piece of sociological extrapolation ("The Last of the Winnebagos"), a story difficult to imagine anyone else having even conceived, she needs only to win for best novel to become the first writer to win in every category. (Others on that threshold include Samuel R. Delany, Robert Silverberg, Fritz Leiber, and Greg Bear—although the late Alice Sheldon, aka James Tiptree, Jr., was also there before her death by suicide in 1987.)

Willis's novels include *Lincoln's Dreams*, the winner of the John W. Campbell Memorial Award, and, with Cynthia Felice, *Water Witch* and *Light Raid*. Her collection *Fire Watch* contains twelve stories (including two early award winners) first published between 1979 and 1984. Her latest novel is *Doomsday Book*, and two recent stories are "At the Rialto" and "Time Out."

About her award-winning novella, she writes: " 'The Last of the Winnebagos' was inspired by parvovirus, which killed half the dogs in our town and which my vet just recently told me appears to be mutating again; by the lumbering recreation vehicles that jam Ute Pass every summer, taking up two lanes and going fifteen miles an hour; by all the things that are gone before you know it and all the things you wish would hurry up and go. And by Aberfan.

"Science fiction is full of stories about disaster, but most of them don't really deal with loss. It isn't that the loss isn't there—in many stories, the entire world lies in shambles—it's just that the characters are so busy trying to salvage what's left, trying to find canned goods and salt and nurse the wounded and keep from getting killed by looters or radiation or walking plants, that mourning is a luxury there isn't time for.

"Aberfan wasn't like that. It wasn't a worldwide disaster. When the slag heap came down and killed the children, it didn't even destroy the whole village, just seventeen houses and the school. And Aberfan wasn't alone. The Red Cross sent in food and the neighboring towns sent in men and earthmoving equipment. Prime Minister Harold Wilson flew in, and people from all over the world sent flowers and money and toys. And all the children weren't killed. A few of them had been home with the measles or out playing hooky, and the older children went to another school, so it was just the children between seven and ten. After the funerals, the townspeople razed the school and enclosed the site with railings and wire, and the British government conducted an investigation that concluded the slag heap had been built on a mountain spring and that the disaster was 'a terrifying tale of bungling ineptitude . . . of failure to heed clear warnings.'[1]

"The mines opened up again, and life went on pretty much as before except for the new bicycles the surviving children had been given by well-meaning Americans and the pulled curtains, a Welsh tradition when there has been a death in the family, on nearly every house. And the pictures the townspeople showed every reporter and sightseer: 'In the school play she was the angel. And the teacher said they certainly picked the right girl for the part, oh, she was a pretty thing.' "[2]

If originality is one of the hallmarks of good science fiction, this story has it in abundance, without sacrificing intelligibility or resorting to stylistic and/or structural tricks.

On the way out to Tempe I saw a dead jackal in the road. I was in the far left lane of Van Buren, ten lanes away from it and its long legs were facing away from me, the squarish muzzle flat against the pavement so it looked narrower than it really was, and for a minute I thought it was a dog.

I had not seen an animal in the road like that for fifteen years.

[1]"The Vulnerable Eyes of Coal-Dusted Faces," *Life,* November 4, 1966.
[2]"The Village That Lost Its Children," *Redbook,* January 1968.

They can't get onto the divideds, of course, and most of the multiways are fenced. And people are more careful of their animals.

The jackal was probably somebody's pet. This part of Phoenix was mostly residential, and after all this time people still think they can turn the nasty, carrion-loving creatures into pets. Which was no reason to have hit it and, worse, left it there. It's a felony to strike an animal and another one to not report it, but whoever had hit it was long gone.

I pulled the Hitori over onto the center shoulder and sat there awhile, staring at the empty multiway. I wondered who had hit it and whether they had stopped to see if it was dead.

Katie had stopped. She had hit the brakes so hard she sent the car into a skid that brought it up against the ditch, and jumped out of the jeep. I was still running toward him, floundering in the snow. We made it to him almost at the same time. I knelt beside him, the camera dangling from my neck, its broken case hanging half open.

"I hit him," Katie had said. "I hit him with the jeep."

I looked in the rearview mirror. I couldn't even see over the pile of camera equipment in the back seat with the eisenstadt balanced on top. I got out. I had come nearly a mile, and looking back, I couldn't see the jackal, though I knew now that's what it was.

"McCombe! David! Are you there yet?" Ramirez's voice said from inside the car.

I leaned in. "No," I shouted in the general direction of the phone's receiver. "I'm still on the multiway."

"Mother of God, what's taking you so long? The governor's conference is at twelve, and I want you to go out to Scottsdale and do a layout on the closing of Taliessin West. The appointment's for ten. Listen, McCombe, I got the poop on the Amblers for you. They bill themselves as '100% Authentic,' but they're not. Their RV isn't really a Winnebago, it's an Open Road. It *is* the last RV on the road, though, according to Highway Patrol. A man named Eldridge was touring with one, also *not* a Winnebago, a Shasta, until March, but he lost his license in Oklahoma for using a tanker lane, so this is it. Recreation vehicles are banned in all but four states. Texas has legislation in committee, and Utah has a full-divided bill coming up next month. Arizona will be next, so take lots of pictures, Davey boy. This may be your last chance. And get some of the zoo."

"What about the Amblers?" I said.

"Their name *is* Ambler, believe it or not. I ran a lifeline on them. He was a welder. She was a bank teller. No kids. They've been doing this since eighty-nine when he retired. Nineteen years. David, are you using the eisenstadt?"

We had been through this the last three times I'd been on a shoot. "I'm not *there* yet," I said.

"Well, I want you to use it at the governor's conference. Set it on his desk if you can."

I intended to set it on a desk, all right. One of the desks at the back, and let it get some nice shots of the rear ends of reporters as they reached wildly for a little clear air space to shoot their pictures in, some of them holding their vidcams in their upstretched arms and aiming them in what they hope is the right direction because they can't see the governor at all, let it get a nice shot of one of the reporter's arms as he knocked it face-down on the desk.

"This one's a new model. It's got a trigger. It's set for faces, full-lengths, and vehicles."

So great. I come home with a hundred-frame cartridge full of passersby and tricycles. How the hell did it know when to click the shutter or which one the governor was in a press conference of eight hundred people, full-length *or* face? It was supposed to have all kinds of fancy light-metrics and computer-composition features, but all it could really do was mindlessly snap whatever passed in front of its idiot lens, just like the highway speed cameras.

It had probably been designed by the same government types who'd put the highway cameras along the road instead of over-head so that all it takes is a little speed to reduce the new side-license plates to a blur, and people go faster than ever. A great camera, the eisenstadt. I could hardly wait to use it.

"Sun-co's very interested in the eisenstadt," Ramirez said. She didn't say goodbye. She never does. She just stops talking and then starts up again later. I looked back in the direction of the jackal.

The multiway was completely deserted. New cars and singles don't use the undivided multiways much, even during rush hours. Too many of the little cars have been squashed by tankers. Usually there are at least a few obsoletes and renegade semis taking advantage of the Patrol's being on the dividers, but there wasn't anybody at all.

I got back in the car and backed up even with the jackal. I turned off the ignition but didn't get out. I could see the trickle of blood from its mouth from here. A tanker went roaring past out of nowhere, trying to beat the cameras, straddling the three middle lanes and crushing the jackal's rear half to a bloody mush. It was a good thing I hadn't been trying to cross the road. He never would have even seen me.

I started the car and drove to the nearest off-ramp to find a phone. There was one at an old 7-Eleven on McDowell.

"I'm calling to report a dead animal on the road," I told the woman who answered the Society's phone.

"Name and number?"

"It's a jackal," I said. "It's between Thirtieth and Thirty-Second on Van Buren. It's in the far right lane."

"Did you render emergency assistance?"

"There was no assistance to be rendered. It was dead."

"Did you move the animal to the side of the road?"

"No."

"Why not?" she said, her tone suddenly sharper, more alert.

Because I thought it was a dog. "I didn't have a shovel," I said, and hung up.

I got out to Tempe by eight-thirty, in spite of the fact that every tanker in the state suddenly decided to take Van Buren. I got pushed out onto the shoulder and drove on that most of the way.

The Winnebago was set up in the fairgrounds between Phoenix and Tempe, next to the old zoo. The flyer had said they would be open from nine to nine, and I had wanted to get most of my pictures before they opened, but it was already a quarter to nine, and even if there were no cars in the dusty parking lot, I was probably too late.

It's a tough job being a photographer. The minute most people see a camera, their real faces close like a shutter in too much light, and all that's left is their camera face, their public face. It's a smiling face, except for Saudi terrorists and senators, but, smiling or not, it shows no real emotion. Actors, politicians, people who have their pictures taken all the time are the worst. The longer the person's been in the public eye, the easier it is for me to get great vidcam footage and the harder it is to get anything approaching a real photograph, and the Amblers had been at this for nearly twenty years. By a quarter to nine they would already have their camera faces on.

I parked down at the foot of the hill next to the clump of ocotillas and yucca where the zoo sign had been, pulled my Nikon longshot out of the mess in the back seat, and took some shots of the sign they'd set up by the multiway: "See a Genuine Winnebago. 100% Authentic."

The Genuine Winnebago was parked longways against the stone banks of cactus and palms at the front of the zoo. Ramirez had said it wasn't a real Winnebago, but it had the identifying W with its extending stripes running the length of the RV, and it seemed to me to be the right shape, though I hadn't seen one in at least ten years.

I was probably the wrong person for this story. I had never had any great love for RVs, and my first thought when Ramirez called with the assignment was that there are some things that should be extinct, like mosquitoes and lane dividers, and RVs are right at the top of the list. They had been everywhere in the mountains when I'd lived in Colorado, crawling along in the left hand lane, taking up two lanes even in the days when a lane was fifteen feet wide, with a train of cursing cars behind them.

I'd been behind one on Independence Pass that had stopped cold while a ten-year-old got out to take pictures of the scenery with an Instamatic, and one of them had tried to take the curve in front of my house and ended up in my ditch, looking like a beached whale. But that was always a bad curve.

An old man in an ironed short-sleeved shirt came out the side
door and around to the front end and began washing the Winnebago with a sponge and a bucket. I wondered where he had
gotten the water. According to Ramirez's advance work about
the Winnebago, which she'd sent me over the modem, it had
maybe a fifty-gallon water tank, tops, which is barely enough for
drinking water, a shower, and maybe washing a dish or two, and
there certainly weren't any hookups here at the zoo, but he was
swilling water onto the front bumper and even over the tires as
if he had more than enough.

I took a few shots of the RV standing in the huge expanse
of parking lot and then hit the longshot to full for a picture of
the old man working on the bumper. He had large reddish-
brown freckles on his arms and the top of his bald head, and he
scrubbed away at the bumper with a vengeance. After a minute
he stopped and stepped back, and then called to his wife. He
looked worried, or maybe just crabby. I was too far away to tell
if he had snapped out her name impatiently or simply called her
to come and look, and I couldn't see his face. She opened the
metal side door, with its narrow louvered window, and stepped
down onto the metal step.

The old man asked her something, and she, still standing on
the step, looked out toward the multiway and shook her head,
and then came around to the front, wiping her hands on a dishtowel, and they both stood there looking at his handiwork.

They were 100% Authentic, even if the Winnebago wasn't,
down to her flowered blouse and polyester slacks, probably also
100%, and the cross-stitched rooster on the dishtowel. She had
on brown leather slip-ons like I remembered my grandmother
wearing, and I was willing to bet she had set her thinning white
hair on bobby pins. Their bio said they were in their eighties, but
I would have put them in their nineties, although I wondered if
they were too perfect and therefore fake, like the Winnebago.
But she went on wiping her hands on the dishtowel the way my
grandmother had when she was upset, even though I couldn't see
if her face was showing any emotion, and that action at least was
authentic.

She apparently told him the bumper looked fine because he

dropped the dripping sponge into the bucket and went around behind the Winnebago. She went back inside, shutting the metal door behind her even though it had to be already at least a hundred and ten out, and they hadn't even bothered to park under what scanty shade the palms provided.

I put the longshot back in the car. The old man came around the front with a big plywood sign. He propped it against the vehicle's side. "The Last of the Winnebagos," the sign read in somebody's idea of what Indian writing should look like. "See a vanishing breed. Admission—Adults: $8.00, Children under twelve: $5.00 Open 9 A.M. to Sunset." He strung up a row of red and yellow flags, and then picked up the bucket and started toward the door, but halfway there he stopped and took a few steps down the parking lot to where I thought he probably had a good view of the road, and then went back, walking like an old man, and took another swipe at the bumper with the sponge.

"Are you done with the RV yet, McCombe?" Ramirez said on the car phone.

I slung the camera into the back. "I just got here. Every tanker in Arizona was on Van Buren this morning. Why the hell don't you have me do a piece on abuses of the multiway system by water haulers?"

"Because I want you to get to Tempe alive. The governor's press conference has been moved to one, so you're okay. Have you used the eisenstadt yet?"

"I told you, I just got here. I haven't even turned the damned thing on."

"You don't turn it on. It self-activates when you set it bottom down on a level surface."

Great. It had probably already shot its 100-frame cartridge on the way here.

"Well, if you don't use it on the Winnebago, make sure you use it at the governor's conference," she said. "By the way, have you thought any more about moving to investigative?"

That was why Sun-co was really so interested in the eisenstadt. It had been easier to send a photographer who could write stories than it had to send a photographer and a reporter, especially in the little one-seater Hitoris they were ordering now, which was how I got to be a photo-journalist. And since that had worked out so well, why send either? Send an eisenstadt and a DAT deck and you won't need an Hitori and way-mile credits to get them there. You can send them through the mail. They can sit unopened on the old governor's desk, and after a while somebody in a one-seater who wouldn't have to be either a photographer *or* a reporter can sneak in to retrieve them and a dozen others.

"No," I said, glancing back up the hill. The old man gave one last swipe to the front bumper and then walked over to one of the zoo's old stone-edged planters and dumped the bucket in on a tangle of prickly pear, which would probably think it was a spring shower and bloom before I made it up the hill. "Look, if I'm going to get any pictures before the touristas arrive, I'd better go."

"I wish you'd think about it. And use the eisenstadt this time. You'll like it once you try it. Even *you'll* forget it's a camera."

"I'll bet," I said. I looked back down the multiway. Nobody at all was coming now. Maybe that was what all the Amblers' anxiety was about—I should have asked Ramirez what their average daily attendance was and what sort of people used up credits to come this far out and see an old beat-up RV. The curve into Tempe alone was three point two miles. Maybe nobody came at all. If that was the case, I might have a chance of getting some decent pictures. I got in the Hitori and drove up the steep drive.

"Howdy," the old man said, all smiles, holding out his reddish-brown freckled hand to shake mine. "Name's Jake Ambler. And this here's Winnie," he said, patting the metal side of the RV, "last of the Winnebagos. Is there just the one of you?"

"David McCombe," I said, holding out my press pass. "I'm a photographer. Sun-co. Phoenix *Sun,* Tempe-Mesa *Tribune,* Glendale *Star,* and affiliated stations. I was wondering if I could take some pictures of your vehicle?" I touched my pocket and turned the taper on.

"You bet. We've always cooperated with the media, Mrs. Ambler and me. I was just cleaning old Winnie up," he said. "She got pretty dusty on the way down from Globe." He didn't make any attempt to tell his wife I was there, even though she could hardly avoid hearing us, and she didn't open the metal door again. "We been on the road now with Winnie for almost twenty years. Bought her in 1989 in Forest City, Iowa, where they were made. The wife didn't want to buy her, didn't know if she'd like traveling, but now she's the one wouldn't part with it."

He was well into his spiel now, an open, friendly, I-have-nothing-to-hide expression on his face that hid everything. There was no point in taking any stills, so I got out the vidcam and shot the TV footage while he led me around the RV.

"This up here," he said, standing with one foot on the flimsy metal ladder and patting the metal bar around the top, "is the luggage rack, and this is the holding tank. It'll hold thirty gallons and has an automatic electric pump that hooks up to any waste hookup. Empties in five minutes, and you don't even get your hands dirty." He held up his fat pink hands palms forward as if to show me. "Water tank," he said, slapping a silver metal tank next to it. "Holds forty gallons, which is plenty for just the two of us. Interior space is a hundred fifty cubic feet with six feet four of headroom. That's plenty even for a tall guy like yourself."

He gave me the whole tour. His manner was easy, just short of slap-on-the-back hearty, but he looked relieved when an ancient VW bug came chugging catty-cornered up through the parking lot. He must have thought they wouldn't have any customers either.

A family piled out, Japanese tourists, a woman with short black hair, a man in shorts, two kids. One of the kids had a ferret on a leash.

"I'll just look around while you tend to the paying customers," I told him.

I locked the vidcam in the car, took the longshot, and went up toward the zoo. I took a wide-angle of the zoo sign for Ramirez. I could see it now—she'd run a caption like, "The old zoo stands empty today. No sound of lion's roar, of elephant's trumpeting, of children's laughter, can be heard here. The old Phoenix Zoo, last of its kind, while just outside its gates stands yet another last of its kind. Story on page 10." Maybe it would be a good idea to let the eisenstadts and the computers take over.

I went inside. I hadn't been out here in years. In the late

eighties there had been a big flap over zoo policy. I had taken the pictures, but I hadn't covered the story since there were still such things as reporters back then. I had photographed the cages in question and the new zoo director who had caused all the flap by stopping the zoo's renovation project cold and giving the money to a wildlife protection group.

"I refuse to spend money on cages when in a few years we'll have nothing to put in them. The timber wolf, the California condor, the grizzly bear, are in imminent danger of becoming extinct, and it's our responsibility to save them, not make a comfortable prison for the last survivors."

The Society had called him an alarmist, which just goes to show you how much things can change. Well, he was an alarmist, wasn't he? The grizzly bear isn't extinct in the wild—it's Colorado's biggest tourist draw, and there are so many whooping cranes Texas is talking about limited hunting.

In all the uproar, the zoo had ceased to exist, and the animals all went to an even more comfortable prison in Sun City—sixteen acres of savannah land for the zebras and lions, and snow manufactured daily for the polar bears.

They hadn't really been cages, in spite of what the zoo director said. The old capybara enclosure, which was the first thing inside the gate, was a nice little meadow with a low stone wall around it. A family of prairie dogs had taken up residence in the middle of it.

I went back to the gate and looked down at the Winnebago. The family circled the Winnebago, the man bending down to look underneath the body. One of the kids was hanging off the ladder at the back of the RV. The ferret was nosing around the front wheel Jake Ambler had so carefully scrubbed down, looking like it was about ready to lift its leg, if ferrets do that. The kid yanked on its leash and then picked it up in his arms. The mother said something to him. Her nose was sunburned.

Katie's nose had been sunburned. She had had that white cream on it, that skiers used to use. She was wearing a parka and jeans and bulky pink-and-white moonboots that she couldn't run in, but she still made it to Aberfan before I did. I pushed past her and knelt over him.

"I hit him," she said bewilderedly. "I hit a dog."

"Get back in the jeep, damn it!" I shouted at her. I stripped off my sweater and tried to wrap him in it. "We've got to get him to the vet."

"Is he dead?" Katie said, her face as pale as the cream on her nose.

"No!" I had shouted. "No, he isn't dead."

The mother turned and looked up toward the zoo, her hand shading her face. She caught sight of the camera, dropped her hand, and smiled, a toothy, impossible smile. People in the public eye are the worst, but even people having a snapshot taken close down somehow, and it isn't just the phony smile. It's as if that old superstition is true, and cameras do really steal the soul.

I pretended to take her picture and then lowered the camera. The zoo director had put up a row of tombstone-shaped signs in front of the gate, one for each endangered species. They were covered with plastic, which hadn't helped much. I wiped the streaky dust off the one in front of me. "Canis latrans," it said, with two green stars after it. "Coyote. North American wild dog. Due to large-scale poisoning by ranchers, who saw it as a threat to cattle and sheep, the coyote is nearly extinct in the wild." Underneath there was a photograph of a ragged coyote sitting on its haunches and an explanation of the stars. Blue—endangered species. Yellow—endangered habitat. Red—extinct in the wild.

After Misha died, I had come out here to photograph the dingo and the coyotes and the wolves, but they were already in the process of moving the zoo, so I couldn't get any pictures, and it probably wouldn't have done any good. The coyote in the picture had faded to a greenish-yellow and its yellow eyes were almost white, but it stared out of the picture looking as hearty and unconcerned as Jake Ambler, wearing its camera face.

The mother had gone back to the bug and was herding the kids inside. Mr. Ambler walked the father back to the car, shaking his shining bald head, and the man talked some more, leaning on the open door, and then got in and drove off. I walked back down.

If he was bothered by the fact that they had only stayed ten minutes and that, as far as I had been able to see, no money had

changed hands, it didn't show in his face. He led me around to
the side of the RV and pointed to a chipped and faded collection
of decals along the painted bar of the W. "These here are the
states we've been in." He pointed to the one nearest the front.
"Every state in the Union, plus Canada and Mexico. Last state we
were in was Nevada."

Up this close it was easy to see where he had painted out the
name of the original RV and covered it with the bar of red. The
paint had the dull look of un-authenticity. He had covered up the
"Open Road" with a burnt-wood plaque that read, "The Amblin'
Amblers."

He pointed at a bumper sticker next to the door that said, "I
got lucky in Vegas at Caesar's Palace," and had a picture of a
naked showgirl. "We couldn't find a decal for Nevada. I don't
think they make them anymore. And you know something else
you can't find? Steering wheel covers. You know the kind. That
keep the wheel from burning your hands when it gets hot?"

"Do you do all the driving?" I asked.

He hesitated before answering, and I wondered if one of
them didn't have a license. I'd have to look it up in the lifeline.
"Mrs. Ambler spells me sometimes, but I do most of it. Mrs.
Ambler reads the map. Damn maps nowadays are so hard to read.
Half the time you can't tell what kind of road it is. They don't
make them like they used to."

We talked for a while more about all the things you couldn't
find a decent one of anymore and the sad state things had gotten
in generally, and then I announced I wanted to talk to Mrs.
Ambler, got the vidcam and the eisenstadt out of the car, and
went inside the Winnebago.

She still had the dishtowel in her hand, even though there
couldn't possibly be space for that many dishes in the tiny RV.
The inside was even smaller than I had thought it would be, low
enough that I had to duck and so narrow I had to hold the Nikon
close to my body to keep from hitting the lens on the passenger
seat. It felt like an oven inside, and it was only nine o'clock in
the morning.

I set the eisenstadt down on the kitchen counter, making sure its concealed lens was facing out. If it would work anywhere, it would be here. There was basically nowhere for Mrs. Ambler to go that she could get out of range. There was nowhere I could go either, and sorry, Ramirez, there are just some things a live photographer can do better than a preprogrammed one, like stay out of the picture.

"This is the galley," Mrs. Ambler said, folding her dishtowel and hanging it from a plastic ring on the cupboard below the sink with the cross-stitch design showing. It wasn't a rooster after all. It was a poodle wearing a sunbonnet and carrying a basket. "Shop on Wednesday," the motto underneath said.

"As you can see, we have a double sink with a hand-pump faucet. The refrigerator is LP-electric and holds four cubic feet. Back here is the dinette area. The table folds up into the rear wall, and we have our bed. And this is our bathroom."

She was as bad as her husband. "How long have you had the Winnebago?" I said to stop the spiel. Sometimes, if you can get people talking about something besides what they intended to talk about, you can disarm them into something like a natural expression.

"Nineteen years," she said, lifting up the lid of the chemical toilet. "We bought it in 1989. I didn't want to buy it—I didn't like the idea of selling our house and going gallivanting off like a couple of hippies, but Jake went ahead and bought it, and now I wouldn't trade it for anything. The shower operates on a forty-gallon pressurized water system." She stood back so I could get a picture of the shower stall, so narrow you wouldn't have to worry about dropping the soap. I dutifully took some vidcam footage.

"You live here full-time then?" I said, trying not to let my voice convey how impossible that prospect sounded. Ramirez had said they were from Minnesota. I had assumed they had a house there and only went on the road for part of the year.

"Jake says the great outdoors is our home," she said. I gave up trying to get a picture of her and snapped a few high-quality detail stills for the papers: the "Pilot" sign taped on the dashboard in front of the driver's seat, the crocheted granny-square afghan on the uncomfortable-looking couch, a row of salt and pepper shakers in the back windows—Indian children, black scottie dogs, ears of corn.

"Sometimes we live on the open prairies and sometimes on the seashore," she said. She went over to the sink and hand-pumped a scant two cups of water into a little pan and set it on the two-burner stove. She took down two turquoise melmac cups and flowered saucers and a jar of freeze-dried and spooned a little into the cups. "Last year we were in the Colorado Rockies. We can have a house on a lake or in the desert, and when we get tired of it, we just move on. Oh, my, the things we've seen."

I didn't believe her. Colorado had been one of the first states to ban recreational vehicles, even before the gas crunch and the multiways. It had banned them on the passes first and then shut them out of the national forests, and by the time I left they weren't even allowed on the interstates.

Ramirez had said RVs were banned outright in forty-seven states. New Mexico was one, Utah had heavy restricks, and daytime travel was forbidden in all the western states. Whatever they'd seen, and it sure wasn't Colorado, they had seen it in the dark or on some unpatrolled multiway, going like sixty to outrun the cameras. Not exactly the footloose and fancy-free life they tried to paint.

The water boiled. Mrs. Ambler poured it into the cups, spilling a little on the turquoise saucers. She blotted it up with the dishtowel. "We came down here because of the snow. They get winter so early in Colorado."

"I know," I said. It had snowed two feet, and it was only the middle of September. Nobody even had their snow tires on. The aspens hadn't even turned yet, and some of the branches broke under the weight of the snow. Katie's nose was still sunburned from the summer.

"Where did you come from just now?" I asked her.

"Globe," she said, and opened the door to yell to her husband. "Jake! Coffee!" She carried the cups to the table-that-converts-into-a-bed. "It has leaves that you can put in it so it seats six," she said.

I sat down at the table so she was on the side where the

eisenstadt could catch her. The sun was coming in through the cranked-open back windows, already hot. Mrs. Ambler got onto her knees on the plaid cushions and let down a woven cloth shade, carefully, so it wouldn't knock the salt and pepper shakers off.

There were some snapshots stuck up between the ceramic ears of corn. I picked one up. It was a square Polaroid from the days when you had to peel off the print and glue it to a stiff card: the two of them, looking exactly the way they did now, with that friendly, impenetrable camera smile, were standing in front of a blur of orange rock—the Grand Canyon? Zion? Monument Valley? Polaroid had always chosen color over definition. Mrs. Ambler was holding a little yellow blur in her arms that could have been a cat but wasn't. It was a dog.

"That's Jake and me at Devil's Tower," she said, taking the picture away from me. "And Taco. You can't tell from this picture, but she was the cutest little thing. A chihuahua." She handed it back to me and rummaged behind the salt and pepper shakers. "Sweetest little dog you ever saw. This will give you a better idea."

The picture she handed me was considerably better, a matte print done with a decent camera. Mrs. Ambler was holding the chihuahua in this one, too, standing in front of the Winnebago.

"She used to sit on the arm of Jake's chair while he drove and when we came to a red light she'd look at it, and when it turned green she'd bark to tell him to go. She was the smartest little thing."

I looked at the dog's flaring, pointed ears, its bulging eyes and rat's snout. The dogs never come through. I took dozens of pictures, there at the end, and they might as well have been calendar shots. Nothing of the real dog at all. I decided it was the lack of muscles in their faces—they could not smile, in spite of what their owners claimed. It is the muscles in the face that make people leap across the years in pictures. The expressions on dogs' faces were what breeding had fastened on them—the gloomy bloodhound, the alert collie, the rakish mutt—and anything else was wishful thinking on the part of the doting master, who would also swear that a color-blind chihuahua with a brain pan the size of a Mexican jumping bean could tell when the light changed.

My theory of the facial muscles doesn't really hold water, of course. Cats can't smile either, and they come through. Smugness, slyness, disdain—all of those expressions come through beautifully, and they don't have any muscles in their faces either, so maybe it's love that you can't capture in a picture because love was the only expression dogs were capable of.

I was still looking at the picture. "She is a cute little thing," I said and handed it back to her. "She wasn't very big, was she?"

"I could carry Taco in my jacket pocket. We didn't name her Taco. We got her from a man in California that named her that," she said, as if she could see herself that the dog didn't come through in the picture. As if, had she named the dog herself, it would have been different. Then the name would have been a more real name, and Taco would have, by default, become more real as well. As if a name could convey what the picture didn't— all the things the little dog did and was and meant to her.

Names don't do it either, of course. I had named Aberfan myself. The vet's assistant, when he heard it, typed it in as Abraham.

"Age?" he had said calmly, even though he had no business typing all this into a computer, he should have been in the operating room with the vet.

"You've got that in there, damn it," I shouted.

He looked calmly puzzled. "I don't show any Abraham . . ."

"Aberfan, damn it. Aberfan!"

"Here it is," the assistant said imperturbably.

Katie, standing across the desk, looked up from the screen. "He had the newparvo and lived through it?" she said bleakly.

"He had the newparvo and lived through it," I said, "until you came along."

"I had an Australian shepherd," I told Mrs. Ambler.

Jake came into the Winnebago, carrying the plastic bucket. "Well, it's about time," Mrs. Ambler said. "Your coffee's getting cold."

"I was just going to finish washing off Winnie," he said. He wedged the bucket into the tiny sink and began pumping vigorously with the heel of his hand. "She got mighty dusty coming down through all that sand."

"I was telling Mr. McCombe here about Taco," she said, getting up and taking him the cup and saucer. "Here, drink your coffee before it gets cold."

"I'll be in in a minute," he said. He stopped pumping and tugged the bucket out of the sink.

"Mr. McCombe had a dog," she said, still holding the cup out to him. "He had an Australian shepherd. I was telling him about Taco."

"He's not interested in that," Jake said. They exchanged one of those warning looks that married couples are so good at. "Tell him about the Winnebago. That's what he's here for."

Jake went back outside. I screwed the longshot's lens cap on and put the vidcam back in its case. She took the little pan off the miniature stove and poured the coffee back into it. "I think I've got all the pictures I need," I said to her back.

She didn't turn around. "He never liked Taco. He wouldn't even let her sleep on the bed with us. Said it made his legs cramp. A little dog like that that didn't weigh anything."

I took the longshot's lens cap back off.

"You know what we were doing the day she died? We were out shopping. I didn't want to leave her alone, but Jake said she'd be fine. It was ninety degrees that day, and he just kept on going from store to store, and when we got back she was dead." She set the pan on the stove and turned on the burner. "The vet said it was the newparvo, but it wasn't. She died from the heat, poor little thing."

I set the Nikon down gently on the formica table and estimated the settings.

"When did Taco die?" I asked her, to make her turn around.

"Ninety," she said. She turned back to me, and I let my hand come down on the button in an almost soundless click, but her public face was still in place: apologetic now, smiling, a little sheepish. "My, that was a long time ago."

I stood up and collected my cameras. "I think I've got all the pictures I need," I said again. "If I don't, I'll come back out."

"Don't forget your briefcase," she said, handing me the eisenstadt. "Did your dog die of the newparvo, too?"

"He died fifteen years ago," I said. "In ninety-three."

She nodded understandingly. "The third wave," she said.

I went outside. Jake was standing behind the Winnebago, under the back window, holding the bucket. He shifted it to his left hand and held out his right hand to me. "You get all the pictures you needed?" he asked.

"Yeah," I said. "I think your wife showed me about everything." I shook his hand.

"You come on back out if you need any more pictures," he said, and sounded, if possible, even more jovial, open-handed, friendly than he had before. "Mrs. Ambler and me, we always cooperate with the media."

"Your wife was telling me about your chihuahua," I said, more to see the effect on him than anything else.

"Yeah, the wife still misses that little dog after all these years," he said, and he looked the way she had, mildly apologetic, still smiling. "It died of the newparvo. I told her she ought to get it vaccinated, but she kept putting it off." He shook his head. "Of course, it wasn't really her fault. You know whose fault the newparvo really was, don't you?"

Yeah, I knew. It was the communists' fault, and it didn't matter that all their dogs had died, too, because he would say their chemical warfare had gotten out of hand or that everybody knows commies hate dogs. Or maybe it was the fault of the Japanese, though I doubted that. He was, after all, in a tourist business. Or the Democrats or the atheists or all of them put together, and even that was 100% Authentic—portrait of the kind of man who drives a Winnebago—but I didn't want to hear it. I walked over to the Hitori and slung the eisenstadt in the back.

"You know who really killed your dog, don't you?" he called after me.

"Yes," I said, and got in the car.

I went home, fighting my way through a fleet of red-painted water tankers who weren't even bothering to try to outrun the cameras and thinking about Taco. My grandmother had had a chihuahua. Perdita. Meanest dog that ever lived. Used to lurk behind the door waiting to take Labrador-sized chunks out of my leg. And my grandmother's. It developed some lingering chihuahuan ailment that made it incontinent and even more illtempered, if that was possible.

Toward the end, it wouldn't even let my grandmother near it, but she refused to have it put to sleep and was unfailingly kind to it, even though I never saw any indication that the dog felt anything but unrelieved spite toward her. If the newparvo hadn't come along, it probably would still have been around making her life miserable.

I wondered what Taco, the wonder dog, able to distinguish red and green at a single intersection, had really been like, and if it had died of heat prostration. And what it had been like for the Amblers, living all that time in a hundred and fifty cubic feet together and blaming each other for their own guilt.

I called Ramirez as soon as I got home, breaking in without announcing myself, the way she always did. "I need a lifeline," I said.

"I'm glad you called," she said. "You got a call from the Society. And how's this as a slant for your story? 'The Winnebago and the Winnebagos.' They're an Indian tribe. In Minnesota, I think—why the hell aren't you at the governor's conference?"

"I came home," I said. "What did the Society want?"

"They didn't say. They asked for your schedule. I told them you were with the governor in Tempe. Is this about a story?"

"Yeah."

"Well, you run a proposal past me before you write it. The last thing the paper needs is to get in trouble with the Society."

"The lifeline's for Katherine Powell." I spelled it.

She spelled it back to me. "Is she connected with the Society story?"

"No."

"Then what is she connected with? I've got to put something on the request-for-info."

"Put down background."

"For the Winnebago story?"

"Yes," I said. "For the Winnebago story. How long will it take?"

"That depends. When do you plan to tell me why you

ditched the governor's conference? *And* Taliessin West. Jesus Maria, I'll have to call the *Republic* and see if they'll trade footage. I'm sure they'll be thrilled to have shots of an extinct RV. That is, assuming you got any shots. You did make it out to the zoo, didn't you?"

"Yes. I got vidcam footage, stills, the works. I even used the eisenstadt."

"Mind sending your pictures in while I look up your old flame, or is that too much to ask? I don't know how long this will take. It took me two days to get clearance on the Amblers. Do you want the whole thing—pictures, documentation?"

"No. Just a resume. And a phone number."

She cut out, still not saying goodbye. If phones still had receivers, Ramirez would be a great one for hanging up on people. I highwired the vidcam footage and the eisenstadts in to the paper and then fed the eisenstadt cartridge into the developer. I was more than a little curious about what kind of pictures it would take, in spite of the fact that it was trying to do me out of a job. At least it used high-res film and not some damn two hundred thousand-pixel TV substitute. I didn't believe it could compose, and I doubted if the eisenstadt would be able to do foreground-background either, but it might, under certain circumstances, get a picture I couldn't.

The doorbell rang. I answered the door. A lanky young man in a Hawaiian shirt and baggies was standing on the front step, and there was another man in a Society uniform out in the driveway.

"Mr. McCombe?" he said, extending a hand. "Jim Hunter. Humane Society."

I don't know what I'd expected—that they wouldn't bother to trace the call? That they'd let somebody get away with leaving a dead animal on the road?

"I just wanted to stop by and thank you on behalf of the Society for phoning in that report on the jackal. Can I come in?"

He smiled, an open, friendly, smug smile, as if he expected me to be stupid enough to say, "I don't know what you're talking about," and slam the screen door on his hand.

"Just doing my duty," I said, smiling back at him.

"Well, we really appreciate responsible citizens like you. It makes our job a whole lot easier." He pulled a folded readout from his shirt pocket. "I just need to double-check a couple of things. You're a reporter for Sun-co, is that right?"

"Photo-journalist," I said.

"And the Hitori you were driving belongs to the paper?"

I nodded.

"It has a phone. Why didn't you use it to make the call?"

The uniform was bending over the Hitori.

"I didn't realize it had a phone. The paper just bought the Hitoris. This is only the second time I've had one out."

Since they knew the paper had had phones put in, they also knew what I'd just told them. I wondered where they'd gotten the info. Public phones were supposed to be tap-free, and if they'd read the license number off one of the cameras, they wouldn't know who'd had the car unless they'd talked to Ramirez, and if they'd talked to her, she wouldn't have been talking blithely about the last thing she needed being trouble with the Society.

"You didn't know the car had a phone," he said, "so you drove to—" He consulted the readout, somehow giving the impression he was taking notes. I'd have bet there was a taper in the pocket of that shirt. "—the 7-Eleven at McDowell and Forti-eth Street, and made the call from there. Why didn't you give the Society rep your name and address?"

"I was in a hurry," I said. "I had two assignments to cover before noon, the second out in Scottsdale."

"Which is why you didn't render assistance to the animal either. Because you were in a hurry."

You bastard, I thought. "No," I said. "I didn't render assistance because there wasn't any assistance to be rendered. The—it was dead."

"And how did you know that, Mr. McCombe?"

"There was blood coming out of its mouth," I said.

I had thought that that was a good sign, that he wasn't bleeding anywhere else. The blood had come out of Aberfan's mouth when he tried to lift his head, just a little trickle, sinking into the hard-packed snow. It had stopped before we even got him into the car. "It's all right, boy," I told him. "We'll be there in a minute."

Katie started the car, killed it, started it again, backed it up to where she could turn around.

Aberfan lay limply across my lap, his tail against the gear shift. "Just lie still, boy," I said. I patted his neck. It was wet, and I raised my hand and looked at the palm, afraid it was blood. It was only water from the melted snow. I dried his neck and the top of his head with the sleeve of my sweater.

"How far is it?" Katie said. She was clutching the steering wheel with both hands and sitting stiffly forward in the seat. The windshield wipers flipped back and forth, trying to keep up with the snow.

"About five miles," I said, and she stepped on the gas pedal and then let up on it again as we began to skid. "On the right side of the highway."

Aberfan raised his head off my lap and looked at me. His gums were gray, and he was panting, but I couldn't see any more blood. He tried to lick my hand. "You'll make it, Aberfan," I said. "You made it before, remember?"

"But you didn't get out of the car and go check, to make sure it was dead?" Hunter said.

"No."

"And you don't have any idea who hit the jackal?" he said, and made it sound like the accusation it was.

"No."

He glanced back at the uniform, who had moved around the car to the other side. "Whew," Hunter said, shaking his Hawaiian collar, "it's like an oven out here. Mind if I come in?" which meant the uniform needed more privacy. Well, then, by all means, give him more privacy. The sooner he sprayed print-fix on the bumper and tires and peeled off the incriminating traces of jackal blood that weren't there and stuck them in the evidence bags he was carrying in the pockets of that uniform, the sooner they'd leave. I opened the screen door wider.

"Oh, this is great," Hunter said, still trying to generate a breeze with his collar. These old adobe houses stay so cool. He glanced around the room at the developer and the enlarger, the couch, the dry-mounted photographs on the wall. "You don't have any idea who might have hit the jackal?"

"I figure it was a tanker," I said. "What else would be on Van Buren that time of morning?"

I was almost sure it had been a car or a small truck. A tanker would have left the jackal a spot on the pavement. But a tanker would get a license suspension and two weeks of having to run water into Santa Fe instead of Phoenix, and probably not that. Rumor at the paper had it the Society was in the water board's pocket. If it was a car, on the other hand, the Society would take away the car and stick its driver with a prison sentence.

"They're all trying to beat the cameras," I said. "The tanker probably didn't even know it'd hit it."

"What?" he said.

"I said, it had to be a tanker. There isn't anything else on Van Buren during rush hour."

I expected him to say, "Except for you," but he didn't. He wasn't even listening. "Is this your dog?" he said.

He was looking at the photograph of Perdita. "No," I said. "That was my grandmother's dog."

"What is it?"

A nasty little beast. And when it died of the newparvo, my grandmother had cried like a baby. "A chihuahua."

He looked around at the other walls. "Did you take all these pictures of dogs?" His whole manner had changed, taking on a politeness that made me realize just how insolent he had intended to be before. The one on the road wasn't the only jackal around.

"Some of them," I said. He was looking at the photograph next to it. I didn't take that one.

"I know what this one is," he said, pointing at it. "It's a boxer, right?"

"An English bulldog," I said.

"Oh, right. Weren't those the ones that were exterminated? For being vicious?"

"No," I said.

He moved on to the picture over the developer, like a tourist in a museum. "I bet you didn't take this one either," he said, pointing at the high shoes, the old-fashioned hat on the stout old woman holding the dogs in her arms.

"That's a photograph of Beatrix Potter, the English children's author," I said. "She wrote *Peter Rabbit.*"

He wasn't interested. "What kind of dogs are those?"

"Pekingese."

"It's a great picture of them."

It is, in fact, a terrible picture of them. One of them has wrenched his face away from the camera, and the other sits grimly in her owner's hand, waiting for its chance. Obviously neither of them liked having its picture taken, though you can't tell that from their expressions. They reveal nothing in their little flat-nosed faces, in their black little eyes.

Beatrix Potter, on the other hand, comes through beautifully, in spite of the attempt to smile for the camera and the fact that she must have had to hold onto the Pekes for dear life, or maybe because of that. The fierce, humorous love she felt for her fierce, humorous little dogs is all there in her face. She must never, in spite of *Peter Rabbit* and its attendant fame, have developed a public face. Everything she felt was right there, unprotected, unshuttered. Like Katie.

"Are any of these your dog?" Hunter asked. He was standing looking at the picture of Misha that hung above the couch.

"No," I said.

"How come you don't have any pictures of your dog?" he asked, and I wondered how he knew I had had a dog and what else he knew.

"He didn't like having his picture taken."

He folded up the readout, stuck it in his pocket, and turned around to look at the photo of Perdita again. "He looks like he was a real nice little dog," he said.

The uniform was waiting on the front step, obviously finished with whatever he had done to the car.

"We'll let you know if we find out who's responsible," Hunter said, and they left. On the way out to the street the uniform tried to tell him what he'd found, but Hunter cut him off. The suspect has a house full of photographs of dogs, therefore he didn't run over a poor facsimile of one on Van Buren this morning. Case closed.

I went back over to the developer and fed the eisenstadt film in. "Positives, one two three order, five seconds," I said, and watched as the pictures came up on the developer's screen. Ramirez had said the eisenstadt automatically turned on whenever it was set upright on a level surface. She was right. It had taken a half-dozen shots on the way out to Tempe. Two shots of the Hitori it must have taken when I set it down to load the car, open door of same with prickly pear in the foreground, a blurred shot of palm trees and buildings with a minuscule, sharp-focused glimpse of the traffic on the expressway. Vehicles and people. There was a great shot of the red tanker that had clipped the jackal and ten or so of the yucca I had parked next to at the foot of the hill.

It had gotten two nice shots of my forearm as I set it down on the kitchen counter of the Winnebago and some beautifully composed still lifes of Melmac With Spoons. Vehicles and people. The rest of the pictures were dead losses: my back, the open bathroom door, Jake's back, and Mrs. Ambler's public face.

Except the last one. She had been standing right in front of the eisenstadt, looking almost directly into the lens. "When I think of that poor thing, all alone," she had said, and by the time she turned around she had her public face back on, but for a minute there, looking at what she thought was a briefcase and remembering, there she was, the person I had tried all morning to get a picture of.

I took it into the living room and sat down and looked at it awhile.

"So you knew this Katherine Powell in Colorado," Ramirez said, breaking in without preamble, and the highwire slid silently forward and began to print out the lifeline. "I always suspected you of having some deep dark secret in your past. Is she the reason you moved to Phoenix?"

I was watching the highwire advance the paper. Katherine Powell. 4628 Dutchman Drive, Apache Junction. Forty miles away.

"Holy Mother, you were really cradle-robbing. According to my calculations, she was seventeen when you lived there."

Sixteen.

"Are you the owner of the dog?" the vet had asked her, his face slackening into pity when he saw how young she was.

"No," she said. "I'm the one who hit him."

"My God," he said. "How old are you?"

"Sixteen," she said, and her face was wide open. "I just got my license."

"Aren't you even going to tell me what she has to do with this Winnebago thing?" Ramirez said.

"I moved down here to get away from the snow," I said, and cut out without saying goodbye.

The lifeline was still rolling silently forward. Hacker at Hewlett-Packard. Fired in ninety-nine, probably during the unionization. Divorced. Two kids. She had moved to Arizona five years after I did. Management programmer for Toshiba. Arizona driver's license.

I went back to the developer and looked at the picture of Mrs. Ambler. I had said dogs never came through. That wasn't true. Taco wasn't in the blurry Polaroids Mrs. Ambler had been so anxious to show me, in the stories she had been so anxious to tell. But he was in this picture, reflected in the pain and love and loss on Mrs. Ambler's face. I could see him plain as day, perched on the arm of the driver's seat, barking impatiently when the light turned green.

I put a new cartridge in the eisenstadt and went out to see Katie.

I had to take Van Buren—it was almost four o'clock, and the rush hour would have started on the dividers—but the jackal was gone anyway. The Society is efficient. Like Hitler and his Nazis.

"Why don't you have any pictures of your dog?" Hunter had asked. The question could have been based on the assumption that anyone who would fill his living room with photographs of dogs must have had one of his own, but it wasn't. He had known about Aberfan, which meant he'd had access to my lifeline, which meant all kinds of things. My lifeline was privacy-coded, so I had to be notified before anybody could get access, except, it appeared, the Society. A reporter I knew at the paper, Dolores Chiwere, had tried to do a story a while back claiming that the Society had an illegal link to the lifeline banks, but she hadn't been able to come up with enough evidence to convince her editor. I wondered if this counted.

The lifeline would have told them about Aberfan but not about how he died. Killing a dog wasn't a crime in those days, and I hadn't pressed charges against Katie for reckless driving or even called the police.

"I think you should," the vet's assistant had said. "There are less than a hundred dogs left. People can't just go around killing them."

"My God, man, it was snowing and slick," the vet had said angrily, "and she's just a kid."

"She's old enough to have a license," I said, looking at Katie. She was fumbling in her purse for her driver's license. "She's old enough to have been on the roads."

Katie found her license and gave it to me. It was so new it was still shiny. Katherine Powell. She had turned sixteen two weeks ago.

"This won't bring him back," the vet had said, and taken the license out of my hand and given it back to her. "You go on home now."

"I need her name for the records," the vet's assistant had said.

She had stepped forward. "Katie Powell," she had said.

"We'll do the paperwork later," the vet had said firmly.

They never did do the paperwork, though. The next week the third wave hit, and I suppose there hadn't seemed any point.

I slowed down at the zoo entrance and looked up into the parking lot. The Amblers were doing a booming business. There were at least five cars and twice as many kids clustered around the Winnebago.

"Where the hell are you?" Ramirez said. "And where the hell are your pictures? I talked the *Republic* into a trade, but they insisted on scoop rights. I need your stills now!"

"I'll send them in as soon as I get home," I said. "I'm on a story."

"The hell you are! You're on your way out to see your old girlfriend. Well, not on the papers' credits, you're not."

"Did you get the stuff on the Winnebago Indians?" I asked her.

"Yes. They were in Wisconsin, but they're not anymore. In the mid-seventies there were sixteen hundred of them on the reservation and about forty-five hundred altogether, but by 1990, the number was down to five hundred, and now they don't think there are any left, and nobody knows what happened to them."

I'll tell you what happened to them, I thought. Almost all of them were killed in the first wave, and people blamed the government and the Japanese and the ozone layer, and after the second wave hit, the Society passed all kinds of laws to protect the survivors, but it was too late, they were already below the minimum survival population limit, and then the third wave polished off the rest of them, and the last of the Winnebagos sat in a cage somewhere, and if I had been there I would probably have taken his picture.

"I called the Bureau of Indian Affairs," Ramirez said, "and they're supposed to call me back, and you don't give a damn about the Winnebagos. You just wanted to get me off the subject. What's this story you're on?"

I looked around the dashboard for an exclusion button.

"What the hell is going on, David? First you ditch two big stories, now you can't even get your pictures in. Jesus, if something's wrong, you can tell me. I want to help. It has something to do with Colorado, doesn't it?"

I found the button and cut her off.

Van Buren got crowded as the afternoon rush spilled over off the dividers. Out past the curve, where Van Buren turns into Apache Boulevard, they were putting in new lanes. The cement forms were already up on the eastbound side, and they were building the wooden forms up in two of the six lanes on my side.

The Amblers must have just beaten the workmen, though at the rate the men were working right now, leaning on their

shovels in the hot afternoon sun and smoking stew, it had probably taken them six weeks to do this stretch.

Mesa was still open multiway, but as soon as I was through
downtown, the construction started again, and this stretch was
nearly done—forms up on both sides and most of the cement
poured. The Amblers couldn't have come in from Globe on this
road. The lanes were barely wide enough for the Hitori, and the
tanker lanes were gated. Superstition is full-divided, and the old
highway down from Roosevelt is, too, which meant they hadn't
come in from Globe at all. I wondered how they had come
in—probably in some tanker lane on a multiway.

"Oh, my, the things we've seen," Mrs. Ambler had said. I
wondered how much they'd been able to see skittering across the
dark desert like a couple of kangaroo mice, trying to beat the
cameras.

The roadworkers didn't have the new exit signs up yet, and
I missed the exit for Apache Junction and had to go halfway to
Superior, trapped in my narrow, cement-sided lane, till I hit a
change-lanes and could get turned around.

Katie's address was in Superstition Estates, a development
pushed up as close to the base of Superstition Mountain as it
could get. I thought about what I would say to Katie when I got
there. I had said maybe ten sentences altogether to her, most of
them shouted directions, in the two hours we had been together.
In the jeep on the way to the vet's I had talked to Aberfan, and
after we got there, sitting in the waiting room, we hadn't talked
at all.

It occurred to me that I might not recognize her. I didn't
really remember what she looked like—only the sunburned nose
and that terrible openness, and now, fifteen years later, it
seemed unlikely that she would have either of them. The Arizona
sun would have taken care of the first, and she had gotten married
and divorced, been fired, had who knows what else happen to her
in fifteen years to close her face. In which case, there had been
no point in my driving all the way out here. But Mrs. Ambler had
had an almost impenetrable public face, and you could still catch
her off-guard. If you got her talking about the dogs. If she didn't
know she was being photographed.

Katie's house was an old-style passive solar, with flat black panels on the roof. It looked presentable, but not compulsively neat. There wasn't any grass—tankers won't waste their credits coming this far out, and Apache Junction isn't big enough to match the bribes and incentives of Phoenix or Tempe—but the front yard was laid out with alternating patches of black lava chips and prickly pear. The side yard had a parched-looking palo verde tree, and there was a cat tied to it. A little girl was playing under it with toy cars.

I took the eisenstadt out of the back and went up to the front door and rang the bell. At the last moment, when it was too late to change my mind, walk away, because she was already opening the screen door, it occurred to me that she might not recognize me, that I might have to tell her who I was.

Her nose wasn't sunburned, and she had put on the weight a sixteen-year-old puts on to get to be thirty, but otherwise she looked the same as she had that day in front of my house. And her face hadn't completely closed. I could tell, looking at her, that she recognized me and that she had known I was coming. She must have put a notify on her lifeline to have them warn her if I asked her whereabouts. I thought about what that meant.

She opened the screen door a little, the way I had to the Humane Society. "What do you want?" she said.

I had never seen her angry, not even when I turned on her at the vet's. "I wanted to see you," I said.

I had thought I might tell her I had run across her name while I was working on a story and wondered if it was the same person or that I was doing a piece on the last of the passive solars. "I saw a dead jackal on the road this morning," I said.

"And you thought I killed it?" she said. She tried to shut the screen door.

I put out my hand without thinking to stop her. "No," I said. I took my hand off the door. "No, of course I don't think that. Can I come in? I just want to talk to you."

The little girl had come over, clutching her toy cars to her pink T-shirt, and was standing off to the side, watching curiously.

"Come on inside, Jana," Katie said, and opened the screen door a fraction wider. The little girl scooted through. "Go on in the kitchen," she said. "I'll fix you some Kool-Aid." She looked up at me. "I used to have nightmares about your coming. I'd dream that I'd go to the door and there you'd be."

"It's really hot out here," I said and knew I sounded like Hunter. "Can I come in?"

She opened the screen door all the way. "I've got to make my daughter something to drink," she said, and led the way into the kitchen, the little girl dancing in front of her.

"What kind of Kool-Aid do you want?" Katie asked her, and she shouted, "Red!"

The kitchen counter faced the stove, refrigerator, and water cooler across a narrow aisle that opened out into an alcove with a table and chairs. I put the eisenstadt down on the table and then sat down myself so she wouldn't suggest moving into another room.

Katie reached a plastic pitcher down from one of the shelves and stuck it under the water tank to fill it. Jana dumped her cars on the counter, clambered up beside them, and began opening the cupboard doors.

"How old's your little girl?" I asked.

Katie got a wooden spoon out of the drawer next to the stove and brought it and the pitcher over to the table. "She's four," she said. "Did you find the Kool-Aid?" she asked the little girl.

"Yes," the little girl said, but it wasn't Kool-Aid. It was a pinkish cube she peeled a plastic wrapping off of. It fizzed and turned a thinnish red when she dropped it in the pitcher. Kool-Aid must have become extinct, too, along with Winnebagos and passive solar. Or else changed beyond recognition. Like the Humane Society.

Katie poured the red stuff into a glass with a cartoon whale on it.

"Is she your only one?" I asked.

"No, I have a little boy," she said, but warily, as if she wasn't sure she wanted to tell me, even though if I'd requested the lifeline I already had access to all this information. Jana asked if she could have a cookie and then took it and her Kool-Aid back down the hall and outside. I could hear the screen door slam.

Katie put the pitcher in the refrigerator and leaned against the kitchen counter, her arms folded across her chest. "What do you want?"

She was just out of range of the eisenstadt, her face in the shadow of the narrow aisle.

"There was a dead jackal on the road this morning," I said. I kept my voice low so she would lean forward into the light to try and hear me. "It'd been hit by a car, and it was lying funny, at an angle. It looked like a dog. I wanted to talk to somebody who remembered Aberfan, somebody who knew him."

"I didn't know him," she said. "I only killed him, remember? That's why you did this, isn't it, because I killed Aberfan?"

She didn't look at the eisenstadt, hadn't even glanced at it when I set it on the table, but I wondered suddenly if she knew what I was up to. She was still carefully out of range. And what if I said to her, "That's right. That's why I did this, because you killed him, and I didn't have any pictures of him. You owe me. If I can't have a picture of Aberfan, you at least owe me a picture of you remembering him."

Only she didn't remember him, didn't know anything about him except what she had seen on the way to the vet's, Aberfan lying on my lap and looking up at me, already dying. I had had no business coming here, dredging all this up again. No business.

"At first I thought you were going to have me arrested," Katie said, "and then after all the dogs died, I thought you were going to kill me."

The screen door banged. "Forgot my cars," the little girl said and scooped them into the tail of her T-shirt. Katie tousled her hair as she went past, and then folded her arms again.

" 'It wasn't my fault,' I was going to tell you when you came to kill me," she said. " 'It was snowy. He ran right in front of me. I didn't even see him.' I looked up everything I could find about newparvo. Preparing for the defense. How it mutated from parvovirus and from cat distemper before that and then kept on mutating, so they couldn't come up with a vaccine. How even before the third wave they were below the minimum survival population. How it was the fault of the people who owned the last survivors because they wouldn't risk their dogs to breed them. How the scientists didn't come up with a vaccine until only the jackals were left. 'You're wrong,' I was going to tell you. 'It was the puppy mill owners' fault that all the dogs died. If they hadn't kept their dogs in such unsanitary conditions, it never would have gotten out of control in the first place.' I had my defense all ready. But you'd moved away."

Jana banged in again, carrying the empty whale glass. She had a red smear across the whole lower half of her face. "I need some more," she said, making "some more" into one word. She held the glass in both hands while Katie opened the refrigerator and poured her another glassful.

"Wait a minute, honey," she said. "You've got Kool-Aid all over you," and bent to wipe Jana's face with a paper towel.

Katie hadn't said a word in her defense while we waited at the vet's, not, "It was snowy," or, "He ran right out in front of me," or, "I didn't even see him." She had sat silently beside me, twisting her mittens in her lap, until the vet came out and told me Aberfan was dead, and then she had said, "I didn't know there were any left in Colorado. I thought they were all dead."

And I had turned to her, to a sixteen-year-old not even old enough to know how to shut her face, and said, "Now they all are. Thanks to you."

"That kind of talk isn't necessary," the vet had said warningly.

I had wrenched away from the hand he tried to put on my shoulder. "How does it feel to have killed one of the last dogs in the world?" I shouted at her. "How does it feel to be responsible for the extinction of an entire species?"

The screen door banged again. Katie was looking at me, still holding the reddened paper towel.

"You moved away," she said, "and I thought maybe that meant you'd forgiven me, but it didn't, did it!" She came over to the table and wiped at the red circle the glass had left. "Why did you do it? To punish me? Or did you think that's what I'd been doing the last fifteen years, roaring around the roads murdering animals?"

"What?" I said.

"The Society's already been here."

"The Society?" I said, not understanding.

"Yes," she said, still looking at the red-stained towel. "They said you had reported a dead animal on Van Buren. They wanted to know where I was this morning between eight and nine A.M."

I nearly ran down a roadworker on the way back into Phoenix. He leaped for the still-wet cement barrier, dropping the shovel he'd been leaning on all day, and I ran right over it.

The Society had already been there. They had left my house and gone straight to hers. Only that wasn't possible, because I hadn't even called Katie then. I hadn't even seen the picture of Mrs. Ambler yet. Which meant they had gone to see Ramirez after they left me, and the last thing Ramirez and the paper needed was trouble with the Society.

"I thought it was suspicious when he didn't go to the governor's conference," she had told them, "and just now he called and asked for a lifeline on this person here. Katherine Powell. 4628 Dutchman Drive. He knew her in Colorado."

"Ramirez!" I shouted at the car phone. "I want to talk to you!" There wasn't any answer.

I swore at her for a good ten miles before I remembered I had the exclusion button on. I punched it off. "Ramirez, where the hell are you?"

"I could ask you the same question," she said. She sounded even angrier than Katie, but not as angry as I was. "You cut me off, you won't tell me what's going on."

"So you decided you had it figured out for yourself, and you told your little theory to the Society."

"What?" she said, and I recognized that tone, too. I had heard it in my own voice when Katie told me the Society had been there. Ramirez hadn't told anybody anything, she didn't even know what I was talking about, but I was going too fast to stop.

"You told the Society I'd asked for Katie's lifeline, didn't you?" I shouted.

"No," she said. "I didn't. Don't you think it's time you told me what's going on?" Ramirez said.

"Did the Society come see you this afternoon?"

"No. I told you. They called this morning and wanted to talk to you. I told them you were at the governor's conference."

"And they didn't call back later?"

"No. Are you in trouble?"

I hit the exclusion button. "Yes," I said. "Yes, I'm in trouble."

Ramirez hadn't told them. Maybe somebody else at the paper had, but I didn't think so. There had after all been Dolores Chiwere's story about them having illegal access to the lifelines. "How come you don't have any pictures of your dog?" Hunter had asked me, which meant they'd read my lifeline, too. So they knew we had both lived in Colorado, in the same town, when Aberfan died.

"What did you tell them?" I had demanded of Katie. She had been standing there in the kitchen still messing with the Kool-Aid-stained towel, and I had wanted to yank it out of her hands and make her look at me. "What did you tell the Society?"

She looked up at me. "I told them I was on Indian School Road, picking up the month's programming assignments from my company. Unfortunately, I could just as easily have driven in on Van Buren."

"About Aberfan!" I shouted. "What did you tell them about Aberfan?"

She looked steadily at me. "I didn't tell them anything. I assumed you'd already told them."

I had taken hold of her shoulders. "If they come back, don't tell them anything. Not even if they arrest you. I'll take care of this. I'll . . ."

But I hadn't told her what I'd do because I didn't know. I had run out of her house, colliding with Jana in the hall on her way in for another refill, and roared off for home, even though I didn't have any idea what I would do when I got there.

Call the Society and tell them to leave Katie alone, that she had nothing to do with this? That would be even more suspicious than everything else I'd done so far, and you couldn't get much more suspicious than that.

I had seen a dead jackal on the road (or so I said), and instead of reporting it immediately on the phone right there in my car, I'd driven to a convenience store two miles away. I'd called the

Society, but I'd refused to give them my name and number. And then I'd cancelled two shoots without telling my boss and asked for the lifeline of one Katherine Powell, whom I had known fifteen years ago and who could have been on Van Buren at the time of the accident.

The connection was obvious, and how long would it take them to make the connection that fifteen years ago was when Aberfan had died?

Apache was beginning to fill up with rush hour overflow and a whole fleet of tankers. The overflow obviously spent all their time driving dividers—nobody bothered to signal that they were changing lanes. Nobody even gave an indication that they knew what a lane was. Going around the curve from Tempe and onto Van Buren they were all over the road. I moved over into the tanker lane.

My lifeline didn't have the vet's name on it. They were just getting started in those days, and there was a lot of nervousness about invasion of privacy. Nothing went online without the person's permission, especially not medical and bank records, and the lifelines were little more than puff bios: family, occupation, hobbies, pets. The only things on the lifeline besides Aberfan's name was the date of his death and my address at the time, but that was probably enough. There were only two vets in town.

The vet hadn't written Katie's name down on Aberfan's record. He had handed her driver's license back to her without even looking at it, but Katie had told her name to the vet's assistant. He might have written it down. There was no way I could find out. I couldn't ask for the vet's lifeline because the Society had access to the lifelines. They'd get to him before I could. I could maybe have the paper get the vet's records for me, but I'd have to tell Ramirez what was going on, and the phone was probably tapped, too. And if I showed up at the paper, Ramirez would confiscate the car. I couldn't go there.

Wherever the hell I was going, I was driving too fast to get there. When the tanker ahead of me slowed down to ninety, I practically climbed up his back bumper. I had gone past the place where the jackal had been hit without ever seeing it. Even without the traffic, there probably hadn't been anything to see. What the Society hadn't taken care of, the overflow probably had, and anyway, there hadn't been any evidence to begin with. If there had been, if the cameras had seen the car that hit it, they wouldn't have come after me. And Katie.

The Society couldn't charge her with Aberfan's death—killing an animal hadn't been a crime back then—but if they found out about Aberfan they would charge her with the jackal's death, and it wouldn't matter if a hundred witnesses, a hundred highway cameras had seen her on Indian School Road. It wouldn't matter if the print-fix on her car was clean. She had killed one of the last dogs, hadn't she? They would crucify her.

I should never have left Katie. "Don't tell them anything," I had told her, but she had never been afraid of admitting guilt. When the receptionist had asked her what had happened, she had said, "I hit him," just like that, no attempt to make excuses, to run off, to lay the blame on someone else.

I had run off to try to stop the Society from finding out that Katie had hit Aberfan, and meanwhile the Society was probably back at Katie's, asking her how she'd happened to know me in Colorado, asking her how Aberfan died.

I was wrong about the Society. They weren't at Katie's house. They were at mine, standing on the porch, waiting for me to let them in.

"You're a hard man to track down," Hunter said.

The uniform grinned. "Where you been?"

"Sorry," I said, fishing my keys out of my pocket. "I thought you were all done with me. I've already told you everything I know about the incident."

Hunter stepped back just far enough for me to get the screen door open and the key in the lock. "Officer Segura and I just need to ask you a couple more questions."

"Where'd you go this afternoon?" Segura asked.

"I went to see an old friend of mine."

"Who?"

"Come on, come on," Hunter said. "Let the guy get in his own front door before you start badgering him with a lot of questions."

I opened the door. "Did the cameras get a picture of the tanker that hit the jackal?" I asked.

"Tanker?" Segura said.

"I told you," I said, "I figure it had to be a tanker. The jackal was lying in the tanker lane." I led the way into the living room, depositing my keys on the computer and switching the phone to exclusion while I talked. The last thing I needed was Ramirez bursting in with, "What's going on? Are you in trouble?"

"It was probably a renegade that hit it, which would explain why he didn't stop." I gestured at them to sit down.

Hunter did. Segura started for the couch and then stopped, staring at the photos on the wall above it. "Jesus, will you look at all the dogs!" he said. "Did you take all these pictures?"

"I took some of them. That one in the middle is Misha."

"The last dog, right?"

"Yes," I said.

"No kidding. The very last one."

No kidding. She was being kept in isolation at the Society's research facility in St. Louis when I saw her. I had talked them into letting me shoot her, but it had to be from outside the quarantine area. The picture had an unfocused look that came from shooting it through a wire-mesh-reinforced window in the door, but I wouldn't have done any better if they'd let me inside. Misha was past having any expression to photograph. She hadn't eaten in a week at that point. She lay with her head on her paws, staring at the door, the whole time I was there.

"You wouldn't consider selling this picture to the Society, would you?"

"No, I wouldn't."

He nodded understandingly. "I guess people were pretty upset when she died."

Pretty upset. They had turned on anyone who had anything to do with it—the puppy mill owners, the scientists who hadn't come up with a vaccine, Misha's vet—and a lot of others who hadn't. And they had handed over their civil rights to a bunch of jackals who were able to grab them because everybody felt so guilty. Pretty upset.

"What's this one?" Segura asked. He had already moved on to the picture next to it.

"It's General Patton's bull terrier Willie."

They fed and cleaned up after Misha with those robot arms they used to use in the nuclear plants. Her owner, a tired-looking woman, was allowed to watch her through the wire-mesh window but had to stay off to the side because Misha flung herself barking against the door whenever she saw her.

"You should make them let you in," I had told her. "It's cruel to keep her locked up like that. You should make them let you take her back home."

"And let her get the newparvo?" she said.

There was nobody left for Misha to get the newparvo from, but I didn't say that. I set the light readings in the camera, trying not to lean into Misha's line of vision.

"You know what killed them, don't you?" she said. "The ozone layer. All those holes. The radiation got in and caused it."

It was the communists, it was the Mexicans, it was the government. And the only people who acknowledged their guilt weren't guilty at all.

"This one here looks kind of like a jackal," Segura said. He was looking at a picture I had taken of a German shepherd after Aberfan died. "Dogs were a lot like jackals, weren't they?"

"No," I said, and sat down on the shelf in front of the developer's screen, across from Hunter. "I already told you everything I know about the jackal. I saw it lying in the road, and I called you."

"You said when you saw the jackal it was in the far right lane," Hunter said.

"That's right."

"And you were in the far left lane?"

"I was in the far left lane."

They were going to take me over my story, point by point, and when I couldn't remember what I'd said before, they were going to say, "Are you sure that's what you saw, Mr. McCombe? Are you sure you didn't see the jackal get hit? Katherine Powell hit it, didn't she?"

"You told us this morning you stopped, but the jackal was already dead. Is that right?" Hunter asked.

"No," I said.

Segura looked up. Hunter touched his hand casually to his pocket and then brought it back to his knee, turning on the taper.

"I didn't stop for about a mile. Then I backed up and looked at it, but it was dead. There was blood coming out of its mouth."

Hunter didn't say anything. He kept his hands on his knees and waited—an old journalist's trick, if you wait long enough, they'll say something they didn't intend to, just to fill the silence.

"The jackal's body was at a peculiar angle," I said, right on cue. "The way it was lying, it didn't look like a jackal. I thought it was a dog." I waited till the silence got uncomfortable again. "It brought back a lot of terrible memories," I said. "I wasn't even thinking. I just wanted to get away from it. After a few minutes I realized I should have called the Society, and I stopped at the 7-Eleven."

I waited again, till Segura began to shoot uncomfortable glances at Hunter, and then started in again. "I thought I'd be okay, that I could go ahead and work, but after I got to my first shoot, I knew I wasn't going to make it, so I came home." Candor. Openness. If the Amblers can do it, so can you. "I guess I was still in shock or something. I didn't even call my boss and have her get somebody to cover the governor's conference. All I could think about was—" I stopped and rubbed my hand across my face. "I needed to talk to somebody. I had the paper look up an old friend of mine, Katherine Powell."

I stopped, I hoped this time for good. I had admitted lying to them and confessed to two crimes: leaving the scene of the accident and using press access to get a lifeline for personal use, and maybe that would be enough to satisfy them. I didn't want to say anything about going out to see Katie. They would know she would have told me about their visit and decide this confession was an attempt to get her off, and maybe they'd been watching the house and knew it anyway, and this was all wasted effort.

The silence dragged on. Hunter's hands tapped his knees twice and then subsided. The story didn't explain why I'd picked Katie, who I hadn't seen in fifteen years, who I knew in Colorado, to go see, but maybe, maybe they wouldn't make the connection.

"This Katherine Powell," Hunter said, "you knew her in Colorado, is that right?"

"We lived in the same little town."

We waited.

"Isn't that when your dog died?" Segura said suddenly. Hunter shot him a glance of pure rage, and I thought, it isn't a taper he's got in that shirt pocket. It's the vet's records, and Katie's name is on them.

"Yes," I said. "He died in September of eighty-nine."

Segura opened his mouth.

"In the third wave?" Hunter asked before he could say anything.

"No," I said. "He was hit by a car."

They both looked genuinely shocked. The Amblers could have taken lessons from them. "Who hit it?" Segura asked, and Hunter leaned forward, his hand moving reflexively toward his pocket.

"I don't know," I said. "It was a hit and run. Whoever it was just left him lying there in the road. That's why when I saw the jackal, it . . . that was how I met Katherine Powell. She stopped and helped me. She helped me get him into her car, and we took him to the vet's, but it was too late."

Hunter's public face was pretty indestructible, but Segura's wasn't. He looked surprised and enlightened and disappointed all at once.

"That's why I wanted to see her," I said unnecessarily.

"Your dog was hit on what day?" Hunter asked.

"September thirtieth."

"What was the vet's name?"

He hadn't changed his way of asking the questions, but he no longer cared what the answers were. He had thought he'd found a connection, a cover-up, but here we were, a couple of dog lovers, a couple of good Samaritans, and his theory had collapsed. He was done with the interview, he was just finishing up, and all I had to do was be careful not to relax too soon.

I frowned. "I don't remember his name. Cooper, I think."

"What kind of car did you say hit your dog?"

"I don't know," I said, thinking, not a jeep. Make it something besides a jeep. "I didn't see him get hit. The vet said it was something big, a pickup maybe. Or a Winnebago."

And I knew who had hit the jackal. It had all been right there in front of me—the old man using up their forty-gallon water supply to wash the bumper, the lies about their coming in from Globe—only I had been too intent on keeping them from finding out about Katie, on getting the picture of Aberfan to see it. It was like the damned parvo. When you had it licked in one place, it broke out somewhere else.

"Were there any identifying tire tracks?" Hunter said.

"What?" I said. "No. It was snowing that day." It had to show in my face, and he hadn't missed anything yet. I passed my hand over my eyes. "I'm sorry. These questions are bringing it all back."

"Sorry," Hunter said.

"Can't we get this stuff from the police report?" Segura asked.

"There wasn't a police report," I said. "It wasn't a crime to kill a dog when Aberfan died."

It was the right thing to say. The look of shock on their faces was the real thing this time, and they looked at each other in disbelief instead of at me. They asked a few more questions and then stood up to leave. I walked them to the door.

"Thank you for your cooperation, Mr. McCombe," Hunter said. "We appreciate what a difficult experience this has been for you."

I shut the screen door between us. The Amblers would have been going too fast, trying to beat the cameras because they weren't even supposed to be on Van Buren. It was almost rush hour, and they were in the tanker lane, and they hadn't even seen the jackal till they hit it, and then it was too late. They had to know the penalty for hitting an animal was jail and confiscation of the vehicle, and there wasn't anybody else on the road.

"Oh, one more question," Hunter said from halfway down the walk. "You said you went to your first assignment this morning. What was it?"

Candid. Open. "It was out at the old zoo. A sideshow kind of thing."

I watched them all the way out to their car and down the street. Then I latched the screen, pulled the inside door shut, and locked it, too. It had been right there in front of me—the ferret sniffing the wheel, the bumper, Jake anxiously watching the road. I had thought he was looking for customers, but he wasn't. He was expecting to see the Society drive up. "He's not interested in that," he had said when Mrs. Ambler said she had been telling me about Taco. He had listened to our whole conversation, standing under the back window with his guilty bucket, ready to come back in and cut her off if she said too much, and I hadn't tumbled to any of it. I had been so intent on Aberfan I hadn't even seen it when I looked right through the lens at it. And what kind of an excuse was that? Katie hadn't even tried to use it, and she was learning to drive.

I went and got the Nikon and pulled the film out of it. It was too late to do anything about the eisenstadt pictures or the vidcam footage, but I didn't think there was anything in them. Jake had already washed the bumper by the time I'd taken those pictures.

I fed the longshot film into the developer. "Positives, one two three order, fifteen seconds," I said, and waited for the image to come on the screen.

I wondered who had been driving. Jake, probably. "He never liked Taco," she had said, and there was no mistaking the bitterness in her voice. "I didn't want to buy the Winnebago."

They would both lose their licenses, no matter who was driving, and the Society would confiscate the Winnebago. They would probably not send two octogenarian specimens of Americana like the Amblers to prison. They wouldn't have to. The trial would take six months, and Texas already had legislation in committee.

The first picture came up. A light-setting shot of an ocotillo.

Even if they got off, even if they didn't end up taking away the Winnebago for unauthorized use of a tanker lane or failure to purchase a sales tax permit, the Amblers had six months left at the outside. Utah was all ready to pass a full-divided bill, and Arizona would be next. In spite of the road crews' stew-slowed pace, Phoenix would be all-divided by the time the investigation was over, and they'd be completely boxed in. Permanent residents of the zoo. Like the coyote.

A shot of the zoo sign, half-hidden in the cactus. A close-up of the Amblers' balloon-trailing sign. The Winnebago in the parking lot.

"Hold," I said. "Crop." I indicated the areas with my finger. "Enlarge to full screen."

The longshot takes great pictures, sharp contrast, excellent detail. The developer only had a five-hundred-thousand-pixel screen, but the dark smear on the bumper was easy to see, and the developed picture would be much clearer. You'd be able to see every splatter, every grayish-yellow hair. The Society's computers would probably be able to type the blood from it.

"Continue," I said, and the next picture came on the screen. Artsy shot of the Winnebago and the zoo entrance. Jake washing the bumper. Redhanded.

Maybe Hunter had bought my story, but he didn't have any other suspects, and how long would it be before he decided to ask Katie a few more questions? If he thought it was the Amblers, he'd leave her alone.

The Japanese family clustered around the waste-disposal tank. Close-up of the decals on the side. Interiors—Mrs. Ambler in the galley, the upright-coffin shower stall, Mrs. Ambler making coffee.

No wonder she had looked that way in the eisenstadt shot, her face full of memory and grief and loss. Maybe in the instant before they hit it, it had looked like a dog to her, too.

All I had to do was tell Hunter about the Amblers, and Katie was off the hook. It should be easy. I had done it before.

"Stop," I said to a shot of the salt and pepper collection. The black scottie dogs had painted, red-plaid bows and red tongues. "Expose," I said. "One through twenty-four."

The screen went to question marks and started beeping. I should have known better. The developer could handle a lot of

orders, but asking it to expose perfectly good film went against
its whole memory, and I didn't have time to give it the step-by-
steps that would convince it I meant what I said.

"Eject," I said. The scotties blinked out. The developer spat
out the film, rerolled into its protective case.

The doorbell rang. I switched on the overhead and pulled the
film out to full length and held it directly under the light. I had
told Hunter an RV hit Aberfan, and he had said on the way out,
almost an afterthought, "That first shoot you went to, what was
it?" And after he left, what had he done, gone out to check on
the sideshow kind of thing, gotten Mrs. Ambler to spill her guts?
There hadn't been time to do that and get back. He must have
called Ramirez. I was glad I had locked the door.

I turned off the overhead. I rerolled the film, fed it back into
the developer, and gave it a direction it could handle. "Permanganate bath, full strength, one through twenty-four. Remove one
hundred percent emulsion. No notify."

The screen went dark. It would take the developer at least
fifteen minutes to run the film through the bleach bath, and the
Society's computers could probably enhance a picture out of two
crystals of silver and thin air, but at least the detail wouldn't be
there. I unlocked the door.

It was Katie.

She held up the eisenstadt. "You forgot your briefcase," she
said.

I stared blankly at it. I hadn't even realized I didn't have it.
I must have left it on the kitchen table when I went tearing out,
running down little girls and stewed roadworkers in my rush to
keep Katie from getting involved. And here she was, and Hunter
would be back any minute, saying, "That shoot you went on this
morning, did you take any pictures?"

"It isn't a briefcase," I said.

"I wanted to tell you," she said, and stopped. "I shouldn't
have accused you of telling the Society I'd killed the jackal. I
don't know why you came to see me today, but I know you're
not capable of—"

"You have no idea what I'm capable of," I said. I opened the
door enough to reach for the eisenstadt. "Thanks for bringing it

back. I'll get the paper to reimburse your way-mile credits."

Go home. Go home. If you're here when the Society comes back, they'll ask you how you met me, and I just destroyed the evidence that could shift the blame to the Amblers. I took hold of the eisenstadt's handle and started to shut the door.

She put her hand on the door. The screen door and the fading light made her look unfocused, like Misha. "Are you in trouble?"

"No," I said. "Look, I'm very busy."

"Why did you come to see me?" she asked. "Did you kill the jackal?"

"No," I said, but I opened the door and let her in.

I went over to the developer and asked for a visual status. It was only on the sixth frame. "I'm destroying evidence," I said to Katie. "I took a picture this morning of the vehicle that hit it, only I didn't know it was the guilty party until a half an hour ago." I motioned for her to sit down on the couch. "They're in their eighties. They were driving on a road they weren't supposed to be on, in an obsolete recreation vehicle, worrying about the cameras and the tankers. There's no way they could have seen it in time to stop. The Society won't see it that way, though. They're determined to blame somebody, anybody, even though it won't bring them back."

She set her canvas carryit and the eisenstadt down on the table next to the couch. "The Society was here when I got home," I said. "They'd figured out we were both in Colorado when Aberfan died. I told them it was a hit and run, and you'd stopped to help me. They had the vet's records, and your name was on them."

I couldn't read her face. "If they come back, you tell them that you gave me a ride to the vet's." I went back to the developer. The longshot film was done. "Eject," I said, and the developer spit it into my hand. I fed it into the recycler.

"McCombe! Where the hell are you?" Ramirez's voice exploded into the room, and I jumped and started for the door, but she wasn't there. The phone was flashing. "McCombe! This is important!"

Ramirez was on the phone and using some override I didn't

even know existed. I went over and pushed it back to access. The lights went out. "I'm here," I said.

"You won't believe what just happened!" She sounded outraged. "A couple of terrorist types from the Society just stormed in here and confiscated the stuff you sent me!"

All I'd sent her was the vidcam footage and the shots from the eisenstadt, and there shouldn't have been anything on those. Jake had already washed the bumper. "What stuff?" I said.

"The prints from the eisenstadt!" she said, still shouting. "Which I didn't have a chance to look at when they came in because I was too busy trying to work a trade on your governor's conference, not to mention trying to track you down! I had hardcopies made and sent the originals straight down to composing with your vidcam footage. I finally got to them half an hour ago, and while I'm sorting through them, this Society creep just grabs them away from me. No warrant, no 'would you mind?' nothing. Right out of my hand. Like a bunch of—"

"Jackals," I said. "You're sure it wasn't the vidcam footage?" There wasn't anything in the eisenstadt shots except Mrs. Ambler and Taco, and even Hunter couldn't have put that together, could he?

"Of course I'm sure," Ramirez said, her voice bouncing off the walls. "It was one of the prints from the eisenstadt. I never even saw the vidcam stuff. I sent it straight to composing. I told you."

I went over to the developer and fed the cartridge in. The first dozen shots were nothing, stuff the eisenstadt had taken from the back seat of the car. "Start with frame ten," I said. "Positives. One two three order. Five seconds."

"What did you say?" Ramirez demanded.

"I said, did they say what they were looking for?"

"Are you kidding? I wasn't even there as far as they were concerned. They split up the pile and started through them on *my* desk."

The yucca at the foot of the hill. More yucca. My forearm as I set the eisenstadt down on the counter. My back.

"Whatever it was they were looking for, they found it," Ramirez said.

I glanced at Katie. She met my gaze steadily, unafraid. She had never been afraid, not even when I told her she had killed all the dogs, not even when I showed up on her doorstep after fifteen years.

"The one in the uniform showed it to the other one," Ramirez was saying, "and said, 'You were wrong about the woman doing it. Look at this.'"

"Did you get a look at the picture?"

Still life of cups and spoons. Mrs. Ambler's arm. Mrs. Ambler's back.

"I tried. It was a truck of some kind."

"A truck? Are you sure? Not a Winnebago?"

"A truck. What the hell is going on over there?"

I didn't answer. Jake's back. Open shower door. Still life with Sanka. Mrs. Ambler remembering Taco.

"What woman are they talking about?" Ramirez said. "The one you wanted the lifeline on?"

"No," I said. The picture of Mrs. Ambler was the last one on the sheet. The developer went back to the beginning. Bottom half of the Hitori. Open car door. Prickly pear. "Did they say anything else?"

"The one in uniform pointed to something on the hardcopy and said, 'See. There's his number on the side. Can you make it out?'"

Blurred palm trees and the expressway. The tanker hitting the jackal.

"Stop," I said. The image froze.

"What?" Ramirez said.

It was a great action shot, the back wheels passing right over the mess that had been the jackal's hind legs. The jackal was already dead, of course, but you couldn't see that or the already drying blood coming out of its mouth because of the angle. You couldn't see the truck's license number either because of the speed the tanker was going, but the number was there, waiting for the Society's computers. It looked like the tanker had just hit it.

"What did they do with the picture?" I asked.

"They took it into the chief's office. I tried to call up the originals from composing, but the chief had already sent for them *and* your vidcam footage. Then I tried to get you, but I couldn't get past your damned exclusion."

"Are they still in there with the chief?"

"They just left. They're on their way over to your house. The chief told me to tell you he wants 'full cooperation,' which means hand over the negatives and any other film you just took this morning. He told *me* to keep my hands off. No story. Case closed."

"How long ago did they leave?"

"Five minutes. You've got plenty of time to make me a print. Don't highwire it. I'll come pick it up."

"What happened to 'The last thing I need is trouble with the Society'?"

"It'll take them at least twenty minutes to get to your place. Hide it somewhere the Society won't find it."

"I can't," I said, and listened to her furious silence. "My developer's broken. It just ate my longshot film," I said, and hit the exclusion button again.

"You want to see who hit the jackal?" I said to Katie, and motioned her over to the developer. "One of Phoenix's finest."

She came and stood in front of the screen, looking at the picture. If the Society's computers were really good, they could probably prove the jackal was already dead, but the Society wouldn't keep the film long enough for that. Hunter and Segura had probably already destroyed the highwire copies. Maybe I should offer to run the cartridge sheet through the permanganate bath for them when they got here, just to save time.

I looked at Katie. "It looks guilty as hell, doesn't it?" I said. "Only it isn't." She didn't say anything, didn't move. "It would have killed the jackal if it had hit it. It was going at least ninety. But the jackal was already dead."

She looked across at me.

"The Society would have sent the Amblers to jail. It would have confiscated the house they've lived in for fifteen years for an accident that was nobody's fault. They didn't even see it coming. It just ran right out in front of them."

Katie put her hand up to the screen and touched the jackal's image.

"They've suffered enough," I said, looking at her. It was getting dark. I hadn't turned on any lights, and the red image of the tanker made her nose look sunburned.

"All these years she's blamed him for her dog's death, and he didn't do it," I said. "A Winnebago's a hundred square feet on the inside. That's about as big as this developer, and they've lived inside it for fifteen years, while the lanes got narrower and the highways shut down, hardly enough room to breathe, let alone live, and her blaming him for something he didn't do."

In the ruddy light from the screen she looked sixteen.

"They won't do anything to the driver, not with the tankers hauling thousands of gallons of water into Phoenix every day. Even the Society won't run the risk of a boycott. They'll destroy the negatives and call the case closed. And the Society won't go after the Amblers," I said. "Or you."

I turned back to the developer. "Go," I said, and the image changed. Yucca. Yucca. My forearm. My back. Cups and spoons.

"Besides," I said. "I'm an old hand at shifting the blame." Mrs. Ambler's arm. Mrs. Ambler's back. Open shower door. "Did I ever tell you about Aberfan?"

Katie was still watching the screen, her face pale now from the light blue 100% formica shower stall.

"The Society already thinks the tanker did it. The only one I've got to convince is my editor." I reached across to the phone and took the exclusion off. "Ramirez," I said, "wanta go after the Society?"

Jake's back. Cups, spoons, and Sanka.

"I did," Ramirez said in a voice that could have frozen the Salt River, "but your developer was broken, and you couldn't get me a picture."

Mrs. Ambler and Taco.

I hit the exclusion button again and left my hand on it. "Stop," I said. "Print." The screen went dark, and the print slid out into the tray. "Reduce frame. Permanganate bath by one percent. Follow on screen." I took my hand off. "What's Dolores Chiwere doing these days, Ramirez?"

"She's working investigative. Why?"

I didn't answer. The picture of Mrs. Ambler faded a little, a little more.

"The Society *does* have a link to the lifelines!" Ramirez said, not quite as fast as Hunter, but almost. "That's why you requested your old girlfriend's line, isn't it? You're running a sting."

I had been wondering how to get Ramirez off Katie's trail, and she had done it herself, jumping to conclusions just like the Society. With a little effort, I could convince Katie, too: Do you know why I really came to see you today? To catch the Society. I had to pick somebody the Society couldn't possibly know about from my lifeline, somebody I didn't have any known connection with.

Katie watched the screen, looking like she already half-believed it. The picture of Mrs. Ambler faded some more. Any known connection.

"Stop," I said.

"What about the truck?" Ramirez demanded. "What does it have to do with this sting of yours?"

"Nothing," I said. "And neither does the water board, which is an even bigger bully than the Society. So do what the chief says. Full cooperation. Case closed. We'll get them on lifeline tapping."

She digested that, or maybe she'd already hung up and was calling Dolores Chiwere. I looked at the image of Mrs. Ambler on the screen. It had faded enough to look slightly overexposed but not enough to look tampered with. And Taco was gone.

I looked at Katie. "The Society will be here in another fifteen minutes," I said, "which gives me just enough time to tell you about Aberfan," I gestured at the couch. "Sit down."

She came and sat down. "He was a great dog," I said. "He loved the snow. He'd dig through it and toss it up with his muzzle and snap at the snowflakes, trying to catch them."

Ramirez had obviously hung up, but she would call back if she couldn't track down Chiwere. I put the exclusion back on and went over to the developer. The image of Mrs. Ambler was still on the screen. The bath hadn't affected the detail that much. You could still see the wrinkles, the thin white hair, but the guilt, or blame, the look of loss and love, was gone. She looked serene, almost happy.

"There are hardly any good pictures of dogs," I said. "They lack the necessary muscles to take good pictures, and Aberfan lunged at you as soon as he saw the camera."

I turned the developer off. Without the light from the screen, it was almost dark in the room. I turned on the overhead.

"There were less than a hundred dogs left in the United States, and he'd already had the newparvo once and nearly died. The only pictures I had of him had been taken when he was asleep. I wanted a picture of Aberfan playing in the snow."

I leaned against the narrow shelf in front of the developer's screen. Katie looked the way she had at the vet's, sitting there with her hands clenched, waiting for me to tell her something terrible.

"I wanted a picture of him playing in the snow, but he always lunged at the camera," I said, "so I let him out in the front yard, and then I sneaked out the side door and went across the road to some pine trees where he wouldn't be able to see me. But he did."

"And he ran across the road," Katie said. "And I hit him."

She was looking down at her hands. I waited for her to look up, dreading what I would see in her face. Or not see.

"It took me a long time to find out where you'd gone," she said to her hands. "I was afraid you'd refuse me access to your lifeline. I finally saw one of your pictures in a newspaper, and I moved to Phoenix, but after I got here I was afraid to call you for fear you'd hang up on me."

She twisted her hands the way she had twisted her mittens at the vet's. "My husband said I was obsessed with it, that I should have gotten over it by now, everybody else had, that they were only dogs anyway." She looked up, and I braced my hands against the developer. "He said forgiveness wasn't something somebody else could give you, but I didn't want you to forgive me exactly. I just wanted to tell you I was sorry."

There hadn't been any reproach, any accusation in her face when I told her she was responsible for the extinction of a species that day at the vet's, and there wasn't now. Maybe she didn't have the facial muscles for it, I thought bitterly.

"Do you know why I came to see you today?" I said angrily. "My camera broke when I tried to catch Aberfan. I didn't get any pictures." I grabbed the picture of Mrs. Ambler out of the developer's tray and flung it at her. "Her dog died of newparvo. They left it in the Winnebago, and when they came back, it was dead."

"Poor thing," she said, but she wasn't looking at the picture. She was looking at me.

"She didn't know she was having her picture taken. I thought if I got you talking about Aberfan, I could get a picture like that of you."

And surely now I would see it, the look I had really wanted when I set the eisenstadt down on Katie's kitchen table, the look I still wanted, even though the eisenstadt was facing the wrong way, the look of betrayal the dogs had never given us. Not even Misha. Not even Aberfan. How does it feel to be responsible for the extinction of an entire species?

I pointed at the eisenstadt. "It's not a briefcase. It's a camera. I was going to take your picture without your even knowing it."

She had never known Aberfan. She had never known Mrs. Ambler either, but in that instant before she started to cry she looked like both of them. She put her hand up to her mouth. "Oh," she said, and the love, the loss was there in her voice, too. "If you'd had it then, it wouldn't have happened."

I looked at the eisenstadt. If I had had it, I could have set it on the porch and Aberfan would never have even noticed it. He would have burrowed through the snow and tossed it up with his nose, and I could have thrown snow up in big glittering sprays that he would have leaped at, and it never would have happened. Katie Powell would have driven past, and I would have stopped to wave at her, and she, sixteen years old and just learning to drive, would maybe even have risked taking a mittened hand off the steering wheel to wave back, and Aberfan would have wagged his tail into a blizzard and then barked at the snow he'd churned up.

He wouldn't have caught the third wave. He would have lived to be an old dog, fourteen or fifteen, too old to play in the snow any more, and even if he had been the last dog in the world I would not have let them lock him up in a cage, I would not have let them take him away. If I had had the eisenstadt.

No wonder I hated it.

It had been at least fifteen minutes since Ramirez called. The Society would be here any minute. "You shouldn't be here when the Society comes," I said, and Katie nodded and smudged the tears off her cheeks and stood up, reaching for her carryit.

"Do you ever take pictures?" she said, shouldering the carryit. "I mean, besides for the papers?"

"I don't know if I'll be taking pictures for them much longer. Photo-journalists are becoming an extinct breed."

"Maybe you could come take some pictures of Jana and Kevin. Kids grow up so fast, they're gone before you know it."

"I'd like that," I said. I opened the screen door for her and looked both ways down the street at the darkness. "All clear," I said, and she went out. I shut the screen door between us.

She turned and looked at me one last time with her dear, open face that even I hadn't been able to close. "I miss them," she said.

I put my hand up to the screen. "I miss them, too."

I watched her to make sure she turned the corner and then went back in the living room and took down the picture of Misha. I propped it against the developer so Segura would be able to see it from the door. In a month or so, when the Amblers were safely in Texas and the Society had forgotten about Katie, I'd call Segura and tell him I might be willing to sell it to the Society, and then in a day or so I'd tell him I'd changed my mind. When he came out to try to talk me into it, I'd tell him about Perdita and Beatrix Potter, and he would tell me about the Society.

Chiwere and Ramirez would have to take the credit for the story—I didn't want Hunter putting anything else together—and it would take more than one story to break them, but it was a start.

Katie had left the print of Mrs. Ambler on the couch. I picked it up and looked at it a minute and then fed it into the developer. "Recycle," I said.

I picked up the eisenstadt from the table by the couch and took the film cartridge out. I started to pull the film out to expose it, and then shoved it into the developer instead and turned it on. "Positives, one two three order, five seconds."

I had apparently set the camera on its activator again—there were ten shots or so of the back seat of the Hitori. Vehicles and people. The pictures of Katie were all in shadow. There was a still life of Kool-Aid Pitcher With Whale Glass and another one of Jana's toy cars, and some near-black frames that meant Katie had laid the eisenstadt face-down when she brought it to me.

"Two seconds," I said, and waited for the developer to flash the last shots so I could make sure there wasn't anything else on the cartridge and then expose it before the Society got here. All but the last frame was of the darkness that was all the eisenstadt could see lying on its face. The last one was of me.

The trick in getting good pictures is to make people forget they're being photographed. Distract them. Get them talking about something they care about.

"Stop," I said, and the image froze.

Aberfan was a great dog. He loved to play in the snow, and after I had murdered him, he lifted his head off my lap and tried to lick my hand.

The Society would be here any minute to take the longshot film and destroy it, and this one would have to go, too, along with the rest of the cartridge. I couldn't risk Hunter's being reminded of Katie. Or Segura taking a notion to do a print-fix and peel on Jana's toy cars.

It was too bad. The eisenstadt takes great pictures. "Even you'll forget it's a camera," Ramirez had said in her spiel, and that was certainly true. I was looking straight into the lens.

And it was all there, Misha and Taco and Perdita and the look he gave me on the way to the vet's while I stroked his poor head and told him it would be all right, that look of love and pity I had been trying to capture all these years. The picture of Aberfan.

The Society would be here any minute. "Eject," I said, and cracked the cartridge open, and exposed it to the light.

My Alphabet Starts Where Your Alphabet Ends

▌▐▌

Paul Di Filippo

Paul Di Filippo is a crazy person. He loves to write. He has been writing half his life, which began almost, but not quite, on Halloween, early in the second full year of Eisenhower's first term, 1954. He has written three novels—none yet published—titled *Harp, Pipe, and Symphony; El Mundo Primero* (which might fare better with editors if he translated the title); and *Ciphers.* Bloodied but unbowed, he is at work on a fourth novel, *Spondulix: A Romance of Hoboken.* I can't speak for others, but *I* would pay to read a novel subtitled "A Romance of Hoboken."

Di Filippo's short fiction *has* been published—in *Unearth, Twilight Zone, Fantasy & Science Fiction, New Pathways, Amazing Stories, Night Cry,* George Zebrowski's *Synergy,* and *Pulphouse.* Bruce Sterling reprinted his story "Stone Lives" in *Mirrorshades: The Cyberpunk Anthology.* Di Filippo's nonfiction has appeared in *SF Eye,* Charles Platt's *SF Guide, New Pathways,* the SFWA *Bulletin,* and in the first incarnation of *Astral Avenue,* an urban-guerrilla one-man fanzine that often reached me in an envelope so colorfully ornamented with gonzo rubber-stamp artwork that I had to wash my hands after opening it. Last year, Di Filippo's "Kid Charlemagne" was a Nebula finalist for best short story.

"My Alphabet Starts Where Your Alphabet Ends" is a tribute to an unsung Grand Master of the SF field. I commissioned this essay after reading an abstract of its main points in an issue of *New Pathways* featuring "Astral Avenue" as a recurring column. To say more would be to steal Mr. Di Filippo's thunder, the quiet rumbling of your own appreciative laughter.

Works Discussed in This Essay

And to Think That I Saw It
on Mulberry Street

Dr. Seuss's Sleep Book
Fox in Socks

Green Eggs and Ham
Hop on Pop
Horton Hatches the Egg
Horton Hears a Who
How the Grinch Stole
Christmas
I Can Lick 30 Tigers Today!
If I Ran the Circus
If I Ran the Zoo
Oh Say Can You Say?
Oh, the Thinks You Can
Think
On Beyond Zebra

One Fish Two Fish Red Fish
Blue Fish
Scrambled Eggs Super
The Butter Battle Book
The Cat in the Hat
The Cat in the Hat Comes
Back
The Lorax
There's a Wocket in My
Pocket
Yertle the Turtle and Other
Stories

In 1989, the year the awards in this volume were given, amid the pomp and splendor of the annual Nebula Banquet, attended by tuxedoed and begowned authors, agents, and publishers, the greatest author of SF and fantasy that the twentieth century has yet produced turned eighty-five years old—alone, without fanfare, neglected by his "peers."

Chances are, most SF fans and writers haven't even thought of this author in twenty years. Chances are, most SF fans and writers, even after examining the evidence assembled in this essay, will still try to deny him his accomplishments. Chances are, most SF fans and writers are dead wrong.

We are going to discuss now—belatedly, but perhaps in time to do him justice—a man who has covered more territory more thoroughly and brilliantly; who has influenced more people in their formative years and so throughout their adult lives; who has been truest to his vision of the world, never varying it to suit marketplace forces, than any other author one can point to.

The man's name?

Theodor Geisel.

Who?

Dr. Seuss.

In the limited space available in this volume, any examination of the Good Doctor's fifty-year career, which has resulted in an equal number of books, must perforce be perfunctory. Yet even such an overview will, I believe, establish the man at the pinnacle of SF writers, where he belongs.

Barry Malzberg has a theory that the totality of an SF writer's themes and gifts are present in embryo in his or her first published work. Malzberg's theory is borne out in Dr. Seuss's debut, *And to Think That I Saw It on Mulberry Street,* published in 1937.

Like many authors, Seuss, as he has recounted in his few interviews, had to struggle to get published at all. And when one reads this first subversive text of his, the reason is evident. A publishing milieu that considered *The Little Engine That Could* and Campbell's *The Black Star Passes* to be state-of-the-art SF would hardly have been ready for Seuss's book.

And to Think That I Saw It on Mulberry Street asserts the supremacy of the human imagination over mere physical and social constraints. The child's mental transformation of mundane early-twentieth-century reality (symbolized by horse and cart) into an extravagant, otherworldly procession is as clear a statement of Seuss's recurring main theme as one could want: the unfettered human mind is the final frontier, the source of ultimate reality, and it must always be in opposition to society (as symbolized by the boy's obtuse father). (Seuss's vision has remained remarkably consistent over the years. Compare his much later, *Oh, the Thinks You Can Think.*) In this, Seuss not only echoes the Surrealists and Dadaists who preceded him, but clearly presages Ballard and the New Wave SF of the 1960s, not to mention foreshadowing the generation-gap tumult taking place in the streets at that time.

The fact that *And to Think That I Saw It on Mulberry Street* remains in print, along with all the Doctor's other books, is further testament to its relevance to today and its place in the continuing dialogue about the role of the individual in an increasingly constricted and totalitarian social matrix.

After this initial hurdle, Seuss's career soared from one conquest to another, as his powers matured and flourished. He quickly found his audience, which proved itself loyal and appreciative. Seuss's readers love him. He speaks directly to their unconscious fears, desires, and dreams. Once someone discovers

Dr. Seuss, he never really lets him go, and his life is never thereafter the same.

But, of course, reader affection and social impact, while somewhat valid, are not true measures of literary merit. Let us continue to examine how the Doctor meets the conventional criteria of fictional excellence.

After his first book, Seuss went on to invent the modern fantasy trilogy, years before Tolkien, proving himself an innovator in form as well as content. The three books in this groundbreaking series are *The 500 Hats of Bartholomew Cubbins, Bartholomew and the Oobleck,* and the tangential, yet clearly linked third volume, *The King's Stilts.*

The first volume is notable for its foreshadowing of such Borgesian concerns as infinity and regression, which would recur in later Seuss works. (Seuss has much in common with Borges.) The latter two books deal with Seuss's vision of biological forces. For while Seuss's work features many examples of the strange machines, gadgets, and technology typifying SF, it is primarily for his bizarre organic conceptions that he is known, his living creatures and landscapes. The cosmic, Lovecraftian horror of a rain of oobleck shows up again as the sea of "blue goo" in *Fox in Socks* and the "blue goo" weapon in *The Butter Battle Book.* Seuss was decades ahead of his time in dealing with this deadly protoplasm, which Eric Drexler, in his book *The Engines of Creation,* calls "grey goo," and which figures in such SF works as Ellison and Sheckley's "I See a Man Sitting on a Chair, and the Chair Is Biting His Leg" and Bear's *Blood Music.* The last book in the trilogy marks the initial appearance of another perennial Seuss topic (again, decades ahead of his "peers") that would crop up later in *The Lorax:* ecology. The ring of Dike Trees holding back the sea from the Land of Didd—menaced by Nizzards, protected by Patrol Cats with clearly augmented intelligence, the whole supervised by the all-seeing King on Stilts—well, this is a forceful vision of man working in harmony with nature, and what goes wrong when society is literally deracinated.

These books, however successful, mark a detour into prose for Seuss, a detour that thankfully was only temporary. Seuss's linguistic skills and his desire for verbal experimentation strain at the fetters of this limited medium, as such failed experiments as Joyce's *Finnegans Wake* did too. (Seuss can, indeed, be seen to have triumphed where Joyce failed: he is a genius who has followed his vision to its ultimate limits without losing his audience. Such books as *There's a Wocket in My Pocket* and *Oh Say Can You Say?* have no plot per se, but exist instead for their linguistic puzzles.) Only poetry offered Seuss the means to continue his daring verbal forays, his innovations in language, and he was not to abandon it again.

Neologisms abound in Seuss's work, along with dazzling reworking of conventional words. He truly exemplifies Pound's dictum, "Make it new." Poetry's appeal to the hardwiring in the human brain explains Seuss's incredible staying power in the reader's mind. "Red fish, blue fish." "Hop on pop." "I do not like green eggs and ham / I do not like them, Sam I Am." It brings to mind that other poet of SF, Cordwainer Smith, author of "Think Blue, Count Two" and "Mother Hitton's Littul Kittens." (In fact, there are many intriguing similarities between these two authors. Could it possibly be that the unseen "Paul Linebarger" was really . . . ? But no, it would be too much. . . .)

In short, the man is a supreme stylist. No sentence of his could ever be mistaken for someone else's. There are few other SF authors about whom one could make this claim.

In the 1940s and 1950s, Seuss's work took on a more political stance, as he sought to remake society (*If I Ran the Circus* and *If I Ran the Zoo*), and as he dabbled in social issues, especially in the two Horton books, and in *Yertle the Turtle.* In *Horton Hatches the Egg,* he cleverly explores the issue of child care, as well as demonstrating more of his patented biological polymorphous perversity (the "elephant-bird"). But *Horton Hears a Who* and *Yertle the Turtle* are Seuss's most *engagé* works.

Horton Hears a Who, published in 1954, is nothing less than a clever parable about Joe McCarthy and HUAC. Horton claims to hear the inhabitants of "another world" (Russia) shouting from a speck of dust. His persecution by the beasts of the jungle— especially by the cretinous tribe of monkeys—is repulsive, but its presentation constitutes one of the finest examples of satiric allegory of 1950s' SF. By all rights, Horton's slogan—"A person's a person, no matter how small"—should have branded Seuss a one-worlder and a fellow-traveler. That it did not is a testimony to the ignorance of tyrants.

Yertle the Turtle—written in 1950, a mere year or two after Orwell's *1984*—is clearly a response to that book. It remains one of the century's most poignant, yet hopeful, dystopias. Once again, Seuss chose a biological image to anchor his text: the living throne formed by the stack of turtle subjects, atop which King Yertle perches. The upsetting of this cruel chair by the simple actions of the bottom turtle, Mack, offers hope that the common man will triumph, through the simple quirks of his nature.

(*Yertle*'s significance has been recognized in recent years, notably in a song by the Red Hot Chili Peppers. Moreover, it was cited in a recent brouhaha involving Mayor Koch of New York.)

These works represent the high-water mark of Seuss's political involvement. Never one for joining mass movements, he advanced in the 1960s into a kind of poetic anarchy best exemplified by *The Cat in the Hat* books, which assert as subtext that the sole measure of social justice is the unqualified freedom of the individual. (However, Seuss did later rewrite *Yertle* in a less powerful version, *King Looie Katz,* in which a kingdom of cats is locked in a ring of protocol, each subject carrying another's tail, until the lowest cat refuses.)

What can we say about Seuss's power of invention, his creation of new plots and incidents, alien societies and cultures? No one can fault Seuss here. As already noted, his diverse universes and swift-moving stories possess all the nightmare logic and fecundity of the best Surrealists, placing him squarely in the mainstream of twentieth-century thought. He leaves clear descendants in such SF figures as Jack Vance, with whom he shares a love of music, language, and biological profligacy.

Seuss also exhibits links to the existentialists and such writers as Beckett and Sartre. His *oeuvre* features more long-suffering, undeservedly tormented characters than all of Kafka. Why does the Fox in Socks torment Knox? Why do children hop on Pop? Why does Sam I Am (with a name like that could he be ... God?) insist on force-feeding his dish of green eggs and ham? And we have already mentioned Horton's Christ-like woes. Paranoia also figures extensively in Seuss's work. (See *There's a Wocket in My Pocket.*)

Seuss's work, like much SF, derives additional power from the explicit and implicit interrelatedness of the various books. It means so much more, after reading *Horton Hears a Who,* to realize that *How the Grinch Stole Christmas,* set in Whoville, must take place entirely on a speck of dust resting on a stalk of clover! Seuss's work gains even deeper resonances from the fact that his odd lands are directly linked to the fields we know. It is always only a short step from Weehawken to the edge of the universe in the cosmos of Seuss. (See *Scrambled Eggs Super.*)

Nor does Seuss fail in that area traditionally reserved to SF: the dramatic embodiment of exciting ideas. The infinite regression of that which is contained within the hat of that ultimate anarchist, the Cat in the Hat. (Note also the recurring hat theme in *The Five Hundred Hats of Bartholomew Cubbins.*) The Chippendale Mupp, (from *Dr. Seuss's Sleep Book*), a creature with a long, slow tail (shades of Bob Shaw's slow glass!), where a bite at the tip serves as a wake-up signal eight hours later. Having barely scratched the surface here, we could go on and on. But perhaps most astonishing and deserving of mention is the notion developed in *On Beyond Zebra* that supplies this essay's title: that there could be letters beyond the end of the mundane alphabet. Here is another metaphysical conceit worthy of Borges. Who else in the literature of SF has dared to dream so boldly?

We cannot finish with Seuss without mentioning two recent works. Produced when the artist was in his late sixties and late seventies, these books, by any rational measure, should have each won him Nebula Awards in their respective years of eligibility.

In 1971 (Nebula winner for best novel: Robert Silverberg's *A Time of Changes*), Seuss published *The Lorax.* This tale of ecological devastation concerns the extinction of the Truffala trees and their dependent ecosystem by a family of greedy industrialists (the Once-lers), despite the best efforts of the Lorax, a nature deity, to prevent the destruction. The bleak landscapes are heartbreaking; the portrayal of the Once-ler clan as mere hands connected to never-seen individuals is brilliant; the sweeping indictment of industrialism and its useless products (Thneeds) is stunning. Today, in light of recent assaults on the biosphere, the book is a more powerful experience than ever.

In 1984 (Nebula winner for best novel: William Gibson's *Neuromancer*), at the age of eighty, Seuss published *The Butter Battle Book.* Like Wells's *Mind at the End of Its Tether,* this story is clearly a product of the elderly artist in a moment of despair. The insane arms buildup conducted between the Butter-Up and Butter-Down camps echoes the tale of Swift's Big-Endians and Little-Endians. Only by leaving the ending in doubt does Seuss spare the reader the emotional trauma of mass carnage; simultaneously, he poses a moral dilemma and calls us to worldly action.

Needless to say, these two scathing books did not even make the preliminary Nebula ballot.

In closing—and it's almost unfair to cite this, for it is a skill that none of his "peers" possesses—there's Seuss's visual art. His poetry stands by itself, of course, but the drawings elevate his work beyond emulation. The alien physiology of even his ostensibly human characters, the feathery toes and fingers, the plumed appendages, the hidden sexual organs that must be there . . . or must they? (Seuss, by the way, is never shy about sex. Consider how much of the action of his books occurs in beds or bedrooms.) In Seuss, then, is a re-creation of our familiar world in the transfiguring terms of a true artist's unique vision. His transcendent stories and satires, adventures and allegories color the reader's perceptions indelibly.

Dr. Seuss.

Where is thy Nebula, thy Grand Master, thy Hugo, thy Howard, thy British Fantasy Award, thy Prix Apollo, thy Balrog?

He needs them not. He has our hearts.

The Year of the Pratfall:
SF Movies of 1988

' ' '

Bill Warren

Over the past few years, in the absence of a Nebula for best
film or best screenplay, these volumes have looked to Bill
Warren to keep us abreast of what is happening in the bizarre
world of science fiction film.

As the author of a comprehensive two-volume survey of SF
films from 1950 to 1962, *Keep Watching the Skies!,* Warren has
the skill, the background, and the patience to sit through and
document both the triumphs and the horrors of Hollywood's
sci-fi movie mill. In fact, I fear that too few of us realize just
what a heroic effort—and I am not kidding—researching and
preparing this report actually is.

Warren emphasizes that his essay is a *survey* of the year in
SF film, not an analysis. He believes that it is the only survey
of its kind and that its value lies in chronicling SF-related activity that would otherwise go unnoted. And he wants to acknowledge again his indebtedness to researcher Bill Thomas.

The year 1988 is probably the worst year for filmed science
fiction since, oh, maybe 1948. Of typical SF movies, only *The Blob*
was really any good, and it was a box office failure, despite being
funny and exciting. The number of sequels was up, but *all* of
them were only the second entry in their would-be series: *Cocoon:
The Return, Phantasm II, Return of the Living Dead Part 2, Short
Circuit 2, Critters 2, Return of the Killer Tomatoes,* and every one
of these failed to earn back its cost, though the *Cocoon* and *Short
Circuit* sequels weren't bad as movies.

The number of other imitations remained about the same;
there were knockoffs on *E.T.* (*Mac and Me*), *Gremlins* (*Hobgoblins*), *Alien* (*Deep Space*), and, inevitably, the *Mad Max* films
(there were five of these, tucked away in their own little niche

in the report that follows). More original films than ever had scant theatrical distribution and went swiftly to videotape; a couple of these had some interest, but not enough to warrant wide distribution.

One problem, of course, is that in the last few years there has been a general decline of interest in science fiction movies— because the films themselves are uninteresting. Instead of blaming poor productions, or bad advertising, which would really mean blaming their own judgment, the Money People behind the films choose instead to blame the genre. So why is *Star Trek: The Next Generation* doing well in syndication on television? They have an answer for that, too: it is *Star Trek,* and has its built-in fans.

The Money People may even be right. Bright, inventive SF films, with no trend to latch onto, no series to belong to, have not done well. Every major SF hit of the last few years can just as easily be placed in another category; *RoboCop,* for example, is an action picture, and action pictures do well. *Star Trek* is *Star Trek.* It's not at all impossible that the public's appetite for SF has severely dwindled, because of all the crud they've been forced to swallow.

Turning to written SF is of no help, at least based on the films of that nature in 1988: *Nightfall* was an overintellectualized bore; *Watchers* was barely released. There's no hope that way.

And none from me, either. The following is a report, film by film, of the SF movies of 1988, big films to small, theatrical to videotape. If it sounds like a trip through the Fifty Worst Films of All Time, with Some Exceptions, you're not far wrong. But I open and close with the best SF of the year. And the last one discussed, was, in my opinion, the best Hollywood movie of *any* sort in 1988.

Thirty years ago, *The Blob* oozed its way across the United States. The Blob was a gelatinous mass of protoplasm that arrived from outer space inside a meteor; it was a monster at its most basic. It was alive, it moved, and it ate. Mostly it ate people, growing with each meal. In the summer of 1988, *The Blob* slimed back in the form of a multimillion-dollar remake, written by Frank Darabont and Chuck Russell, and directed by Russell, the same team who made the third *Nightmare on Elm Street* movie. Bless their black little hearts, Darabont and Russell have not forgotten the B-movie origins of their monster: the new *The Blob* is a big B-movie, a humdinger of a horror thriller, fast-paced, amusing, and colorful.

The story is much the same as before: a meteor lands near a small town, and the Blob emerges, engulfing people as it grows. This time, however, the meteor is a crashed U.S. satellite, and the Blob is some kind of biological warfare experiment gone awry. This adds complexity to the plot, but not much else. The special effects are variable but often excellent, and most of the time the Blob seems malignant, alive, and fleshy, as if a pile of raw meat had come to hungry life. The movie is peppered with major set pieces, show-stopping scenes of the Blob gobbling up people, but it's not a grossout contest.

Accepting the familiar plot but battling predictability, Darabont and Russell frequently set up what seems to be a standard scene, a cliché of the genre, then stand it on its head, popping up with a bright surprise. Nobody will ever mistake *The Blob* '88 for a work of art; it's an efficient, entertaining science fiction–horror adventure, but it's a relief to see a movie that honors its 1950s roots without slavishly imitating them. *The Blob* is clever, sleek, and speedy, a perfect drive-in movie, and the best standard SF movie of 1988.

Cocoon: The Return was an unexpectedly responsible sequel. *Cocoon* accidentally said that the only way for old folks to be happy was to be rejuvenated by aliens, then sent into space to live forever. This sequel directly addresses that idea.

The cast from *Cocoon* reunites for *Cocoon: The Return.* And though the story is contrived in getting the six old folks who flew off to Antares back to Earth, even the contrivance works in terms of other plot elements. It's true that Daniel Petrie's direction doesn't build up any suspense at the climax, but this isn't a director's movie anyway. Nor, despite competent work by Stephen McPherson, is it a writer's movie.

It's an actors' movie. And the actors, even bland Steve Guttenberg (*why* is this guy a star?), are all marvelous. The actor who made the biggest impression in the first film, Don Ameche, takes a back seat here to his compatriots, Jack Gilford, Hume Cronyn, and Wilford Brimley; of the actresses, Jessica Tandy predominates over Maureen Stapleton and Gwen Verdon.

Cocoon: The Return asserts that we must take what fate offers us; for everyone here, it will be gradual old age and eventual death, but sometimes that's the right choice to make—still, old age doesn't have to make you stop enjoying yourself. This is a more positive, more humanistic message than the one inadvertently sent by the original film. Though *Cocoon: The Return* is rather aimless in terms of structure, and never becomes very exciting, it's charming because of the cast, and touching because of the decisions they make.

The first *Short Circuit* was merely a restaging of *E.T.* with Number Five, a robot, standing in for the alien; it was negligible, but had one major virtue—the robot himself. Thanks to the voice of Tim Blaney and impressive special effects tricks by a large crew, Number Five was endearing and believable, a lot more than could be said for the movie around him. There was room for a sequel to *Short Circuit,* and *Short Circuit 2* is better than the first film. Once again, the human beings around him are far less interesting than Johnny himself, but at least this time they have a lot to do.

This is an authentic children's movie; the target audience is probably fourteen and under, but it does have value for others. Number Five is still endearing, so perfectly realized by robotics supervisor Eric Allard and his crew that occasional slight reminders that he is, after all, just a special effect, are disappointing. Director Kenneth Johnson blunders occasionally: he has the human characters play too broadly much of the time, as if overplaying *is* comedy. But *Short Circuit 2* belongs body and soul to Johnny Five, the living robot. Many adults will regard the film as simpleminded junk, but it is done with some care and some skill; it has charm and intelligence.

Alien Nation isn't just a conventional cop action thriller, it's a *painfully* conventional cop action thriller. It has, in fact, basically the same storyline as *The Presidio* or, for that matter, *Who Framed Roger Rabbit.* A loner cop is forced to accept as a partner a member of a minority group, one of whom just killed his partner. But now here's the High Concept kicker: *the minority are ALIENS.* Not like from Guadalajara, but from Outer Space. Yow! How's that for different?

Not a lot. You see, these aliens are just like you and me—*very much* like you and me. They have heads like cantaloupes and they get drunk on sour milk, they are already assimilated thoroughly into our culture, and they've only been here three years. There isn't a trace of their own culture left, except an occasional sign in alien lettering, and fast-food joints that serve raw beaver.

This is cowardly science fiction. Director Graham Baker was nervous about alienating, shall we say, a large chunk of the audience by making the Newcomers (as the aliens are unimaginatively called) *too* alien. One has the feeling that this film is not quite what screenwriter Rockne S. O'Bannon originally intended.

Despite his stereotyped role, James Caan, as the human cop, gives an involved and sincere performance. Mandy Patinkin, as the alien partner, only shows that Patinkin's increasingly annoying mannerisms can come right through five pounds of latex. Though gorgeously photographed on real Los Angeles locations by Adam Greenberg, this bland, ordinary movie plays like a TV pilot film. And sure enough, Fox announced an *Alien Nation* TV series.

Alien Nation wasn't the only cop-and-odd-partner SF movie of 1988; there was also *Dead Heat.* This time the odd partner is a zombie. Tough L.A. cops Roger Mortis—get it?—and Doug Bigelow find themselves pitted against holdup men who can't be killed by normal means. They rather easily discover a rejuvenation machine, just in time to temporarily revive Roger after he's decompressed to death—of course, he has only a few hours before he disintegrates. In the course of fairly standard investigation stuff, they discover a sinister conspiracy including coroner Darrin McGavin, supposedly dead industrialist Vincent Price, and Chinese restaurateur Keye Luke. The three veteran performers deserve a lot better treatment than they get here, though McGavin's kind of amusing.

Rumors abounded that Joe Piscopo, as Doug, was uncooperative and egocentric; certainly his smug, narcissistic performance is deadly for the film. Treat Williams, as Roger, is a lot better, entering into things with humor that manages to be both impish and grim. You keep having the feeling that there was something better in Terry Black's screenplay, something that eluded first-time director Mark Goldblatt. The film itself is repellent and gratuitous.

They Live, John Carpenter's latest, has a terrific premise, from a short story by Ray Faraday Nelson, who likes to claim he introduced propellor beanies to science fiction conventions. But something seems to have gone awry in Frank Armitage's screenplay. The solid satirical surface has nothing holding it up in terms of logical motivations, and what starts as a tale of a unique alien invasion disappointingly turns into a bang-bang action piece. ("Armitage" is apparently John Carpenter.)

In Los Angeles, Roddy Piper learns that special dark glasses reveal that ghoul-faced aliens, by use of a secret signal broadcast over television sets, and subliminal lettering in advertising, have forced the "seek the good life" mentality on humanity. But more important, Roddy discovers that about a third of the populace *are* aliens.

Carpenter's prowling camera and unexpectedly effective score provide an eerie sense of unease and tension—right up until we see the aliens. Frank Carriosa's makeup is disastrous, outrageous, unbelievable. The aliens resemble human skulls from which the flesh has fallen, with ball bearings for eyes—they look like the walking dead.

But there's a bigger problem: Carpenter/Armitage never explains just what the aliens want. What are they getting out of exploiting the Earth, promoting consumerism? We're told that they are turning our atmosphere into theirs—but there seem to be *thousands* (if not millions) of aliens already here, so they must be breathing our air just fine right now.

Carpenter believes effect is all. It doesn't matter that at heart the story has no logic, because we will be carried along by the action and thrills. But *They Live* is science fiction; the logic has to be stringent, and that has always been Carpenter's weakest area. There's a real satirical, critical intent to much of *They Live,* with its attack on consumerism at all costs. But though this is a very good, amusing idea for an alien invasion story, Carpenter's illogic and pandering to the action crowd undermine and finally collapse *They Live.*

Vibes was a misfired attempt at a New Age comedy involving pyramid power and ESP. The script by Lowell Ganz and Babaloo Mandel is inferior to their work on *Splash;* it is basically that of a TV movie, both in content and in results. *Vibes* is flatly directed by Ken Kwapis and seems oddly unpopulated.

Jeff Goldblum is psychometric—touching an object gives him knowledge about people who have previously handled it—and Cyndi Lauper seems slightly precognitive, but mainly she's followed around by Louise, an invisible ghost who feeds her important information. Rascally fortune hunter Peter Falk induces them to come to Ecuador, where he hopes to find a treasure.

The plot is loose and sloppy, an attempt at a comic variation on the Indiana Jones movies. The title *Vibes* harks back to the 1960s and implies a kind of high energy, but the film has no relation to any time period and is lacking in almost all energy. Goldblum, Lauper, and Falk deserve another chance to appear together, but *Vibes* itself is so bland that it will probably kill any reunion.

The single-line concept of *Twins* is "Arnold Schwarzenegger and Danny DeVito play twin brothers." Though the film is a routine, clumsily plotted comedy, it was very popular, due entirely to the two leads, who have charm to spare. The central joke was exhausted once you saw the poster for the film, with DeVito leaning against Schwarzenegger like the lower leg on a letter K. The tepid script is credited to two writing teams, William Davies and William Osborne, and Timothy Harris and Herschel Weingrod. Producer-director Ivan Reitman has directed at a medium pace throughout; the film never becomes exciting or very interesting, but also never quite tumbles off the cliff into dull.

Science fiction was required to explain just how Arnold and Danny could be brothers in the first place. In an experiment in eugenics in the early 1950s, donations from six notable men are combined into one sperm, and an exceptional young woman is impregnated. To everyone's highly unlikely surprise, two sons are born. There's a cheap, obvious subplot about a stolen scientific device; the film should have stuck to the idea of the brothers' search for their long-lost mother. If you get any fun out of this, it will be because Arnold Schwarzenegger and Danny DeVito are a nice pair of guys to spend a couple of hours with, not because the film itself has anything to offer.

The unconscious message of *Monkey Shines,* adapted from a novel by Michael Stewart, is that all monkeys are evil. And another, even more distasteful, idea that the film unintentionally promulgates is that if you are quadriplegic, you're better off dead. George Romero wrote and directed, and struggled to structure things solidly and to build logically on characterization. But the effort shows, and the film dawdles when it should rush ahead. At the climax, things get so far out of hand that what's intended to induce terror in shuddering audiences is more likely to prompt scornful laughter.

Despondent quadriplegic Allan is given a monkey as his servant and companion (this is a real practice), but she's a super-monkey, the result of brain cell experiments by Allan's scientist friend. Ella, the monkey, soon comes to jealously guard Allan against everyone, resorting to murder when needed. As the attachment between Ella and Allan grows, they become telepathically linked; she somehow magnifies Allan's anger into homicidal rages, but when she's gone, he can't wait to get rid of her. Ella, the fiend, manages to overpower both of the would-be rescuers, who are accustomed to handling monkeys; it is up to a man paralyzed from the neck down to save the day.

Some of the dialogue, though occasionally too theatrical, has pop and sizzle—Romero has always been a better writer than a director. It wouldn't have been an easy film to do, with its heavy dependence on a monkey, but it's too bad that at some point someone didn't decide that it really was not worth doing.

Paul Mayersberg's script for *The Man Who Fell to Earth* was elliptical, subtle, and sophisticated; Nicholas Roeg's direction was equally daring, but his powerful images, plus the effective performances of the cast, kept the film engrossing even when it was puzzling. In adapting Isaac Asimov's short story "Nightfall" as a film of the same title, Mayersberg turned director and used the same disjointed style in telling this very straight-line narrative. It was appropriate for adapting Walter Tevis's novel, but not for the Asimov story, partly because Mayersberg lacks Roeg's flair, and his film lacks the vivid characters of the earlier story.

Nightfall is verbose, outrageously expository. It overcorrects a fault of the story, in which the society depicted was pretty much like that of the period in which the story was written. Here, the society has no discernible relationship to any human society, past or present, though the film vaguely resembles an early 1950s SF movie, only set in ancient Rome.

Asimov's story had a powerful central idea, a good metaphor for any major change facing society: on a planet with three suns, true night comes only once every thousand years, and for reasons no one really knows, at each of those times, society plunges back into barbarism. At last, we discover that the planet is in the center of a star cluster, so that not only does night descend, but millions of brilliant stars appear in the sky. Society suffers a psychotic sense of insignificance.

In the film, as in the story, night is about to fall, but Mayersberg ignores the issues facing society and the mystery of the collapse of civilization. Instead, his two central characters, played by David Birney and Alexis Kanner (in a hammy, stylized performance), lock horns over ill-defined religious matters. When night does at last fall, there are few consequences for anyone; people seem more impressed that it is snowing . . . or something.

Mayersberg's fragmented editing fractures whatever interest the story itself develops. He grotesquely mistakes pompous pretentiousness for seriousness, trying to force meaning out of style. He does take a classic SF story seriously, but instead of expanding upon the ideas the story raises, he jettisons them in favor of his own concepts—and then fails to make those clear.

Sometimes scripts wind their way through Hollywood for years, picking up and dropping stars, writers, and directors. *My Stepmother Is an Alien* began as Jerico Stone's dead-serious script about an evil alien stepmother intent on destroying the world; Stone claimed it was based on a real-life experience. But when Bette Midler was cast, the script was rewritten as a comedy. After Midler left the project and new stars came in, the script was changed to accommodate the personae of successive actresses. In order, they were Julie Andrews, Raquel Welch, Bette Midler (again), Joan Rivers, Cybill Shepherd, Shelley Long, and, finally, Kim Basinger. At last, the stepmother was both comic and sexy. By this time, the script had gone through at least eight writers; those finally credited were Stone (billed under his first name, Jerico), Herschel Weingrod, Timothy Harris, and Jonathan Reynolds. All this effort for a film plotted a lot like *Splash.*

Nerdy, pudgy scientist Steve Mills (Dan Aykroyd) accidentally zaps a planet in another solar system, damaging its gravity; two aliens, Celeste (Basinger) and a literal one-eyed handbag snake, arrive to get him to duplicate the experiment, which will save their world. They can't just ask him, because the head aliens (treated much like gods) on the damaged planet intend to destroy the Earth once Aykroyd sets things right. Basinger vamps Aykroyd, and after one wild night they're married, arousing the suspicions of Steve's daughter Jessie (Alyson Hannigan). Celeste goes through a lot of the usual Ma and Pa Kettle in New York routines, only this time sex is involved. She studies a porn film to learn technique.

The movie is way over the top in plotting and directing. Director Richard Benjamin slams every laugh home, apparently afraid that otherwise no one will know that laughs are intended. Aykroyd plays his role like a *Saturday Night Live* sketch character, but Basinger, despite some overplaying on her part, manages to actually be both sexy and funny. However, like virtually all comic aliens in movies, Celeste might as well have come from Faerie as from outer space. The movie ends with both Aykroyd and Basinger badly doing Jimmy Durante routines in an effort to prevent the destruction of the Earth; this effort doesn't pay off, though they do save the Earth. The movie self-destructs.

The minor SF films of the year had more bright spots among them than the major films, as used often to be the case, but even the brightest spots were of low wattage.

Most reviewers greeted *Killer Klowns from Outer Space* with weary disgust, such as "Cart" in *Variety,* who concluded, "If sci-fi has come to this, it's time for a break." Undeniably, the film is routinely plotted, unevenly acted, and cheaply produced; Stephen Chiodo's direction is lumpy and unexciting. But all that aside, *Killer Klowns* is a brassy, funny, and imaginative aberration, the kind of thing that a high school class cutup might manufacture. The Chiodo Brothers—Stephen, Charles, and Edward—produced the film; Stephen and Charles wrote it; and all three did the effects, which range from average to good.

In a spaceship that looks like a circus tent, Klowns from outer space land near a small town. These Klowns are indeed Killers; their faces aren't *made up* with white greasepaint and colossal grins, they *really look that way,* in elaborate, unsettling masks. They wear the usual clown garb: baggy, colorful satin, with ruffled collars and tiny hats. The Chiodos have hardly missed a clown cliché: to track down the fugitive heroes, the Klowns fashion a dog out of balloons, which yarks and snuffles its way through the forest. Their guns shoot living popcorn, apparently embryonic Klowns; they encase people in big balls of cotton candy, then drink blood through twisting straws. Their pies are deadly, they ride on invisible motorcycles, they clout people with candy-striped mallets, they turn up as pizza deliverymen and hand-puppeteers. Even though they behave like clowns, with broad gestures and silly walks, they're genuinely murderous, and the film is not really a comedy, though it's often very funny. *Killer Klowns* meanders, the dialogue is lame, and in terms of actual plot there are no surprises—but it's cheerful, wackily designed, and altogether original in concept. And those are major virtues.

In addition to *Nightfall,* several other SF films were released in 1988 by Roger Corman's company, Concorde. Terence H. Winkless made his directing debut with *The Nest* (from a novel by Eli Cantor), a suspenseful, lean model for a good low-budget B-movie thriller, this time dealing with killer cockroaches. Robert Lansing was the star. The film overextends itself at the end, but until then is very well done. Jim Wynorski remade Roger Corman's own *Not of This Earth,* about a vampiric alien, as a vehicle for porn-star-going-straight Traci Lords. It was brisk, vulgar, and unpretentious; Lords was not bad at all. Concorde's shot-in-Peru *Crime Zone* was a nice try, a profane, satiric underworld melodrama set in a repressive future. David Carradine coerces Peter Nelson and Sherilyn Fenn into committing crimes for him; his motivation is a genuine surprise. The film collapses before the end, however. Producer-director Luis Llosa exhibits a moody, stylish talent that could go far, *The Purple People Eater* was a children's movie based on the Sheb 'Wooley hit of thirty years before; *Variety* called it "silly and juvenile," though it did star two respected character actors, Ned Beatty and Shelley Winters.

Although extravagantly tasteless, Frank Henenlotter's *Brain Damage* is vivid, unusual, and intelligent. However, it's an ultimately failed attempt to comment metaphorically on drug addiction through the medium of a freakish monster movie. The message seems to be simply that addiction is bad for you. The result was an instant cult fave-rave, but swiftly hit the video shops, probably its best venue anyway.

A talking eel-like parasite called Elmer invades the skull of New York City resident Brian, and in the voice of John "Zacherly" Zacherle, Elmer promises Brian great things—and delivers by excreting a blue fluid into the tissues of Brian's brain. (Seen in loving close-up.) Brian, hallucinating in LSD-like fashion, wanders around the city. Elmer uses Brian as a mobile base to leap forth and devour the brains of victims.

Brian's state of euphoria and the horrible withdrawal symptoms when Elmer withholds the fluid are very explicitly compared with those of both drug and alcohol addiction. But a problem is that the movie is so gruesome that many to whom it might appeal will be repelled. It's also impishly grotesque—Elmer sings, natch, "Elmer's Tune"—but not entirely a black comedy. Writer-director Henenlotter seems scornful of the material, yet passionately embraces its most gruesome aspects and still wants the film to be a serious statement on addiction. But the seriousness is compromised by the horror, and the horror by the idea of an intelligent, sardonic parasite (an Aylmer). Still, the film is impressive on its own scrambled level, with Elmer's characterization being especially strong: he insists upon Brian's complicity in the murders.

The other SF films of the year included a movie that its own director, Mick Garris, described as "not bad for a sequel to a ripoff." And *Critters 2* was in fact a sequel to *Critters,* an imitation of *Gremlins.* The voracious "krites," the alien critters of the title, are back to bedevil the same small town, with mostly predictable results. Garris, who co-wrote with D. T. Twohy, is obviously more at ease with the violence and action than with the awkward sentimentality of the ending. The movie was reasonably entertaining.

Phantasm II began very well; the opening half hour was disciplined filmmaking, with a disquieting mood. But director Don Coscarelli let things run down badly in the last half, and it becomes simply an excuse for extravagant gore effects.

Mac and Me, directed by Stewart Raffill, was just a cumbersome imitation of *E.T.,* faking that film's genuine warmth, and featuring a big-eyed alien family from what seems to be Titan, although the credits call them Martians. It heavily plugged McDonald's; the hamburger chain returned the mandated favor. The relationship between the little-boy alien and the "me" of the title, a boy who is really confined to a wheelchair, takes forever to be established, and is taken for granted thereafter.

The Pia Zadora star vehicle, *Voyage of the Rock Aliens,* sat on the shelf for a long time, but aging didn't improve it. However, it's harmless at worst in its story of emotionless aliens seeking the source of rock music. There's also a pollution-spawned tentacled monster in a polluted lake near the town of Spielburg—these being the film's nods toward social activism and satire. The songs are just thumpathumpa noise, but the choreography is good. And Pia Zadora is charming. The film will be enjoyed by those who appreciate self-conscious camp; I can't imagine who else would even want to watch it.

Ken Wiederhorn's *Return of the Living Dead Part II* lacks all the nasty wit that made Dan O'Bannon's *Return of the Living Dead* exceptional, as well as any real attempt to terrify. The movie is a repellent catastrophe, so unfunny that it seems as though Wiederhorn doesn't even know what comedy *is,* but merely read about it somewhere.

It wasn't even as funny as *The Invisible Kid,* which wasn't funny at all. Or anything else. Writer-director Avery Crounse explored new lows in taste: in the story, pigeon crap is the secret ingredient in an invisibility formula. Although the film is about teenagers, it doesn't exploit any of the obvious jokes, except for one quick scene in a girls' locker room—nor is it otherwise funny. The story would have been just about the same if invisibility had not been involved. It does set a landmark, however—it contains Karen Black's worst performance.

Galactic Gigolo is *almost* the worst SF comedy of 1988, a year notable for bad ones. It's as close to unwatchable as any film I have ever seen. This is not a recommendation.

Universal's *Watchers,* from the Dean R. Koontz novel, played only a few locations. Reviews were harsh, even hostile, but the story doesn't seem promising in the first place. A dog, its intelligence raised to genius level by experimenters, escapes from a lab and becomes friendly with Corey Haim. But it's pursued by a monster called Oxcom, who hates the dog, though they were designed to be partners. Also on their trail is Michael Ironside, a murderous government agent assigned to get the experimental creatures back. The script was by Bill Freed and Damian Lee; the director was Jon Hess. *Variety*'s "Har" said, "It's never very clear who the watchers are, what they are watching or why, but it's quickly certain nobody will be watching the *Watchers* for long."

In the last few years, feature-length animation films have made a comeback, and a few producers have been using the medium as a vehicle for science fiction, or SF-styled stories. So far, the batting average has been as low as for live-action films. For instance, although Don Bluth's *The Land Before Time* is better than *An American Tail,* it was still a weakly picaresque tale, involving baby dinosaurs seeking a better life. It was innovative in terms of subject matter, but cowardly in terms of approach: there's no real sense of menace. It needed more spunk, but it was successful. The animation, however, is outstanding, lacking the fussy, overdone quality of *An American Tail.*

Isaac Asimov rewrote the translation of the French script of *Light Years* (you follow that?), and so got to be credited as "presenting" this film from Rene Laloux and Philippe Caza, the director and designer, respectively. It's set on another world and involves time travel, but the film is labored, with an overemphasis on pastel blue in the color scheme, and actually too much imagination in the design of the characters. The film suffers from a cluttered landscape with no governing logic. Like the earlier film from the same team, *Fantastic Planet, Light Years* was made for adults, but unfortunately is slow and uninteresting.

Bravestarr was just a TV cartoon moved into theaters, centering on a planet with a lot of Old West elements. The result is of interest only to the most indulgent (and youngest) children.

At the Last Trump, George *Mad Max* Miller is going to have to answer for showing exploitative producers the way to make a science fiction movie without actually spending any money: set it in the future after the collapse of civilization (or a war, or a plague), have everyone dress in leather or thrift-shop wardrobe, and drive around in cheaply obtained old cars. Shoot it in the desert to avoid having to build miniatures or do expensive matte paintings. At least 1988 didn't bring any new *Italian* ripoffs of the *Mad Max* films.

World Gone Wild is better than the vast majority of post-holocaust films, though that should not be regarded as a major recommendation—the best word for it is "funky." But it has spirit and a pleasing self-awareness.

In the late twenty-first century, rain hasn't fallen for fifty years, so water is a precious commodity. But not in the small community of Lost Wells, where everyone lives in derelict cars; they have a working well. The head of the community is laid-back, spacey Ethan (Bruce Dern)—half real, half charlatan. The community is raided by vicious visionary Derek (Adam Ant) and his regimented young followers dressed in white. In a city where it's always night, Ethan finds old pal George (Michael Paré), and in *Magnificent Seven* tradition, they round up a group of mercenaries who're willing to protect Lost Wells from Derek, who vowed to return. In keeping with the idea that this is really a Western, the heroine is virginal schoolmarm Catherine Mary Stewart, who shows a nice ability with comedy.

But it's Dern who steals the film. He seems more relaxed these days, more willing to have fun on screen. He loves making movies, and it shows now more than ever. His Ethan is one of the most entertaining roles he's had in ten years, and you miss him whenever he's off screen.

The movie is played out in several big, ineptly connected

chunks, but Jorge Zamacona's funny, jokey script gives some pleasure anyway. Lee H. Katzin directed, reasonably well. Katzin isn't a stylist, he's an action director, and *World Gone Wild,* loose and rawboned as it is, has enough action to satisfy. It seems very underproduced, but at heart is a disposable movie, the kind of thing that plays off quickly and then vanishes, which it did.

Of the several other post-holocaust films, *Cherry 2000* was the best, although it went to video several years after it was made, after only scant releases around the country. It's again set in that *Mad Max*–ized future, although here there doesn't seem to have been a war. Seeking a new body for his sex robot Cherry—he carries her memory chip faithfully—Sam (David Andrews) hires "Tracker" E Johnson (Melanie Griffith) to lead him to the desolate Zone where the bodies are stored in an old, sand-covered casino. The film wasn't cheap, and involves an exciting action scene set near Hoover Dam, but Griffith was wildly miscast as the tough, strong Tracker. Director Steve de Jarnatt directed Michael Almereyda's awkwardly satirical script too straight; only actor Tim Thomerson entered into the spirit of things properly; he's grand. The central idea is mossy with age: at the end, of course, Sam has fallen for E, proving once again that a live person, complete with flaws, is preferable to cold robotic perfection. As if anyone ever really has to make that choice. Brion James is seen briefly.

Hell Comes to Frogtown has a great title and excellent humanoid frog masks by Steve Wang, but two directors, R. J. Kizer and Donald Jackson, can't bring the cliché-ridden script by Randall Frakes to life. The conflicts are trite, and characterization is snowed under by a blizzard of double entendres, few of them clever. It involves the only fertile man (Roddy Piper again), being hauled around by tough Sandahl Bergman, as they attempt to rescue the only fertile women from the frogs. It's routine, but does rate some points for brassy outrageousness.

Dead Man Walking features Brion James as an orange-haired "Zero Man," a noncontagious victim of the plague that has devastated the world by 2004; dying, he angrily kidnaps an industrialist's daughter. Another Zero Man, Wings Hauser, goes into one of those omnipresent desolate areas to bring her back.

Although the movie is not set in the usual post-holocaust future, it has the same junk-apocalypse set design; the color is washed out, and the film seems almost unfinished. But director Gregory Brown shows glimmerings of promise, though writers John Weidner and Rick Marx toe the clichéd line.

The sole distinction of *Phoenix the Warrior* was that in *this* *Mad Max*–ish future, all men (but one, as it turns out) are dead. But writers Robert Hayes and Dan Rotblatt otherwise do the same things the same way, and so does Hayes as director. It's shot in the desert to save money, and features dune buggies and assault rifles, while everyone—all gorgeous young women— dresses in skimpy rags and furs. In the leading role, Kathleen Kinmont (Abby Dalton's daughter) is very attractive, and certainly enters into things with energy, but needs to learn more about grace for future action roles.

It's still not impossible that movies made exclusively, or at least primarily, for videotape will be the savior of science fiction. All they have to do is have a spiffy ad on the box, attractive enough to get a customer to plunk down a couple of bucks for rental. The films have to be cheap, of course, but that's all—they *can* be inventive, literate, and imaginative. So far, however, those commodities are in even shorter supply on videotape than in theaters. Not always, though.

Pulse is so persuasively directed by Paul Golding, who also wrote, that for a while you're swept up in the absurd story, but eventually it loses its grip—because it's just too hard to believe in an inimical electrical short circuit. A pulse of electricity travels into the television set in a suburban home; slowly the boy living there learns that it has killed others in the neighborhood, and is now infecting more appliances in his home. This idea, almost Ray Bradburyesque, is better developed in written fiction; despite excellent scenes within the set of soldered circuits melting and reforming, and a bang-up finale as the TV's electron gun fires laserlike beams all around the house, the story becomes less convincing as it proceeds. But it is a nice try, overall; the story is visually very well told from the boy's point of view. Golding is a writer-director to keep an eye on.

Slugs, a Spanish film set in the United States, is the first movie based on the gleefully sleazy subgenre of horror known as "British Nasties," which often center on some icky woodland creature gone amok, or multiplying like mad. There is an entire *series* of novels centering on giant crabs. In *Slugs*, common garden slugs are enlarged a little by toxic waste, multiply under a small town, then start gobbling up those who can't outrun a one-footed mollusc. The courage of some of the actors, in allowing themselves to be covered with slugs, is impressive. Juan Riquer Simon directed from Ron Gantman's script, and rather well, too. It's just a cheap little monster picture, but not bad for what it is.

Even Oscar winners have to keep themselves in Reeboks and jogging suits, so you can't really blame George Kennedy for making *Demonwarp, Nightmare at Noon,* and *Uninvited.* He probably worked only two or three days on *Demonwarp,* the most dismal of the three. This mess involved Bigfoot, the walking dead, and an alien stranded in Griffith Park's Bronson Caverns. It's hopeless

Nightmare at Noon was more ambitious, and a bit better. Kennedy played a sheriff in a small town where inhabitants suddenly go berserk and kill others. This is because Brion James (this time an albino) has dumped something weird in the town's water supply, which turns people's blood into green acid. The survivors recover at the end. The cast, also including Wings Hauser and Bo Hopkins, would be great for a Western, which the film turns into. Nico Mastorakis directed from the script he wrote with Kirk Ellis; it has a desert-town setting, but is otherwise much like earlier films in which small town inhabitants go berserk, such as *The Crazies* and *Impulse.*

Greydon Clark's *Uninvited* featured Kennedy as the glum, taciturn henchman to millionaire financier Alex Cord (who's quite good, though a good performance is unnecessary here); another henchman is freakish Clu Gulager. Along with some college students, they're all trapped on Cord's yacht at the mercy of a pretty orange tabby cat. It's an escaped lab animal, though what the experiments (involving an old favorite, radiation) were aimed at is anyone's guess: at times of stress the cat gags, and out of its mouth crawls a vicious creature resembling a bat. It expands in size and bites a bystander; the person's blood expands i volume, the person explodes, the monster shrinks and crawls back inside the cat. Clark produced and directed as well as wrote. But why? In any event, Kennedy landed a role on TV's *Dallas* and doesn't need to look back.

Jeff Lieberman's *Remote Control* doesn't work, but the idea is unusual and interesting; it's the only mainstream movie I know of to address the popularity of movies on videotape. If Lieberman had paid more attention to logic, written an ending for his premise, and found a unified tone for the film, it might have been a winner. As it is, it's a bright, confused curiosity.

The new movie *Remote Control* is very popular at the video store where Kevin Dillon works. He soon learns that while watching the movie, people suddenly see themselves in it, then kill their companions. It's a 1950s SF movie that predicted home video; the plot of the movie involved aliens using a home videotape called *Remote Control* to take over the minds of human beings and force them to murder. Which, of course, is the plot of *this* *Remote Control* as well.

This twisting of perception back on itself could have led to something interesting, but it's really just a joke, like the 1950s movie-within-the-movie—it's nothing at all like real 1950s SF movies. At the Japanese-owned factory where the killer tapes are manufactured, Dillon and his friend Jennifer Tilly are almost caught by Bert Remsen, a slave of the aliens, but they destroy all the tapes. All but one, a triumphant Japanese alien points out. But that's just a punchline, not an ending. Lieberman is intelligent, but has difficulty developing his premises. The movie is slickly made, however, and quite watchable.

Attack of the Killer Tomatoes was a deliberately schlocky little cheapie that gained notoriety for its title alone; certainly the film itself warranted no fame, as it was sophomoric and heavy. But the sequel, *Return of the Killer Tomatoes!,* is somewhat better. The script was by Constantine Dillon, J. Stephen Peace, and John De Bello, who directed.

After the onslaught of the vicious vegetables in the first film, the world has become terrified of tomatoes. This does not discourage mad scientist John Astin, who is turning tomatoes into ʾamboid tomato men, who guard him. The story is pretty aimless, involving a pizza delivery man (Anthony Starke) falling in love with winsome Tara (Karen Mistal), unaware that she is a were-tomato.

The movie ambles along, setting up and paying off gags, tossing out cheap puns, and working overtime at spoofing everything possible. The film is pretty deadly as a comedy for a solitary viewer, but might provide laughs for a group. The script is much better than the first film, but the direction is still clunky and obvious.

Everybody loves a good disembodied brain movie, of course (don't they?), but *The Brain* isn't good. It's certainly wild-eyed, because this disembodied brain grows eyes and a fangy mouth, then gobbles people up whole, growing like The Blob all the time. It's dispatched by a flung bottle of sodium, a rather ignoble end for such an extravagant critter. It's apparently from outer space, and seeks "action" as it dominates the minds of the residents of a small city. The movie is plodding and silly, dull and predictable; Barry Pearson seems to have intended some jokes in his script, but director Edward Hunt misses them. The one good joke is that the mad scientist's cultish group "The Independent Thinkers" are all brainwashed zombies. David Gale, who lost his head in *Re-Animator,* does it again here. He should find a good way to keep it fastened down.

R.O.T.O.R. (Robotic Officer Tactical Operation Research) is the first American-made imitation of *RoboCop* and was shot in Texas on videotape. Those are all its distinguishing traits; it has no virtues, just the old Watchbird plot, as the robot cop goes berserk and spends most of the movie trying to kill just one speeder. Budd Lewis wrote it and Cullen Blaine directed, not very well. It's heavily padded, set in a future that looks exactly like today, and sports the worst pseudoscientific gobbledegook since *Teenagers from Outer Space.*

Busy director Fred Olen Ray had only one SF film out in 1988, *Deep Space* (which doesn't have a single frame set in deep space), a too-slavish imitation of *Alien.* L.A. cops Charles Napier and Ron Glass battle a monstrous creature created by scientists, which falls to Earth in Southern California. There's some indication that the film was intended to be a spoof, but there's not enough of this. Ray, not a bad director, would be better off with original material.

Miami Horror was an Italian film set in the United States and dealing with Atlantis, Martians, ancient Etruscans, and a strange embryo being grown by unheeding scientists. This is best left to die-hard buffs.

"Once upon a time there lived a little girl named Wanda," the movie begins, and eons later ends with, ". . . and they lived happily ever after." No one who manages to sit all the way through Albert Pyun's *Alien from L.A.* is likely to think in terms of happiness for hours. The film has no appeal, and all the pace of cold honey, so it's not likely anyone will reach the end of the picture anyway. The story is awful, and Pyun's dark-yet-gaudy, vaguely punkish visuals sour things further. It was written by women, Debra Ricci and Regina Davis, but that is no recommendation.

Model Kathy Ireland plays Wanda Saknussemm, a female nerd living in Los Angeles who loses her asshole boyfriend because she's boring. Ireland's performance is charmless, and her squeaky voice sounds like Rocky the Flying Squirrel after emasculation.

Receiving a message from her long-lost father in Africa, Wanda rushes off to find him. He believed that aliens founded Atlantis centuries before and set off to prove this. Wanda promptly falls down a hole to the center of the Earth. (Arne Saknussemm was the subterranean explorer followed ever downward in Verne's *Journey to the Center of the Earth.*) She finds an English-speaking, urban/frontier/totalitarian society, something like a cross between *Mad Max Beyond Thunderdome, 1984,* and a rock video. The crude satire is soured by Pyun's murky, overripe photography, with lots of rotten yellow light. His control of actors is poor, and crowd scenes are just that—movement with no choreography.

With *Frankenstein General Hospital,* writers Michael Kelly and Robert Deel, and director Deborah Roberts, have achieved a major distinction: the worst Frankenstein film ever shot in English. Easily. Mark Blankfield is Dr. Bob Frankenstein, a hospital resident tinkering together a monster in the basement. Roberts thinks she's parodying 1930s Frankenstein movies in shooting all the basement scenes in black and white, using long takes and no close-ups, but she's out of her league. The movie is slow and stupid, full of dully vulgar sex jokes and potty humor, including the first farting Frankenstein monster (Irwin Keyes). This is particularly worthless dreck.

So is *Hobgoblins,* another *Gremlins* imitation, written, produced, directed, photographed, and edited by Rick Sloane, who makes a full miss in every category. Murderous, wish-granting imps from a flying saucer terrorize a nightclub. The movie is wretchedly amateurish, with poor color and effects; it's so dreadful that the fact that it's a comedy isn't apparent until the film is nearly over—and that's when you have the sick realization that a man burning to death is supposed to be funny.

Lawrence Cohn, *Variety*'s "Lor," called *Rejuvenatrix*—a cross between *Sunset Boulevard* and *The Wasp Woman*—"a pleasantly old-fashioned horror film." An aging actress seeking rejuvenation achieves it, but at the cost of occasionally turning into a Medusa-like monster. Cohn also reviewed *Midnight Movie Massacre* and *Invasion Earth: The Aliens Are Here,* which had very similar premises: monsters attack an audience watching old SF films. In the first of the two, the film they're watching is actually re-created footage from the TV series *Space Patrol;* in the second, it's real scenes from 1950s SF movies. Neither film was considered anything much.

And so we at last, wearily, come to the end of this onslaught of ordure, this marching band of mediocrity. And what do we arrive at? A film that may actually be a masterpiece. Though many will disagree, I'm sure, I consider *Who Framed Roger Rabbit* to be, in some senses, the very model of a science fiction film. It is set in an alternate reality in which animated cartoon characters live in a garish, alarming ghetto called Toontown and interact with people on a regular basis. The abilities of the 'Toons are fantastical, but limited and defined. These are hallmarks of science fiction, in, as I said, some senses. Also, the movie is terrific, and I wanted to mention it.

Everyone flipped for the wonderful animation, directed by Richard Williams, so beautifully integrated into the live action, directed by Bob Zemeckis. But as great as that aspect is, it's not what I consider the major virtue of *Who Framed Roger Rabbit.* After all, this technical wizardry is largely a matter of money and time: spend enough money, take enough time, and these problems can be solved, however painstakingly.

Nor is the best thing the movie's fast pace, a-gag-a-microsecond timing, Bob Hoskins's sympathetic but funny performance as a tough private eye, Christopher Lloyd's weirdo Judge Doom, the zappity-pow action, or the cliffhanger ending. Nor yet the guest star appearances by many Disney and Warner Bros. cartoon characters.

The most impressive, even astonishing, thing about *Who Framed Roger Rabbit* is Roger himself. What's terrific about Roger, and ultimately the most impressive aspect of the movie, is that he is a fully developed, believable, and winning character who is unabashedly an animated cartoon character, perhaps the first time this has ever been done in movie history. Previously, fully believable characters in feature cartoons have been people in funny suits, with the motivations and temperaments of people. Roger Rabbit is a 'Toon bunny rabbit. He was created to make people laugh, and that's his purpose in life, even when it *threatens* his life. But he's warmhearted, passionate, generous, friendly, frightened, touching, heroic; Roger is a star.

The film was freely adapted by Jeffrey Price and Peter S. Seaman from Gary K. Wolf's novel *Who Censored Roger Rabbit?* and is an improvement on the novel, which centered on comic strips rather than cartoons. It's a good spoof of *film noir,* following classic *film noir* traditions. The story could have done better by being a little less obvious, and the climax goes on far too long. Not all the gags work; at times, you find yourself appreciating the effort, but also realize that you aren't laughing. On the other hand, the film is so fast that you can end up concentrating on it so hard that you refrain from laughing, just to avoid stepping on the *next* laugh.

But *Who Framed Roger Rabbit* is *unique.* There has never been another film like it, and probably never will be again. It's a genuine must-see for everyone; families will love it for Roger, movie buffs for its neat cross-references, and everyone else for the dizzyingly fast action and bellylaffs. It's the best movie of 1988.

Appendixes

About the Nebula Awards

The twenty-fourth annual Nebula Awards were presented at the traditional banquet, held this year at the New York Penta Hotel in New York City on April 22, 1989. As usual, the final ballot was the result of votes cast by the members of the Science Fiction Writers of America on a preliminary ballot, itself the product of recommendations made throughout the year by SFWA members. The final ballot consisted of the five works receiving the most votes in each of four categories: novel, novella, novelette, and short story. The number of works was more than five if there were ties in the voting, or if the Nebula Awards jury elected to add a work to one or more of the categories.

For purposes of the Nebula Awards, a novel is 40,000 words or more; a novella, 17,500 to 39,999 words; a novelette, 7,500 to 17,499 words; and a short story, 7,499 words or less.

Active members of the Science Fiction Writers of America decide the Nebula Awards. Founded in 1965 by Damon Knight, SFWA's first president, the organization began with a charter membership of seventy-eight writers; it now has nearly a thousand members.

Lloyd Biggle, Jr., SFWA's first secretary-treasurer, proposed in 1965 that the organization publish an annual anthology of the best stories of the year. This notion, wrote Damon Knight in his introduction to *Nebula Award Stories: 1965* (Doubleday, 1966), "rapidly grew into an annual ballot of SFWA's members to choose the best stories, and an annual Awards Banquet." Judith Ann Lawrence designed the trophy, from a sketch by Kate Wilhelm; it is a block of lucite containing a rock crystal and a spiral nebula made of metallic glitter. No two handmade trophies are exactly alike.

Since 1965, the Nebula Awards have been given each year for the best novel, novella, novelette, and short story published during the preceding year. An award for Best Dramatic Presentation first given in 1972 lasted only three years, the membership later voting to restrict the Nebula to published literary works. An anthology including the winning short fiction and selected runners-up is published each year. The Nebula Awards Banquet takes place every spring, its location alternating between New York City and the West Coast.

The Grand Master Nebula Award goes to a living author for a lifetime's achievement. The membership bestows it no more than six times in a decade. In accordance with SFWA bylaws, the president, who traditionally consults with past presidents and the board of directors, nominates a candidate. This nomination then goes before the officers; if a majority approve, that candidate becomes a Grand Master.

To date, ten writers have received the Grand Master Nebula: Robert A. Heinlein in 1974, Jack Williamson in 1975, Clifford D. Simak in 1976, L. Sprague de Camp in 1978, Fritz Leiber in 1981, Andre Norton in 1983, Arthur C. Clarke in 1985, Isaac Asimov in 1986, Alfred Bester in 1987, and Ray Bradbury in 1988. Seven of SFWA's ten officially designated Grand Masters are still alive at this writing.

Past Nebula Award Winners

1965

Best Novel: *Dune* by Frank Herbert
Best Novella: "The Saliva Tree" by Brian W. Aldiss
"He Who Shapes" by Roger Zelazny (tie)
Best Novelette: "The Doors of His Face, the Lamps of His Mouth" by Roger Zelazny
Best Short Story: "Repent, Harlequin!' Said the Ticktockman" by Harlan Ellison

1966

Best Novel: *Flowers for Algernon* by Daniel Keyes
Babel-17 by Samuel R. Delany (tie)
Best Novella: "The Last Castle" by Jack Vance
Best Novelette: "Call Him Lord" by Gordon R. Dickson
Best Short Story: "The Secret Place" by Richard McKenna

1967

Best Novel: *The Einstein Intersection* by Samuel R. Delany
Best Novella: "Behold the Man" by Michael Moorcock
Best Novelette: "Gonna Roll the Bones" by Fritz Leiber
Best Short Story: "Aye, and Gomorrah" by Samuel R. Delany

1968

Best Novel: *Rite of Passage* by Alexei Panshin
Best Novella: "Dragonrider" by Anne McCaffrey
Best Novelette: "Mother to the World" by Richard Wilson
Best Short Story: "The Planners" by Kate Wilhelm

1969

Best Novel: *The Left Hand of Darkness* by Ursula K. Le Guin
Best Novella: "A Boy and His Dog" by Harlan Ellison
Best Novelette: "Time Considered as a Helix of
Semi-Precious Stones" by Samuel R. Delany
Best Short Story: "Passengers" by Robert Silverberg

1970

Best Novel: *Ringworld* by Larry Niven
Best Novella: "Ill Met in Lankhmar" by Fritz Leiber
Best Novelette: "Slow Sculpture" by Theodore Sturgeon
Best Short Story: No Award

1971

Best Novel: *A Time of Changes* by Robert Silverberg
Best Novella: "The Missing Man" by Katherine MacLean
Best Novelette: "The Queen of Air and Darkness" by Poul
Anderson
Best Short Story: "Good News from the Vatican" by Robert
Silverberg

1972

Best Novel: *The Gods Themselves* by Isaac Asimov
Best Novella: "A Meeting with Medusa" by Arthur C. Clarke
Best Novelette: "Goat Song" by Poul Anderson
Best Short Story: "When It Changed" by Joanna Russ

1973

Best Novel: *Rendezvous with Rama* by Arthur C. Clarke
Best Novella: "The Death of Doctor Island" by Gene Wolfe
Best Novelette: "Of Mist, and Grass, and Sand" by Vonda N.
McIntyre
Best Short Story: "Love Is the Plan, the Plan Is Death" by
James Tiptree, Jr.
Best Dramatic Presentation: *Soylent Green*

1974

Best Novel: *The Dispossessed* by Ursula K. Le Guin
Best Novella: "Born with the Dead" by Robert Silverberg
Best Novelette: "If the Stars Are Gods" by Gordon Eklund
and Gregory Benford
Best Short Story: "The Day Before the Revolution" by
Ursula K. Le Guin
Best Dramatic Presentation: *Sleeper*
Grand Master: Robert A. Heinlein

1975

Best Novel: *The Forever War* by Joe Haldeman
Best Novella: "Home Is the Hangman" by Roger Zelazny
Best Novelette: "San Diego Lightfoot Sue" by Tom Reamy
Best Short Story: "Catch That Zeppelin!" by Fritz Leiber
Best Dramatic Presentation: *Young Frankenstein*
Grand Master: Jack Williamson

1976

Best Novel: *Man Plus* by Frederik Pohl
Best Novella: "Houston, Houston, Do You Read?" by James
Tiptree, Jr.
Best Novelette: "The Bicentennial Man" by Isaac Asimov
Best Short Story: "A Crowd of Shadows" by Charles L. Grant
Grand Master: Clifford D. Simak

1977

Best Novel: *Gateway* by Frederik Pohl
Best Novella: "Stardance" by Spider and Jeanne Robinson
Best Novelette: "The Screwfly Solution" by Raccoona
Sheldon
Best Short Story: "Jeffty Is Five" by Harlan Ellison
Special Award *Star Wars*

1978

Best Novel: *Dreamsnake* by Vonda N. McIntyre
Best Novella: "The Persistence of Vision" by John Varley
Best Novelette: "A Glow of Candles, a Unicorn's Eye" by
Charles L. Grant
Best Short Story: "Stone" by Edward Bryant
Grand Master: L. Sprague de Camp

1979

Best Novel: *The Fountains of Paradise* by Arthur C. Clarke
Best Novella: "Enemy Mine" by Barry Longyear
Best Novelette: "Sandkings" by George R. R. Martin
Best Short Story: "giANTS" by Edward Bryant

1980

Best Novel: *Timescape* by Gregory Benford
Best Novella: "The Unicorn Tapestry" by Suzy
McKee Charnas

Best Novelette: "The Ugly Chickens" by Howard Waldrop
Best Short Story: "Grotto of the Dancing Deer" by Clifford D. Simak

1981

Best Novel: *The Claw of the Conciliator* by Gene Wolfe
Best Novella: "The Saturn Game" by Poul Anderson
Best Novelette: "The Quickening" by Michael Bishop
Best Short Story: "The Bone Flute" by Lisa Tuttle*
Grand Master: Fritz Leiber

1982

Best Novel: *No Enemy But Time* by Michael Bishop
Best Novella: "Another Orphan" by John Kessel
Best Novelette: "Fire Watch" by Connie Willis
Best Short Story: "A Letter from the Clearys" by Connie Willis

1983

Best Novel: *Startide Rising* by David Brin
Best Novella: "Hardfought" by Greg Bear
Best Novelette: "Blood Music" by Greg Bear
Best Short Story: "The Peacemaker" by Gardner Dozois
Grand Master: Andre Norton

1984

Best Novel: *Neuromancer* by William Gibson
Best Novella: "PRESS ENTER ■" by John Varley
Best Novelette: "Bloodchild" by Octavia E. Butler
Best Short Story: "Morning Child" by Gardner Dozois

*This Nebula Award was declined by the author.

1985

Best Novel: *Ender's Game* by Orson Scott Card
Best Novella: "Sailing to Byzantium" by Robert Silverberg
Best Novelette: "Portraits of His Children" by George R.R.
Martin
Best Short Story: "Out of All Them Bright Stars" by Nancy
Kress
Grand Master: Arthur C. Clarke

1986

Best Novel: *Speaker for the Dead* by Orson Scott Card
Best Novella: "R & R" by Lucius Shepard
Best Novelette: "The Girl Who Fell Into the Sky" by Kate
Wilhelm
Best Short Story: "Tangents" by Greg Bear
Grand Master: Isaac Asimov

1987

Best Novel: *The Falling Woman* by Pat Murphy
Best Novella: "The Blind Geometer" by Kim Stanley
Robinson
Best Novelette: "Rachel in Love" by Pat Murphy
Best Short Story: "Forever Yours, Anna" by Kate Wilhelm
Grand Master: Alfred Bester

$228.90

Advanced Health
Act. Recovery
act. 28 ID 9579979
3031 N. 114th
Milw. 53222